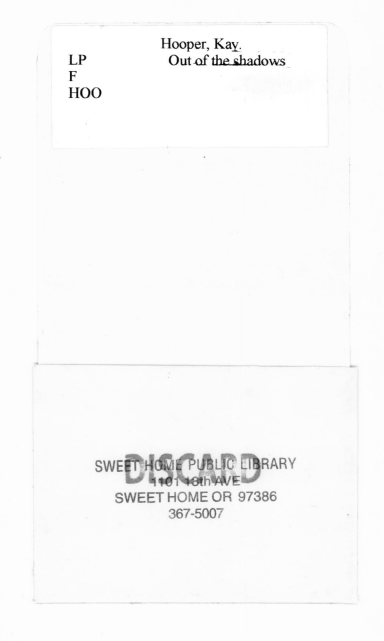

OUT
OF THE
SHADOWS

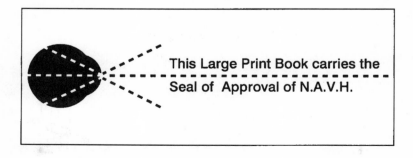

OUT
OF THE
SHADOWS

Kay Hooper

Thorndike Press • Thorndike, Maine

Published in 2001 by arrangement with Bantam Books,
an imprint of The Bantam Dell Publishing Group, a division
of Random House, Inc.

Thorndike Press Large Print Basic Series.

The tree indicium is a trademark of Thorndike Press.

The text of this Large Print edition is unabridged.
Other aspects of the book may vary from the original edition.

Set in 16 pt. Plantin by Elena Picard.

Printed in the United States on permanent paper.

Library of Congress Cataloging-in-Publication Data

Hooper, Kay.
    Out of the shadows / Kay Hooper.
      p. cm.
    ISBN 0-7862-3059-2 (lg. print : hc : alk. paper)
    ISBN 0-7862-3060-6 (lg. print : sc : alk. paper)
    1. Government investigators — Fiction. 2. Serial
murders — Fiction. 3. Policewomen — Fiction.
4. Tennessee — Fiction. 5. Sheriffs — Fiction.
6. Large type books. I. Title.
PS3558.O587 O9 2001
  813'.54—dc21
                                  00-048937

For my sister Linda
and her brave new ventures
both personal and professional

PROLOGUE

Wednesday, January 5, 2000

Lynet Grainger had no real reason to feel afraid. Gladstone was a safe town, had always been a safe town. The rest of the world might be going nuts, with students shooting up their schools and disgruntled employees shooting up their workplaces, with cars being jacked and children being stolen, but in Gladstone none of that stuff ever happened.

Ever.

Of course, nothing much else happened either, at least not until recently.

Even before they'd built the new highway bypass last year — which had quite effectively bypassed Gladstone — the little town had been no more than a place where people stopped for gas and an occasional weary night at the Bluebird Lodge out on Main Street, pausing as briefly as possible in their journey through to Nashville. Otherwise, it was just a wide place in the road, not high enough in the mountains to offer skiing as a tourist attraction — though the Bluebird Lodge defiantly had as its logo a pair of crossed skis — and not far enough out of the mountains to boast much decent farming or pastureland.

It was just a little valley. The bedrock core of the local economy was a smelly paper mill out on the river where a healthy majority of the town's blue-collar workers toiled. And in town, there were a few small businesses, the sort of car dealerships and real estate offices and stores that dotted all small towns.

Thankfully, Gladstone wasn't so small that absolutely everybody knew the business of their neighbors — but nearly so. Gossip was second only to the video store downtown as a source of entertainment.

So when Kerry Ingram, barely fourteen, seemingly ran away from home a couple of months ago, it was big news. Lots of people were heard to say they'd expected as much, since Kerry's older brother had done the same thing several years before to try his luck as a singer in Nashville (and ended up trying to support a wife and two little kids on a mechanic's pay). It was that sort of family, the gossips said, not the kind to raise up kids loyal to the town.

But there had been uneasiness beneath

the confidence even then, even before they found out what had really happened to Kerry, because at about the same time she disappeared there had been something creepy going on hardly more than a hundred miles away, in Concord. Lynet wasn't entirely sure of the details, but it was whispered that a horrible man had been stalking and raping women, and it had only been when a special FBI task force had been called in that he was caught.

Lynet would like to have seen a special FBI task force in action. She was interested in law enforcement, and since the sheriff had patiently answered her questions on Career Day back last spring, that interest had only grown. At least until Kerry Ingram's body had been found, and some of the details had gotten around.

Lynet had felt more than a little sick upon hearing those details. She'd told herself it was only because she had actually *known* Kerry that the whole thing had upset her, not because she had a weak stomach unsuited for the work of a police officer or, better yet, an FBI agent just like Scully.

No, it was only because she'd known Kerry, been just a year ahead of her in school and ridden on the same school bus. Because she remembered so vividly how

Kerry had worn a bright ribbon in her hair every day, and smiled shyly whenever one of the boys tried to talk to her, and had been so proud of making the honor roll because math was difficult for her and she had to try really, really hard in that class. . . .

Lynet shook off the memories and glanced around warily as she walked briskly along the sidewalk. Just about all the stores downtown had closed early as usual on this Wednesday, and now at nine o'clock at night there was almost no traffic and virtually no one about.

Still, Lynet had no real reason to be afraid. The sheriff had said it was likely poor Kerry had slipped and fallen into that nasty ravine where people used to dump their trash and where her bruised body had been found. But Lynet had heard a few whispers about what might have been done to Kerry before she'd died, and even if it was just speculation, it was the kind to make a girl worried about being alone on the streets after dark.

She paused on the corner of Main and Trade streets and briefly considered taking the usual shortcut through the park. Very briefly. Much better, she thought, to stay on the sidewalk under the streetlights, even if it would take an extra fifteen minutes to get home.

So she walked on, wishing she hadn't lingered at the library so late, wishing her sixteenth birthday would come so she could drive her mom's battered Honda instead of having to hoof it everywhere.

"Lynet, what on earth are you doing out so late?"

She nearly jumped out of her skin, and actually put a hand to her breast in an unconsciously dramatic gesture of near heart failure. "Oh, it's you! God, don't scare me like that!"

"I'm sorry — but you shouldn't be out here so late. Why aren't you at home?"

"I had to use the computer at the library — you know I don't have one of my own yet."

"Well, next time have somebody drive you."

"I will." Lynet smiled winningly. "We can walk together as far as the next corner. You're going that way, aren't you?"

"Yes."

"Great. Nobody would bother the two of us."

"No, nobody would bother the two of us."

"I'm surprised you're out here," Lynet said chattily. "Are you just walking? I know some people do, around town to get exercise, but I thought that was just in the summer."

"It's not cold tonight."

"You aren't cold? Oh, I am. Walking fast helps, though. If we hurry —" Lynet took another step, then stopped as she recognized what was being held out toward her. "Oh," she said numbly. "Oh, no. You —"

"You know what this is. And what it can do."

"Yes," Lynet whispered.

"Then you'll come along with me and not make trouble, won't you, Lynet?"

"Don't hurt me. Please, don't —"

"I'm sorry, Lynet. I really am."

ONE

Thursday, January 6

The body had been exposed to the elements for at least two or three days. And before last night's heavy rain had washed them away, the tracks of dozens of paws and claws must have crisscrossed the clearing.

It was shaping up to be a long, cold winter, and the animals were hungry.

Deputy Alex Mayse shivered as he picked his way gingerly past the town's single forensics "expert," a young doctor who'd been elected coroner because nobody else had wanted the job. The doctor was crawling around the clearing on his hands and knees, his nose inches from the wet ground as he found and flagged the scattered bones and other bits the animals had left.

"You don't have to hum to yourself, Doc," Alex muttered sourly. "We all know how happy you are."

Remaining in his crouched position, Dr.

Peter Shepherd said cheerfully, "If a murdered teenager made me happy, Alex, I'd be worse than a ghoul. I'm just fascinated by the puzzle, that's all."

Waiting patiently just a few steps behind the doctor, camera in hand as he waited to take pictures of each flagged spot, Deputy Brady Shaw rolled his eyes at Alex.

Alex grimaced in sympathy, but all he said to Shepherd was, "Yeah, yeah. Just find something helpful this time, will you?"

"Do my best," the doctor replied, studying what appeared to be a bleached twig.

Alex walked to the area where most of the body had been found, noticing with a certain amount of sympathy that Sandy Lynch was over behind a tree puking her guts out. She was having a lousy introduction to the job, poor kid. Not that the old hands were handling it any better, really. Carl Tierney had had the misfortune to find Adam Ramsay's mortal remains, and the ten-year veteran of the Sheriff's Department had promptly lost his morning Egg McMuffin.

Alex himself had suffered through a few teeth-grittingly queasy moments during the last couple of hours.

In fact, the only member of the Cox County Sheriff's Department who had shown no signs of being sickened by the gory sight was the sheriff.

There was an irony there somewhere, Alex thought as he joined the sheriff, who was hunkered down several feet from what was left of Adam Ramsay, elbows on knees and fingers steepled. In its entire history, the small town of Gladstone had seldom been troubled by murder. A long line of sheriffs had grown old in their jobs, dealing with petty crime and little else of consequence, needing no more police training than how to load a gun, which would in all likelihood never be fired except at targets or the occasional unlucky rabbit. It was a local saying that all the Cox County sheriff had to be good at was filling out the Santa suit for the annual Christmas parade down Main Street.

Until last year, anyway. The town finally elected a sheriff with an actual law degree and a minor in criminology — and what happened? Damned if they didn't start having real crimes.

But they were blessed in that this particular sheriff had very quickly displayed an almost uncanny ability to get to the bottom of things with a minimum of time wasted.

At least until recently.

"This makes two," Alex said, judging that

the silence had gone on long enough.

"Yeah."

"Same killer, d'you think?"

Startling blue eyes slanted him a look. "Hard to tell from the bones."

Alex started to reply that there was a bit of rotting flesh here and there, but kept his mouth shut. There was little remaining on the skeleton of Adam Ramsay, that was true enough, and what was there didn't immediately offer up any evidence as to who had killed him and how. Impossible to tell if the boy's body had borne the same bruises and cuts as they had found on Kerry Ingram. Still, it was a fair guess that two bodies turning up in less than a month had to be connected in some way.

With a sigh, Alex said, "We won't be able to quiet the gossip by suggesting this death was an accident. We might not know how he died yet, but it's a cinch a victim of an accident wouldn't have buried his own body. And you can bet that little fact won't stay out of circulation for long."

"I know."

"So we have a problem. A big problem."

"Shit," the sheriff said quietly after a moment.

Alex wondered if that was guilt he heard. "Announcing that Kerry Ingram had been murdered wouldn't have saved this one," he reminded. "I may not be an expert, but my guess is that Adam died more than a couple of weeks ago."

"Yeah, probably."

"And his own mother didn't report him missing until just before Halloween, even though he'd already been gone for weeks by then."

"Because they'd had a big fight and he'd run off to live with his father in Florida just like he'd done at least twice before — or so she thought."

"My point," Alex said, "is that there's nothing we could have done to save Adam Ramsay."

"Maybe," the sheriff said, still quiet. "But maybe we could have saved Kerry Ingram."

Breaking the ensuing silence, Alex said, "Good thing he was wearing his class ring. And that he had that gold tooth. Otherwise we'd never have been able to identify him. But what kid his age has a gold tooth? I meant to ask before now, but —"

"Not a tooth, just a cap. He had a ring of his father's melted down, and a dentist in the city did the work."

"Why, for God's sake?"

"His mother didn't know or wouldn't say. And we can't ask him now." Still hunkered down, the sheriff added, "I doubt it's important, at least to the question of who killed him and why."

"Yeah, I guess. You have any ideas about that, by the way?"

"No."

Alex sighed. "Me either. The mayor isn't going to like this, Randy."

"Nobody's going to like it, Alex. Especially not Adam Ramsay's mother."

"You know what I mean."

"Yeah. I know." Sheriff Miranda Knight sighed and rose from the crouched position, absently stretching cramped muscles. "Shit," she said again, softly.

Deputy Sandy Lynch, still very pale, ventured a step toward them but kept her gaze studiously away from the remains. "I'm sorry, Sheriff," she said nervously, new enough at the job that she feared losing it.

Miranda looked at her. "Don't worry about it, Sandy. There's nothing you can do here anyway. Go on back to the office and help Grace deal with all the phone calls."

"Okay, Sheriff." She paused. "What should we tell people?"

"Tell them we have no information at this time."

"Yes, ma'am."

As the young deputy retreated to her car

in visible relief, Alex said, "That won't hold 'em for long."

"Long enough, with a little luck. I'd like a few more answers before I have to face John with a recommendation."

"Since that flap over in Concord spooked him, you know he'll overreact and declare we have a serial killer on our hands."

"Two murders don't make a serial killer."

"You know that and I know that. His Honor will prefer to err on the side of caution. He likes his job and he wants to keep it. Concord's mayor was practically run out of town for not insisting that task force be called in sooner. John MacBride is not going to make the same mistake."

Miranda nodded, frowning. "I know, I know."

"So get the jump on him. Tell him your recommendation is to call in the task force now."

Her frown deepened. "You read the bulletin, same as I did. The task force was set up to handle unusual crimes with inexplicable elements, crimes ordinary police work can't solve. For all we know, what we have here are two teenage victims of grudges or impulsive violence. Both of them were probably killed by someone they knew, and for depressingly mundane reasons. We don't know there's anything unusual."

"Randy, nobody'd blame you for calling in the feds whether these murders are unusual or not. We're a small-town sheriff's department with little manpower and almost no high-tech toys. Before we found the Ingram girl, the last murder any Cox County sheriff had to investigate was twenty years ago — when a cuckolded husband shot his wife's lover while the man was trying to escape out the bedroom window. Hardly a tricky investigation. The cases you've handled so far were demanding, and God knows you dealt with them well, but what they required was skill, intelligence, and instinct, all of which you certainly have. What you don't have are state-of-the-art crime scene investigation tools, a computer system that isn't five years out of date, enough deputies to effectively cover the county you're responsible for, and a medical examiner whose specialty — not his hobby — is forensics."

"I heard that," Doc Shepherd called out.

Unrepentant, Alex called back, "I meant you to hear it." He returned his attention to Miranda and went on in a lower voice. "Call in the feds, Randy. Nobody'll think less of you. And, goddammit, we need the help."

"They don't help, they take over."

"Then I say let 'em have it."

She shook her head. "I can't say that, Alex. I can't just hand this problem over to somebody else because I'm afraid it might be too difficult for me."

"MacBride can pull rank — and you know he will. Randy, there were just enough doubts about electing a woman sheriff to make him very, very nervous of any criticism from the voters. First sign this department can't handle the investigation, and he'll be yelling for help as loud as he can."

"No," she said. "He won't do that, not publicly."

"Then he'll pressure you to do it."

"Maybe."

"Randy —"

"We don't know there's anything unusual here," Miranda repeated stubbornly. "And just because we've gotten nowhere investigating Kerry Ingram's murder doesn't mean we won't have better luck with this case. One thing I'm sure of is that I'm damned well planning to give it my best shot. I'm not calling in outsiders unless we have no other choice." She lifted one hand and rubbed the nape of her neck, where tension had undoubtedly gathered, and scowled at the remains of Adam Ramsay.

Alex watched her, not bothering to be

subtle about it because he had long ago realized that Miranda was never conscious of masculine scrutiny. Not on the job, at any rate. She tended to wear sweaters and jeans, kept her black hair pulled back severely from her face, her nails short and unpolished, and her makeup to a minimum. And none of it mattered one little bit.

Miranda Knight was one of those rare women who would have been beautiful even if you wrapped her in a burlap feed sack and dipped her in mud.

She wasn't in uniform even on duty, a perk she had more or less demanded before taking on the job, and the snug jeans and bulky sweater she wore today did little to hide either the gun on her hip or measurements of true centerfold proportions.

Alex had never been sure which attracted Gladstone's mayor more, the gun or the body, but it was an open secret that John MacBride had had his eye on Miranda long before they'd both been voted into office over a year before.

What Miranda thought of the mayor, on the other hand, was a secret known only to her. She might refer to him casually when speaking to Alex, but in public she was invariably formal, polite, and respectful to His Honor, and if she had so much as allowed him to buy her a cup of coffee she'd managed to drink it where nobody in this very curious town had been able to observe.

Still, Alex couldn't help but wonder if MacBride's determined pursuit of the last few months would change if Miranda refused to ensure the mayor's political safety by handing the investigation over to the feds with all speed.

"We don't *know* there's anything unusual here," she said again, the emphasis making Alex look at her in sudden awareness.

"Have you noticed something?" he asked.

Obviously conscious of his stare, Miranda nonetheless didn't meet his eyes. "I just said —"

"I know what you said. I also heard how you said it. And I know that sometimes you see things everybody else misses. What do you see that I don't, Randy?"

"Nothing. I see nothing."

Alex thought she was lying to him. But before he could press her, Doc Shepherd came up to them.

"I have a preliminary report," he told Miranda. "I'll write it up as soon as I get back to the office, of course, but if you want to hear what'll be on it while Brady's getting shots of everything —"

"Let's hear it."

"No way to tell if the boy was strangled

like the Ingram girl, but there is evidence that a few bones were broken prior to death."

"Could they have been broken in an accidental fall?" Miranda asked.

"Not likely. I'd say his arms were twisted hard enough to snap, which would require considerable, deliberate force. And two bones in his left hand were crushed, probably by a hammer or similar tool."

Alex offered a reluctant question. "Are you saying he was tortured?"

"I wouldn't rule it out, but there isn't enough evidence for me to be absolutely sure."

"What are you sure of?" Miranda asked.

"I'm sure he's been dead at least three or four weeks, possibly longer. I'm sure he was killed somewhere else, then brought here and buried in a shallow grave that didn't protect the body very long from scavenging animals." Peter Shepherd paused briefly. "Now let me ask you something: Are you sure these are the remains of Adam Ramsay?"

Alex was surprised by the question, but when he looked at Miranda he realized she wasn't.

"We found his class ring here," she said neutrally. "And the gold crown on that front tooth matches our information. Height and estimated weight in the right range. And the patch of scalp still attached to the skull has red hair like Adam Ramsay. We have every reason to believe the I.D. is accurate." It was her turn to pause, and when she went on, she asked what sounded like an unwilling question. "You think it isn't him?"

Clearly enjoying his role, Shepherd said, "I think if it is him, his mother must be a hell of a lot older than she looks. I'll know more after I conduct a few tests, but I'll be surprised if I find out those bones belonged to any man less than forty years old."

Again, Miranda didn't seem surprised, but all she said, in the same dispassionate tone of before, was, "We have complete dental records, so verifying identity — if it is Adam — shouldn't take long."

Bewildered, Alex said, "Adam was seventeen."

"Those bones are older," Shepherd answered with a shrug.

"There's barely enough of him left to put in a shoe-box," Alex objected. "How can you possibly know —"

Miranda lifted a hand to stop Alex. "Why don't we wait until we have a few more facts before we start arguing? Doc, if you'll take the remains back to the morgue, I'll have the dental records sent over."

"I don't know who his family doctor was, but if you could get those records as well . . ."

"I'll send them along."

Alex followed as Miranda retreated several yards to give the doctor room to work, and said accusingly, "You knew what he was going to say, didn't you?"

"How could I have known that?" Her tone wasn't so much evasive as matter-of-fact. She watched Shepherd work the remains into a black body bag.

"That's what I'm asking you, Randy. How did you know? You been hiding a degree in medicine or forensics?"

"Of course not."

"Well then?"

"I didn't see anything you didn't see, Alex."

"But you knew that skeleton wasn't Adam Ramsay?"

Miranda finally turned her head and looked at Alex. There was something in her face he couldn't quite read and didn't like one bit, a shuttered expression he'd never seen before. For the first time in the nearly five years he'd known her, Alex felt he was looking at a stranger.

"On the contrary," she said quietly. "What I knew — what I *know* — is that we've found all that's left of Adam Ramsay."

"I don't get it."

"It's Adam Ramsay, Alex. The dental records will prove it."

"But if the bones belonged to an older man —" Alex broke off and made his voice low. "So Doc is wrong about that?"

"I hope so."

Alex didn't make the mistake of thinking Miranda was engaged in a game of one-upmanship with the doctor. Thinking aloud, he mused, "If Doc's right about the age of the bones, it'd mean this victim is someone nobody reported missing. And it would mean we might still find Adam Ramsay's body. If you're right —"

"If I'm right, it would mean something else," Miranda cut in. "It would mean we have a much bigger puzzle than who killed two teenage runaways."

Liz Hallowell had lived in Gladstone all of her thirty years, which meant she knew just about everybody. And since the bookstore she'd inherited from her parents was centrally located in town *and* boasted the recent addition of a coffeeshop where people could sit and chat as long as they liked, she tended to know everything that was going on within hours of its happening.

So she knew the latest news on this cold January morning. She knew that a body — or bones, anyway — had been found in the woods just outside town by an off-duty sheriff's deputy trying to get in a little early-morning hunting. She knew it was believed the bones were Adam Ramsay's. And she knew there was something decidedly odd about the whole thing.

Not that murder wasn't odd, of course. But something else was going on, she was certain of it. The leaves in her morning cup of tea had made a chill go through her entire body, and even before that there had been several other unsettling omens. She'd heard a whippoorwill last night and afterward dreamed about riding a horse — which was supposed to be sexual, hardly surprising to Liz given her frustrations of late — and about a door she couldn't open, which wasn't a good sign at all.

She'd been awakened twice by a dog howling, and just before dawn thunder had rumbled even though there was no storm. This morning her neighbor's pet rooster had faced her own front door while crowing, which meant a stranger was coming. She'd spilled salt three times in the last two days, so even doing what she could to immediately negate the bad luck wouldn't get rid of it all.

And a bird had struck the window of her breakfast room, a dove no less, breaking its poor little neck. Since she lived alone, Liz assumed she was the one whom death was hovering near.

Alex would shake his head when she told him, but Liz's grandmother had been Romany and she herself had been born with a caul — and she knew what she knew.

Bad was here, and worse was coming.

So before Liz had ventured out of her house today, she'd made damned sure to put several amulets in the medicine bag that hung around her neck on a black thong: a couple of ash-tree leaves, a clove of garlic, bits of lucky hand root and oak bark, and several small stones — bloodstone, carnelian, cat's eye, garnet, black opal, staurolite, and topaz. She also carried a rabbit's foot in her purse, and her earrings were tiny gold wishbones.

None of which protected her from Justin Marsh, which was a pity.

"This is blasphemy, Elizabeth," he declared, waving a book beneath her nose.

She pushed the book gently back far enough to bring the title into focus, then said mildly, "It's a novel, Justin. A made-up story. I doubt very much if the author is trying to persuade anyone to actually believe that Christ was a woman. But if it makes you feel any better, you're the first one I've seen even pick it up."

His pale brown eyes glittered in his perpetually tanned face. The healthy thatch of white hair and the customary white suit made him look like a televangelist, she thought. He sounded like one too.

"Books like this one should be banned!" he told her stridently.

Liz noted that few of her other early-morning customers even looked up, as accustomed to his tirades as she was herself. "We don't ban books around here, Justin."

"If innocent minds should read this — !"

"Trust me, innocent minds don't venture into that section of the store. They're all three rows over reading stuff about ninjas and how to hack into computer systems."

He missed the irony, just as she had expected.

"Elizabeth, you're responsible for protecting impressionable young minds from corruption such as this." He waved the book under her nose again.

Behind him, a deep voice said dryly, "No, their parents are responsible for that. Liz just runs a bookstore."

"Morning, Alex," she said.

"Hi. Coffee would be heaven, Liz."

"You got it." Leaving Alex to deal with Justin, she went behind the counter to pour a couple of cups of the Swiss-chocolate-flavored coffee Alex had recently become addicted to. By the time she joined him at their customary table near the front window, Justin had vanished.

"If he's over there tearing up another book . . ."

"I warned him the next episode would mean a fine and jail time, for all the good it'll do." He blew on the coffee automatically, but began sipping before it had a chance to cool. "I don't know why he can't go away somewhere and start a nice pseudo-religious cult, leave us the hell alone."

"He isn't charismatic enough," Liz said definitely. "Just a not-too-bright kook, and it's obvious. It's Selena I feel sorry for."

Alex grunted. "I never heard she was forced to marry him. Besides, the way she looks at him it's obvious she considers him the Second Coming — if you'll forgive the blasphemy."

"I guess every town has to have at least one Justin Marsh. What else would we have to talk about otherwise?"

"Murder?" he suggested dryly.

Liz looked at his tired, drawn face and

said slowly, "I heard it was Adam Ramsay's body this time."

"Sheriff says it is. Doc says it isn't. We'll know for sure when Doc compares the dental records."

"What do you think?"

"I think Randy isn't often wrong." He shrugged, frowning down at his coffee. "But if she's right this time, something very weird is going on, Liz."

Without thinking, Liz said, "The leaves told me that this morning."

Alex looked at her with resignation. "Uh-huh. Did they happen to tell you anything else? Like maybe if we have a vicious killer in this nice little town of ours?"

"You don't think it's one of us?" she exclaimed, genuinely shocked.

He smiled at her with an odd expression she couldn't quite define. "Liz, Gladstone might as well be the town that time forgot. Or at least the town travelers bypass. How many strangers do you notice in any given week?"

"Well . . . not many."

"Not many?"

"All right, so strangers are rare, especially if you discount insurance salesmen. But that doesn't have to mean one of us is doing these terrible things, Alex."

"I don't like to think it either, you know. But how likely is it that a stranger picked Gladstone as his base of operations to begin killing teenagers?"

"When you put it like that . . ."

"Yeah."

After a moment of silence, Liz said reluctantly, "Whatever is going on, it isn't over, Alex."

"Tea leaves again?"

"I know what I know." It was her standard response to doubt or disbelief.

"Because your grandmother was a gypsy? Liz —"

"I know you don't believe, but you have to listen to me this time. I've never seen so many dark omens and portents. There's evil here, real, literal evil hanging over this town."

"That much I'll buy. Have you checked your crystal ball lately to see how it'll all turn out?"

"You know I don't have one of those." She hesitated. "But I do know someone's coming. The leaves showed me that. A dark man with a mark on his face. An outsider. He'll come to help, but for some other reason too, a secret reason. And I think . . . I know . . . he'll give his life to save one of us."

TWO

Miranda let herself into the small, quiet house not far from downtown Gladstone and went directly to the kitchen. It was a bright room most of the time, but last night's rain had left the sky overcast, and not even the airy yellow-and-white color scheme and gleaming white appliances could do much to cheer the room.

Or Miranda.

She went to the coffeemaker and turned it on, warming the remains of last night's pot because there hadn't been time earlier that morning to make fresh, and Mrs. Task was coming in late because of a doctor's appointment. The reheated coffee would be unbearably bitter, she knew.

But it would suit her mood.

Fresh coffee awaited her at the office, but she'd wanted to stop here first, if only for a few precious minutes, away from ringing telephones and anxious deputies and frightened townspeople. She thought Alex had probably detoured as well, though he would have gone to Liz's place rather than his own home.

They all took their comfort where they could.

"Randy?" A girl of about sixteen, her resemblance to Miranda striking, came hesitantly into the room. She was wearing a nightgown and robe even at ten in the morning on a school day, but that was explained when Miranda spoke.

"You shouldn't have gotten up, Bonnie. Doc said sleep would help you more than anything."

"I feel much better, honest. It's only a cold, nothing major." Bonnie watched Miranda pour very black coffee into a cup. "Was it . . . ?"

Miranda sipped her coffee, then nodded.

"Adam Ramsay? Just like you saw?"

"Just like I saw," Miranda confirmed bitterly.

Bonnie shivered and bit her lip, then walked to the table in the center of the room and sat down. "I didn't really know him. Still . . ."

"Still," Miranda agreed.

"It's all going to happen now, isn't it?"

"I'm afraid so."

Bonnie's lip quivered before she bit it again. "Then we'll leave, that's all. We'll just —"

"It wouldn't matter, Bonnie. It wouldn't change anything. Some things have to happen just the way they happen."

"You can't stop it?" Her vivid blue eyes were desperately worried.

"No, I can't stop it." Miranda drew a breath. "Not alone."

"Maybe Alex can —"

"No. Not Alex."

Their eyes met, held, then Bonnie said, "You could ask them to send somebody else."

"I need *him*." Bitterness had crept back into Miranda's voice, and reluctance, and something that might have been loathing.

"You're sure?"

"Yeah, I'm sure."

"It's been a long time, Randy. Eight years —"

"Eight years, four months, and an odd number of days." Miranda's laugh held no amusement. "I know how long it's been, believe me."

"I only meant that things change, Randy. People change, you know they do. Even he must have changed. It'll be different this time."

"Will it?"

Bonnie hesitated. "You've seen something else, haven't you? What is it? What have you seen?"

Miranda looked down at her coffee, and her mouth twisted. "Inevitability," she said.

Friday, January 7

"I can't explain it," Dr. Shepherd said, his habitual cheery smile replaced by a baffled frown. "The dental records match, without question. What we found are the remains of Adam Ramsay."

"But," Miranda said.

"Yeah — but. The bones show all the signs of belonging to a man at least forty years old. The sutures of the skull were filled in. Calcium deposits and other changes in bone structure also indicate forty to fifty years of life." He paused. "This one's beyond my knowledge, Randy. Obviously someone with more training and experience in forensics, a forensic pathologist or anthropologist, should examine the remains. I must have missed something somehow, misread the results or performed the wrong tests — something."

Miranda looked at him across her desk. "Setting that aside for the moment, maybe we're losing sight of the point. The point is that we found the remains of a seventeen-year-old runaway. Do you know how he died?"

"Enough of the skull was intact to reveal evidence of blunt-force trauma in at least two spots, and I don't believe it was post-mortem."

"Not accidental blows?"

"If you're asking for my opinion, I'd say not. For the record, a blow to the head probably killed him. Whether that blow was deliberate or accidental is impossible for me to state with any medical — or legal — certainty."

Miranda made a note on the pad in front of her. "I appreciate you coming into the office to report, Doc."

"No problem. I knew you had your hands full. Any word on Lynet Grainger?"

"Not yet. I've got all my deputies, Simon's bloodhounds, and every volunteer I could get my hands on out searching for her, but no luck so far. She left the library Wednesday night and vanished into thin air." Her mouth tightened. "If her mother hadn't been drunk that night and failed to report Lynet missing until yesterday afternoon, we might have had a better shot at finding her. As it is, with nearly forty-eight hours gone now, the trail is ice-cold."

Shepherd studied her. "You look like hell, if you don't mind me saying so."

"Thanks a lot."

"Did you even go to bed last night, Randy?"

Miranda drew a breath and let it out slowly. "Doc, I've got two teenagers dead and a third one missing, and no evidence to persuade me we're just in the middle of a series of tragic accidents and random disappearances. I also have no evidence pointing me toward the killer — or killers — of the two dead kids, and no clue to help me find Lynet Grainger. I spent half the morning arguing with the mayor and the other half fielding calls from terrified parents. Somebody in my nice, safe little town has apparently decided to start torturing, maiming, and killing teenagers. And I have a sixteen-year-old sister at home. What do you think?"

"I think you didn't go to bed."

She straightened in her chair as if to refute his accusation, then lifted a hand to rub the back of her neck wearily. "Yeah, well, I couldn't have slept anyway. I don't want to find another dead teenager, Peter."

"Do you think you will?"

"Do you?"

He hesitated for a beat. "Honestly? Yes. I

don't know what's going on, Randy, or who's behind it, but I think you're right about one thing. Someone is after our teenagers. And that someone has some very strange . . . appetites."

In an abrupt turnabout, Miranda shook her head. "We don't know that's what's going on."

"Don't we?"

"No."

"I see. Then I guess you have a reasonable explanation for why Kerry Ingram's body was drained of almost all its blood."

"Don't tell me you think the killer drank it," Miranda objected dryly.

"No — although that sort of thing is more common than most people would like to believe."

"I wonder why."

Ignoring the muttered aside, Shepherd went on, "I believe that the killer had some need for the blood, undoubtedly one a rational person could never understand. And — not that you missed this detail, I'm sure — it's interesting to note that we actually found only a small percentage of Adam Ramsay's bones out there."

"The animals. Scavengers."

"Maybe. Or maybe he wasn't all there to begin with. Maybe the killer took his blood as well as the girl's. And a few bones to go with it. And maybe he took Lynet Grainger because he didn't get all he needed from the first two."

"Speculation," Miranda said firmly. "We don't even know that Kerry and Adam were killed by the same person, and Lynet's disappearance doesn't have to end with us finding her body."

"That's true enough." Shepherd got to his feet. "But here's something just as true: It's not like you to hide your head in the sand, Randy."

"I don't know what you mean."

"I think you do." He smiled faintly. "I also think you're honest enough — maybe especially with yourself — to face up to it sooner rather than later. At least I hope so. I don't read tea leaves like Liz Hallowell, but I don't need to have gypsy blood to know there's something very strange going on in Gladstone."

"Yes. Yes, I know that."

"Nobody will think less of you for calling in help, not when something like this is going on."

"So everyone keeps telling me."

"And they're telling the truth." He paused. "We need to get an expert in to look at those bones, Randy. Tell me who, and I'll make the call."

She looked at him for a long while, then sighed. "No, it's my job. I'll make the call, Doc."

But she didn't pick up the phone after Shepherd left. Instead, she went through the case files one more time, studying every piece of information gathered on Kerry Ingram and Adam Ramsay. She fixed all her will on finding something, some tiny, previously overlooked clue, that would tell her these were ordinary murders, committed in anger or for some other perfectly tragic, perfectly human reason.

But no matter how many times she went over it all, the photos of a young, battered body and skeletal remains, the medical reports and the interviews with relatives and acquaintances, the traced movements of the two teenagers during the last weeks before they disappeared — no matter how many times she went over the information in the files, only the same unalterable, inescapable chilling facts jumped out at her.

Kerry Ingram's exsanguinated body.

The bones missing from Adam Ramsay's remains.

The aged condition of the bones they had found.

Miranda closed the last file and stared

across the room at nothing. "Goddammit," she whispered.

Inevitability.

Some people called it fate.

He watched the girl as she lay in a drugged stupor on the cot where he had placed her. She was pretty. That was a shame. And she'd been trying to improve her lot in life, working hard in school, doing her best to keep her lush of a mother from driving drunk or burning down the house.

Definitely a shame.

But there was nothing he could do to change things.

He hoped Lynet would understand that.

Saturday, January 8

"So when're the feds due in?" Alex asked Miranda. They stood near the top of the hill and watched as half a dozen small boats slowly crisscrossed the lake down in the hollow. The last light of day was shining just over the mountains and painting the lake shimmering silver; another few minutes and they'd have to put up floodlights or stop the search for the night.

"Any time now."

Alex turned to her. "So how come you're out here instead of back at the office waiting for them? Dragging the lake is a good idea — anonymous tip or not — since we haven't found a trace of the Grainger girl anywhere else in the area, but I can call in if we find anything."

Miranda's shoulders moved in an irritable shrug. "They'll have to drive in from Nashville, so it could be late tonight. Anyway, I left Brady on duty at the office with instructions to send them out here if they arrive before I get back."

"Do you have any idea how many are coming? I mean, isn't this crack new unit of theirs supposed to be made up of a dozen or more agents?"

"I don't know for sure. There isn't much information available, even for law enforcement officials. We'll get what we get, I guess." She sounded restless, uneasy.

Alex was about to ask another question when he saw Miranda stiffen. He wasn't sure how he knew, but looking at her he was certain that all her attention, all her *being*, was suddenly focused elsewhere. She no longer saw the lake or the people below, and wasn't even aware of him standing beside her.

Then he saw her eyes shift to one side, as

if she was suddenly, intensely aware of some sound, some thing, behind her and didn't want to turn her head to look.

"Randy?"

She didn't respond, didn't seem to hear him.

Alex looked behind them. At first, all he saw was the hilltop flooded with light because the sun had not yet set. Then there was an abrupt, curiously fluid shifting of the light, and the silhouette of a tall man appeared.

Alex blinked, startled because he hadn't heard a sound. Two more silhouettes appeared on either side of the first, another man and a woman. They paused on the crest of the hill, looking at the activity below, then lost the blinding halo of light as they moved down the slope toward Alex and Miranda.

The man on the left was about six feet tall. He was maybe thirty, on the thin side, with nondescript brown hair. The woman was likely the same age, medium height, slender, and blond. Both were casually dressed in dark pants and bulky sweaters.

But it was the man in the center who caught and held Alex's attention. Dressed as casually as the other two in jeans and a black leather jacket, he was a striking figure, over six feet tall and very dark. His black hair gleamed in the last of the day's light, and a distinct widow's peak crowned his high forehead. He was wide shouldered and moved with the ease and grace of a trained athlete, navigating the rock-strewn slope with far more dexterity than his slipping and sliding companions. As he neared them, Alex saw a vivid scar on the left side of his coldly handsome face.

Liz's dark stranger, Alex thought, with a lack of surprise that would have surprised her.

He looked back at Miranda and saw that her gaze was fixed once more on the lake below. But her breath came quickly through parted, trembling lips, and her face was pale and strained. He was astonished at how vulnerable she looked. For a moment. Just a moment.

Then she closed her eyes, and when she opened them a moment later all the strain was gone. She looked perfectly calm, indifferent even.

Quietly, he said, "Randy, I think the feds are here."

"Are they?" She sounded only mildly interested. She slid her hands into the front pockets of her jeans. "They're early."

"Guess they had a fast car."

"Guess so."

Intrigued, but willing to await events, Alex returned his attention to the approaching agents. When they were close, the tall man in the center spoke, his voice deep and cool but with an undercurrent of tension that was audible.

"Sheriff Knight?" It wasn't quite a question, and his pale, oddly reflective eyes were already fixed on Miranda.

She turned to face the newcomers. "Hello, Bishop."

Bishop's companions didn't seem surprised that this small-town sheriff knew him, so it was left to Alex to ask, "You two know each other?"

"We've met," Miranda said. She introduced Alex, and just as calmly Bishop introduced Special Agents Anthony Harte and Dr. Sharon Edwards. Nobody offered to shake hands, possibly because Miranda and Bishop kept their hands in their pockets the entire time.

"I'm the forensic pathologist you requested," Edwards said cheerfully. Alex thought that Doc Shepherd was about to meet a kindred spirit.

"My specialty is interpretation of data," Harte explained when Miranda's gaze turned questioningly toward him.

"Good," she said. "We have some puzzling data for you to interpret. In the meantime, just to catch you up on events, we're following a tip that our missing teenager might be found here in the lake."

"A tip from whom, Sheriff Knight?" Bishop asked.

"An anonymous tip."

"Phoned in to your office?"

"That's right."

"Male or female?"

Her hesitation was almost unnoticeable. "Female."

"Interesting," he said.

His voice held no accusation, hers no defensiveness, but Alex felt both existed and was even more puzzled. Then he realized something else. "Hey, you're both chess pieces. Knight and Bishop."

Miranda looked at him, one brow rising. "How about that," she said dryly.

Alex cleared his throat. "Well, anyway. We're losing the light down on the lake, Sheriff. Want to call off the search for the day?"

"Might as well." She glanced at the agents. "If you'll excuse me for a few minutes?" Without waiting for a response, she made her way down to the shore where the boats were gathering.

Bishop never took his eyes off Miranda. Alex was curious enough to be nosy, but something in Bishop's face made him stick to professional inquiries. "So what's your specialty, Agent Bishop?"

"Profiler. Who took the anonymous call, Deputy Mayse?"

Alex wasn't sure he liked the question but answered it anyway. "Sheriff Knight." Then he found himself defending where Miranda had refused to. "That's not at all unusual, in case you think it is. The sheriff makes a point of being accessible, so lots of people call her directly if they have information or questions."

Those cool, pale eyes turned to him at last, and Bishop said almost indifferently, "Typical of small towns, in my experience. Tell me, has this area been searched?"

"No. Until we got the tip about the lake, there was no reason to think the Grainger girl would be this far out of town."

"And do you think she's here?"

"The sheriff thinks there's a chance. That's good enough for me."

Bishop continued to gaze at him for a long moment, making Alex uncomfortable. Then the agent nodded, exchanged glances with his two companions, and moved several yards away to a rocky outcropping.

From there he could see most of the hollow, the lake, and the surrounding hills.

"What's he doing?" Alex asked, keeping his voice low.

Sharon Edwards answered. "Getting the lay of the land, I guess you'd call it. Looking for . . . signs."

"Signs? It's nearly dark already, especially down there; what can he possibly see?"

"You might be surprised," Tony Harte murmured.

Alex wanted to question that, but instead said, "I gather he's in charge?"

"He's the senior agent," Edwards confirmed. "But your sheriff is the one in charge. We're just here to help, to offer our expertise and advice."

"Uh-huh."

She smiled. "Really. We have a mandate never to interfere with local law enforcement. It's the only way we can be truly useful *and* be certain we're called in when the situation warrants. We're a lot more likely to be contacted when police are confronted with our sort of cases if word gets around that we never ride roughshod over local authorities."

Alex looked at her curiously. "Your sort of cases?"

"I'm sure you saw the bulletin the Bureau

sent out."

"I saw it. Like most Bureau bulletins, it didn't tell me a hell of a lot."

Edwards smiled again. "They can be cryptic when they want to be. Basically, we get called in on cases where the evidence just doesn't add up or is nonexistent, or there are details that seem to smack of the paranormal or inexplicable. Often those elements show up only after local law enforcement has exhausted all the usual avenues of investigation."

"So you guys pursue *un*usual avenues?"

"We . . . look for the less likely explanations. And some of the methods we use are more intuitive than scientific. We try to keep things informal."

"Is that why no trench coats?"

She chuckled, honestly amused. "We are considered something of a maverick group within the Bureau, so when it was suggested that we dress more casually, the powers that be gave their permission."

Alex wanted to know more, but Miranda hailed him from the lake and he went down to help the search teams get their gear ashore.

Gazing after him, Tony Harte said, "Think you told him enough?"

"To satisfy him?" Edwards shook her

head. "Only for the moment. According to his profile, he's curious and possesses a high tolerance for unconventional methods — probably why he hasn't questioned his sheriff too closely about all the hunches and intuitions since she took office. But he's protective of her, and he's wary of us. He'll be cooperative as long as he's sure we're contributing to the investigation without making Sheriff Knight look bad."

Harte grunted, then glanced at Bishop, still standing several yards away and looking down at the lake. "What about this sheriff? Did you know who she was?"

"I had my suspicions when I went to do a deep background check on her — and found she didn't have one."

"So it is her?"

"I think so."

"No wonder he was in such a hurry to get here. But I've seen warmer greetings between mortal enemies."

"What makes you so sure that isn't what they are — at least from her point of view?"

"Never thought I'd feel sorry for Bishop."

"I imagine he can handle his own problems." Edwards smiled faintly. "In the meantime, there's this little problem we're supposed to be helping with. Are you getting anything?"

"Nope. I was blocked just about the time we topped the hill. You?"

"The same. Remarkable, isn't it?"

Harte watched as Sheriff Knight made her way up the slope. Her lovely face was singularly without expression. "Poor Bishop," he murmured.

If he knew his subordinates were discussing him, Bishop gave no sign, but he joined them only moments before the sheriff and her deputy reached them.

Deputy Mayse said, "Nothing more we can do here tonight, so —"

"We can search for an abandoned well," Bishop said. "There's one nearby."

Mayse stared at him. "How can you possibly know that?"

"He knows," Sheriff Knight said. She looked at her deputy matter-of-factly. "Most of the men are probably exhausted, Alex, but ask for volunteers to search around the lake. The moon will be rising, so we'll have some light."

The deputy clearly wanted to question or argue, but in the end just shook his head and went back down to talk to the searchers.

Harte exchanged looks with Edwards, then said, "The more people we have searching, the quicker we're likely to find something. Our gear's in the car. We'll go change into boots and get our flashlights, some rope — whatever else looks like it might be helpful."

"Better have a compass or two," Sheriff Knight said. "This is tricky terrain. It's easy to get turned around, especially in the dark."

"Understood." Harte glanced at Bishop, who was already wearing boots, then traded another look with Edwards and shrugged. They both turned and trudged back up the slope toward the top and their rental car on the other side.

With one last glance back at the two people standing several feet and a light-year or so apart, Harte muttered, "I guess it could be worse. She could have shot him on sight."

Bishop knew it would be up to him to break the silence between them, but when it came down to it, all he could think of was an absurdly lame comment.

"I never thought you'd be in law enforcement."

"It was a logical choice. With a law degree I couldn't use . . . and the right kind of experience."

"And it kept you . . . plugged in, didn't it?

54

Connected to all the right sources of information."

"It did that."

He let the silence drag on as long as he could bear, then made one more inadequate comment. "Knight. Another interesting choice."

"I thought it was apt."

He waited for elaboration, but she coolly changed the subject.

"I see your spider-sense is working as well as ever."

She kept her gaze fixed on the lake as if the barely visible movements of the men were fascinating. He wondered what she was thinking but dared not touch her to find out. She had been the first to call it his spider-sense, this ability he had to sharpen and amplify his sight and hearing to the point that he was often able to see and hear far beyond what was considered normal. He wondered if she had any idea that now he seldom thought of this ancillary skill by any other name.

"We'll know that if we find a well," he said finally.

"Oh, there's a well."

He really wished she would look at him. "And a body?"

Miranda nodded. "And a body."

"There was no anonymous tip, was there, Miranda?"

"No."

"You had a vision."

Her shoulders moved in a faint, restless shrug that belied her calm expression. "I had a . . . very vivid daydream. I saw this lake. I knew she was here somewhere. I know it now. A well . . . feels right."

"Still reluctant to call them visions, I see."

"Visions? I'm the elected sheriff of a small, conservative town where the churches actually outnumber the car dealerships. Just how long do you suppose I'd keep my job if word got out that I was seeing visions?"

"Have you been able to hide it that well?"

"It's amazing how many nice, logical reasons one can find for possessing surprising knowledge." She drew a breath and let it out slowly. "I'm intuitive. I have hunches. I'm lucky. I'm very good at my job. I make sure there's evidence to support me. If all else fails, I rely on the traditional anonymous tip. And I'm very, very careful."

After a moment he said, "You have very loyal deputies."

"To take me at my word? I suppose. But I've been right before, and they've learned to trust me."

"Any idea who's behind these killings?"

Miranda's smile was twisted. "If I knew that, you wouldn't be here."

The bitterness in her voice was unmistakable, telling him with certainty for the first time that she was hardly as indifferent as she seemed on the surface. She didn't want him there. She hated him. And the strength of his own reaction to that surprised him.

"I never meant to hurt you," he said abruptly.

The light was going fast, but they could both see Alex Mayse on his way back up toward them.

"Hurting me," Miranda said, "was the least of it." Then she moved to meet her deputy.

THREE

It took less than two hours to find the well.

It took two more to bring up the hideously battered body of Lynet Grainger.

They had rigged several battery-powered lights to illuminate the clearing around the well, and that made it possible for Dr. Edwards to perform a preliminary exam at the scene. While she was doing that, the area was cordoned off and meticulously searched.

"Not that we'll find anything useful," Alex said to Miranda. "It rained again last night, and I'm betting she was dropped in there either before or during the rain. Nice way to wash away all the evidence. Doesn't miss a trick, our guy."

"You think it's the same killer?"

"I think you noticed the same thing I did."

"Yeah."

"Well then?"

She nodded slowly. "I think we have only one killer here. But . . . there's something different about this victim."

"What?"

"I don't know."

Alex waited a beat. "She's fully clothed, is that it? The other two were naked, or near enough."

"No . . . not that. Something else." She met his gaze and grimaced slightly. "Nothing I can explain, obviously. A hunch, I suppose."

"Your hunches are generally pretty sound."

"They haven't helped us much on this case." Miranda rubbed the back of her neck in a characteristic gesture of weariness.

Alex checked his watch. "Nearly ten. You've been out here more than eight hours, Randy. No supper, no lunch — and I'll bet you hardly slept last night."

Her gaze shifted to the other side of the cordoned-off area where Bishop stood talking to Agent Harte, but all she said was, "I'll sleep tonight. Too tired not to."

"Is Mrs. Task staying with Bonnie?"

"Till I get home, yeah. As usual. I don't know what I'd do without her."

"It goes both ways," Alex said. "She would have been in bad shape if you and

Bonnie hadn't come here eight years ago. Widowed and left up to her ears in debt by that louse she was married to, no other family, no skills, no friends. Taking care of the two of you gave her a new lease on life."

"If that's the case, she's more than repaid me. I just hate keeping her up all hours waiting for me."

"She doesn't mind. It's not like you make a habit of it — I mean, before the last couple of months."

That was true enough, Miranda admitted silently. Being the sheriff of a small and generally peaceful town was a nine-to-five job for the most part. There were occasional town council meetings and other evening commitments, but she was usually able to spend her nights home with Bonnie.

Even when she'd been a deputy serving under the last sheriff, the hours had been reasonable and the work mostly pleasant and undemanding.

But that was before a killer began stalking Gladstone.

Before the visions had returned.

Before Bishop came back into her life.

She looked at the doctor to avoid the temptation of watching Bishop, and saw Edwards make a subtle gesture toward him. By the time the doctor reached her and Alex,

Bishop and Agent Harte had also joined them.

"I have a preliminary report, Sheriff," Edwards said briskly. "I'll know more later, of course, but . . ."

"Go ahead, Doctor."

"Death occurred approximately twelve to twenty-four hours ago. She's in complete rigor, and judging by the position in which we found the body, she was probably dropped into the well no more than two or three hours after death but certainly well before rigor commenced. In these colder temperatures, of course, rigor would have been retarded for some time."

"Yes," Miranda said. "Go on."

"There are no external signs of rape or other sexual abuse. No signs she was tied up or otherwise bound or physically restrained. No defensive injuries. Nothing under the fingernails. She's been severely beaten by a blunt object, something wooden, possibly a baseball bat. The cause of death, I believe, will prove to be internal injuries caused by the beating. The body's been completely exsanguinated, and by someone who knew what they were doing."

Alex said, "There are people who specialize in draining blood? If anybody mentions vampires, I'll —"

61

Edwards shook her head, but showed no mockery. "Morticians, doctors, even a vet would know. But it's not just a matter of knowledge. This wasn't done out in a field somewhere. He had to have the right place and the right equipment."

"Running water," Miranda said. "Tubing, drains. Containers for the blood, if he kept it."

"Exactly." Edwards nodded. "He might have read up on the procedures, at least enough to have done a professional job, but we can be sure he had to have enough uninterrupted time and privacy to get the job done."

Miranda gazed steadily at the forensic expert. "Okay. And you're sure she didn't fight him? No defensive injuries, she wasn't restrained, nothing under her fingernails — she just let somebody beat her to death without a struggle?"

"I doubt she knew what was happening. A tox screen will tell us for certain, but I believe she was drugged, possibly to the point of coma, before she was killed."

"Bingo," Alex said quietly, looking at Miranda. "That's what's different."

"We haven't seen the detailed reports of the two other cases yet," Bishop reminded them.

Miranda answered the implicit question. "We don't know about Adam Ramsay, but the tox screen on Kerry Ingram came back negative, and all indications are that she was awake and aware through most of her ordeal. In fact, our medical examiner believes she was repeatedly strangled to the point of unconsciousness and then allowed to revive. A blow to the head finally killed her."

Agent Harte muttered, "I'll interpret that data to mean this guy is a real sicko."

"Amen," Alex agreed.

Edwards said, "I'll be able to test the remains of the Ramsay boy. We should know fairly quickly if he was drugged. And I'll know more about this one after the post."

Miranda said, "You didn't mention her eyes, Doctor."

"Removed, as you obviously noticed. And, again, by someone who knew what they were doing."

"Meaning?"

"Meaning that the eyes weren't hacked out or gouged out. They were very neatly removed from the sockets. Whoever did it was careful not to damage the surrounding tissue. In fact, that was the only injury above her neck."

"I'm no profiler," Alex said, looking at Bishop, "but that sounds significant to me."

"Could be," Bishop said dispassionately, as if he hadn't noticed the direct challenge. "By blinding his victim and yet leaving her face essentially undamaged, he could be telling us she knew him and he felt something for her, possibly even some kind of affection. He took her eyes because she'd seen him, and probably covered her face with something while he was beating her so he could think of her as a nameless, faceless object. On the other hand, though it's comparatively rare for a killer to take a body part as a trophy, that could also be a valid guess."

"I'm sorry I asked," Alex muttered.

"Why did he take her blood?" Miranda asked. "And Kerry Ingram's blood — possibly the blood of all three of them? What does that signify?"

"A ritualistic or cannibalistic obsession, most likely," Bishop answered promptly. "Assuming he kept it and didn't just drain it from the body, he needs the blood or believes he does. Either to drink it or use it some other way in a ritual that's important to him."

"Then maybe," Miranda suggested, "he needed Lynet's eyes as well."

"It is possible," Bishop agreed. "At this point, I barely have enough information to offer a threshold diagnosis, much less a complete profile."

Edwards said, "And I've learned all I can from this body, at least for the moment. Also, in case the rest of you haven't noticed, it's getting damned cold out here. I suggest we bag the body and take it to your autopsy facility, and I'll get started on the post."

"Our autopsy facility," Alex said, "is the morgue of the county hospital. I think they threw out the leeches a year or so ago."

Edwards smiled faintly. "Fieldwork demands accommodations, Deputy. I always bring my own equipment along."

"Wise of you."

Miranda said, "The hearse we've been using to transport the bodies is back with the other vehicles, Doctor. Take as many of my people as you need to help."

"Thank you, Sheriff."

After Edwards and Harte moved away, Alex said, "Randy, why don't you head on back? It's been a hell of a long day, and tomorrow won't be any better."

Very conscious of Bishop's silent attention, Miranda shook her head. "I still have to go tell Teresa Grainger about her daughter, before she hears it from someone else. Besides, we'll be finished up here in another hour."

"A word, Sheriff?" Bishop's tone was impersonal.

Miranda followed him a few feet away, keeping a careful and deliberate distance between them. She didn't have to wait long to hear what he had to say.

"Miranda, if my team's to be of any real use to you, they have to be able to do their jobs."

She stiffened. "I wasn't aware anyone was interfering with them."

"You are."

She opened her mouth to deny it, but he didn't give her a chance.

"You closed down like a steel trap the moment we got here. And whatever else may have changed in eight years, that hasn't. You're blocking them, Miranda. They can't pick up a damned thing, from the body or from the area, as long as you're here."

"You didn't seem to have any trouble." She refused to look away from those pale sentry eyes of his, refused to give him the satisfaction of knowing he could still get under her skin — even if not inside her head.

"And we both know why," he said flatly. "But my team doesn't have the same . . . advantage."

It took every ounce of her willpower not

to hit him. She couldn't say a word, didn't trust herself to speak at all.

Obviously not suffering from the same paralysis, he said, "Let us do what we came here to do, Miranda. And you do what you have to do. Go tell that kid's mother she won't be coming home. And then get some rest. We'll start fresh in the morning."

She still couldn't say a word, because she knew if she did it would become a torrent of words. Words about betrayal. Words about dishonesty and deception, about hurt and loss and bitterness and rage.

So she didn't say a word. She just turned and headed around the lake to her Jeep. She left Bishop to explain to Alex and the others why she had left so abruptly.

She knew he'd think of something to tell them.

"My God, we do have a serial killer," the mayor said, horrified.

John MacBride was seated across the desk from Miranda, who wished for the third time that she had gone straight home from Teresa Grainger's place. Instead, she had stopped at the office for what she'd thought would be no more than ten minutes. But MacBride showed up and the ten minutes stretched into twenty.

"We don't know that for sure," she told him patiently.

"With three dead teenagers? What else could it be?"

"They used to call serial killers 'stranger killers,' because they seldom had any connection to or prior knowledge of their victims. I don't believe that's the case here. And given the way we found the bodies, I think the task force will eventually classify these as bizarre murders — killings committed to satisfy the needs of some kind of ritual."

MacBride looked more appalled. He was normally a handsome man, but signs of strain had appeared in recent weeks, and his expression of dismay made the dark circles under his eyes and lines on his face much more evident.

"Ritual killings?" he exclaimed. "Do you mean we're dealing with satanism or some other kind of occult shit?"

"I don't know, John. But if you're imagining black-robed figures dancing around a fire out in the woods under a full moon, forget it. We have one killer here, and whatever his reasons for killing, whatever his sick rituals are, I believe we'll find he's acting alone."

"That doesn't make me feel any better,

dammit! The bastard's done a hell of a lot of damage alone." He brooded for a moment. "It has to be a stranger. Someone who doesn't actually live in Gladstone but just —"

"Just hunts here?" Miranda shrugged. "It's possible. And now, with three killings to reference, at least we should be able to note enough commonalities to ask law enforcement in surrounding counties to check their own unsolved cases for similar killings."

"The publicity," MacBride moaned.

Miranda decided she wasn't up to reassuring a worried mayor tonight; no matter what she said, it would only upset him more. With a sigh, she rose to her feet.

"Look, John, let's not borrow more trouble, all right? We'll do our best to limit publicity. Besides, if this FBI task force is as good as their reputation, chances are we'll have this case solved and the killer in custody very soon."

"And if they're not as good?" He got up too, moving stiffly and frowning. "I've already had a dozen calls tonight, Randy. Panic is spreading quickly."

"Then we'll do what we can to calm everybody down, John. We'll recommend reasonable precautions, and we'll make certain the town knows that every resource we can muster is focused on finding this killer."

"And we should make sure those FBI people are visible. Very visible."

Miranda knew that MacBride was prepared to publicly cast the entire responsibility of capturing the killer onto the broader shoulders of the FBI. That didn't bother Miranda so much for her own sake, but she'd be damned if her own people didn't get the credit they deserved. They had already put in long hours of painstaking work.

But all she said was, "I imagine they'll be visible enough, John. Aside from everything else, we only have one motel in town, and since it's on Main Street and seldom has more than a couple of overnight guests in any given week . . ."

He grunted. "Yeah, you're right about that. But look, Randy, I'd appreciate daily reports."

"I'll be sure to keep you informed," she said noncommittally.

He sighed, but didn't insist. Instead, he said, "Why don't you let me give you a ride home? You must be exhausted, and I'm parked out front —"

"So am I," she told him. "Besides, I want to get an early start in the morning, so I'd rather drive home tonight. But thanks, John."

He sighed again. "One of these days, you're going to say yes, Randy."

"Good night, John."

The Bluebird Lodge sucked.

That was Bishop's considered opinion, and not even the "major renovations" in the works, according to the owner/manager, could make the place any better. It boasted two floors but no interior hallways, cramped rooms furnished in decent quality but questionable taste, and unless one chose to visit a restaurant down the street (which closed promptly at 9:00 P.M.), the only options for dining were a couple of vending machines.

Still, at least the place was clean.

It was nearly midnight. Bishop and his team planned to make an early start the following day, and he knew he should sleep. But he was too keyed up.

He unpacked and set his laptop up on the ridiculously small desk near the window. After connecting with Quantico, he downloaded a few potentially useful data files. It was something he usually did long before he was actually on the scene, but in this case . . .

He sat back in the none-too-comfortable chair and stared at an uninspired print on the wall. But he was seeing something else.

She had changed in eight years. Still strikingly lovely, of course, but he'd expected that, had braced himself for it. Or thought he had. But the girl he remembered, dazzling though she had been then, had grown in the years since into a woman of uncommon beauty and rare strength.

Her vivid blue eyes didn't gleam with laughter as readily as before, and they had a depth that hid thoughts and secrets. Her beautiful face revealed only what she chose to reveal, and her splendid body moved with fluid grace. Her voice was measured, controlled, a voice one could hardly imagine spitting out shaking curses in grief and rage and pain.

"You ruthless, coldhearted bastard! You'll use anything and anyone you have to, won't you? As long as you get what you want, as long as you win, you don't give a shit what happens to anyone else!"

He wondered if now, under the same circumstances, Miranda would simply shoot him.

Not that the circumstances would ever be the same.

He never made the same mistake twice.

No, this Miranda, this woman he had faced today across a gulf of eight years and too much pain and loss, was not the girl he remembered. She had perfected her previously erratic control and learned not only to shield herself but to extend that bubble of protection outside herself to enclose others.

He knew why, of course. Because of Bonnie.

The human mind was a remarkable instrument, the human will even more so. Miranda had needed to protect Bonnie, and that intense, desperate need had driven her to hone her extraordinary ability.

He wondered if she had any idea just how extraordinary.

It was . . . an unanticipated complication. He was confident of getting through her shields by touch; after all, his spider-sense had, as she had noted, functioned normally despite them. And he did have an advantage over most other people when it came to her. But her strength had surprised him. It told him Miranda would give up nothing against her will.

If he forced his way past her shields, he doubted either of them would emerge from the battle without untold damage.

Bishop allowed himself a moment of grimly amused self-mockery. For eight years, he had focused on the simple need to find her, deluding himself that the wounds he had inflicted could be healed quickly once he was able to face her again, to talk to her. He had imagined that her pain and bitterness had faded with time, making it even easier for him.

But it was not going to be easy to earn Miranda's forgiveness. If it would even be possible.

"Hurting me was the least of it."

She was wrong about that, as far as he was concerned. What he had done could not be undone; the dead could not be brought back to life. For that, he expected no forgiveness, because he would never forgive himself. But he meant to make things right between him and Miranda.

Whatever it cost him.

Miranda broke the news to her sister and Mrs. Task when she got home, but she kept it brief. Lynet Grainger's body had been found, that's all they needed to know. For now, at least.

Bonnie wasn't surprised; Miranda had told her before she'd gone to the lake that she was certain they would find another body.

The housekeeper was horrified; she'd been saying over and over "that Grainger girl" had just run away, most likely, and would probably come home any day now.

Whistling in the graveyard.

Like everyone in town, she didn't want to believe that a monster lurked nearby. A monster that looked human.

"Poor Teresa," Mrs. Task murmured as she put on her coat. "You told her?"

"Yes, before I came home," Miranda said. "And called her sister to come stay with her."

"She wasn't drinking?"

"Not as far as I could tell. In fact, I think she's been cold sober since she woke up to find Lynet gone. It's just a pity she didn't wake up sooner."

"I'll take something over tomorrow." Like many of her generation, Mrs. Task believed life's hurts and death's shocks could be eased with food.

"I'm sure she'd appreciate that," Miranda murmured, sure only that lots of neighbors would bring lots of food to try to fill the terrible void left by the death of a child.

Mrs. Task shook her head as she picked up her purse. "Poor thing. To lose a child . . ."

Bonnie waited until after the housekeeper had left, then said, "One of Mrs. Task's friends called and told her the FBI agents had come. Had they?"

Miranda nodded.

"Well? Is it him?"

"Three agents. Naturally, he's the one in charge."

Bonnie looked at her anxiously. "Did you talk to him?"

"About the investigation." Miranda shrugged. "He was entirely professional. So was I."

"But he remembered you."

"Oh, yes. He remembered." *Too damned well.*

"Did he ask why you'd changed your name?"

"He didn't have to ask."

"Did you tell him what you saw?"

"No. No, of course not. He doesn't need to know about that. Not now. Not yet."

After a moment, Bonnie said, "Why don't you shower and get ready for bed while I heat up supper?"

"I'm not very hungry."

"You have to eat, Randy."

Miranda was too tired to argue. She went upstairs and took a long, hot shower, trying to soothe weary muscles and wash away tension and the stink of death. She did feel better afterward, at least physically. When she returned to the kitchen in robe and slippers she felt a twinge of appetite as she smelled stew.

Automatically, Miranda reached for a coffee cup, but found herself holding a glass of milk instead.

"The last thing you need tonight," Bonnie said, "is more caffeine."

Again, Miranda didn't argue. She drank her milk and ate the stew without tasting it, wondering how long she could delay the conversation her sister undoubtedly wanted to have.

"Has Bishop changed much?"

Not long at all.

"He's older. We're all older."

"Does he look different?"

"Not that I noticed."

"Is he married?"

The question startled Miranda. "No," she said quickly, then added, "I don't know. He isn't wearing a ring."

"And you didn't talk about personal things."

I never meant to hurt you.

"No," Miranda said steadily. "We didn't talk about personal things."

"Because you're all closed up?"

"Because there's no reason for us to discuss personal things, Bonnie. He's here to do a job, and that's all."

"Can he still . . ."

"What?"

"Can he still get in even when you're all closed up?"

Miranda stared down at her empty milk glass. "I don't know."

"But —"

"We didn't touch."

"Not at all?"

"No."

Bonnie frowned. "You have to find out, Randy. If he can't get in, he won't be able to help you when the time comes."

"I know."

Bonnie hesitated, then said gently, "If he can't get in, you'll have to *let* him in."

"I know that too."

"Can you do it?"

"You said it. I'll have to."

Bonnie bit her lip. "I know you said leaving wouldn't change anything, but —"

"Even if we could, it's too late." Because Bishop was here now. Because events had been set in motion and there was no stopping them, not until they reached their inevitable conclusion.

Not until it was finally over.

fOUK

Sunday, January 9

The Cox County Sheriff's Department was housed in a building less than twenty years old. And back when it was designed, the city fathers had envisioned continued economic growth along the happy lines of what the town had then been experiencing. Unfortunately, they'd been wrong, but at least their optimism had led to a building with numerous offices and a spacious conference room, which was used mostly for storage.

Miranda had left orders, and by the time she and two of the three FBI agents met there early the following morning, the conference room had been cleared of boxes of old files and supplies, and provided a decent base of operations for the task force. Extra phone lines were already in place, as were fixed blackboards and bulletin boards, and the three large partner desks contained all the usual supplies. There was a conference table big enough to seat six, several pieces of antiquated audiovisual equipment, and one five-year-old desktop computer hastily shifted from one of the outer offices.

The coffeemaker, at least, was new.

Miranda didn't bother to apologize for the inadequacies of her department; since Dr. Edwards had brought her own equipment along, and both Bishop and Harte arrived this morning with the latest thing in laptop computers, she figured they'd expected small-town deficiencies from the get-go.

And if they didn't like it, tough.

She got them settled in the room with all the files on the investigation, assigned a regrettably awed and nervous young deputy to fetch and carry for them, and retreated to her office to handle the morning's duties.

She called the morgue first and was told by Dr. Edwards that the postmortem on Lynet Grainger was well under way.

"By the way, I've studied Dr. Shepherd's report on the post he performed on Kerry Ingram, and I don't believe there'll be any need to exhume the body."

Kerry was the only victim whose body had been released to the family for burial, and Miranda was intensely grateful that she probably wouldn't have to return to those grieving relatives and ask to dig up their little girl for another session on the autopsy table.

"Dr. Shepherd was quite thorough," Edwards said cheerfully, "and careful in preserving the slides and tissue samples, so there should be no trouble in verifying his findings."

In the background, Peter Shepherd could be heard to say that he appreciated that.

Miranda was relieved yet again by that little aside. Not that she'd expected trouble from him since calling in a more experienced forensics expert had been his suggestion — but you just never knew about professionals, especially doctors. So jealous of their authority.

"Thank you, Doctor," she said to Edwards. "If there's anything you need, please call me here at the office."

"I will, Sheriff, thanks. I should have a written report for you by the end of the day."

Miranda hung up, then turned to the stack of messages that had come in already this morning. She spent considerable time returning calls and soothing, as best she could, the fears and worries of the people who had voted her into office.

Not that there was much she could really say to reassure anyone.

She did try, though, listening patiently to suggestions ranging from a dusk-to-dawn curfew of everyone in town under the age of eighteen to the calling in of the National Guard, and offering her own brand of calm confidence.

They would catch the killer, she was certain of it.

She told no one what else she was certain of — that more teenagers would have to die first. Unless she found a way to frustrate fate.

That was possible. She had done it once before, after all.

By eleven o'clock, Miranda couldn't listen to one more anxious voice, so she went back to the conference room to escape the ceaseless ringing of her telephone.

At least, that's what she told herself.

Bishop and Harte had been busy. Files were lying open or stacked neatly on the conference table, alongside legal pads covered with notes. Their laptops and the old desktop were humming, and an even older printer was laboring in the corner to produce a hard copy of somebody's request.

The big bulletin board on the wall had been divided into three sections, one for each victim, and all the photos of the bodies at the crime scenes were tacked up, along with autopsy reports. Agent Harte was writing a time line on the blackboard, printing in block letters the names and ages of the victims, when and where they'd disappeared, and when and where the bodies had been found.

Bishop, who was half sitting on one end of the conference table and watching Harte, greeted Miranda by saying, "You saw the time pattern, of course."

Miranda wasn't especially flattered that he expected her to see the obvious. "You mean that the disappearances were almost exactly two months apart? Of course. Any ideas as to why that particular amount of time?"

"I wouldn't want to hazard an opinion until we find all the commonalities between the victims and start developing a reasonable profile of the killer."

That made sense and was what Miranda had expected. Still, she had to make a comment. "He does seem to be killing them quicker each time."

Bishop consulted the legal pad beside him. "Your M.E. estimates the Ramsay boy was killed as much as six weeks after he disappeared, the Ingram girl less than four weeks. And since Lynet Grainger disappeared only a few days ago, we know she was killed in a matter of hours."

Tony Harte stepped back to view his work. "So we have several possibilities. He might have drastically stepped up his timetable for some reason important to him and his ritual. He might have discovered soon after he grabbed her that the Grainger girl didn't fit his requirements as he'd expected, and therefore killed her in rage. Killing her quickly might have *been* part of his ritual, a new step. Or there was something different about Grainger, something that made him treat her unlike the other victims."

Miranda thought those were pretty good possibilities.

"So we don't know if we have two months before he grabs another kid."

Harte shook his head soberly. "Ask me, he could grab another one today or tomorrow. Then again, he could also wait two months or six — or move to a new hunting ground. We don't know enough yet."

Since she was alone with the agents, she said point-blank, "Did any of you pick up anything last night after I left?" She looked at Harte but it was Bishop who answered.

"Tony thinks the killer knew the girl, probably quite well. He got a strong sense of regret, even sadness."

Miranda regarded the agent with genuine interest. "So that's your other specialty, huh? You pick up emotional vibes?"

He laughed softly. "That's as good a definition as any, I guess."

Miranda sat in a chair at the opposite end of the conference table from Bishop. "What about Dr. Edwards? What's her nonmedical specialty?"

"Similar to mine. Only she picks up bits of information rather than feelings, hard facts. Tunes in to the physical vibes, I guess you'd say. We lump both abilities under the heading of 'adept.' "

"I see. And did she pick up any physical vibes out at the well last night?"

"None to speak of. She thinks he lingered only long enough to dump the body. I agree." It was his turn to look at her with interest. "And I must say, it's a nice change to deal with local law enforcement without having to find alternate explanations for how we gather some of our information."

"If you use unconventional methods," Miranda said, "you've got to expect that sort of suspicion and disbelief."

"But not from you."

"No. Not from me." She smiled faintly. "And don't try to tell me you don't know why."

"Because you're pretty good at picking up vibes yourself?"

"Picking up vibes isn't really my strong suit. It's what Bishop used to call an ancillary ability," she said, keeping her gaze fixed on Harte. "Like his spider-sense, only not nearly so focused."

"Ah. One of the rare psychics possessing more than a single skill. And your primary ability?"

"Once upon a time, it was precognition. But I burned that one out pretty thoroughly years ago. The . . . visions . . . are few and far between these days."

Harte's spaniel-brown eyes widened, and he looked at Bishop with something like wonder. "My God," he said softly. "Three separate abilities?"

"Four," Bishop said. "Aside from being adept, precognitive, and able to project a shield, she's also a pretty fair touch telepath. On our scale . . . probably eighth degree."

"Wow," Harte said, again very softly.

Miranda wasn't entirely sure she liked Bishop's frankness, but knew only too well that she herself had opened the door. It just felt odd to be discussing it so openly after so many years of careful silence. She didn't want to admit even to herself that it also felt sort of nice to talk to people who understood and accepted.

But curiosity drove her to ask, "Eighth degree? What the hell kind of scale are we talking about?" Since Harte still appeared a bit stunned, she had no choice but to look, finally, at Bishop.

He gazed at her steadily, his pale eyes unreadable. "A scale we developed at Quantico while putting the program together the last few years."

"Being anal feds," she said dryly, "you just had to weigh, measure, and evaluate even the paranormal, huh?"

"Something like that."

She realized he wasn't going to tell her unless she asked, and it annoyed her. "Okay, I'll bite. So how high does this scale of yours go?"

"To twelve."

"Which, I suppose, is your degree?"

Bishop shook his head. "We have yet to encounter a psychic with any kind of twelfth-degree ability. I rank at a little above ten telepathically."

"How about the spider-sense? What does that rank?"

"Maybe six. On a good day."

"To put things into perspective," Harte murmured, "Sharon and I both come in around three on the scale as adepts. Most of the other members of the unit, in fact, don't go above five. And only one other agent besides Bishop has even an ancillary ability, far less a full-blown secondary ability. This is the first time I've ever met *anybody* with more than two. In fact, it's the first time I've even heard of it."

"Yeah, well. I come from a long line of overachievers." Miranda wasn't as impressed with herself as Harte was. Familiarity had not bred contempt, but it had bred acceptance; to Miranda, the paranormal was just a part of life.

"Why in hell are you stuck way out here in the boonies instead of playing on our team?" Harte exclaimed, then winced and sent an apologetic look to Bishop. "Yikes. Sorry, boss."

"Tony," Bishop said mildly, "I think the coffeepot is empty. Why don't you go fill it?"

"Hey, you don't have to drop a house on me to get me to go away. I'm psychic — I can take a more subtle hint than that." He grabbed the coffeepot and beat a hasty retreat, closing the door gently behind him.

Miranda didn't know which emotion was stronger, furious embarrassment that her past was not, apparently, as private as she had supposed, or furious pain that Bishop had evidently discussed her with at least one member of his team.

"I'm sorry, Miranda."

She forced herself not to look away, and called on all her self-control to present an indifferent front. "About what? Discussing me with your agents? Should I have expected anything else?"

"I hope so. It isn't what you obviously think."

"Isn't it?"

"Miranda, they're psychics. And even though my walls are fairly solid, I can't project an impenetrable shield the way you can — even around my own mind."

She was glad her shield was firmly in place just then, glad he had no idea of her thoughts and emotions. But all she said was, "So whose idea was this new unit of yours? It doesn't sound at all typical of the Bureau."

For a moment, she thought he would fight her, but finally he answered.

"It isn't. There was a great deal of resistance at first, until it was proved that unconventional methods and abilities could produce tangible results."

"And who proved that? You?"

"Eventually."

"Really? How?"

He drew a breath. "I tracked down the Rosemont Butcher."

Miranda rose to her feet slowly, staring

at him. "What?" she whispered.

"Lewis Harrison. I got him, Miranda. Six and a half years ago."

Alex had been more or less ordered not to come into the office on Sunday. He'd been working nearly three weeks without a break, and Miranda claimed the town council would have her head on a platter if she didn't see to it that he took time off whether he wanted to or not. Overtime was one thing, she said, but he was carrying it to extremes — even if they *did* have a serial killer to find.

He hated days off. He wasn't a sporting man, so hunting and fishing held no appeal for him. Neither did golf. Watching sports on television was an enjoyable pastime only during baseball season. He ran and worked out to keep in shape, but a man could hardly do that all day.

And then there was the house. It was too big and too damned empty. He should get rid of it, he knew. But Janet had loved the house, had decorated it with painstaking care, and in the year since her death he hadn't been able to face the thought of someone else living in Janet's house.

But living in the house alone had its own kind of pain, and though sleeping there was, finally, possible, Alex could seldom spend much time in it when he was awake.

Unfortunately, Sundays in Gladstone didn't offer a lot in the way of entertainment once church let out. And even less if one wasn't particularly interested in church.

He finally drove to town, resisting the urge to stop by the office and find out what was going on. Instead, he parked near Liz's bookstore and coffeeshop, forced to wait nearly forty-five minutes for Liz to unlock the doors at two o'clock.

"I heard about Lynet," she said.

"Yeah, poor kid." Alex sat at the counter rather than his usual booth, since Liz worked alone on Sundays.

"And I heard the FBI is in town."

"Well, three agents anyway." He smiled. "Your dark man with a mark on his face is one of them. And Randy knows him." Then Alex recalled what Liz had said about the fate of that man, and his smile faded. "You don't still think —"

Liz chewed on her bottom lip. "When I read the leaves again, it was more fuzzy, less definite, but I'm sure it was the same thing, Alex. Does — does Randy like him?"

Alex considered the question. "To be honest, the only thing I'm sure of is that she feels a lot about him. Whether it's like or dislike, positive or negative, I can't tell."

"Maybe I should talk to her about what I saw," Liz suggested hesitantly. "She's never scoffed. Never let me read the leaves for her, but —"

Alex shook his head. "Not right now, Liz. Randy has enough on her plate, I think, without having to worry about something that might not happen."

"I knew it would be a strange year, new millennium and all, but I really don't like all these bad omens, Alex."

"More dogs howling at night?"

Before she could answer, Justin Marsh stormed into the coffeeshop, his thin little wife, Selena, on his heels like a mute shadow.

"Elizabeth, I'm asking you again not to conduct business on the Sabbath!" he thundered as though from a pulpit.

Alex sighed. "Justin, why're you picking on Liz? Half the retail businesses and all the restaurants and cafe's open up after church. Afternoon, Selena."

"Hello." She smiled timidly, holding her Bible with both hands as though she feared it would escape any minute. She might have been pretty once, but Selena had been married to Justin Marsh for nearly thirty years and the ordeal had worn her down. She was seldom seen in public without him, and Alex couldn't recall hearing her say much more than hello and goodbye, with an occasional Praise the Lord or Amen thrown in at appropriate pauses in Justin's oratory.

"As a matter of fact," Alex went on, "didn't you use to open up your car lot on Sundays before you retired and sold out?"

"I saw the error of my ways," Justin declared piously, his face reddening. "And now I'm commanded by the Lord to guide the others of his flock toward the light of salvation!"

Alex almost gave that one an Amen himself. He always appreciated a good dramatic performance.

Gravely, Liz said, "Can I get you two some coffee, Justin? Purely on the house, you understand — not a business transaction."

He leaned across the counter, eyes intent on her face. "Elizabeth, I will place your feet upon a godly path. You must not be allowed to follow the evil way. A good woman such as you should have an honored place in the house of our Lord."

Normally Alex was patient with Justin's excesses, but with the memory of poor little Lynet's battered body vivid in his mind, he snapped. "Justin, if you want to seek out evil, you might begin with whoever killed our teenagers. I'd think that would be a damned sight more important to any god than whether Liz should sell coffee and books on Sunday!"

Justin made a choked sound, then turned away. Selena, out of long practice, skipped nimbly aside, then shadowed him faithfully as he stalked out of the store.

"I don't like that man," Alex said.

"But you shouldn't have said that, Alex. You know he'll go straight to the mayor."

"Oh, don't worry about it. Right now, even the mayor has more to worry about than Justin Marsh's ruffled feathers."

Sharon Edwards stripped off her rubber gloves and looked across the table at Peter Shepherd. "No question about it."

Shepherd grunted. "I don't get it," he said. "What would be the point?"

"We'll add that to our list of questions to ask this lunatic when we catch him. In the meantime, if you'll box up all the slides and tissue samples, I'll get started on the report for the sheriff."

"Six and a half years ago," Miranda repeated numbly. "But . . . there was nothing about it on the news."

"Not the national news, no. Coincidentally, a far more famous killer was captured that week — a mass murderer out in Texas — and he got all the national media attention."

"I checked NCIC," Miranda protested. "As soon as I joined the Sheriff's Department here and had access, I checked every month to see if he'd been caught."

"I'm sorry," Bishop said. "Some inside the Bureau were convinced Harrison had a partner, that one man couldn't have done everything he'd confessed to doing. The decision was made to keep the case file open, to list him as at large to make certain any similar crimes would send up a flag."

"But how could they do that unless —" She sat back down in her chair. "He's dead?"

Bishop nodded.

"You?"

"Yes."

She was, on some level, surprised to feel so little about the death of Lewis Harrison. For so long, he had been a part of her life, a continual threat, the monster hiding in the closet ready to spring out when darkness came.

She doubted there had been a single night in the last eight years that she had not thought of him in the instant before she turned off her bedside lamp. As for Bonnie, the poor kid still had nightmares, horrible ones. Not so often now, but it was clear she had forgotten nothing of terror.

Miranda couldn't help but wonder how her life might have been different if she'd known Lewis Harrison could never take anything away from her ever again.

What would have changed?

"I wanted to tell you, Miranda. I tried to find you."

"I didn't want to be found," she murmured.

"That became obvious sooner rather than later. Not even FBI resources can locate an angry psychic if she doesn't want to be found."

Miranda didn't explain the methods she had used to start her life over again, though she knew he was curious. Even with the threat of Harrison gone, she was wary enough to want to protect secrets she might need again someday.

Always assuming she survived the next few weeks.

She looked across the table at Bishop and suddenly a dark, chilling doubt twisted inside her. He was ruthless, always had been. When it came to doing his job, he believed the end justified the means, and he was perfectly capable of doing whatever it took to accomplish his objectives.

God, how well she knew that.

So what were his objectives now? To persuade her to drop her guard, her shields, so he could use her abilities to track down a vicious killer? To convince her there was no threat to her and Bonnie, no reason for her to protect herself and her sister?

Would he lie to convince her?

Even though he certainly couldn't read her thoughts, Miranda saw a change in his face, as if he realized what she was thinking.

"I am not lying," he said evenly.

She conjured a brittle smile. "You'll have to forgive me if I don't take your word for that."

Bishop moved slightly, an unconscious shifting of his weight in protest or denial, but all he said, in that same level voice, was, "I'll make sure you're allowed access to the sealed records concerning Harrison."

"You do that," Miranda said.

FIVE

It was after noon when Tony Harte stuck his head cautiously into the conference room. He found Bishop alone, still sitting on the table, still staring at the blackboard. He appeared perfectly calm, but the scar on his face stood out whitely from the tanned flesh surrounding it and Harte took due note of a warning sign he had learned to be wary of.

"Um . . . the sheriff left a few minutes ago," Harte offered.

"I know."

"I mean, she left the building."

Bishop looked at him briefly. "Yes. I know."

"She seemed to be in an awful hurry. Couldn't wait to get out of here, was my take."

Bishop kept his gaze on the blackboard.

Harte came in and got a fresh pot of coffee brewing. He debated with himself silently, then sighed and ventured where many before him hadn't dared to tread.

"Back when I joined up, the word was you didn't get official approval for the new unit until you threatened to quit. Even after all the stuff you did unofficially, the years of planning and testing and building the program, after all the fieldwork and a growing list of closed cases, the Bureau still didn't want to openly sanction — or appear to sanction — highly unorthodox investigative methods. Even after you gave them results they couldn't deny. But they didn't want to lose one of their top profilers, so they finally gave the unit their official seal of approval — even if it did make them queasy to do it."

"If you get anywhere near a point, Tony, make it."

Harte didn't let that warning voice dissuade him. "I was just thinking that Sheriff Knight probably has no idea that because of her there are a lot of monsters in cages where they belong."

Bishop didn't respond.

"And I was thinking maybe you should tell her."

"If you think it would even the score," Bishop said, "you're wrong."

"Maybe. But she might feel better

knowing something positive came out of tragedy."

"You mean she might hate me a little less?" Bishop's smile was hardly worthy of the name. "Don't count on it."

"If you'll excuse me for saying so, boss, letting things go on the way they are between you is just going to slow us down. If we're going to catch this bastard, we'll need every ace we can pull out of our sleeves — and that includes an incredibly gifted psychic with singular abilities who right now is very much shut inside herself."

"She couldn't sense him before we got here," Bishop argued.

"Probably because of her shield. Because she's had to hide what she can do, had to be careful. And . . . because she was hiding here herself. Hiding her sister." Harte paused. "I gather she knows she doesn't have to do that anymore."

"She knows what I've told her. Whether she believes I told her the truth is something else entirely."

"You can prove it's the truth." Then Harte shook his head. "Except that official records have the bastard still alive and at large. You'll have to get her access to the sealed records."

"I know."

Harte eyed him, wondering if Bishop wanted Sheriff Knight to believe him without proof. Definitely a proud man, was Bishop. But not a stupid man. He had to know that his past actions made Miranda Knight nothing but suspicious.

Harte tentatively sensed the emotions in the room, much as a trained hunting dog would sniff the air for telltale scent, and was startled by the turmoil he detected in his normally composed boss. The feelings went deep and sharp, a confusion of anger and guilt, hunger and regret, pain and need and shame.

Slowly, Harte said, "Proof or no, it'll take her some time to get used to the idea, I imagine. But once she gets past that, once she realizes she can open up . . . then there's you."

"Then there's me. Keeping her closed." Bishop sighed and stared at his subordinate with grim eyes. "Sometimes I hate working with psychics."

"Ninety-eight-percent success rate," Harte reminded him.

"Yeah, yeah. Just stay the hell out of my head, will you, please?"

"Hey, boss, I can't get into your head. That's not my forte, remember? I just pick things up from the air. Not my fault if you're tossing 'em out there."

"I'll try to watch that," Bishop said dryly.

"Yeah, you might want to," Harte murmured, fixing his attention on a small and unnecessary adjustment to the coffeemaker.

A tinge of hot color stole into Bishop's cheeks. "Any idea where she went?"

"Nope. But it is lunchtime, more or less; maybe she has a usual haunt. Being the sheriff, I'd assume she has to always leave word where she'll be. Or wear a pager, I suppose, though I didn't notice one earlier. I saw her speak to the receptionist — what's her name, Grace? — before she went out."

Bishop didn't bother to invent an excuse for leaving the conference room; there really were precious few secrets among a team of psychics, and if it disturbed him to have his thoughts and emotions plucked out of hiding, at least it also made prevarication useless and explanation unnecessary.

Grace hesitated when he stopped at her desk to ask, but the sheriff had, after all, instructed that the task force be given any assistance requested.

"She's at Tim's. Karate school. Main Street, downtown, you can't miss it." Grace Russell had worked with cops for too many years to be easily intimidated, but this federal agent made her feel uneasy. Maybe it was his pale eyes, looking right through a body the way they did. Or maybe it was the wicked scar that twisted down the left side of his face and suggested an odd duality about the man — one side of him perfect, the other side marred, by mischance or failure. From a purely female perspective, she thought it was a real pity; without that scar, he would have been drop-dead gorgeous, and not many men could carry that off while still being uncompromisingly masculine.

At the same time, the scar lent him a dangerous air that was also immensely fascinating. Grace had seen the female deputies eyeing him unobtrusively, and the interest in their faces had little to do with professional wariness of a federal cop in their midst.

"A karate school? Open on Sunday?" Bishop's voice was perfectly courteous, his expression entirely unreadable, but Grace had the uncomfortable idea that he knew exactly what she was thinking.

"Not officially open, no, but a few of Tim's students work out there in the afternoons, even sometimes on Sunday. Sheriff Knight usually takes part of her lunch hour." Not that he could help the scar, she supposed, though cosmetic surgery could do wonders these days, and why such a good-looking man would choose to wear his one physical flaw right on his face for all to see baffled her.

"Thank you, Mrs. Russell." Perfectly aware of her thoughts even without touching her, Bishop left her to speculate as to when and how he had gotten the scar. The speculation didn't bother him any more than her wariness did; he had grown accustomed to both over the years.

She was right in saying that he couldn't miss the karate school; the line of trophies and ribbons in the front window would have made it obvious even without the sign proclaiming the Tim Skinner School of Karate. Bishop contemplated the name for a moment, then shrugged and went inside.

He found himself in a huge classroom where six students ranging in age from eight to sixteen worked out in pairs under the watchful eye of an instructor. No one noticed him as he walked to the half-open door and looked into the other, smaller classroom.

Only two people were there, each barefoot and wearing a white gi so associated with karate. One of them was a man of perhaps forty-five who moved with such expertise, it was hard to imagine that anyone could offer him a decent challenge.

Miranda clearly could.

Balance exceptional and concentration absolute, she compensated for less muscle with speed and agility that were mesmerizing to watch and kept her opponent on his toes.

Bishop wasn't surprised by her skill or the black belt she wore, though he knew she must have begun studying karate only in the past eight years. He watched her through the door, not calling attention to his presence — and saw the change in her the instant she sensed him there.

Her shoulders tensed and her head turned just a bit toward him. Then her workout partner moved in with a flying kick, and all her attention was taken up by the necessity of defending herself.

It bothered Bishop that Miranda could sense him even through her shields — and yet he could not sense her. Once, he had been able to. Once, he had known whenever she was anywhere near him. When she had been hurt or upset, he had felt it instantly.

Once.

Now she might as well be a stranger. He was aware of her only if he saw or heard her. If she walked silently into a room behind him, he would be completely oblivious of her arrival.

That was a cold realization.

It didn't help to remind himself that she was a far more experienced telepath and that her version of a spider-sense had always been more defensive than his own. On top of which, she had been hunted by a deadly predator. Living for years in fear for her life had, without doubt, sharpened her immediate awareness of any threat.

He was a threat.

Bishop turned around and walked back to the front door. He went outside and stood on the sidewalk, his back to the school, and his gaze fixed on nothing.

Miranda had been closed before his arrival, but her intuition and spider-sense had functioned; even her precognitive abilities had allowed her to "see" Lynet Grainger being found in water near the lake. She had been closed just enough to protect herself and her sister.

But now Miranda was willfully making herself blind and deaf in a psychic sense, cutting off the extra abilities that made her who she was. It was a drastic, desperate act, and it told Bishop more clearly than words ever could that he had done much more than simply hurt her eight years before.

The question was . . . how could he atone for a mistake that had cost them both so much?

In a rare unguarded gesture of vulnerability, he reached up and fingered the scar marking his left cheek. Then he swore beneath his breath and shoved his hands in the pockets of his jacket. And stared at nothing.

It was quite a while before he became aware that drivers were slowing down to get a better look at him and that the very few pedestrians were eyeing him warily.

"When the churchgoers start heading for the café and bookstore, you'll be drawing quite a crowd," Miranda said dryly.

He had been right. She had silently joined him on the sidewalk and he hadn't realized she was near.

Bishop half turned to look at her, angered by that — and angry at her because of it. "I'm surprised you didn't go to church," he said, the words biting. "I thought all small-town sheriffs had their own pew."

"Not the atheists." Her brows rose. "Or had you forgotten that?"

He had. Ignoring her question, he asked one of his own. "How did you manage to get elected in this conservative town with that on your résumé?"

Miranda shrugged. "Oddly enough, nobody asked. Are you here for a reason, Bishop, or just window shopping?"

"We need to talk."

"About the investigation?"

"No."

"Then," she said, "we don't need to talk."

"Miranda —"

Her voice still pleasant, she said, "I'm on my way back to the office. See you there."

For an instant, Bishop was tempted to grab her arm, to force her to talk to him here and now. He wanted to find out if he could still read her while he was touching her, but thought better of the idea. For one thing, Miranda was a black belt.

And she had a gun.

So he stood there and watched her walk a few yards down the sidewalk to where her Jeep was parked, and he didn't say another word.

But, for the first time in his life, Bishop faced the cold and certain realization that not everything carelessly broken could be repaired. Ever.

"If my mother finds out about this," Amy Fowler said with a giggle, "she'll skin me alive."

Steve Penman grinned at her. "Then let's make sure she doesn't find out. And make sure your dad doesn't find out either. He'd do more than skin me." He toyed with the top button of her pretty Sunday blouse while his other hand pulled the tail of his shirt from his pants. "We don't have much time, honey. Seth says his boss comes in sometimes after church and Sunday dinner."

Amy looked around at the dirty, greasy-smelling back room of Cobb's garage and stifled a sigh. It had seemed exciting at first, meeting her eighteen-year-old boyfriend in whatever odd place he or his friends could recommend for an hour or two of privacy, but after two months both the secrecy and the inevitably tacky surroundings were beginning to depress her.

"Steve, don't you think —"

He kissed her, cutting off the beginnings of a problem he didn't want to hear, much less deal with. Not today. Maybe tomorrow, or next week, but for now she was still fun and eager and willing to try things he'd only read about in the magazines hidden under his mattress.

She let him push her back on the cot and unbutton her blouse, and didn't object when he unfastened the front clasp of her otherwise prim white bra and pushed the cups aside. He lay half on top of her, his body hard from the rough season of football behind him and heating with a fever she recognized.

Amy closed her eyes and stroked the back of his neck, enjoying the sensations of his mouth on her, but it didn't last long enough for her to get anywhere near his level of arousal. It never did. Too quickly, he was pushing up her skirt and working her panties down her legs.

She tried to slow things, reaching for his fly but taking her time about it, sliding the zipper down and unfastening the snap, reaching inside. He was hard and hot, and she held him in her hand, using a gentle touch rather than the rougher one he preferred, because it excited her more. He was still new and strange to her, still a fascinating alien creature to be explored and savored — but he never seemed to understand that.

He groaned and wrapped his hand around hers, forcing her to hold him harder, rub him more roughly. He thrust his tongue into her mouth and shoved his pants down over his thighs.

Slow down! she wanted to plead, but already he was kneeing her legs wide apart and preparing to mount her, muttering a few hoarse words that might have been encouragement or endearments or just raw want.

She thought he might forget, but at the

last minute fumbled in his pocket for the rubber and managed to get it on before he plunged inside her. Amy gripped him hard with her legs and tried to slow him that way, knowing from experience that the friction would be pleasant even if not as wildly exciting for her as Steve seemed to find it. But she could tell from the look of blind striving on his red face that this would be one of those times when he just wanted or needed to come quickly. She had resigned herself to that when his jerk and shuddering groan told her he'd already finished.

She lay there underneath him, blouse and bra open, skirt hiked up and panties God only knew where, feeling little except his weight on her and his moist panting against her neck, smelling grease and oil, and watching dust motes float in the shaft of light from the one dirty window in this dirty little back room.

When he raised his head at last, he said, "You all right, honey?" It was his usual question, uttered with the usual self-satisfied smile that anticipated her answer. Amy didn't disappoint him.

"I'm fine, Steve." She slid her fingers into his hair. "Just fine."

He was already checking his watch. "Guess we'd better get a move on. Didn't you tell your mom you'd spend the afternoon with Bonnie?"

"She wouldn't have let me go otherwise," Amy said. "She's spooked by what happened to Kerry Ingram and Lynet."

Steve grunted as he rose to his knees and pulled up his pants. He dealt with the used condom by dropping it to the stained concrete floor between the cot and the wall.

Amy wondered how many other used condoms lay under the cot, shriveled, their guilty contents petrified by time, a forlorn reminder of other girls who had lain on that scratchy wool blanket with their skirts hiked up and panties discarded.

She felt horribly exposed for the first time — and he wasn't even *looking* at her. She sat up and scooted backward in the same motion so her skirt would at least partially cover her, and hastily reached to fasten her bra and button her blouse.

Nervously, she said, "Bonnie says the sheriff might declare a curfew to keep kids in after dark." Where were her panties?

"Maybe." Steve got off the cot and tucked his shirt into his pants. "Probably wouldn't be a bad idea, at least for you girls."

His absent tone irritated her, and she heard her voice take on a shrill note she despised. "What makes you so sure we're the only ones in danger? What about Adam Ramsay?"

"From what I've heard, nobody can be sure he was killed by the same bastard who got the girls."

Amy didn't want to think about what she'd heard. "I haven't seen the FBI agents yet. Have you?"

"Nah, not yet. Get a move on, honey, we need to get out of here."

Amy slid off the bunk and finished buttoning her blouse. Where were her panties? She didn't want to ask Steve; there was something painfully tawdry about asking a man what he'd done with your panties . . .

Steve barely waited for her to finish buttoning her blouse. He pushed aside the box of spare engine parts that had kept the flimsy plywood door closed, then grabbed her hand and pulled her along through the silent garage.

"I'll drop you off at Bonnie's," he said briskly, "and pick up Seth. We're supposed to go look at a car he wants."

Amy wasn't surprised that neither she nor Bonnie was invited on the errand, but she was annoyed. Not that going to look at a stupid old car would have been much fun, but he might have *asked*.

Steve put her into the passenger seat of his

Mustang and closed her door, the automatic courtesy one of the things that had first attracted her to him. Amy waited until he was behind the wheel and they were on their way before she spoke again.

"Steve, aren't you worried about what's going on?"

"What, with these killings?" He shrugged. "I just don't see any reason to panic, is all. Probably just some nut passing through got the girls, and as for Adam Ramsay, I know half a dozen guys wanted to burn his ass."

"Why?"

"Never you mind," Steve said.

"But —"

"You and Bonnie just need to be careful, that's all you need to worry about, honey. Stay at the sheriff's house today until your mom comes to pick you up. Don't go anywhere by yourself, especially after dark. And I'll see you tomorrow at school." He shrugged again. "Bet on it, whoever did those killings is long gone by now."

She looked at him searchingly. "Do you really think so, Steve?"

"Bet on it."

It was nearly four o'clock when Miranda heard her office door open without warning. Since she had been trying to cope with a blinding headache and had both hands pressed against her face, she felt at a distinct disadvantage. Even more so when she removed her hands and saw that her visitor was Bishop. "House rules. If that door is closed, you knock first and wait to be invited in," she told him, trying not to sound as tense as she felt.

"Is that what you told your deputies?"

"Like I said, house rules. Applies to everybody."

He stood in the doorway, frowning at her. "Headache, Miranda?"

She knew better than to lie. "Yeah, a real corker. Is there something you wanted?"

Bishop didn't answer for a moment, but finally said, "Sharon's here with her report on the Grainger girl. I thought we should all discuss it."

"All right. I'll be there in a minute." Miranda opened the file on her blotter and stared at the top sheet until the door closed quietly behind him.

Alone again, she took slightly more than the promised minute to work on her control. There wasn't much she could do about the pallor or the fact that the light bothered her so much she wished she could put on sunglasses. But she was able to bury the pain deep enough that she doubted Bishop or his

115

psychics would sense anything unusual.

Maybe the price is too high to pay. Maybe . . .

But she knew it wasn't. Some things had to happen, events had to unfold in their proper order, or the results could be catastrophic. Instead of merely tragic.

Miranda got to her feet and grimly rode out the wave of dizziness. Then she squared her shoulders, pulled on the mask of professional detachment, and went to join the task force in the conference room.

Alex was there, in defiance of orders, though he did grimace apologetically when Miranda came in.

"I ought to fire you," she said.

"I'm not on the clock."

"You're here, you're on the clock." She sat down at the table beside him, across from the three agents, and focused on Sharon Edwards. "Doctor. Please tell me you found something to point to our killer."

"I wish I could." Edwards pushed a manila folder toward the sheriff.

Miranda didn't open it. "So what did you find? Did the post verify your preliminary conclusions?"

"More or less. She died approximately sixteen to eighteen hours before the body was discovered, which would put time of death at between two and four A.M. on

Friday. And — it took her a long time to die, probably hours. I believe his weapon of choice was a baseball bat — I found a few slivers of wood embedded in her skin. Judging by the bruising, I believe he went at her on at least three occasions with pauses in between, perhaps to rest."

Alex muttered something under his breath, but Miranda kept her gaze on the doctor and her sickened reaction off her face. "Go on."

"She wasn't raped, and there are no signs she was ever bound or physically restrained. She had been drugged — I found a more than toxic level of chloral hydrate, most probably given to her in a cup of sweet tea. I believe she was comatose before he began beating her, and that she never woke up. She died of internal injuries caused by the beating, though the dose of chloral hydrate would most probably have killed her eventually.

"Her eyes were removed postmortem, and her body exsanguinated, both the carotid and femoral arteries opened."

"I didn't see any blood on her clothes," Miranda said.

"No, there wasn't so much as a drop I could find. That added to the wood slivers embedded in her skin tells me that he stripped her naked before beating her, and dressed her after it was all over. Not only that, but he washed the body. I found traces of a mild liquid soap, the kind you can buy in any pharmacy, grocery, or department store. Peter — Dr. Shepherd — checked with her mother, and the soap they use at home is something entirely different."

Miranda didn't bother to comment on Shepherd's overstepping his authority. "I see."

"There's one last thing, Sheriff. The killer had inserted a tampon into the girl's vagina."

A moment of silence followed, then Alex said uncomfortably, "How do you know she didn't —"

"She wasn't menstruating, Deputy. And I think we can be fairly certain she didn't insert it herself." She looked at Miranda. "It was still sealed in its plastic wrapper."

SIX

The silence this time lasted much longer. Then Miranda ventured a reluctant question. "Are we talking about an act of rape, even if symbolic?"

Dr. Edwards frowned. "I don't believe so. I mean, I don't believe it was about power or domination, as we all know rape generally is. There was nothing to indicate that any violence or force was used. No bruising, no tearing — in fact, no signs of irritation whatsoever. He was careful. He was even, one could argue, gentle. The wrapped tampon was lubricated with K-Y before it was inserted."

"I don't get it," Alex said blankly.

Miranda looked at Agent Harte. "Any idea how to interpret that data?"

He leaned back in his chair and clasped his hands together over his middle, frowning. "Maybe he was . . . closing her, blocking her off. Making it impossible for anyone — including him — to have sex with her."

"Because he wanted to?" Miranda mused.

"Maybe. If he drugged her and covered her face while he was beating her because he knew her, even cared about her in some twisted way, then he might have been fighting the temptation to have sex with her — maybe for a long time."

"You mean before he abducted her?"

Harte nodded. "She was just barely fifteen, but pretty well developed for her age, physically more woman than child. It's possible he watched her, thought about her, a long time before he finally grabbed her."

Plaintively, Alex said, "But what does it *mean?* Will knowing any of this help us catch the bastard?"

Miranda said, "Eventually, it has to." She didn't wait for a response to that determined optimism, but went on broodingly, "There was no sign of sexual activity or even that sort of interest in Kerry Ingram. And if we add Adam Ramsay's murder, assume it's the same killer —"

"I say we do," the doctor broke in. "I have a hunch about the appearance of those bones, though I'd rather wait until my tests are complete to comment. But one thing I am sure of is that the Ramsay boy was also exsanguinated. I doubt you'd have two killers operating at the same time in the same small town, both draining the blood of their victims."

Miranda agreed to that with a grimace. "And as long as we manage to keep that detail quiet, it virtually rules out a copycat killer. I know you didn't have much to work with in examining the Ramsay boy's remains, but did you find any evidence of sexual activity?"

"No, none. But I'm sure you know such evidence would be difficult if not impossible to find with almost no soft tissue left, especially when the remains had been out in the elements for such a long time."

Miranda realized she was rubbing her temple only when she felt Bishop's eyes on her, and at once stopped the betraying gesture. "Okay, so our killer grabbed a seventeen- year-old boy and apparently tortured him to death over a period of weeks. Then he grabbed a fourteen-year-old girl whom he also tortured by repeatedly strangling her, also over a period of weeks. Then he grabbed a fifteen-year-old girl and drugged her senseless, and beat her to death with a baseball bat — within a matter of hours. No sign of sexual interest in the first two —

though we can't be sure about the boy — and possible signs of some kind of reluctant or abortive sexual interest in the third. He killed the first two with blows to the head, but killed the third by beating her to death. Slowly."

"That sounds about right," Harte said. "If you want my . . . hunch . . . I'd say we have an incredibly conflicted killer here. He feels he has to do this, and he won't let anything stop him, but at the same time regrets the necessity. Now, whether he feels remorse in any genuine sense is open to debate; my take is that he's sorry as hell he has to kill these kids, but not because they die — only because he has to disarrange his life and dirty his hands in order to kill them."

Alex stared at him. "You get all that from the little bit we know so far?"

Harte smiled. "It's just a hunch."

"Tony's hunches," Bishop said neutrally, "are generally pretty reliable."

Alex looked from one to the other, then shook his head. "What I don't get is that there doesn't seem to be any rhyme or reason to how he's picking them. The victims have nothing in common."

"Except that all three were teenagers," Miranda said.

Bishop rose and went to the bulletin

board, where he studied the reports and photos.

Miranda watched him for a moment, then turned back to Edwards. "You went over the postmortem on Kerry Ingram?"

Edwards nodded. "Peter was quite thorough, and I agree with his conclusions. She was repeatedly strangled to the point of unconsciousness and then allowed or made to revive, and she was beaten — though with a fist, I believe, and certainly not with the force used on the Grainger girl. A blow to the head finally killed her — a single very powerful blow."

Musing aloud, Harte said, "The first victim stands out because he was male, but Lynet Grainger is the one who really stands out in my mind — because of the way he treated her. I say he knew her, and possibly very well."

Alex sent Miranda a rueful glance, then said to the agent, "Trouble is, most every single adult male in town knew Lynet, if only by association with her mother. Teresa Grainger drinks too much and likes to party — and she isn't real particular who she parties with. To say that she dates a lot is definitely an understatement. And she was in the habit of bringing her dates home for the night. In that kind of environment,

Lynet could have gone either way, I guess, but she was apparently pretty straightlaced. Didn't drink, didn't smoke or do drugs, didn't screw around — in fact, I heard it said she was proud of being a virgin."

"She died a virgin," Dr. Edwards said.

"So did Kerry Ingram," Miranda said slowly. "Could that be something?"

"If it were just girls, I'd say maybe," Harte said. "Could be some kind of obsession about sexual purity. But factoring in the male victim makes that less likely. I suppose the killer could be bisexual, attracted to both, but the Ramsay boy —"

"Seems to have led a very active sex life for a boy his age," Miranda finished dryly.

"According to your report." Harte nodded. "So the idea of the killer trying to preserve purity is out, unless he killed the boy for an entirely different reason."

"He did." Bishop spoke finally, turning toward them. "He wasn't tempted by the Ingram girl. Her body was still childlike, undeveloped. He could take his time with her, enjoy what he was doing without the distraction of being attracted to her. But Lynet Grainger tempted him. He wanted her, and his own need frightened him. That's why he killed her so quickly. I think . . . Lynet was a mistake. I think he grabbed her on impulse,

124

maybe just because the opportunity was there, and once he had her he knew he had to go through with it, had to kill her. But he wanted to do other things to her as well, so he drugged her to make sure she couldn't speak to him, and covered her face so that wouldn't tempt him either. The tampon — Sharon, was it inserted postmortem?"

"Hard to say for certain, but I'd guess he did that while she was still alive."

Bishop nodded. "Maybe as soon as he stripped her. Her body tempted him, and he had to do something to prevent himself from giving in to the temptation. Inserting the tampon not only effectively closed her sexual passage, it was also an act of penetration that probably took the edge off his need."

"Why did he take her eyes?" Miranda asked. "Because she knew him?"

Bishop shook his head. "Because she had seen what he did to her, or he thought she had. Maybe her eyes partially opened at some point, and he thought she was looking at him. He took her eyes because . . . they had seen him tempted by her. They had seen his shame."

Alex was staring at Bishop in unconscious fascination. "You say he killed Adam Ramsay for a different reason. What?"

"He needed something from him."

"Other than his blood?"

"Yes."

"And you know this — how?" It wasn't quite a challenge.

Bishop glanced over his shoulder at the pictures behind him, then smiled at Alex. "Call it a hunch."

"A hunch? You wouldn't happen to have anything solid to back that up, would you?"

Bishop's smile remained, but his eyes narrowed slightly. "One or two things, Deputy. People always betray who they are, what their lives are like, and what their motives are, however unconsciously or accidentally. Little things, mostly. For instance, the way you tie your running shoes tells me that you run daily, that you're committed to it. The way you hold that pencil between your fingers tells me you're an ex-smoker, and I know from the way you're sitting that you pulled a muscle in your back fairly recently."

He did not, Miranda noted, quite explain what "signs" had led him to deduce that their killer had wanted something of Adam Ramsay. But the performance had the desired effect of distracting Alex from wondering about it.

Not quite under his breath, Alex muttered, "You must be loads of fun at parties."

Miranda felt a flicker of reluctant, rueful amusement, and when she looked at Bishop she saw the same understanding alight in his eyes. For just an instant, they shared the knowledge that they were set apart from others, that their abilities gave them insights into everything from the recent events and habits of an ordinary life to the dark corners of the human mind, where shadows and monsters lurked.

Then Miranda realized whom she was smiling at, and forced herself to look away from him. She met the doctor's calm gaze, and said the first thing that came into her head. "I guess there isn't much hope he left fingerprints on the tampon?"

"No hope at all. I believe he wore latex gloves, probably from the moment he grabbed the kids."

"And since the time of death for Lynet means he was dropping her into that well before dawn, we're unlikely to find anyone who saw anything."

Edwards sighed. "He's careful, I'll say that for him. If Bishop is right and grabbing Lynet was a mistake, then that's the only one he's made, as far as I can see."

"No," Bishop said. "He's made one more. He didn't bury Adam Ramsay deep enough."

★ ★ ★

"Oh, come on, Bonnie, it'll be fun." Amy kept her voice low even though Mrs. Task was downstairs getting supper ready.

"I don't think Randy would like it," Bonnie protested.

Exasperated, Amy said, "Bon, it's very boring how you always do what your sister wants. I mean, come on — what's the harm? It's just a game."

Bonnie looked at the Ouija board lying on the bed between them. It made her feel very nervous, a reaction she could hardly explain to Amy; there were some secrets even best friends couldn't share. Stalling for time, she said, "I can't believe you sat through church with that in your backpack. Reverend Seaton would call it a tool of the devil, you know he would."

"It was out in Steve's car," Amy said. "Besides, Reverend Seaton isn't going to know. And neither is Miranda, unless you tell her." Amy read the hesitancy in Bonnie's expression and added quickly, "Even if you did tell her, Miranda isn't religious, so why would it bother her? It isn't a tool of the devil, it's just a game. Come on."

"You just want to find out if Steve means to ask you to the prom," Bonnie said dryly.

"No," Amy said, feeling heat rise in her

face, "I want to find out if he gives a damn about me."

Bonnie's clear, startlingly blue eyes suddenly turned gentle. "He isn't dating anyone else. You'd know if he was."

"That doesn't mean he cares about me. I give him what he wants, Bonnie. And maybe that's all he wants."

It was a question Bonnie could have answered, but that was a rule she dared not break. She glanced down at the Ouija board, wondering guiltily if just bending the rule was really so bad when her intentions were good.

"Please?" Amy begged. Confident of the response she wanted, she moved one of the tables Bonnie used as a nightstand to the side of the bed so she could place the board on it. She put the planchette in position in the center of the board and placed her fingertips on it.

Bonnie wavered for a moment longer. "Oh, all right. But keep the questions very specific, Amy."

Amy laughed. "Why? Is it a dumb board?"

Secrets really were amazingly restrictive, Bonnie reflected, wondering how to explain to her friend that when you opened a door you couldn't always control what came in. "Just don't wander off the point, all right? Ask about you and Steve, and that's all."

"I thought you'd never played this game before," Amy said suspiciously.

"I told you I'd never used a Ouija board, and I haven't." Bonnie drew a breath and placed her fingertips lightly on the planchette. "Let's get on with it."

Amy began, "What I want to know —"

The planchette jerked violently and centered itself over the word NO.

"Hey! You're not supposed to *make* it move," Amy exclaimed indignantly.

"I didn't." Bonnie stared down at the planchette and the adamant word showing through it.

"But I didn't even ask —" Amy shook her head and guided the planchette back to the center. "We'll try again. What I want to know is —"

The planchette jerked again, and again decisively indicated the word NO.

"Bonnie . . ." Every time Amy moved the planchette back to the center, it returned immediately to NO. "You swear you aren't —"

"I'm not moving it." Not consciously at least. Not deliberately. Staring down at the board, she said softly, "Who are you?" The planchette moved instantly.

L . . . Y . . . N . . . E . . . T.

Amy jerked her fingers away. "That isn't funny, Bonnie!"

Bonnie removed her own fingers and looked at them as if they belonged to someone else. "I didn't do it."

Amy opened her mouth to argue, then realized with a little chill that this was hardly the sort of joke Bonnie would find amusing. "You mean . . ."

"I think we'd better stop, Amy."

"You don't really think . . . It's just a *game.*"

"Some games are dangerous."

Amy felt a thrill of fear not unmixed with excitement. "But if there's a chance . . . Bonnie, what if we can find out who killed her? Everybody wants to know that, and if we can find out —"

Bonnie chose her words carefully. "Amy, Randy says the one thing you can never afford to do in this life is assume. You're assuming that whoever — or whatever — spelled out that name really is Lynet."

"But who else could it be?"

"If her . . . spirit . . . could reach out to us, don't you think other spirits could as well? Maybe bad spirits?"

"Are there bad spirits?"

Bonnie looked at her sadly. "There are bad people. Why wouldn't there be bad spirits?"

"Well, but . . . spirits can't hurt us. Can they?"

"I don't know," Bonnie lied. "But I imagine it's not a good idea to open a door for them."

Amy bit her lip. "Bonnie, aren't you scared there's some maniac running around killing kids? Don't you want to look back over your shoulder every time you're somewhere by yourself? And just before you turn a corner, aren't you afraid there might be something awful waiting for you?"

Half-consciously, Bonnie fingered the small, oddly shaped scar on her right forearm. "Yes," she said. "Yes to all that. But, Amy, doing anything because we're scared is bound to be a bad idea. We have to trust Randy and the deputies and the FBI agents to find the killer. It's what they do."

Amy looked at her friend searchingly. "You really don't want to play this game anymore, do you, Bon?"

"I really don't," Bonnie said steadily.

"Okay, then we won't." Amy reached for her backpack to put the board away, and when she picked up the planchette neither she nor Bonnie noticed that it had once again centered itself over the word NO.

Miranda glanced at Bishop with a frown, trying to ignore the increasingly frequent stabs of pain behind her eyes. "Why was the killer's mistake not burying Adam Ramsay deep enough? Because we found him?"

Bishop nodded. "I don't think that boy's body was ever meant to be found — unlike the other two."

Alex said, "Granted, Kerry Ingram was found lying openly in a ravine like discarded trash, but Lynet was pretty thoroughly hidden at the bottom of that well."

"Yes, but for how long? I did a little checking, and it seems your local paper reported just a week or so ago that the property around the lake had been sold to a group of buyers from Florida who plan to build vacation homes there. Clearing off the home sites in preparation is due to start in just a couple of weeks. And according to the land surveys, one of those sites is within twenty yards of the well."

"So the body probably would have been found," Miranda agreed. "Okay. But did he want us to find the girls, or just not care whether we did?"

"You tell me," Bishop said, looking at her steadily.

"Me? How would I know?" She was practically daring him to say something about extra senses in front of Alex, and both of them knew it.

Instead, Bishop said, "You know the basics of how to profile a killer, Sheriff. Why would one victim among three be transported miles farther than the others and buried in a forest where even hunters seldom go?"

She thought about it. "Because something about the victim or the way he was killed points to the killer."

"Exactly." Bishop reached back over his shoulder and tapped his knuckles against the photographs on the bulletin board. Photographs of Adam Ramsay's remains. "He took the boy first and kept him alive longest, and when he was finished he buried the remains where he had every reason to expect they would be hidden indefinitely."

"Unfortunately, they nearly were," Alex said. "And by the time we found them, there wasn't much left. How're we supposed to find any evidence pointing to the killer when all we have are bones — and precious few of them?"

"Those bones." Miranda looked at Edwards. "Are you sure there isn't something you can tell us now about those bones, Doctor?"

"Sheriff, to be honest, all I have is a hunch — and it's pretty far out. I need a few days to finish my tests. All I can tell you right now is that the Ramsay boy's bones had been . . . altered."

"Aged," Miranda said.

Edwards nodded. "Artificially aged."

Alex said, "Why, for God's sake?"

"That's the question, isn't it, Deputy? Why — and how. I hope to find those answers, but I need time."

"I hope we have time," Miranda said. "But if Lynet *was* a mistake, killing her might have altered his needs and his rituals in ways we can't begin to understand let alone predict."

"He could be hunting again," Harte said. "And since we all seem to be having hunches, another one of mine is that he's looking around for his next victim even as we speak."

"In a county with several thousand teenagers." This time, Miranda didn't stop herself from rubbing her temples. "Shit. At the very least, I'm going to have to declare a dusk-to-dawn curfew for everybody under eighteen, try to keep the kids at home, at school — and off the streets."

"I doubt you'll get an argument," Alex told her. "Except from the kids, of course. The mayor will be thrilled to announce any action that sounds like he's helping to keep the town safe."

Miranda sent him a faint smile, then glanced at her watch. Addressing the three agents but looking only at Edwards, she said, "I don't know if you three plan on working tonight, but I do know the café and most of our better restaurants will be closing in less than two hours. If you want my advice, you'll go get something to eat while you can."

"Sounds like a good idea to me." Harte stood up and stretched. "If I don't get something besides caffeine in my system, somebody'll have to peel me off the ceiling."

Edwards nodded agreement and looked at Bishop as she rose too. "I'll need a couple more hours at the morgue tonight, then there's nothing I can do until tomorrow."

Bishop, his gaze on Miranda, seemed about to say something, but finally just followed his agents out of the conference room.

Mildly, Alex said, "I guess we could offer to feed them now and then, since they're here to help us."

"I had Grace send for takeout for their lunch and made it a standing order for the remainder of their time here," Miranda said. "Even had something sent over to the hospital for Edwards. I'm not being inhospitable, Alex. But I also don't intend to socialize with them. They're here to do a job, and I sincerely hope they're very good at what they do."

"We all hope that. And I'm not saying we have to make nice outside the office. You may not have noticed, but I don't especially care for Bishop."

"No, really?" Miranda murmured.

"Okay, so maybe it was a little more obvious than I thought." He paused. "Was it?"

"Let's just say I can't see the two of you going running together at dawn like best buds."

"Oh, he runs?" Alex's tone was innocent.

Miranda drew a breath and rubbed her temple again. "Now? I couldn't say. But he used to, and he looks to be in good shape, so I'd guess he still runs."

"Oh, yeah, I'd say he was in fair shape. Is he any good with that gun he wears?"

"Yes," Miranda replied without elaborating.

"Uh-huh. And I guess he earned that scar fighting bad guys?"

"In the best heroic tradition," she said, only half mockingly.

"What about his hunch about the killer? How close is that likely to be?"

"Let's just say I wouldn't bet against him. He was always . . . very good at his job."

There was a short silence, then Alex said

casually, "So you two knew each other pretty well, huh?"

She laughed under her breath. "Are you asking me if we were lovers, Alex?"

"Just tell me if I'm being too nosy."

"It was a long time ago."

"And I guess . . . it ended badly?"

"You could say that." She shrugged, very conscious of the tightness in her shoulders.

"Working with him now can't be a whole hell of a lot of fun."

"No," Miranda said. "I wouldn't call it fun." A sudden stab of pain made her breath catch.

Alex stared at her, his brows drawing together in a frown. "Are you all right? You look pale."

"Headache, that's all." Miranda pretended the momentary pause wasn't caused by a surge of nausea. "I'm going home. You too. And don't come back tonight."

"Randy? This killer. Do you suppose it's somebody we know? I mean, know well?"

"I don't think we know him, Alex. I don't think we know him at all."

Tony Harte leaned back to let the waitress set his plate before him, and waited until she had left before saying, "Granted, I only had the use of the usual five senses, but am I the only one who thought the sheriff was in pain? A lot of pain?"

"She said it was a headache," Bishop said.

"That," Sharon Edwards said, "was no ordinary headache. Her pupils were dilated. Is she subject to migraines?" That last brisk question was aimed directly at Bishop.

He hesitated. "Not as far as I know."

Edwards watched him intently. "But?"

"You know as well as I do. Better than I do." Bishop wished this weren't Sunday in a small town where he couldn't even buy a beer, much less the raw whiskey he craved at the moment. "One theory is that psychic ability is caused when some of the electrical impulses in the brain misfire and forge new pathways to previously unused areas."

Harte frowned. "Yeah, I remember reading about that. So?"

"So," Bishop said unemotionally, "if that theory is true, then it follows that especially frequent or especially powerful misfires could, instead of forging new pathways, begin to destroy old ones. Begin to destroy the brain itself."

"Miranda Knight," Harte said slowly, "is definitely what I'd call an especially powerful psychic. Since she has four separate abilities to call her own, there must be an awful lot of electrical activity in her brain. Especially since she's using an incredible amount of energy to shield herself — and block us."

"Yes," Bishop said.

Edwards put down her fork. Reluctantly, she said, "In such a case, the early symptoms would most likely be intense headaches, sensitivity to light and noise, dilated pupils. Like a migraine, but growing worse and causing more damage with each event."

"Until?" Harte asked warily.

Edwards avoided his gaze and picked up her fork again. "There hasn't been enough research to offer any definitive answers to something so theoretical. Even if we had the technical knowledge to understand it, the instruments to measure and evaluate . . ."

Harte looked at Bishop and didn't like what he saw. Or what he felt. "Until?" he repeated.

"Until she's a vegetable." Bishop's voice was stony. He turned his head to stare out the window at the dark, chilly winter night. "Of course . . . it's only a theory."

SEVEN

Tuesday, January 11

Seth Daniels eased into second gear, babying the car, aiming for a smooth transition, and scowled at the betraying jerk. He knew Bonnie was watching him in amused understanding but refused to meet her eyes. It was hard enough on a guy that his girlfriend was the sheriff's sister; it was downright embarrassing to have that same girlfriend teaching him how to drive a stick shift.

"It just takes practice," she said, her carefully neutral voice doing nothing except underline the fact that she was trying not to further damage his fragile male ego.

"I know that," he said.

"And coordination."

"I know that too, Bonnie."

"All I'm saying is that you'll get the hang of it. It can't be harder than playing football, and you do that."

Seth winced as the shift into third was ac-

141

complished with another jerk and a grinding noise. "Oh, yeah — how hard can it be?" he muttered. A sideways glance showed him Bonnie was biting her lip, and he struggled with himself for a moment before finally laughing. "Okay, okay. I'll get the hang of it. Just tell me Miranda didn't teach you how to hunt bears or fly a jet."

"You want to learn how to hunt bears?" she asked innocently. "Because if so —"

"Bonnie."

She laughed. "No, she didn't teach me either of those things. Just the more usual stuff. Cooking, sewing, driving a stick . . . sharpshooting."

"Jesus."

Bonnie smiled at him. "Well, she was trying to be mother and father, you know."

"Well, yeah, I understand that — but sometimes I wonder if she wasn't also trying to be a commando. Sharpshooting?"

"With a gun in the house, she just thought I should know how to handle it."

"But *sharpshooting?* Knowing how not to shoot yourself in the foot is one thing, but how often in life will you need to blow the wings off a fly at a hundred yards?"

"The light's yellow, Seth — use the clutch and downshift."

He obeyed, eventually bringing the car to a halt at the traffic light in a maneuver smooth enough to partially soothe his ruffled feathers. "You changed the subject," he told her.

"There was nothing more to say. Randy taught me what she thought might be useful someday. So I can bake biscuits and sew on a button, and I can also change a tire and handle a gun."

Seth looked at her for a moment, then eased the car forward when the light changed. "I'm surprised she let you come out with me today."

"We have to be back home by curfew, Seth."

"Yeah, I know that." He was seventeen, which put him in the age group required to be off the streets and under parental or employer supervision by 5:00 P.M. "But she's always been so protective of you, and with a killer running loose —"

"I promised her I wouldn't go anywhere alone even before curfew, that I'd either be with you or home with Mrs. Task. She likes you, and she trusts you."

"She does?"

"Why are you so surprised by that? You could be the poster child for good teenagers."

"Thanks a lot."

"It's true and you know it. Your grades are good enough that you tutor other students, and we all know you'll go to medical school. You work part-time in Cobb's garage *and* in your father's clinic every chance you get. You even help teach a Sunday-school class and have a paper route."

"I've had that route since I was ten," he said defensively, then glanced at her and found her smiling at him. It was a smile that never failed to raise his blood pressure and make him think so many absurd things he dared not say aloud. Even if he could say anything coherent, which he doubted.

Bonnie didn't seem to notice the effect she had on him. "Well, anyway, Randy trusts you. She knows I'm safe with you."

Glancing at her again, Seth saw a shadow cross her face, and it distracted him from surging hormones. "Every time you say something like that, I get the feeling . . ."

"What?" Bonnie said, but more like she was just responding brightly than because she really wanted to know.

Seth listened to the tone rather than the words and backed off. "Nothing." He was honest enough to ask himself if he did it because he knew she didn't want to confide whatever it was — or because he was afraid to hear it. And he didn't know the answer.

Distracting them both, he said, "Hey, there's Steve. Want to stop and say hi?"

"He looks like he's in a hurry. Doesn't he have to go in to work?"

"At six, yeah." Seth downshifted and heard the gears grind. "Damn. Maybe I'd better concentrate on what I'm doing."

"Maybe you'd better." She sounded amused again, but her tone sobered when she added, "Steve is planning to dump Amy, isn't he?"

"I don't know what Steve is planning to do."

"Don't you?"

"No. Honest, Bonnie, I don't." He hesitated. "He's a great guy, it's just that he likes . . ."

"Variety?" she supplied wryly.

"I'm not saying it's a good thing — just his thing. Come on, Amy must have known that going in. It's not like Steve's reputation is lily white. She did know, right?"

"Knowing is one thing. Believing and understanding are something else."

Seth grimaced. "She thinks she can change him?"

Bonnie sighed. "I guess so."

"She won't change him, Bonnie."

"I know." She checked her watch. "It's after four, Seth."

He accepted the change of subject with relief. Keeping his own romantic relationship on an even keel was difficult enough; trying to manage someone else's was beyond him. "Yeah, I know. Time to head for home. Do you want to stop by and see Miranda first?"

"No. She'll probably be home by seven or so. There isn't much they can do at night except keep going over and over all the reports and information, and after a while it's like . . ."

"Like a dog chasing its tail?"

"Pretty much."

"Must be driving Miranda crazy. She's always been so good at solving crimes quickly. But I guess there's never been anything like this killer."

"No," Bonnie said. "There's never been anything like him."

Hearing an odd note in her voice, Seth shot her a glance. She was unconsciously rubbing the scar on her forearm, something he knew she only did when she was worried or anxious about something. "They'll get him, Bonnie."

"I know. I know they will."

"You're worried about Miranda?"

"Of course I am."

"She'll be all right. I don't know anybody

better able to take care of herself than Miranda."

"You'd think so," Bonnie said, "wouldn't you."

They had taken to locking the conference room whenever it was empty, keeping their reports and speculations away from the eyes of the curious. Even Miranda's deputies, with the exception of Alex Mayse, knew only as much as necessary. So Bishop was not happy when Miranda came in at nearly six o'clock Tuesday evening accompanied by the mayor.

Bishop had met John MacBride the day before and hadn't been terribly impressed — but that might have been because MacBride had made a point of touching Miranda in a casual manner guaranteed to alert the instincts of any other man. Miranda had been polite, professional, and unresponsive to the attention — but she hadn't objected.

When His Honor stood staring at the gruesome display on the bulletin board with a sickened expression on his face as Tony explained their procedures, Bishop moved as close to Miranda as he dared. "This isn't a good idea," he said quietly.

"I know," she said, equally quiet. "But he

insisted. And if this visit reassures him that we're doing everything we can to find the killer, then maybe he'll be able to reassure the town council and all the other worried citizens. Right now, no one is bringing any undue pressure to bear on the investigation, much less trying to run things. I'd like to keep it that way."

Bishop was politically savvy enough to get the point, but it didn't make him like the situation any better. "If some of these details get out, you'll have a major panic on your hands — and our job won't get any easier."

"He won't talk about the details."

"How can you be so sure?"

Miranda sat on the edge of the conference table and lifted an eyebrow at him. "Because I told him not to."

Bishop didn't know whether to be amused or irritated. "And he always does what you tell him to?"

"He does when it's my job."

A glance showed Bishop that MacBride and Tony were still occupied. "Can you read him?"

Miranda shook her head.

"Even when he touches you?"

"Even then."

Bishop silently debated if it would be wise to ask about this touching, then forced himself to remain professional. "Because of your shields or his?"

"His." Miranda shrugged. "It's not an uncommon trait in small towns. You must have noticed."

"I have. Yesterday when Tony and I were walking around downtown meeting the merchants, I couldn't read two-thirds of them. Neither could Tony."

"Like I said, it's not so extraordinary. In small towns, privacy is especially hard to come by, so the tendency is to guard oneself. Over a lifetime, that could easily and logically equate to mental and emotional shields and walls."

"Is that why you settled here?"

"It was one of the reasons."

"And because small-town life would be good for Bonnie?"

"That too."

Bishop reflected somewhat bitterly that she was only willing to talk to him like this when there were other people around. He had tried to take advantage of such moments, but since he could hardly say some of the things he wanted to say when there was every chance of being overheard, he had forced himself to bide his time, to concentrate on the investigation and keep their conversations relatively professional.

It wasn't getting any easier.

Hoping to make a breakthrough of sorts, he reached into his jacket pocket for a folded piece of paper and held it out to her. "I meant to give you this earlier."

She didn't move. "What is it?"

"Access to those sealed files we talked about."

Still, she didn't move.

He pretended not to notice her hesitation. "The files have been copied from the Bureau's database into a separate, secured area, and you've been granted temporary access. Nothing can be downloaded or copied, you'll have to agree to that. The computers here are capable of establishing the link. These are the codes you'll need."

Finally, Miranda took the paper from him without, needless to say, touching him.

Bishop didn't wait to find out if she would thank him, since he suspected he'd be waiting a long time. He joined the two men at the bulletin board.

He didn't have to be a telepath to interpret Tony's quick roll of the eyes, and when he heard the nervousness in MacBride's voice he realized the other agent was probably holding on to his patience with both hands.

"But why aren't you doing more to catch

him? Roadblocks, or searching with dogs, or —"

Bishop cut him off. "No trail was left for dogs to follow. And roadblocks can only catch a suspected killer when he's trying to leave town. This one lives here."

"You can't possibly know that."

"It's my job to know that, Mayor. The killer lives in Gladstone or the surrounding area. He's been very careful not to leave evidence we can use to find him. And we're not likely to catch him unless he makes a mistake."

MacBride looked pained. "That's blunt enough."

"It's the truth."

"But . . . to make a mistake, wouldn't he have to —"

"Kill again. Yes, I'm afraid so." Bishop paused a beat. "So in instituting the curfew, Sheriff Knight has done the only thing she could do to protect the young people of Gladstone. And, in the meantime, we're studying what information we have and are using every scrap of knowledge and experience we have between us to look for and interpret even the most minute detail of the crimes. We will catch him, Mayor. It's only a matter of time."

MacBride glanced again at the bulletin

board and said, "I hope so, Agent Bishop. I hope so." He waved Miranda back when she would have gone to the door to show him out, and quietly left the conference room alone.

In an admiring tone, Tony said, "Why didn't I think to tell him it was only a matter of time? That perked him right up."

"Shut up, Tony."

Tony grinned at him, then looked at Miranda and sobered. "Sorry, Sheriff. Nobody knows better than me how serious this is. It's just . . . I don't deal well with elected officials as a rule."

"Present company excepted, Agent Harte?" she said lightly.

"Present company excepted," he said promptly.

"Then make it Miranda, all right?"

"I'd love to, if you return the favor."

"Tony it is."

"Thanks. So — Miranda — has the canvass of the area around that well turned up anything?"

She shook her head. "Alex is still out with his team, but so far nothing. No one who lived in the area will even admit to having been awake or out of bed between four and six A.M., much less to having seen or heard a car — or anything else."

Tony looked at Bishop and grimaced. "Well, it was a long shot."

Bishop nodded. "A very long shot."

"Reassuring words to the mayor aside," Miranda said, "do we have something useful? Fact, conclusion, speculation . . . hunch?"

"All we know today that we didn't know yesterday," Bishop said, "is that none of the surrounding law enforcement agencies have any similar crimes on their books — solved or unsolved."

"Another indication that he's local," Tony said, taking a chair at the table.

"Which we were virtually certain of anyway," she pointed out.

"Yeah." Tony shrugged. "And I can't see we're going to get anything else unless Sharon comes up with something useful in testing the Ramsay boy's bones. Or unless we're overlooking something about one of the other victims."

"I'd be surprised if all of us had missed anything important. We have all the information we're ever likely to get from the victims. In this life, anyway." Miranda looked at Bishop and said dryly, "Have a good medium on the payroll?"

He took the question seriously. "We've never been able to validate a medium in any credible sense. Talking to the dead isn't an easy thing to prove scientifically."

"I guess not."

Bishop hesitated, then said casually, "I seem to recall that sort of thing was Bonnie's particular talent. Seeing ghosts. Does she still?"

Miranda stiffened. In a very quiet voice, she said, "Bonnie is not part of this. You don't see her, you don't talk to her — in fact, you don't go anywhere near her. Is that clear?"

"She's a teenager, Miranda." The scar on Bishop's cheek stood out starkly. "If for no other reason than fitting the victim profile, she is part of this."

"No. Not as far as you're concerned. You stay away from her." She looked at Tony. "All of you stay away from her." Then she walked out of the room.

"Brrrrr." Tony half zipped his jacket and thrust his hands into the pockets. "I guess we stay away from Bonnie."

Bishop grunted and turned grim eyes to the bulletin board. "If we can. For as long as we can."

Tony looked at him curiously. "Does her sister have more than one ability too?"

"Probably. They all did. But Bonnie was only a kid when I knew her, no more than eight, and her abilities were still developing."

"But she saw ghosts?"

"So she said."

"Her family believed her?"

"Yeah, they believed her." Bishop's voice was suddenly flat. "They were a . . . remarkable family."

"Sorry, boss. Didn't mean to rake up old —"

"Memories? They aren't old and you didn't rake them up, so don't worry about it." Bishop stared at the bulletin board, trying to fill his mind with details of the killings and nothing else. "If I could just figure out what the killer needed from the Ramsay boy . . ."

"You think that's the key?"

"Could be. I'm certain it's a detail vital to understanding the bastard."

"Assuming we don't catch him quick enough, what about his next victim?"

"Male," Bishop said. "Late teens, probably. Strong, maybe even aggressive, but definitely masculine. By all appearances he won't seem vulnerable, and no one could ever think of him as a victim."

"Why?"

Bishop tapped the yearbook picture of Lynet Grainger. "Because of her. She tempted him, Tony, and he didn't want to be tempted. He won't trust himself to grab another girl, not yet. First he'll have to prove to himself that he's powerful and in charge. Prove to himself there's nothing sexual about what he's doing. So he'll pick an older boy, someone he could never feel a sexual attraction to and one who won't be easy to subdue. If he hasn't already chosen him, he will soon. He won't want to spend too much time with his own doubts, letting them prey on his confidence. And he won't kill this boy quickly, not like Lynet. He'll need to make this one suffer a long time."

From the doorway, Miranda said quietly, "Sometimes you're just too goddamned smart for your own good, Bishop."

He and Tony looked at her, alerted by something in her voice. Strain showed in her grim eyes and in the straight, hard line of her mouth.

"We have another missing teenager," she said.

By nine o'clock that night, they were reasonably sure that eighteen-year-old Steve Penman was not going to return from some unannounced trip or errand wondering innocently what all the fuss was about. He had last been seen shortly before four o'clock, when he had dropped off his sixteen-year-old girlfriend at her home.

He'd made sure to get her home before curfew, Amy Fowler numbly told the sheriff and FBI agents, so she'd be safe. Then, not restricted by the curfew himself, he had headed back toward town to pick up something at the drugstore before he reported to work at the paper mill for the six o'clock mini-shift.

When he hadn't reported to work, his supervisor, as requested by the Sheriff's Department, had immediately notified his parents. They had called the sheriff.

His car was found parked near the front of the drugstore, but no one inside remembered seeing him come in. Deputies were questioning other merchants, and the sheriff had gone on the radio to request calls from anyone who had been downtown between four and six and might have seen anything unusual.

The phones were ringing off the hook, but the calls were only from concerned citizens saying they had seen nothing.

"How could he just vanish like that?" Miranda was absently rubbing her temples. "How could he have been taken against his will without a sound or any kind of commotion, without even being noticed? The kid's six feet tall, and he was wearing his bright blue football jacket. Not what you'd call invisible. If he got to town just after four, it wasn't even dark yet."

Alex looked at the legal pad before him on the conference table. "At last count, between four and six o'clock there were a dozen senior boys in town wearing those jackets. They were planning to throw some kind of party for their coach sometime this week, apparently postponed from the end of the season because he was in Nashville having bypass surgery. So several of them were in town getting supplies." He paused. "None of the boys saw Steve Penman or anything they believed to be even remotely suspicious."

Miranda felt Bishop's eyes on her, realized what she was doing, and stopped rubbing her temples. With a certain amount of detachment, she wondered if it was possible for a head to split wide open. "No trail for the dogs to follow. No leads. No witnesses. No clues."

"And we don't have much time," Tony contributed soberly. "If Bishop is right, this boy may be kept alive for a while — but I'm guessing it won't be for long."

Miranda leaned back in her chair, trying to appear at least somewhat relaxed, and looked across the table at Bishop. "Does this abduction alter your profile?"

He shook his head. "We're looking for a white male, thirty to forty-five, in good physical shape. He's probably single, or has a place other than his home where he's assured of privacy and has the means to confine his victims. He's highly intelligent, meticulous and controlled, definitely organized. He either has a business of his own or else works in some administrative or managerial capacity, a position of authority. He understands enough about police procedure to avoid leaving any forensic evidence we can use, but whether that's professional knowledge or just a hobby is impossible to guess."

"Professional knowledge? Are you saying he could be a cop?" Alex asked.

"It's possible."

"But is it likely?" Miranda watched him closely. "What's your hunch?"

"My hunch is he's not. I think it's a hobby of sorts, that he's educated himself in police techniques. He may even have a conduit into this department, a friend or relative who could be, in all innocence, passing on information to him."

"Great," Miranda said.

Bishop shook his head. "It isn't likely to be

restricted information. But if it was, I doubt he'd be stupid enough to let us know he has it by altering his M.O. He's smart enough to know how to leave a body so that nothing can be traced back to him, and cool enough to take his time and make sure it's done right. He's not given to panic or carelessness."

"An expert killer," Alex said.

Musing aloud, Tony said, "I'm wondering what the trigger was. What set him off so suddenly. Most killers of this sort start comparatively young, showing signs of homicidal tendencies all the way back to childhood. Not many reach their thirties or forties with their crimes still completely undiscovered."

"Unless they're very, very lucky," Bishop said slowly. He asked Miranda, "Before the new highway opened, this town was on one of the main routes to Nashville, wasn't it?"

She nodded, a frown drawing her brows together.

"According to your records, there are no unsolved disappearances of locals, but what about transients? Teenagers, either runaways or kids passing through the area. Say . . . within fifty miles of Gladstone. There would have been bulletins of some kind among regional law enforcement agencies, general alerts."

"None since I took office," Miranda said. "Before that, I wouldn't know. Investigating disappearances wasn't one of my duties as a deputy."

"We need to know how many unsolved cases we're really dealing with here," Bishop told her. "I'm hoping like hell we don't find any more missing teenagers, but if we do, every other case gives us one more opportunity to see if this bastard made a mistake we can use to throw a net over him."

Miranda looked at Alex and nodded.

Alex got up. "I'll have Sandy and Greg start checking files. We only have the recent stuff on computers; anything going back further than five years or so will be in storage boxes in the basement. How far back do you want to look?"

"Ten to fifteen years," Bishop replied.

Alex sighed. "It'll take days, probably longer. The last few administrations weren't exactly known for their record-keeping expertise."

"Call in anyone you need to help," Miranda said. "We're all on overtime anyway." After the deputy left, she said to Bishop, "Ten to fifteen years?"

"If the killer is at the high end of that age estimate, he could have been at this fifteen years or longer."

"Christ. And nobody noticed?"

"Maybe because he was hunting somewhere else. Or maybe just because his victims fell through the cracks and were never really missed."

Miranda drew a breath and let it out slowly. "And it seemed like such a nice, safe little town."

"You know there's no such thing."

She was silent.

"There's no such thing," he repeated.

"Yes. I know."

Into the silence, Tony murmured something about helping Alex and slipped from the room.

Before Miranda could follow him, Bishop said, "You have another headache, don't you?"

Lightly, she said, "My entire life is a headache at the moment."

He ignored that. "Miranda, do you understand the danger of what you're doing?"

"I don't know what you're talking about."

"You know exactly what I'm talking about. You're working so hard at keeping me out —"

"Don't flatter yourself," she snapped.

Bishop counted silently to ten. "All right. You're working so hard at keeping *us* out, channeling all your psychic energy into

162

blocking us, that your body is beginning to rebel. Headaches, sensitivity to light and sound, nausea."

"You're imagining things, Bishop."

"It can damage you beyond repair, Miranda, do you understand that? We've learned a lot more about psychic ability in the last few years, and the current understanding is that the electrical impulses that trigger telepathy and precognition can also damage the brain — especially if they aren't allowed to dissipate naturally."

"If you'll forgive a lousy pun," she said, "I'll keep that in mind."

He stared at her for a long moment, then said deliberately, "I suppose you've considered what would happen to Bonnie without you to watch over her."

Miranda wondered why she wasn't getting up and walking out of the room. "Bonnie is not your concern."

He hesitated. "She would be, you know. Not because I owe you, but because I owe her."

She was surprised and tried not to let it show. "It's not a debt you can pay, Bishop."

"I know."

Miranda felt the sudden need to go away somewhere by herself and reinforce her shields. She put her hands on the table as she got to her feet, hoping grimly that the action looked more casual than the necessary support it was.

Abruptly, Bishop reached across the table and grasped her wrist.

For a frozen instant, Miranda stared into those pale, compelling eyes of his with a sense of blind panic. Then she jerked away from him and stepped back.

Bishop remained where he was, his arm stretched out, the long fingers slowly closing into a fist. "You won't let me in."

Miranda uttered a shaken laugh. "And you have the nerve to be surprised by that?"

His scar stood out so starkly that it appeared newly made, raw. "What are you afraid of, Miranda?" he demanded roughly. "What is it you don't want me to see, don't want me to know?"

"Like I said before, don't flatter yourself."

"Miranda —"

She hadn't intended to say anything else. She should have simply turned around and walked out of the room. But the panic drove her to distract, deflect.

"I let you in once, Bishop. Into my life. Into my mind. Into my bed. Even, God help me, into my heart. And that mistake cost me so much I'm not likely to ever repeat it."

He leaned back and spoke with great deliberation. "I'm the one who made the mistake. I was stupid and arrogant, and so obsessed with catching a killer I couldn't see beyond that goal. And I'm *sorry*. Not a day passes that I don't regret what happened eight years ago. But it's done, Miranda. I can't go back and change anything, as much as I'd like to. I have to live with what I did, what I caused to happen. But . . ."

She didn't move, didn't prompt him or do anything except wait.

"But if anything happened now to you or Bonnie because of me, I couldn't live with that. I'm not asking for your forgiveness. I'm just asking you not to hurt yourself trying to keep me out. I'll stay out. I swear to you, I will."

Miranda would have liked to say something cool or mocking, but she didn't trust herself to say a word. Instead, she just turned and walked out, leaving him there.

And wondered how long she could keep the truth from him.

EIGHT

Wednesday, January 12

Liz Hallowell had learned at her grandmother's knee how to read faces. The color and shape of eyes, the angle of jaw and arch of brow, the curve of the mouth. They were all signposts, her gran had said, the outer directions to the soul.

So when she stepped outside her store in the early afternoon for a quick break and one of the rare cigarettes she allowed herself, and saw standing on the sidewalk only a few yards away the FBI agent with the marked face, she studied him intently. They hadn't yet been introduced; the other two agents had been in her coffeeshop, but not this one.

He was talking to Peter Green, who owned the old-fashioned barbershop behind them, and Liz didn't have to read the tea leaves to know what they were discussing. Half of Randy's deputies and two of the three federal agents had been moving methodically through town all day, talking to everyone who might have seen something yesterday when the Penman boy had vanished. Nobody had talked to Liz yet.

Taking advantage of the time granted to her, she smoked and watched the agent, not especially worried if he noticed her stare. Most of the people on the streets were staring at him anyway, so why should she be different?

It was an interesting face. Fascinating, even. Her gran would have loved it. It was both unquestionably hard and unquestionably handsome, and the scar marking his left cheek didn't detract a bit from either quality. It was a face that kept the secrets of the man who wore it, yet to Liz it also revealed much of his character.

Even at a distance, the intensity of his pale gray eyes was almost hypnotic, the outward sign of deep and powerful emotions, and laugh lines at the corners suggested he was at least capable of laughing at himself. His mouth was sensitive and mobile, yet held firm with absolute mastery. His sharp jaw was strong, determined, his forehead high and exotically framed by the perfect widow's peak of gleaming black hair. The flying arch of his eyebrows hinted at quick wit, and the faint kink in the bridge of his aristocratic nose pointed to equally quick fists.

It was, Liz decided, the face of a brilliant, proud, highly perceptive man of considerable courage and acute compassion. It was also the face of a man who could be caustic, arrogant, impatient, and apt to act ruthlessly if he honestly believed the occasion called for it — and the results were important enough to him.

His friends, Liz thought, would never question his absolute loyalty or his willingness to do anything within his power to help in times of trouble. And his enemies would never doubt that once on their trail he simply would not give up.

Liz shivered without really being aware of it and drew her jacket more closely around her. But when the agent left Peter and approached her, she was able to sound perfectly calm. "My turn now?"

His sentry eyes studied her with interest. "You're Liz Hallowell?"

"That's me."

In a virtually automatic gesture, he showed her his I.D. "Noah Bishop."

Liz felt her eyebrows climbing. "Now, that's unexpected."

"What is?"

"Your name. Not the Bishop part, that's definitely you, but the Noah part. Noah was a caretaker, someone who offered comfort. Is that you?"

He smiled faintly. "I'm just a cop, Miss Hallowell." He paused and then, almost as if he couldn't help himself, added, "Why is the Bishop part definitely me?"

"Bishop means overseer." She barely hesitated. "I'm afraid I can't tell you anything about Steve Penman disappearing yesterday. I mean, I know that he did, but I didn't see anything. Not surprising, since the drugstore is at the other end of town."

"Do you know him?"

"Sure, as well as I knew any of the teenagers. To speak to. I didn't like him much."

"Why not?"

"The way he treated his girlfriends," she answered promptly.

"How does he treat them? Is he abusive?"

Liz took a long draw on her cigarette and blew the smoke out slowly before she spoke. "Depends on your definition of abusive, I guess. I never heard he hit any of them, or was physically rough in any other way. But he was a good-looking, charming kid who knew it and took advantage of it to get what he wanted. I don't think many girls said no to him, even though he had a track record of getting bored and moving on fairly quickly. What I didn't like was the way he seemed to view the girls as just something useful he carried along with him — like his backpack."

Bishop nodded and then, softly, said, "You keep using the past tense, Miss Hallowell. Do you know something I don't know?"

"I know he's lost. But you know that too."

"I know he's missing."

She shook her head. "You know more than that, Agent Bishop."

"Do I?"

"Sure. It's your job to know more, isn't it? They call what you do profiling, I hear. Which basically means you try to climb inside the head of the monster, figure out who he is and what he's going to do next. Isn't that right?"

"More or less."

"I wouldn't call that a pleasant job."

"That part of it isn't."

"But you're good at it, aren't you? You understand how the monsters think."

He shrugged. "There's a kind of logic even in insanity. It looks like a jigsaw puzzle, but all the pieces are there and usually fit together. It isn't that difficult to do once you know how."

Liz drew on her cigarette and blew out the smoke in a quick burst. "Maybe, but I'd say it was dangerous. If you go too deep into that insane logic, you might never get out."

Bishop smiled suddenly. "Who's interviewing whom, Miss Hallowell?"

Liz had to laugh. "Sorry. I'm incurably nosy, but I don't mean any harm. What was it you wanted to know? Why I believe Steve Penman won't be coming back? Well, I don't know monsters as well as you do, but one thing I do know about them is that they seldom leave their . . . prey . . . unharmed. Right?"

"Right."

"And this monster didn't leave behind any puzzle pieces for you guys to put together, did he?"

"Not many."

"Then Steve's lost, isn't he?"

Bishop looked at her for a long, steady moment, then smiled again. "I hear you read tea leaves, Miss Hallowell. Have you seen anything in the bottom of a cup lately that could help us?"

Liz listened for scorn or disbelief in his voice, and heard nothing except mild interest. It encouraged her to say, "I don't know how helpful it'll be, but he's trying to distract you — not you personally, I mean the investigation — by taking Steve Penman. There's something about one of the others he doesn't want you to look at closely. I don't know what it is, maybe a mistake he made or just something you have the ability to see more clearly than he bargained for, but it's there. And he's afraid you'll find it."

"So he took Steve Penman?"

Liz hesitated. "That's partly it. He had other reasons for picking Steve. I don't think he liked him." Unconsciously, she cocked her head, trying to hear what her gypsy blood was trying to tell her. "He was a little afraid of Steve — no, he was afraid of something Steve knew."

"What was that?"

She groped mentally, but the elusive knowledge was gone. "I don't know." Surprised at herself, she shook her head. "That was weird. I usually don't get much of anything without tea leaves or cards in front of me." She was just about to add that his spiritual energy must be especially strong to spark hers like that, when she saw him glance past her. Without turning her head or even thinking about it, she knew he had spotted Miranda Knight — and in a sudden flash understood much that had been murky to her before.

Bishop's attention returned to her face. Politely, he said, "Thank you very much for your help, Miss Hallowell. If I have any more questions, I'll be in touch."

Liz dropped the stub of her cigarette to the sidewalk and ground it out beneath her foot. "And I'll be here, Agent Bishop. Right here, usually."

Without actually planning to do it, Liz found herself shaking hands with the agent. She wanted to warn him to be careful, but the certainty that interference usually back-fired kept her silent. What would be would be.

She was about to return to her store when Bishop said, "I will, Miss Hallowell."

"You will what?" she asked blankly.

He smiled. "I'll be careful."

Liz stared after him, murmured, "Wow," under her breath, and went very thought-fully back to work.

"Grandstanding?" Miranda asked. She stood only a few yards away, close enough to hear, waiting on the sidewalk beside her Jeep.

Instead of denying it, Bishop merely said, "I wanted her to know I was someone who would be open to information no matter how it was come by. If something else occurs to her, she might be more willing to contact me."

Miranda put her hands in the pockets of her jacket and leaned back against the door of the Jeep. "Maybe she will. So you could read her?"

"Only partly. No deeper than surface consciousness. She was thinking I needed to be careful, that's all I got."

"An interesting place for a shield, isn't it? Just beneath the surface."

"You read her the same way?"

Miranda nodded. "I don't think she's any more conscious of her shield than she is of her innate abilities. Liz doesn't think of herself as being psychic, just the granddaughter of a gypsy. She has The Sight and her grandmother taught her how to read signs. Tell her she's telepathic and precognitive, and she probably wouldn't believe you. She's into crystals and talismans, omens and portents, crystal balls and tarot cards — and tea leaves. She only reads for friends, doesn't do it very often, and as far as I can tell, she's about seventy-five-percent accurate. So maybe you'd better be careful."

Her voice was perfectly cool and professional, without an ounce of personal concern, and since she'd been speaking to him with the same detachment all day, Bishop was hardly surprised. Which was why it did surprise him when Miranda added, "Sometimes I worry about Liz."

"Oh? Why?"

"Because she doesn't understand the power she has. I mean, she doesn't understand that knowing things about other people, sometimes secret things, can be dangerous."

Bishop chose not to take that personally. "She's spoken of very highly by everyone I've talked to, described as a kind, unfailingly helpful lady — with mildly interesting pagan beliefs nobody else really takes seriously but nobody is particularly offended by. From the sound of it, she has no enemies, no one likely to even listen closely to what she says, much less see her as a threat."

"So far," Miranda said soberly. "But what happens if she says the wrong thing to the wrong person? We're all agreed the killer is one of the supposedly good citizens of Gladstone, and I doubt he has horns or a tail to give away the evil in his soul."

"True."

Miranda glanced at Liz's shop. "I'd like to warn her, but what do I say? Stay away from the tea leaves for the duration?"

"I doubt she'd obey, not with all this going on. It's human nature to try and solve puzzles."

"Yeah, I guess. Anyway, did she tell you anything we didn't already know?"

Bishop had promised himself that he would match Miranda's aloof professionalism, and he intended to keep that promise. At least for the moment. "She said the killer took Steve Penman to distract us from something he didn't want us to notice about one of the other victims, and because he was afraid of something Steve knew."

"Do you think she could be right?"

"Maybe."

"If she is, do you think we've noticed whatever it is he doesn't want us to see?"

"If we have," Bishop said, "it isn't ringing any bells off their hooks, is it? It could be something about the Ramsay boy's bones, but Sharon hasn't been able to tell us anything definitive yet. It could be the fact that Lynet Grainger tempted him, or that she was a mistake all the way across the board — I just don't know. Not yet."

Miranda gazed at Liz's shop again, this time frowning. "Something Steve Penman knew. It's an avenue to explore, I guess. Though finding out what someone might have known about an unknown subject when he isn't here to even tell us the right questions to ask . . ."

"Yeah, it isn't much of a lead. I saw the

dogs out earlier — any luck there?"

"No, same as last night. They track him around the side of the drugstore and to the alley behind — then nothing. Perfect place to have a car waiting, and the angle would have made it all but impossible for anyone to have seen what happened once he was lured — we assume — back there."

"I guess Tony told you neither of us could pick up anything from the area."

Miranda nodded. "And Sharon went by there about an hour ago, but said she didn't get so much as a whisper of anything new."

"Did you try?" Bishop asked bluntly.

"No."

"Miranda —"

"In case you've forgotten, my abilities don't work that way, Bishop. I pick up knowledge if I touch someone I can read — which works out to no more than about forty percent of the people around me. I pick up knowledge if I just happen to catch a glimpse into the future — an occurrence that is extremely rare these days and over which I have absolutely no control. And I pick up knowledge in a very limited and defensive way through my version of your spider-sense — which means that sometimes my sight and hearing are a little better than the average and I can feel it if someone is trying to sneak up on me, if I'm being watched or potentially threatened." She paused, then added dryly, "For instance, I can tell you that most of the people in town today are watching us right now. But you already knew that, so it's fairly useless information."

Bishop did know and it was useless, but he was mildly curious about the reason for the attention. Because he was a stranger and an FBI agent? Or because he was talking to Miranda?

"So the bottom line," she said, "is that it wouldn't do any good if I tried to use my psychic abilities to pick up knowledge from the area where Steve Penman disappeared. I wish I could pick up something, believe me. I don't enjoy just waiting around to find another dead teenager."

Bishop wanted to say that they could still find Penman alive, but the words would ring hollow. They had no evidence pointing to who had abducted Penman or where he was being held. Unless their luck changed in a major way, that boy was, as Liz Hallowell had said, lost.

"Sheriff!"

Bishop saw Miranda wince, then brace herself before she turned and greeted the man striding toward them.

"Hello, Justin. Selena."

Bishop had almost missed the woman moving literally in her husband's shadow.

Miranda said, "Have you met Agent Bishop?"

"We were introduced this morning," Justin Marsh said impatiently. "Sheriff, I would like to address the town council."

"The next council meeting is in two weeks, I believe," Miranda said. "You know the protocol, Justin."

In a tone of simmering resentment, he said, "Knowing the protocol doesn't guarantee me an opportunity to speak, Sheriff, as you well know. The last council meeting was moved up a day without notice — to keep me silent."

Unmoved, she said, "I believe the date was changed due to an illness in a councilman's family, Justin. I wouldn't take it so personally if I were you."

"I was denied my constitutional right to speak my mind, Sheriff, and I do take that personally."

"Nobody's trying to silence you."

"I beg to differ. And I've tried three times since yesterday to reach the mayor, to no avail."

"It's a busy time," she said dryly.

"So busy that John MacBride won't even

speak to someone who helped put him in office?"

"We have this murder investigation going on, Justin." There was nothing at all sarcastic in her voice.

"Which is just what I want to discuss with the mayor."

Miranda didn't seem to find anything peculiar about the conversation, which told Bishop a great deal about Justin Marsh. Curious to observe the man's reaction, Bishop butted in. "If you have any information that could aid the investigation, Mr. Marsh —"

"Information?" He drew himself up stiffly, eyes blazing. "What I know is what any decent citizen of this town knows, Agent Bishop. The wicked have been silenced!"

Bishop saw Miranda's face harden, and wasn't surprised when she spoke in a quiet tone that could have cut steel.

"Lynet Grainger was fifteen, Justin. Kerry Ingram was fourteen. Now just how much wickedness do you suppose they'd had time to learn?"

"Youth cannot excuse iniquity," he said fiercely, holding his Bible aloft in emphasis. Or possibly because he knew what a dramatic gesture it was. "And the sins of the parents will be visited upon them."

"Which is it?" Bishop asked with spurious

interest. "Were they wicked themselves, or paying for the sins of their parents?"

Justin characteristically ignored the direct questions. "The righteous are duty bound to punish the world for their evil and the wicked for their iniquity."

"If you're paraphrasing Isaiah," Bishop said, "I believe it's supposed to be God doing the punishing."

Justin glared at him. "The wicked flee when no man pursueth: but the righteous are bold as a tiger!"

"Bold as a lion," Bishop corrected politely. "Proverbs, chapter twenty-eight, verse one."

"They have sown the wind," Justin snapped, "and they shall reap the whirlwind!"

"Hosea," Bishop said. "Chapter eight, verse seven."

Whether because he was unwilling to match wits with one who might just possibly know the Bible better than he did or simply because he knew he was standing on shaky ground generally, Justin looked away from Bishop with splendid indifference and addressed Miranda in freezing tones.

"I trust the next council meeting will not be rescheduled without due notice, Sheriff."

"Since I don't schedule them," she returned politely, "I really couldn't say, Justin. Good afternoon. Bye, Selena."

Justin gritted his teeth and reddened under his tan, then turned on his heel and stalked away. Selena sidestepped to avoid being run over, offered Miranda and Bishop a timid smile and an unintelligible murmur, and followed her husband.

"I don't suppose we could pin it on him?" Bishop said.

Miranda smiled. "I'd love to. Unfortunately, he wasn't even in the state when Kerry disappeared, and he was in church all evening the night Lynet vanished."

"Besides which," Bishop said, "he's the type who'll always be urging others to take action while doing absolutely nothing himself."

"That too."

"Does his wife ever say anything? I mean, other than that wordless murmur?"

"Seldom in public, as far as I can tell." Miranda shrugged. "It wouldn't be the life I'd choose, but Selena seems content enough. Then again, I'm told she's been with Justin since they were fifteen years old, so maybe it's just that she doesn't know any other way to live."

Bishop thought that was depressing in

and of itself, but it also made him think of something else. "Are there any other religious fanatics in town?"

"Who might have decided to punish the wicked themselves?"

"It's possible, Miranda."

She thought about it for a few moments. "I don't believe so, though I'm probably not the best person to ask. It's always been my impression that most of the people around here aside from Justin take their religion a lot more casually — at least to the extent of leaving it up to God to punish the evil in the world." There was no mockery in her tone, just matter-of-fact tolerance of other people's beliefs.

"We haven't seen any signs of religious mania connected with the crimes," Bishop mused. "Still, if Justin Marsh perceived those kids as wicked, someone else might have as well."

"I would say only a lunatic could have, but since it's obvious this bastard is mad as a hatter, I suppose it goes without saying." Miranda sighed. "One more possibility to throw into the hopper, I guess." The weak winter sun made a sudden appearance in the overcast sky, and she winced and pulled a pair of sunglasses from her jacket pocket.

Bishop hesitated and then, as neutrally as

he could, said, "Before we got here, you had a vision of where Lynet Grainger would be found."

Miranda put the sunglasses on and straightened away from the side of the Jeep, obviously preparing to get in and leave. "If you're implying I could see something useful about Steve Penman, I told you I can't control it."

"I know that. But you aren't open to it either."

She laughed under her breath, but without amusement. "Some things have certainly changed in eight years. From jeering skeptic to dedicated believer is quite a journey for any man to make, even in a lifetime."

"I never jeered."

"About precognition you did. Nobody could see into the future, that's what you said. It was impossible to see what hadn't happened yet, simply impossible. You were absolutely convinced. Until —"

"Until I had a vision," he said steadily. "Your vision."

"Wasn't quite what you expected, was it, Bishop?" Behind the sunglasses, her eyes were invisible, unreadable. "You thought it put you in control, made you master of your fate and the fate of others. You thought seeing the future had given you all the answers."

"And I was wrong. Is that what you want me to say one more time? I was wrong, Miranda." He was conscious of people moving past them and wondered what they made of the obviously intense, low-voiced conversation. If he was lucky, they thought their sheriff was at odds professionally with the FBI agent.

If he was lucky.

"And no matter what you think, I don't envy you that ability." The certainty in his voice sounded convincing because he was telling her the literal truth.

"Then don't ask me to open myself up to it. If I could help that boy, I would, but I can't. Not that way."

"How do you know? Goddammit, you're so closed, nothing can get in. Even your intuition is blocked, smothered —"

"We've been through this, Bishop. However I choose to shield is my business, not yours. I understand my abilities a hell of a lot better than you do, and I don't appreciate this attempt at emotional blackmail —"

"That is not what I'm trying to do. I know you honestly believe you can't control the visions, but I also know you can't think clearly about them, not now. Miranda —"

"You always know what's best, don't you? Always have to make everybody else's decisions for them. No one else is even capable of rational thought, are they?"

He drew a deep breath, trying to hold on to his patience even though he knew she was deliberately goading him, that it was another of her defense mechanisms, at least where he was concerned. "You're not listening to me. All I'm saying is that you're choosing to shut down your abilities at the worst possible time. You can shield yourself without shutting down, without closing yourself off like this."

"You'd love that, wouldn't you?"

"This is *not* about me."

"Isn't it?" She opened the Jeep door, then offered him a mocking smile. "Isn't it, Bishop?"

He stood there and watched her drive away, and didn't give a damn that at least two passersby quite definitely heard him angrily mutter, "Shit."

NINE

Friday, January 14

Alex finished his second cup of Swiss-chocolate-flavored coffee and idly watched Liz moving around behind the counter. He had no business drinking anything with this much caffeine in it so late in the day; another sleepless night lay ahead of him. And he had no business watching Liz either.

Cravings always seemed to be bad for a man.

His, at least.

"More?" Liz asked.

"Better not. I'm off for the day, so staying awake isn't a big concern."

Liz glanced around to make sure none of the other half dozen or so customers needed anything, then leaned her elbows on the counter. "I guess nothing much is happening, huh?"

"Not much, no. We've been trying to find out if Steve Penman knew something that might have made him dangerous to some-body, but —"

"Because of what I said to Agent Bishop?" Liz looked both astonished and disconcerted.

Alex had to smile at her. "You started us asking. And when Amy Fowler told us Steve had made some kind of comment about there being several other guys who'd wanted to get Adam Ramsay, it started to look more likely. But that's as far as we've been able to get. Amy swears Steve wasn't specific, and nobody else we've questioned has added anything useful."

Liz lowered her voice. "I overheard some customers talking, and they said Teresa Grainger came to the Sheriff's Department this morning in hysterics, demanding to be able to bury her little girl."

"Yeah, she did," Alex said grimly. "I've never seen anybody so wild. Her eyes were like saucers and she was talking so fast you could hardly understand her. A couple of deputies were trying to calm her down, but she didn't want to be touched and sure as hell didn't want to calm down. Some of us were afraid she was going to try to grab a gun and shoot somebody."

"What happened?"

"Oddly enough, Bishop took care of it. He got to the reception area about two steps ahead of Randy, and never hesitated. Went right up to Teresa and put his hands on her shoulders, said something to her none of us was close enough to hear — and it was like flipping a switch. She quieted down completely, sat when he led her to a chair, and waited right there without another word until Doc Shepherd and her sister got there to take her back home."

"Maybe the Noah isn't such a surprise after all," Liz murmured.

"What?"

"It's not important." Liz frowned. "How's Randy holding up?"

Alex shook his head. "Maybe it's the pressure of the investigation getting to her, I don't know — but there's definitely something wrong. She's popping aspirin like candy, wearing sunglasses when she never used to before, and when she does let you see her eyes they don't look right."

"In what way?"

He thought about it. "Almost . . . glazed somehow. There's an odd, flat shine to them, like you're looking through something else first. It's weird."

"Have you asked her about it?"

"I've asked her if she's okay. She says it's just a bad headache and for me not to worry about it."

"Maybe that's all it is."

"Yeah. Maybe."

Hesitantly, Liz asked, "How are she and Bishop together? I mean, how do they act around each other?"

"That's another weird thing. At first, they seem fine. Professional, polite, even moments of friendliness as far as I can see. But the longer the two of them are in the same room, the more the tension builds. It's actually a *tangible* thing, I swear to God it is. You feel jittery yourself, catch yourself drumming your fingers against a desk or tapping your foot."

Still tentative, Liz asked, "Has anyone else noticed it?"

Alex knew what she was thinking. "I'm not jealous, if that's what you mean. I've told you I don't think about Randy that way."

"I didn't —"

He waved a dismissive hand, ignoring her flush, and went on. "Yeah, everybody else has noticed it. I've heard some of the other deputies talking about it, in fact. You can't help but notice. If you look around, you see everybody in the room watching them the way you'd watch a crystal vase on a shelf you know is about to give way. And then their voices get this edge to them, and one or the other of them finds some reason to leave the room. And it starts all over again the next time they're together."

"Who usually leaves?" Liz asked, a touch of embarrassment lingering in her voice.

"Randy," he answered promptly. "She shuts herself in her office for a while, that closed door daring any of us to bother her. And every time it happens I get the feeling Bishop wants to kick something."

"You do realize . . . they were involved once."

Alex gazed at her curiously. "Randy more or less admitted it. But how did you know?"

"Yesterday I saw Bishop looking at her."

"And that was enough?" he asked wryly.

"Well . . . for me."

He didn't push her. "I don't know their story, but I do know it isn't over yet. Problem is, they either can't or won't settle things between them. So there's this tension building, like steam inside a pot. And sooner or later the lid's going to blow sky high."

"Is it interfering with work?"

"So far, no." He paused. "Not that there's all that much work going on, to be honest. I mean, constructive work. All we can do is keep going over and over the same ground, trying to pick up something we missed before. Even Bishop and Tony Harte are reduced to rearranging the pictures on the bulletin board to make the puzzle look different."

"I thought the other agent — that doctor — was supposed to be running some kind of tests that might help."

"Yeah, well, it turned out she needed a better lab than what she brought with her, and way more than anything we could offer. She flew back to Quantico last night. And unless they're not telling me everything, she still hasn't told Randy or Bishop what it is she suspects about those bones."

Liz was called away by another customer, and when she came back Alex made getting-ready-to-go motions like leaving money on the counter despite her protests and picking up his hat.

"Carolyn's going to work tonight, so I'm going home in an hour," she said, "and I made a big pot of stew this morning before I came in. If you don't have anything else planned, why not help me eat it?" The invitation was light, but a slight flush rose in her cheeks.

Alex knew he had no business accepting, but the prospect of spending an endless evening alone in his own house held absolutely no appeal. So he closed his mind to the little voice warning him that he'd be sorry. "That sounds great, Liz. Thanks."

"I should have everything ready by seven," she said. "But come earlier if you feel like it."

She was always so careful, he reflected with a pang. So careful to make her invitations casual, companionable, and nothing more. Maybe it was because she and Janet had been friends. Or maybe it was just because the tea leaves had told her he was still in love with his dead wife.

"I'll bring a bottle of wine," he said, matching her nonchalance.

Bonnie moved her fingertips in a gentle circular motion on Miranda's temples. "Better?"

"Yes, much better. Thanks, sweetie."

Standing behind her sister's chair, Bonnie continued the soothing massage. "It's just a temporary fix, you know that. The headaches aren't going away until —"

"I know, I know."

"Are you sure this is the right way, Randy?"

"It's the only way."

"Maybe if you told Bishop —"

"No. Not this time."

"It wasn't your fault. It wasn't even his

fault. How many times have you told me that some things have to happen just the way they happen?"

"Some things. Not everything."

Bonnie came around and sat on the couch. "Even so, how can you be sure he'd react the same way this time?"

Miranda kept her head leaning against the back of her chair, her eyes closed, and her voice was matter-of-fact. "Because he's a coldhearted bastard with only one moral certainty — that the end justifies the means."

"Is he? Is that the man he is today, Randy, or only the man he used to be?"

"Bonnie —"

"What happened changed you. How can you be so sure it didn't change him too?"

"Men don't change. Get that out of your head right now."

"I know they don't just because someone — some woman — wants them to," Bonnie agreed, thinking of Steve Penman and poor Amy, "but life can alter them just like it can us. Experience can change them, especially something so awful."

Miranda was silent.

"All I'm saying is that as long as you're closed up, you can't be sure of anything where Bishop is concerned. You don't know his mind, Randy. Not anymore. And it isn't like you to — to judge without a fair hearing."

Miranda lifted her head, opened her eyes, and frowned at her sister.

Bonnie went on quickly. "You said you hadn't even used the access he gave you to find out about Lewis Harrison." Her voice quivered very slightly on the name.

"There's no need. He wouldn't have given it to me if he hadn't been telling the truth." Miranda shrugged. "So we know that threat is gone. What else is there to find out?"

"I don't know. And neither do you." Bonnie rose. "I think I'll turn in. Do you mind if Amy spends the day here tomorrow? With no news on Steve, she's pretty much pacing the floor and driving her parents crazy. At least here with me she has somebody to talk to, and maybe I can get her busy, keep her mind off things."

"It's fine with me. But don't go anywhere unless Seth or Mrs. Task is with you, okay?"

"Sure. Good night, Randy."

"Night, sweetie."

Alone in the silence of the living room, Miranda tried to relax but found it impossible. The dull pounding in her head wasn't exactly restful, and she couldn't seem to let go of the conversation with her sister.

Bonnie was softhearted, of course. Way too sensitive for her own good, Miranda often thought. She fed stray cats and dogs, cried when even the villain died in the movies, and invariably felt sorry for anyone she felt wasn't being treated fairly.

Even, apparently, Bishop.

"What else is there to find out?"

"I don't know. And neither do you."

Miranda realized she was on her feet only when the sudden movement caused a surge of nausea. She gritted her teeth and waited it out, then went into the little side room off the downstairs hallway she had set up as a home office. The desktop computer was actually a couple years newer than those at the Sheriff's Department, and the modem was top of the line.

She swore, then turned on the machine. While it was booting up, she went to get the paper Bishop had given her from the pocket of her jacket.

He had provided all the information necessary for her to access the file on Lewis Harrison, A.K.A. the Rosemont Butcher, but that didn't mean the process was either quick or easy; the Federal Bureau of Investigation clearly disliked opening any of its files to outsiders, however well authorized, and made her work for the information.

But Miranda's experience with bureaucratic red tape since taking on the job of sheriff stood her in good stead, and she patiently wended her way through the security maze that led her, finally, to the files.

Six and a half years ago, Bishop had been a junior agent, so the bulk of the reports Miranda read had been written by two senior agents and their supervisor in the L.A. field office, as well as by several of the L.A. cops involved. Miranda doubted Bishop had even seen them.

The only report actually written by Bishop was his account of the final confrontation with Lewis Harrison that had resulted in the death of the Rosemont Butcher. One cop and another agent had witnessed what happened, and both agreed without apparent reservation that it had been a justifiable shooting, that Bishop had acted in self-defense and had no other alternative available to him, a judgment the FBI's own review board had concurred with.

But long before Miranda read about that, she had absorbed account after account of one man's relentless, obsessive hunt for a killer. Both the senior agents and their supervisor were generous in their praise of

Bishop, and all three, Miranda noted wryly, used very careful phrasing to note his "hunches" and his "instincts" in tracking down Harrison.

It really did look more like magic.

For nearly eighteen months Bishop had so completely crawled inside Harrison's head that the killer had found himself unable to continue with the meticulously planned murders he had prided himself on. Again and again, no sooner did he choose his victim than Bishop would be there somehow, waiting, protecting the victim even as he set trap after trap, his patience endless.

And Bishop had not moved in secret or even quietly, but boldly and openly, making himself a target Harrison could hardly help but see, a shadow always at his heels, a brilliant mind always second-guessing him, even outthinking him. Until finally the killer had been unable to do anything except turn like a cornered animal and make one desperate, vicious attempt to get the man on his trail.

He had failed.

Miranda slowly closed the file and turned off her computer, then just sat there staring at the monitor's dark screen. She thought about those eighteen months, that dogged pursuit, and wondered what kind of life Bishop could have had then. Not much of one.

For a man of "normal" senses and imagination to so thoroughly immerse himself in the mind of a brutal killer for that length of time would have been traumatic; for a psychic gifted or cursed with a far deeper and more intimate understanding, it must have been devastating.

And to willingly subject himself to that argued a degree of determination and commitment that was incredible.

"He had his own ax to grind," Miranda murmured into the silent room. "His own score to settle. That's why he did it. That's why."

But for the first time, she wondered.

Liz had told herself she wasn't going to push. She'd told herself repeatedly while she was getting supper ready and waiting for Alex. She would be casual and friendly, and that was all. Offer him good food and good company, and hope . . . And hope.

"I am so pathetic," she told her Ragdoll cat Tetley, who was crouched companionably at the end of the breakfast bar watching her move about the kitchen. "He still loves Janet. And who can blame him? She was a

199

wonderful woman, wasn't she?"

Tetley blinked agreeably at her.

Liz sighed. She finished her cup of tea, then sat beside her cat at the bar and studied the leaves. Within seconds, she got a flashing image of a scene she had seen once before plainly and a second time more ambiguously. A dark man with a mark on his face — Bishop — throwing himself in front of someone Liz couldn't see clearly. The bullet hit him squarely in the center of his chest. Scarlet bloomed across his white shirt as he fell heavily to the ground and lay still. Liz knew without any doubt at all that he was dead.

The cup clattered to the bar and Liz pushed it away from her, shaken. "That's three times. But I shouldn't keep seeing that," she told her cat. "It's my cup of tea, not his, why am I seeing *his* fate?"

But was it Bishop's fate? Or did Liz keep seeing it because she was somehow involved, somehow in a position to change what she saw?

Was she the one he would give his life to save?

"Symbolic," she muttered, staring at the cup but not daring to look at the leaves again. "What I see is almost always symbolic. Signs and portents. So what does it mean? What does it portend? Help me, Gran, help me figure it out."

The peal of the doorbell nearly made her jump out of her skin, but she felt relieved as she went to let Alex in. There was such a thing as being alone too long, she thought, and one sign of that was probably talking to one's dead grandmother.

"Is something wrong?" Alex asked immediately, his smile fading.

"No, I was just starting to talk to — myself. Come on in."

He followed her back to the kitchen and uncorked the wine while she set the meal on the table. They were, as usual, quite comfortable together. Casual. They talked about the nervous, frightened mood of the town, and about how unbelievable it was that a killer walked among them, and they soberly pondered the fate of Steve Penman.

"Could he be alive?" Liz asked.

"Sure he could. But if this sick bastard follows what looks like his pattern, the poor kid would probably prefer to be dead. I know I would."

Repeating what she had told Bishop, Liz said, "I think he's doing something different to Steve. Not because he wants to — more because he has to. Maybe because he made a mistake before and now he has to correct it. Or because you cops have figured out more than he bargained for and now he wants to throw you off his scent." Suddenly self-conscious, she added, "It's just a hunch."

"A hunch." Alex grimaced. "You know, I seem to be the only one around here who isn't having hunches about this investigation, and it's beginning to bother me."

"Randy's always had hunches," Liz noted. "It never bothered you before."

"Yeah, but this is different. From the minute the feds got here, it was like there was something going on that everybody but me knew about. It's in the way they all look at each other, the careful way they talk sometimes, the way they suddenly change the subject if I walk into the room."

"You sound a little paranoid, Alex."

"Don't you think I know that? But just because I'm paranoid doesn't mean I'm not also right."

Liz considered it. "Maybe it's just this history between Bishop and Randy. His people could know about it, and —"

"That's part of it, I think, but there's more to it. And it's not just between the two of them, it's all four of them — the three agents and Randy. I noticed it from the very first.

It's like they share a secret."

Quite suddenly, Liz recalled how Bishop had seemingly read her mind, and with that memory came a host of others. "Alex . . . do you remember last summer when Ed and Jean Gordon's little girl wandered away and got lost?"

"Sure. Randy found her."

"Yeah. Even though the dogs lost the trail at the river. Even though that little girl had gotten herself into an old rowboat and floated two miles down the river, and then managed to get out without drowning before hiding in that old shed you couldn't even *see* unless you knew it was there. But Randy found her there, didn't she?"

"Yeah," Alex said slowly. "She said it was a . . . hunch."

"And what about last April when she insisted the school board get a fire inspector to check the temporary classrooms even though it wasn't time to have them inspected again? He said another month and they'd have had a fire for sure with that faulty wiring."

"I remember." Alex was frowning.

Carefully, Liz said, "And there've been other things, other . . . hunches. Yesterday, Bishop said something to me that made me think he — he might have The Sight. What if he does? And what if Randy has it too?"

She more than half expected Alex to scoff, but he only continued to frown. He drained his wineglass, refilled it, then looked at her finally. "After they got here, I went back and reread that Bureau bulletin about the task force. It's cagey as hell, but if you read it carefully, what it says is that the reason this new group of agents is so successful is that they use *unconventional* and *intuitive* investigative methods and tools to solve crimes."

Liz felt her eyes widen. "You mean . . . they all have The Sight? The FBI gathered together a group of agents *because* they have The Sight, and that's what makes them effective?"

"Maybe. I would have said it was damned far-fetched for the Bureau, but more people seem open to the idea of the paranormal these days."

"New millennium," Liz said promptly. "Historically, mysticism and spirituality become more accepted and popular around the turn of a century — and a new millennium just multiplies the effects."

"I'll take your word for it." Alex paused. "If that is what's going on, I can understand their caution. No police department I've ever heard of wants to willingly admit they use psychics in investigations. If it got out publicly that the FBI has an entire unit of them on the government payroll . . ."

"But Randy would know about them if she has The Sight herself, especially if it's really strong in her. She's probably lived all her life with it, and understands the doubt and mistrust they'd face. So they can all talk freely with her — even though they'd still have to be careful around other people."

"Like me." He shook his head. "Hunches. Damn. Things are starting to make more sense. When Bishop said there was a well out near the lake even though he'd never been there before, I asked how he could possibly know that. And all Randy said was — 'he knows.' In spite of the obvious antagonism between them, she didn't hesitate to start looking for that well."

Liz watched him brood for a moment. "Will you confront Randy? Ask her if it's true?"

"I don't know."

"Not telling you was probably more habit than anything to do with trust, you do realize that?"

He half nodded. "Still, if she doesn't want me to know, maybe I should just keep my mouth shut."

Liz hesitated before saying, "Just before

you got here, I saw it again. I saw Bishop die. That's three times, Alex."

With more gravity than he'd ever shown before, Alex said, "Exactly what did you see?"

Liz closed her eyes and tried to bring the details into focus. "It was outside, in the woods, I think, but I didn't recognize the place. There were patches of snow here and there. I saw a gun, a pistol, held out in a black-gloved hand, but I couldn't see who was holding it. Then the scene tilted, almost like a camera falling, and I saw Bishop lunge in front of somebody else, put himself between the gun and whoever it was he was trying to protect. I couldn't see who it was. But I saw the bullet hit him in the center of his chest, saw the blood, saw him fall." She opened her eyes. "He was dead."

"You're certain of that?"

"Yes. What I don't understand is why I keep seeing it when I read my own tea leaves. That isn't the way it's supposed to work, Alex, not unless — unless I'm either the one holding the gun or the one Bishop dies to protect."

"It isn't you holding the gun," Alex said flatly.

"Thanks for the vote of confidence."

He smiled, but said, "Maybe you're not

actively involved in what happens. Maybe you're seeing it because you can change it."

"Maybe." She frowned. "There have been a few times in the past when I saw something that didn't quite happen the way I thought it would. I thought I'd misinterpreted the signs, but maybe what I saw was more like . . . a warning. What could and would happen if I didn't change something."

Alex said, "But the tea leaves gave you no idea what that might be, right?"

"Not that I could see."

He got up to help clear the table, and said somewhat ruefully, "What good is psychic ability if everything is shrouded in symbolism and all the important bits are left out?"

"Gran told me it worked that way because it's an ancient ability we've forgotten how to use properly. She said our modern brains try to process the information and present it to us as best they can, using signs and symbols only our primal instincts can truly interpret."

Alex thought about that while they scraped plates and loaded the dishwasher. "So if you are being . . . invited to change what you see, then there must be a clue buried there somewhere. A sign, a symbol. Right?"

"I assume so." Liz was delighted to find him willing to discuss the subject so calmly, since he'd always scoffed — however gently — in the past.

They carried their wine into her living room, where a crackling fire in the old stone fireplace made it warm and cozy, and sat on the couch. Liz tried to take heart from the fact that there was nothing separating them but the space of half a cushion, but since Alex was clearly preoccupied by signs and portents she didn't count it as much of a victory.

"Signs," he muttered. "Signs are visible, they stand out. What stood out to you in what you saw? Was there anything that seemed . . . out of place?"

"His shirt," Liz said immediately.

"His shirt?"

"Yeah. There was snow on the ground, it was cold — and Bishop wasn't wearing a jacket. Not even a long-sleeved shirt. It was a T-shirt, so white it almost hurt my eyes."

"A T-shirt. A very white T-shirt." Alex drained half his wine. "Symbolic of what — that he does his laundry?"

Liz didn't blame him for feeling frustrated. Gently, she said, "It takes a lot of practice to read signs, Alex, and even then it's often guesswork."

"So what do you guess that white T-shirt means?"

She sipped her wine as she considered it. "If the color is important, white means purity."

"I don't think," Alex said, "that Bishop is all that pure."

She hid a smile. "It might not have anything to do with him personally. The sign is for me to see, remember? So white can mean purity or innocence. It also used to be a color of mourning. On the other hand, it might not be the color at all, but the vivid cleanness of the shirt, or the fact that it's short-sleeved. It might not be the shirt at all, but the lack of a jacket that's important."

"This just keeps getting better," Alex muttered.

"I'm afraid it may take some time to interpret, assuming we can. Alex . . . do you think I should tell Randy about this?"

"Could she do anything to change it?"

"Probably not."

After a moment, he said, "I think Randy's got about all she can handle right now. No matter how she feels about him, telling her Bishop might be slated to get himself shot is just going to pile on the stress."

"I didn't warn Bishop," Liz confessed. "But when we shook hands yesterday, I was thinking he should be careful — and he knew that. He said he would."

"Then let's hope he will. For what it's worth, I can't see anything we know so far in the investigation leading to a shooting like that."

"If it has anything to do with the investigation," Liz reminded him. "It might not."

"Great. Then we really don't have a clue." He drained his glass and set it on the coffee table. "I should get out of here and let you get some rest. Thanks for supper, Liz."

"You're welcome." The part of her Liz couldn't seem to control went on in a casual tone that didn't fool either one of them. "And you're welcome to stay, you know that."

His face changed, and she didn't need The Sight to read reluctance, regret — and a touch of discomfort.

"Liz —"

"It's all right." She was desperate to head him off before he said what she didn't want to hear. "I thought you might want to talk or something, but —"

"Liz, what happened at Christmas was a mistake, you know that. I was lonely, and I'd had too much to drink." His voice was gentle. "Hell, I'm still lonely — and I hate sleeping alone. But you deserve more than gratitude."

She forced herself to say, "Stop apologizing, Alex. I was there too, remember? And I'm a big girl, all grown up and everything. Go on home. I'll see you tomorrow."

He lifted one hand as though he would touch her, then swore under his breath and left.

By the time the fire died down, Liz had emptied the bottle of wine. But it didn't help her sleep.

It didn't help anything at all.

TEN

Saturday, January 15

When Miranda came into the conference room late in the morning, she found Tony Harte writing a list of names on the blackboard, and Bishop sitting at his accustomed place on the end of the table while he studied a file.

"Missing kids?" Miranda asked.

Bishop looked up and frowned slightly, but nodded. "Your deputies are backtracking though the files, and following up on missing persons reports to rule out kids who later turned up somewhere either alive or dead. So far, we have three missing teenagers from '98, five from '97, and two from '96."

Hardly aware of doing it, Miranda sat down in a chair near Bishop. "Ten kids? Ten kids in three years?"

"All either last seen or last known to be within a fifty-mile radius of Gladstone,"

Bishop confirmed. "The youngest was four-teen when she ran away from home in '96 — in the company of her nineteen-year-old boyfriend, who wanted to go to Nashville to become a singer. Nobody reported him missing, but so far we've been unable to trace either of them beyond this area, so we're including him on the list."

Tony turned from the blackboard. "Of course, we have no evidence that any of these kids only got as far as Gladstone. Falling between the cracks of the system is all too easy, especially for kids on the streets. They could have made it to Nashville — or wherever else they were headed. They could have been picked up on the road somewhere along the way and wound up six states from here."

"All we do know," Bishop finished, "is that none of these kids reappears anywhere in the system under these names. We've cross-checked FBI files, NCIC, every data-base available. No sign of them."

Slowly, Miranda said, "Before the new highway, a lot of strangers passed through Gladstone from week to week. Aside from the Lodge on Main Street, we had two more motels just outside town that were usually at least half full."

Tony came to the conference table and

consulted a legal pad. "Let's see . . . The Starlite Motor Lodge and the Red Oak Inn, right?"

Miranda nodded. "The Starlite burned to the ground about six months ago, long after it had been abandoned. The Red Oak closed its doors the day the new highway opened. The town bought the property, and the fire department's been using the building for practice drills."

"Some of these kids may have had a few bucks for a room," Tony noted. "Any way to get our hands on the guest registers?"

"Oh, hell, I don't even know if they still exist." Miranda thought about it. "No problem getting the registers from the Lodge, since they're still doing business, but the owners of the other two places cleared out when they closed. I assume they took their records and other paperwork with them."

Tony made notes on the legal pad. "Well, we can check the Lodge at least. If we can actually place any of these kids here in Gladstone, at least we can ask a few more questions. Maybe somebody will remember something."

Bishop said to Miranda, "I looked through that special edition of *The Sentinel* this morning. Some of the letters to the editor were a bit . . ."

"Bloodthirsty?" She grimaced. "Yeah. We've had to disarm a few citizens, especially since the Penman boy disappeared. I've doubled the usual patrols just to try and keep an eye on things, but if and when suspicion falls on any one person I'm going to have a lynch mob on my hands."

"Justin Marsh isn't helping matters," Bishop said.

"With his street-corner harangues? I know. I've warned him twice, told him he's crossing the line between free speech and yelling fire in a crowded theater. If I catch him one more time urging people to purge the evil in Gladstone with their own hands, I'll see if a night in jail helps him see reason."

"His kind doesn't see reason," Tony said. "Ever."

"Talked to him, have you?" she murmured.

Tony grinned at her. "Oh, yes. I was treated to a ten-minute lecture on the corruption within government agencies."

Miranda sighed. "On a normal day, very few people really listen to him, and he's mostly harmless. But with all this going on . . . I'm afraid he might actually inspire a few of the hotheads to do something stupid."

Bishop said, "We probably don't have too much to worry about as long as they don't have a definite focus for their rage. We certainly haven't a suspect to offer them. And as far as I can tell, not even the gossips have suggested anyone for the role of possible killer."

"That's true enough — today, at least," Miranda agreed. She looked across the table to see Tony drumming his fingers on the legal pad, and said, "Is something bothering you, Tony?"

He looked down at his hand, frowned, and stopped drumming. Bright eyes moved from Bishop's calm face to Miranda. "I'm feeling tense," he said dryly. "I can't imagine why."

Miranda glanced at Bishop, and decided not to venture down that road. To Tony, she said only, "It's a tense time."

"Oh, yeah."

Bishop also ignored Tony's words. "Sharon called. She's flying back down this afternoon. Says she has something interesting for us. Maybe we'll finally get a break."

"That'd be a nice change," Miranda said. "In the meantime, the town council has called an emergency meeting, and I need to be there."

"Does Justin Marsh know about it?" Bishop asked.

"Not if we're lucky," Miranda replied as she walked to the door. "And since I threatened to arrest anybody who told him, I'm feeling lucky today."

Tony chuckled as the door closed behind her. "I had a feeling she could play hardball if she had to."

"I never doubted it," Bishop said.

Tony eyed him. "You know, even being sensitive to emotions around me, I never understood how tension could be so real you could actually cut it with a knife — until now."

"Learn something new every day."

"Boss, I'm not the only one who's noticed. Take another look out in the bullpen next time you walk through — especially if Miranda is in the room. Every deputy in the place watches you two the way they would a ticking bomb."

Bishop went to refill his coffee cup. "Yeah, I know."

"So?"

"So what?"

"So, what're you going to do about it?"

"There's nothing I can do, Tony. She wouldn't even be talking to me if it wasn't a professional duty."

Tony watched him for a moment longer, then said, "Guess you're right. There's nothing you can do about it. I'm sure neither of you could stand raking up old hurts, not at this late stage. Better to just get through this and get out of her life for good. Much better for everyone concerned."

Bishop shot him a look, but Tony was frowning down at the legal pad and seemed oblivious when Bishop said with more force than he'd intended, "Exactly."

"Say yes, Bonnie." Amy's voice shook and her eyes pleaded. "It's almost four days now, and nobody's seen him. I have to do something, I just have to!"

Bonnie kept her own voice calm. "Not this, Amy. This won't help anything."

"I know he's still alive, I know that, but we reached Lynet before and maybe she knows —"

"You two tried this before?" Seth asked.

"I've tried a dozen times on my own," Amy told him. "All week I've tried, but it never worked for me. But Bonnie made it work, she —"

"I didn't *make* anything work, Amy."

"Then it worked through you or something. All I know is that Lynet reached out to us before you made us stop. She knows who killed her, Bonnie, and maybe she knows where Steve is."

"Listen to yourself," Seth said uneasily.

"I'm telling you, it worked for Bonnie." Amy tapped the Ouija board she had set up on the table beside the bed. "Some people are more sensitive than others. I read that last night while I was researching this on the Internet. The really sensitive ones can talk to spirits. They're called mediums. I think Bonnie's a medium."

Bonnie sat beside her on the bed. "Stop talking about me as if I weren't here. I'm not a medium, Amy."

"Does Miranda know about this?" Seth demanded.

Amy's laugh was brittle. "Do you think she'd care if we could tell her where to find Steve? Do you think anybody will care?"

"Amy, it isn't that simple and you know it," Bonnie said. "Randy wouldn't like it, and I don't like it either. It's *dangerous* to play around with this stuff."

Seth frowned. "This is just a game, right? You don't believe the dead speak through this game, do you, Bonnie?"

She returned his gaze steadily. "I believe the dead speak when they realize someone's listening. And I'm telling both of you — it isn't always smart to be the one listening."

Seth would have scoffed, but something in her grave blue eyes stopped him. Not entirely sure he wanted to know any more than he already did, he said to Amy, "Look, I know you want to find Steve. I do, too. But this isn't the way."

"Why? Because you know it won't work? Or because Bonnie believes it will?" Her ferocity challenged them both. "Bonnie, you're my best friend. And you know — you know why I have to find Steve, don't you?"

Seth looked from one to the other and got a sick feeling in the pit of his stomach. "Amy, are you —"

"I have to find Steve. I *have* to." Her trembling fingers rested on the planchette. "Help me, please."

Bonnie surrendered with a sigh. "All right. All right, but remember what I said before. Keep your mind focused on what you want to know. Seth?"

"I think I'll just watch, if you don't mind." He sat down on the stool by the dressing table and folded his arms across his chest, both literally and symbolically removing himself from the attempt.

Bonnie wished she knew whether he'd be able to accept this. The possibility that he wouldn't scared her even more than the very real probability that this entire thing was a terrible mistake. But Amy was her best friend, and for Amy's sake she had to try to help.

Drawing a deep breath, she reached out and placed her fingertips next to Amy's on the planchette.

Instantly, it swung across the board and centered over NO.

Before Bonnie could ask if it was a warning for them to stop, Amy spoke quickly.

"Where is Steve?"

M...I...L...L.

Leaning toward the board unconsciously as Amy spelled out loud, Seth said, "Mill? The paper mill?"

NO.

"Wow," he muttered at the instant response, then watched in fascination as the planchette moved briskly.

M...I...L...L...H...O...U...S...E.

For a moment the teenagers looked blankly at one another, then Seth announced, "I know. That broken-down place out on the river where they used to grind grain. I thought it was barely standing, but I suppose..."

Eagerly, Amy asked, "Is that it? Is Steve at the old millhouse at the river?"

YES.

"We can save him." Amy almost stuttered in her excitement. "We can tell Randy, and —"

The planchette moved frantically.

T . . . O . . . O . . . L . . . A . . . T . . . E.

Amy gasped, her face draining of color.

Bonnie wanted to move her fingers off the planchette, but couldn't somehow. She watched, mesmerized, as the flying indicator repeated the words with almost manic intensity.

TOO LATE . . . TOO LATE . . . TOO LATE.

Seth reached over and knocked the planchette to the floor.

Amy sobbed, as Seth and Bonnie stared at each other, both white-faced. Then a motion caught their attention, and both turned their heads to see the gauzy curtains at her closed window billow inward as though a gust of wind had entered the room.

Or something.

"Oh, shit," Bonnie murmured.

Instead of eating lunch, Bishop went running. He hoped the exercise would work off the tension knotting his shoulders, but even after a forty-five-minute run and a hot shower, the tension remained. And since he was about to walk back into the Sheriff's Department, he didn't expect things to get any better.

He was just outside the front door when it opened. He caught a glimpse of a tall, blond boy with an intelligent face and steady gray eyes who was holding the door for his companion. And then she stepped through.

Bishop hadn't expected it to hit him so hard, but for a moment he couldn't breathe.

She was so like Miranda — or like Miranda had been once. Blue eyes vividly alive in a sweet, lovely face, not quite innocent but not yet cynical and definitely not veiled. A sensitive mouth, which was still vulnerable.

She recognized him instantly, going still in surprise.

He reached out without thought, his fingers closing around her right wrist. "Bonnie."

"Hey," the boy behind her said, bewildered rather than belligerent.

Bonnie stared up at Bishop and half-consciously shook her head. "It's all right, Seth. Hello, Bishop."

All the things he'd wanted to say to the shattered little girl she'd been eight years before crowded into his mind, but the only thing that emerged was a jerky, "I'm sorry, Bonnie —"

Then the words in his head were pushed

out by violent images, and his breath caught in shock. His gaze dropped to her arm, and he knew the sleeve of her sweater hid a peculiar scar, knew how she'd gotten it, what she had done to herself and why, and the wave of pain that washed over him was so intense his knees nearly buckled. "Jesus —"

Bonnie pulled her arm gently from his grasp. She was a little pale but calm, even smiling. "It wasn't your fault," she said quietly. "Even Randy knows it wasn't your fault. Let it go, Bishop."

He couldn't say a word, but she didn't seem to expect any response. She walked past him, followed closely by the boy, who gave Bishop a wary, puzzled look.

Bishop watched them get into a car parked at the curb. He noted the boy's protective body language, the way he looked at her and touched her, the way he carefully put her in the passenger seat and closed her door.

He wondered if Miranda knew.

Pushing that speculation out of his mind, he looked after the car as long as he could see it, then tried to pull himself together enough to go inside. He thought he'd done a fair job, but judging by the stares he got as he walked through the bullpen, maybe not.

He barely remembered to knock first at

Miranda's closed office door, to wait for the muffled response before going in.

She was on her feet behind the desk, leaning over a map spread out on the blotter. And she was wearing a shoulder harness that held her .45 automatic.

She glanced up at him and said briskly, "At least this time you remembered to knock." Then her eyes narrowed and she straightened slowly. In an entirely different tone, she said, "You saw Bonnie."

He closed the door and sat down in a visitor's chair. "I saw Bonnie."

Her mouth tightened, but all she said was, "And read her like a book, I see."

"No. Not like a book. But I saw her nightmare." He paused. "It wasn't in the police report, Miranda. I didn't know."

"That was my decision. She'd been through enough. And it wouldn't have changed anything, wouldn't have helped you get him."

He heard himself say, "She told me it wasn't my fault."

"Yeah, that sounds like her."

"She said you didn't believe it either."

Miranda looked at him for a steady moment, her expression unreadable, then began to fold the map. "I have to go check out a tip."

He was willing to let her change the subject, but only because he felt too raw to push it. "A tip — or a vision?"

She hesitated, then sighed. "Bonnie's best friend Amy was desperate to try to find Steve Penman. So they tried. They used a Ouija board."

Bishop stood up. "And?"

"And if they got the truth, we're already too late. But they were told where to find him. It's an old millhouse out on the river. Abandoned, isolated." She shrugged. "No possible reason or evidence leads me to look there, and I'm not going to claim another anonymous tip unless it pans out first."

"Then I'm going with you," Bishop said. To his surprise, Miranda didn't argue.

"Let's go."

It was nearly two o'clock when Alex carried the most recently discovered files of missing teenagers into the conference room. Tony Harte was at his laptop and spoke wryly before Alex could.

"Your county librarian tells me that the reason so few records are on computer yet is because the city fathers chose to put their upgrade money into making sure existing systems were Y2K compliant."

"That was their excuse," Alex admitted.

"Personally, I think they hoarded money to buy doomsday supplies they probably stashed in the basement of the courthouse, but that's just my opinion."

Tony grinned. "If so, they wouldn't be the only ones who did. But it's making it damned difficult to find information with any speed. Even your newspaper is still storing back issues on microfilm."

"What're you looking for?"

"I wanted to check the newspapers covering the two weeks or so before and after each of these kids was last seen in the area. Probably won't find anything, but it never hurts to look. Sometimes runaways respond to ads in the classifieds — you know, temporary jobs, that sort of thing."

"Good idea." Alex held up the files in his hands. "And here are two more for you, from '95."

"Two for the year?"

"We're not done with the year yet."

Tony grimaced. "Great. Okay, I'll add their names to the list."

Alex put the files on the table, then said, "Sheriff isn't in her office, and I don't see your boss around either."

"They went to check out a tip."

"*They?*"

"Surprised me too," Tony murmured.

"Bishop stuck his head in just long enough to say they were going to some old millhouse, and that they'd call in if they found anything. That was about ten minutes ago."

"An old millhouse?" Alex frowned.

"Yeah. Out on the river, I think he said." Tony eyed the deputy. "You okay? You look sort of ragged, if you don't mind me saying."

"Bad night," Alex replied briefly.

"Ah. I've had my share of those."

"Then you know what my head feels like. I think I'd rather go look at microfilm in the library than go back down into the basement and paw through more files. If you'll give me the relevant dates, I'll see if *The Sentinel* has anything helpful."

"You don't have to offer twice," Tony said.

"You're not shielding Bonnie any longer," Bishop said. "That's how I was able to read her."

At the wheel of her Jeep, Miranda frowned but didn't look at him. "With Harrison no longer a threat, it wasn't necessary. Bonnie can protect herself as long as —"

"As long as she's not being hunted by a deranged psychic?"

"Yes."

He turned in the passenger seat to watch her. "There's no hint that Gladstone's killer has any psychic ability."

"No," she agreed.

"And yet you're shielding yourself. Even more now than you were a week ago."

"I have my reasons."

She had surprised him again by offering at least some kind of answer readily, and he probed carefully. "You said it wasn't . . . us. My team. Something to do with the investigation?"

"We're not going to play twenty questions, Bishop. I have my reasons. And that's all."

"Reasons important enough to risk your life?"

"Check the map, will you? I think we turn left at the next crossroads."

"Jesus, you're a stubborn woman," he said as he got the map off the dashboard. He confirmed that they did indeed turn left, and was silent for several miles before asking, "How did the council meeting go?"

"Badly."

"Are they calling for your job yet?"

"Not yet. Nobody else wants it."

He caught a glimpse of the river and realized they were getting close. Absently, he said, "A Ouija board. I would have thought

Bonnie would know better than that."

"She does. But she wanted to help her friend."

"Where are they now?"

"Seth's father, Colin Daniels, is one of our local doctors. He runs a pediatric clinic. Bonnie and Seth took Amy there before they came to tell me, then they went back there to stay with her. Colin's her doctor, and he's got her sedated."

"Then she's convinced the Penman boy is dead?"

"Apparently it was a pretty convincing scene."

"Who did they reach? Penman?"

"I don't know. And neither do they."

Bishop hesitated. "If Bonnie's that sensitive, maybe —"

"No way, Bishop. *You* should know better than that. Whatever Bonnie opened the door to is likely to be confused and enraged at the very least, and I will not allow my sixteen-year-old sister to subject herself to that kind of negative psychic energy. It could destroy her."

"You're right," he said. He thought he'd surprised her, and the reminder of how ruthless she thought him was unexpectedly painful. "I would never do anything to hurt Bonnie, Miranda. If you don't believe anything else I ever say to you, believe that."

She glanced at him, but all she said was, "The road leading out to the millhouse should be just ahead. There's no way to approach quietly except on foot — and we'd be very visible on foot."

He saw what she meant when she turned the Jeep off the winding two-lane blacktop and onto a rutted dirt road. She stopped, leaving the engine running, and they both studied the scene ahead. A half mile or so down the road, the millhouse was visible. Part of the roof had fallen in on one side, and only shards of glass remained in the few windows not boarded up. The waterwheel had long since become no more than a crumbling skeleton, and overgrown bushes, their branches stripped bare in winter, reached as high as the eaves.

Miranda pulled a pair of binoculars from the center console and got a closer view of the place, then passed them to Bishop. "I don't see anyone. How's the spider-sense?"

He rolled down his window and leaned out with the binoculars, then put them aside and concentrated all his senses. "I don't see anyone either." After a long while, he looked at Miranda and added quietly, "But I smell blood."

She put the Jeep in gear without another

word and drove up the road almost to the millhouse before parking. "The ground's likely softer near the house," she said. "There might be tire tracks, footprints. Something we might be able to use."

"It's a chance," he agreed.

They got out, both automatically drawing and checking their weapons. Miranda got flashlights and latex gloves from a tool kit in the back of the Jeep, and they made their way cautiously to the house.

They had never worked together this way before, and it wasn't until later that Bishop realized how smoothly and in sync they had operated as a team. Nothing had to be said, and neither wasted a motion or a second of time. They split up to bracket the house, each of them treading carefully to avoid trampling any evidence. They tried and failed to see into several windows as they worked their way toward the door.

The smell of blood grew stronger.

Miranda was the first to reach a window that allowed a view of the inside, and Bishop knew instantly that the sight sickened her. She stood there for a moment, her face still and pale, then moved past the window and joined him beside the closed door.

She whispered, "What I saw couldn't try to escape."

Bishop reached out to try the rusted door-knob, and it turned easily, as if recently oiled. Cautiously, making sure they were standing well to the side, he pushed open the door.

The heavy, coppery stench seemed to roll out at them, cloying and sickly sweet.

He already knew nothing alive was in there, but they went in by the numbers anyway, guns ready, alert for threats and protecting each other as partners did.

Whatever machinery had once been contained in the single huge room was long since gone. Half the space was cluttered by rotting beams and broken tiles; the other half, sheltered by the partial roof, was dim and musty, with weeds sprouting here and there between the few remaining floorboards.

Under the crossbeam, a shallow trench had been dug in the ground. It was about three feet long and a foot wide, and no more than ten inches deep. The soft earth had soaked up much of the blood.

Above the trench, suspended from the crossbeam by a rope knotted around both ankles, hung the naked body of Steve Penman.

Blood still dripped from his slashed throat.

ELEVEN

Deputy Sandy Lynch didn't get sick this time, but she was none too happy that the call had come in while she was on duty. Even if all she had to do was fetch and carry for Dr. Edwards, who had returned just in time to examine Steve Penman's butchered body, it meant Sandy was stuck inside the millhouse with that body and all the blood, and she hated the smell of blood, she just hated it —

"Deputy?" Agent Edwards said kindly. "If you could hold the light a little higher, please?"

"Yes, ma'am." She did and tried not to look at what it showed. She also tried to breathe through her mouth only, and tried not to look too desperate when Alex looked in long enough to catch her eye.

Alex retreated from the doorway to where Miranda stood next to Tony Harte, who was making a plaster cast of tire tracks.

"Sandy's about to lose her lunch," Alex said.

Miranda nodded. "Have her switch places with Carl. We need somebody at the end of the road just in case anyone passes by and gets too curious."

"Right." Alex went off to obey orders.

"I know how she feels," Tony commented, sitting back on his heels as he waited for the plaster to harden. "She's — what? — twenty?"

"About that." Miranda shifted her gaze to Bishop, standing near the crumbling waterwheel several yards away. "And she didn't bargain for all this."

Tony noted the direction of her stare, but all he said was, "I guess not. Sometimes fate just loves to knock you back on your ass."

Miranda looked at him, one brow rising slightly.

Innocently, he said, "By the way, thanks for not blocking us anymore. It was giving me a hell of a headache."

"So what can you pick up from the area?" she asked, neatly bypassing any discussion as to why she had retracted her shield to enclose only her own mind.

Tony sighed. "All I got inside was the boy's terror — which gives me a whole new insight into the human mind, since he was unconscious the entire time and shouldn't by any science we've always believed in and relied upon have known or been able to feel what was being done to him."

"But he knew? He felt it?"

"He knew," Tony said soberly. "Knew he was going to die and there wasn't a damned thing he could do about it. And he felt it. The pain."

Miranda tried not to think too much about that. "Did he know who —"

"If he did, he was too terrified of dying to care who was killing him. I just got the emotions, not the thoughts."

"I see. Anything else?"

"About what you'd expect. There was a kind of . . . free-floating rage, I assume the killer's. He wasn't finished here, and I don't think he intended us to find the body here, so if we do find any evidence, it might be worth a lot. That's it for me. Sharon might get more, since this is definitely the scene of the crime and not just a dumping place."

"Yes, this time we got . . . lucky."

"Gotta love those anonymous tips," Tony said.

It was Miranda's turn to sigh. "It would be nice to have some solid evidence from here on out. Too many more anonymous tips I can't explain and we'll all be in trouble."

Bishop joined them. "This was a onetime deal," he said. "The other victims weren't killed here."

"Which begs the question, why did he bring this victim to a different place?" Miranda absently rubbed the nape of her neck. "To throw us off track? He can't be killing them all in different places, surely?"

"Given what he did to each of the other victims, I wouldn't think so," Bishop said. "He had to be someplace where he could feel safe and secure, and he had to have both time and privacy. How many of us have more than one place where we feel really safe? No, I think your guess is right. I think he killed this boy here because he was afraid we were getting too close to wherever he killed the others."

Tony said, "But does that mean he planned to bring future victims here as well? It's obvious we weren't expected to find this place, or at least not so quickly. If it hadn't been for that . . . anonymous tip . . . would we have found this boy's body buried out in the woods somewhere — if we found it at all?"

Miranda was about to say something irritable to Tony about harping on that "anonymous tip" that he knew very well had come from her sister when she saw Alex out of the corner of her eye, and realized how close he was. Close enough to hear. Tony had only been continuing to protect their little secret, she realized.

She also realized something else, and it made her feel more than a little grim. Because she had retracted her shield, energy and effort that had been designed to protect both herself *and* her sister were now focused on a much narrower point — her mind alone. It was a very solid shield that now separated her from those around her. She was beginning to lose even the heightened awareness of her surroundings that was normal for her, her version of Bishop's spider-sense. She always seemed to know where *he* was, feeling him near long before she actually saw or heard him, but that was something different.

She hoped he'd never discover just how it was different.

Feeling his eyes on her, she forced herself to concentrate on what Alex was saying, and it worried her that his voice actually sounded peculiarly hollow to her.

". . . and from what I understand about your profile of the killer, Bishop, wouldn't it be important to him that we did find this victim? I mean, if he was out to prove — to himself and maybe to us — that he was all-powerful and in control, wouldn't he have wanted us to see his handiwork sooner rather than later?"

Bishop nodded slowly. "That's a good point. He would have expected us to know that he had abducted a very masculine, physically powerful kid, but until we found the body we couldn't be sure what he had done to that kid. Without evidence to the contrary, we might speculate that his needs and desires were sexual, something he certainly doesn't want."

Miranda resisted the urge to rub her temples in a vain attempt to soothe the throbbing there. "But why is he so determined not to display — or feel, apparently — sexual desire for his victims? Aren't most murders of this . . . bizarre nature sexual at the core?"

"Virtually always," Bishop answered. "And few murderers bother to try to hide or disguise it. Tony, you said you thought this killer was highly conflicted. I think you were right. I believe this killer has very neatly divided his life. Light and dark. In the light side, he has a normal existence, with friends, maybe family — and a woman or women he's attracted to sexually. He may even have at least one successful ongoing relationship, apparently normal in every way.

In the dark side, he has these violent urges and needs he's driven to satisfy."

"Okay," Miranda said. "But my question stands. Why, as far as he's concerned, may his killings not be sexual or viewed as sexual even by himself? Why is that so important to him?"

"My guess is that he's trying to protect the light side of his life — and the woman or women there. To keep that separate and apart. If what he's doing becomes overtly sexual, then he'll begin to want to do these things to women he's attracted to in the light, sane side of his life. The darkness will spill over, out of his control."

"If this is him in control," Tony said, "I really don't want to be around to see him out of control."

They were all silent for a few moments, then Alex stirred and said, "Speaking of dark, it's getting there. Either we start wrapping this up for the day or else break out the big lights."

Bishop looked at Miranda. "I'll check with Sharon and find out how much more time she needs."

She nodded slightly and watched him walk back to the millhouse.

"Supposed to snow tonight."

Miranda was startled to find Alex looking

at her intently. She hadn't felt it. *She hadn't felt it.* "I haven't seen a weather report," she said.

"Well, the weather people are being fairly cagey, but last I heard, the best we could hope for was two or three inches. Worst is a blizzard."

"Great. That's just dandy." She thought it might at least give the townspeople something else to worry about. But bad weather would also threaten potential problems with electricity, and would demand that most of her deputies be out and about helping people rather than in the office chasing down information that might prove helpful to the investigation.

They weren't moving very fast anyway, but a storm could stop them in their tracks.

"Is that cast going to be helpful?" Alex asked, as Tony tested the plaster.

"After all this work, I certainly hope so. But we'll see. It'll take time to run down the right brand of tire, and more time to match up sales of that brand with cars registered in the area, and then . . . Well, it'll take time. But maybe it'll give us something in the end."

Miranda noticed the heavy clouds rolling in and hoped they'd have time.

"Here, wait a second and I'll give you a

hand." Alex bent to help lift the plaster cast.

"Thanks."

Miranda watched them carry the cast toward the vehicles parked several yards away. She felt the tingle on the nape of her neck, and didn't have to look to know Bishop was approaching her.

"Is she about done in there?" It gave her a certain amount of satisfaction to know that it bugged Bishop when she did that, especially since it had become patently obvious that she could sneak up on him without his awareness — spider-sense notwithstanding. She was glad to know she could shake his composure at least a bit. Even more, she preferred to have him annoyed rather than thinking too much about how she was able to do it.

"Another half hour," Bishop replied, sounding faintly distracted. "She said not to bother rigging the big lights, and that she'd have a preliminary report for us in a few minutes."

"In the meantime," Miranda said, "we'd better take a last look around. Alex says snow's in the forecast. Whatever clue or evidence we leave out here is likely to be buried, at least for a while."

She felt a light touch on her arm, and was confident enough of her shield that she was able to look at Bishop calmly without jerking from his grasp.

"Are you all right?" he asked.

"Oh, sure. I'm getting used to finding dead kids." She was able to keep her voice dry and unemotional, but it required more of an effort than she had expected. And it shook her to realize that what she really wanted to do was confide that she was unutterably weary, and that it tore at her soul to have to discuss with professional detachment the unspeakable evil being committed in her town. To confide that she had nightmares when she could sleep at all, that she was desperately worried about her sister, worried about what was still to come. Worried that she had misread what she'd seen or misunderstood what she was meant to do. Worried that she wouldn't have the strength when the time came.

She wanted to confide all that. In him.

He was frowning slightly. He did not release her arm.

"I'm fine, Bishop." It was, of course, the only thing she could say, the only answer she could give him. She still didn't try to pull away. Even with her shield firmly in place — or perhaps because of that — she knew that he was being true to his word and not trying to read her.

"You're not fine," he argued, keeping his voice low. "You're too pale and your pupils are dilated. And don't you think I can tell you've shut off your defenses? Christ, Miranda, I'm the only one who *couldn't* sneak up and blindside you."

For just an instant, she was tempted to snap that since only he posed a threat to her, her defenses were still in good working order. Instead, she said calmly, "Since nobody's after me, it hardly matters, does it?"

"That's naive and we both know it. You're the sheriff investigating a series of brutal murders, and that sure as hell makes you a threat to the killer."

"I can take care of myself."

"I'm beginning to wonder about that."

"You can stop wondering."

He was silent for a moment, then said, "Your pulse is racing."

Miranda only just stopped herself from jerking her arm away. "You're imagining things. Now, if you don't mind, I'd like to do one last walk-through of the scene before it gets too dark to see anything."

Bishop had the grim face of a man who wasn't finished arguing, but he finally released her. "I want another look around the waterwheel. Something about it is bothering me."

She didn't move immediately but watched him walk away, and it wasn't until she turned herself that she realized Alex was standing several yards away looking at her. That he was there at all startled her, but his expression made her feel decidedly wary, and not only because of her failing defenses. Since he fell into the sixty percent of people she couldn't read, she had never sensed any more of his thoughts than those he was willing to share, but she knew him well enough to be certain something was disturbing him.

"Alex?"

He closed the space between them, speaking before she could ask the half-formed question in her mind. "Greg just called from the office. Word's out, Randy."

"How the hell did that happen? I was at least hoping I could break the news to his parents before somebody else told them."

Alex sighed. "I don't know how, but it might not be the worst of it. Apparently, when her parents came to get her, Amy Fowler was pretty hysterical, and before Dr. Daniels could sedate her again, she was babbling on about Ouija boards and contacting spirits who told her where Steve's body could be found — and claiming Bonnie is a medium. A couple of nurses overheard. You can guess the rest."

"Oh, shit," Miranda said.

Panic was not an emotion he was accustomed to. His life had always been completely under his control; that was what he worked for and planned for. He hated surprises.

Finding cops crawling all over the old millhouse was a distinct and unpleasant shock.

He racked his brains to remember if he'd left anything incriminating behind. He couldn't think of anything; he was always careful. Always.

But they'd found poor Steve before he was ready for them to, and that wasn't good. That wasn't good at all.

The question was . . . how had they found him?

"Death wasn't quite as recent as it appears," Sharon Edwards said briskly. "I may have a closer estimate for you later, but for now you can say time of death was last night between midnight and six A.M."

"Twelve or more hours ago? The blood's still dripping," Miranda said.

"My guess is that he gave the boy — either

orally or by injection — an anticoagulant to prevent the blood from clotting."

Miranda frowned as she watched two of her deputies gingerly carrying the black-bagged body toward the hearse. "He didn't do that to the others, right?"

"No."

"Why this time? Because he was . . . away from home and didn't have his equipment handy? Because using a drug was the fastest and simplest way to drain the body of blood?"

"Maybe."

Alex asked, "Where would he have gotten the drug?"

Sharon sighed. "With what's available on the Internet now? If he knew what to ask for — and practically any physician's or pharmacology reference book would have told him — he could have ordered the stuff from any one of a thousand places. If we find him, we may be able to backtrack from his own computer, but otherwise . . ."

Tony said, "That does argue a certain amount of forethought and planning. It isn't something you'd have on hand unless you needed it yourself. But my guess is this guy's too smart to use anything that could be traced back to him."

"So he had to know or at least believe he'd

need it," Miranda mused. "For the others? Did he think he might need help in draining the bodies, only to find he was able to do it without drugs? And then used the drugs on Steve because he had no other choice?"

"Well," Sharon said, "here's something else to throw into the pot. He took at least some of the blood with him. There's a depression in the trench where a bucket or pail was placed underneath the body. It's difficult to tell how much is missing, though I'd guess not more than a pint or two."

"What else is missing from the body?" Miranda asked. She was aware that Bishop gave her a sharp look, but kept her eyes on the doctor.

Sharon's brows rose. "I'm surprised you caught that, Sheriff. I didn't see it until I examined the body. His tongue is missing, neatly removed with a sharp knife or razor."

"Oh, Christ," Alex muttered.

Slowly, Bishop said, "Lynet Grainger might have seen him, seen his temptation, so he took her eyes. He took Steve Penman's tongue because the boy might have spoken . . . might have told someone something dangerous to him."

"I'd think killing the boy removed that threat," Tony said.

"Maybe he didn't think so," Miranda said

carefully. "Maybe we have a . . . superstitious killer here. Maybe he believes in ghosts."

Surprisingly, it was Alex who said, "If that were true, wouldn't he have done the same thing to the others? I mean, they all had to see him at some point, right, if only when he grabbed them? They all probably knew who he was. So if he believed in ghosts, he had to believe any one of them could have — have named him as their killer."

"That makes sense," Miranda admitted.

Bishop said, "The simplest reason is probably the right one. Punishment. He took Lynet's eyes as punishment because she saw his temptation. He took Steve's tongue as punishment because he would have talked."

"And the blood he took from all of them?" Alex asked.

"He needed it."

Alex sighed. "Great. Sooner or later, that little item is going to get out. Anybody want to bet as to how soon this bastard is nicknamed the vampire killer?"

Bishop was brooding and didn't respond; Tony shook his head solemnly; Miranda returned her attention to the doctor with a question.

"How was Steve subdued?"

"Blow to the head, probably with a bat or something else made of wood. A solid blow. The skull is fractured, and I doubt very seriously if the boy ever regained consciousness."

"There's consciousness," Tony murmured, "and then there's consciousness."

Alex seemed about to ask something, so Miranda spoke quickly. "What was the immediate cause of death?"

"Loss of blood."

"Any signs of torture?"

"No, none. There isn't so much as a bruise or cut anywhere on the body except for the throat and the tongue. Even the ropes around the ankles were no tighter than necessary. It's as if he was very careful not to damage the boy any more than he had to."

"Or," Miranda said, "very careful not to display too great an interest in Steve." She looked at Bishop. "So we wouldn't think it was sexual?"

Bishop nodded. "I'm surprised he stripped the boy. Leaving him naked was taking the chance we might think he enjoyed looking at him that way."

Miranda frowned. "Unless there was a greater risk in leaving the clothes on. Forensic evidence, maybe?"

"Could be. He had to transport the boy

here, and given where he was abducted, there was no opportunity at that end to guard against picking up fibers from whatever vehicle was used."

Miranda looked back at Sharon. "The body was washed?"

"Just like the Grainger girl's," Sharon confirmed. "I found traces of the same mild liquid soap."

Bishop looked toward the millhouse. "No running water inside, but —"

"The waterwheel," Miranda said. "Something about it was bothering you."

"The trough," he said slowly, realizing. "It was still damp. He put the boy in the trough to wash him. The wheel no longer turns, but he could dip water from the river with a bucket and use the trough as a tub."

"Steve Penman was no lightweight," Miranda said. "And there are no signs the killer used anything but a car to transport his victim. Carrying him to and from the water wheel definitely took some muscle."

"Or sheer determination," Bishop said.

Miranda sighed, glanced around at the deepening twilight, then said to the doctor, "There's been no time to discuss it until now, but you said you had found something interesting about the bones of the first victim?"

"You could say that. While he was still alive, the boy had been injected with a chemical compound that leached all the nutrients from his system and forced his bones to appear to age much more rapidly than normal."

Miranda stared at her for a moment. "Why?"

"If I had to guess, knowing what little we do about this killer, I'd say he did it just to see what would happen. I have no doubt the process would have been agonizing for the victim, and if he gets his kicks by causing pain . . ."

"A lab experiment," Alex said incredulously. "A goddamned lab experiment."

Miranda felt too sickened to speak, and it was Bishop who said, "Is there any other reason he might have done it? Anything he could have gained?"

Sharon pursed her lips. "Well, maybe one thing, though I'm damned if I know why. One result of the chemical process would have been to . . . enrich the blood. All the nutrients leached from the bones and organs would have been deposited in the bloodstream. So if he exsanguinated that body — and I believe he did — the blood he got as a result would have been much higher in minerals and nutrients than normal."

After a long silence, Alex said, "Am I the only one starting to believe in vampires?"

"No," Miranda said. "Let's get the hell out of here."

Liz hadn't been thinking much about the weather, but when the flow of customers to the café and bookstore increased dramatically in the late afternoon she knew something was up. People tended to make last-minute runs to the grocery story and — depending on their tastes — either a bookstore or a video store whenever bad weather was expected. Nobody wanted to be stuck at home without food or entertainment.

And in this case, Liz soon realized, they also wanted a last chance to linger in the relative safety of a public place and explore the latest gossip. Word had spread that Steve Penman's body had been discovered, and the mood of those Liz talked to seemed evenly divided between frightened and furious. They wanted the killings to *stop,* wanted this madman caught and punished, and they wanted it now.

Which was why when Alex came in just after six o'clock, three of Liz's customers pounced on him and demanded to know what the Sheriff's Department was doing to make the streets of Gladstone safe again.

"Everything we can," Alex told them patiently.

"Like what? It's getting very scary out there, Alex," Scott Sherman told him, waving his copy of the latest thriller in unconscious irony.

"Then don't be out there, Scott. Go home. There's a storm coming, or haven't you heard?"

"Of course I've heard. Why do you think I'm here looking for a few good books? Alex, I voted for Sheriff Knight, and I really hope she doesn't make me regret it."

"Then leave her alone to do her job — and help her by getting off the streets so we can all put our energy where it needs to go."

"But, Alex," Linda Bolton said anxiously, "if Steve Penman can be taken off Main Street in the middle of the afternoon, how can we expect our kids to be safe even at home?"

"Keep them inside and lock the doors." Alex sighed. "Look, I know it's a nervous time, but there's no sense in imagining a boogeyman around every corner. This killer is being hunted and knows it — and chances are he'll stay inside during bad weather just like the rest of us. So buy a few books and a jigsaw puzzle or two, and wait for the storm to blow over, okay?"

"But what if —"

Liz rescued him, waving the others back to their shopping or coffee and taking Alex to the counter, where he could sit and have a cup of coffee himself. She fixed his favorite and set it before him. "I don't have to ask if it's been a bad day. We heard you'd found Steve."

"Yeah."

Determined not to allow either of them to remember the last time they'd spoken, Liz kept her voice matter-of-fact. "Was there anything out there that might tell you who killed him?"

"Hell, I don't know." Alex sipped his coffee.

Liz hesitated. "I heard something about Steve coming back from the dead to tell his girlfriend where his body could be found."

Alex scowled. "So that's the latest garbled version? Shit. Not but what it's probably for the best that the story is getting outrageous. If we're lucky, nobody'll believe whatever they hear."

Grave, Liz said, "How did you know his body was out there?"

Sourly, Alex said, "How else? Randy got an anonymous tip."

TWELVE

"Her parents wanted to take her home, especially with a storm on the way," Bonnie said into the receiver, "but Dr. Daniels said better not. She's in pretty bad shape, Randy."

"Do her parents know yet?"

Bonnie lowered her voice even though she was alone at the reception desk and not likely to be overheard. "About the baby? I'm afraid so. I think her mom's in shock, and her dad looked . . . well, he looked awful. Like somebody had hit him."

"Somebody did," Miranda said.

"Yeah. Anyway, Dr. Daniels said she needed to sleep, straight through the night at least, and he wants to keep her here where she can be watched closely. I think he's afraid she — she might try to hurt herself or the baby."

"Do you think she could?"

"She's really scared, Randy. I mean, a few

days ago she didn't even suspect she was pregnant, and then Steve disappeared and she started thinking and . . . and now he's gone and there's a baby coming. I don't know what she's capable of doing, I really don't. But I know I want to be here for her."

"You could be stuck there if this storm hits big."

"I know. And so does Seth. His dad and mom are both staying here because there are a few kids that can't he moved without making them worse, and we can help out. Part of the kitchen staff are staying, and two of the nurses. There are plenty of supplies, and a generator if we lose power. We'll be fine here even if we get snowed in."

Miranda sighed, sounding incredibly weary. "Well, I'd rather you were there at the clinic with Seth and his parents than home alone with Mrs. Task, for now at least."

Bonnie hesitated. "Randy, I don't think anybody's going to take what Amy said seriously. She was obviously hysterical and not making much sense at all."

"I hope you're right. But it gives people . . . possibilities . . . to talk about, sweetie. And right now, that's about all they have. Until I can give them a solid suspect with believable evidence, they're bound to speculate."

"I know. I'm sorry, Randy."

"Don't be. Finding Steve before the killer was ready for us might turn out to be a huge break."

"I hope so. Will you stay there tonight?"

"That's the plan. I'll leave before the storm breaks and make sure Mrs. Task gets home safely and the house is battened down, then come back here."

Bonnie felt uneasy for no reason she could explain even to herself. "Be careful, okay? I mean . . . the roads could be bad."

"It isn't even snowing yet. But don't worry, I'll be careful. And you be sure and check in tomorrow morning whether we end up snowbound or not. Don't leave the clinic, even with Seth, without telling me first."

"No, I won't."

"I'll talk to you tomorrow. 'Bye, sweetie."

" 'Bye." Bonnie hung up and went down the hall to look in on Amy, who was sleeping with the utter stillness of sedation or exhaustion — or both. Seth had been standing by her window gazing out at nothing, but when Bonnie looked in he joined her at the door.

"She won't wake for hours," he said, keeping his voice low. He eased Bonnie back out into the hall and pulled the door almost closed.

Restless, Bonnie said, "If there's anything I can do to help your parents with the other patients —"

"Dad said they might need us later, but not now. We have some time to ourselves. I think we should talk, don't you?"

Bonnie wanted to deny that, but she was ruefully aware that Seth had been uncommonly patient and he certainly deserved an explanation. Or two. So she followed him to a small waiting room just down the hall. It wasn't what you'd call the ideal place for a serious conversation, since it was decorated in bright primary colors and boasted decals of cartoon characters on the walls — decor geared to the mostly young patients the clinic treated — but there were a couple of comfortable couches, and lamps turned low kept it from feeling too much like Disney on parade.

"Who's Bishop?" Seth asked as soon as they sat down.

It surprised her that it was his first question given everything that had happened that day, but when she thought about the abrupt and strained meeting with Bishop on the steps of the Sheriff's Department her surprise faded somewhat. From the point of view of someone who didn't know the story, it had quite likely been a decidedly enigmatic meeting.

Cautiously, she said, "You know he's an FBI agent."

"Yeah, I know that. But what is he to you and your sister? What happened that isn't his fault? It has something to do with that scar on your arm, doesn't it?"

Bonnie looked down at her right forearm, absently brushing the sleeve of her sweater back to expose the white, raggedly crescent-shaped scar. She was trying to decide how much to say, worried about overwhelming Seth; given how sensitive and empathetic he was, she was inclined to say as little as possible even if it wasn't the whole story.

"Bonnie?"

She chose her words with care. "When I was a little girl, before we came to Gladstone, I lived outside L.A. with our parents and our sister Kara."

"I didn't know you had another sister."

Bonnie nodded jerkily. "I . . . I did. Randy didn't live with us, she had her own place. She had just finished law school. It was in the spring that year when a man the newspapers called the Rosemont Butcher started killing people. He always chose families, and he got inside their homes so easily it almost seemed like magic. Alarm systems, guard dogs, even armed security guards — nothing could keep the families safe once he'd picked them.

"The police needed help, so they asked the FBI. And that whole summer, agents and cops were trying to figure out how to stop the killer. And he kept on killing."

Seth reached over and took her hand. "What happened?"

"My sister Kara was . . . psychic. And the ability she had was a very unusual one. A dangerous one. Sometimes she had visions, and in those visions she could . . . see through the eyes of someone else. Sometimes she could even make it happen, see through a particular person's eyes by holding something they had touched."

She paused, waiting anxiously for Seth to comment, but he just said, "Go on."

Bonnie drew a deep breath. "Bishop was part of the FBI investigation. He and Randy had met, I don't know how, and had gotten involved that summer. Pretty seriously involved. He found out about what Kara could do, and he thought he could use her abilities to help him catch the Rosemont Butcher."

"Did it work?" Seth asked slowly.

"No. Maybe it would have, but what Bishop didn't know, what nobody knew, was that the killer was psychic too. When Kara tried to see through his eyes, he saw her instead. And he came after our family." She looked down at her arm, at the scar. "I was the only one in the house who survived."

Seth reached for her other hand, his face pale. "Jesus, Bonnie, I'm sorry."

Bonnie hadn't intended to add anything else, but heard her voice, thin and unsteady. "The worst thing . . . the worst thing was that Kara realized too late that he was in the house. There wasn't time for her to do anything except — except hide me. So she did. And I saw . . . everything he did to her."

"Bonnie . . ."

She looked up finally to meet his horrified eyes, and whispered, "She made me promise. When she hid me, she made me promise not to make a sound. No matter what. So I watched him kill her, and I didn't make a sound."

Seth looked at her scar and suddenly realized he was seeing what her own teeth had done to the flesh. In the desperate need to remain silent, she must have bitten down almost to the bone.

"Jesus Christ," Seth said, and pulled her into his arms.

Miranda didn't like storms as a rule. She supposed if she could curl up in front of a roaring fire and sip hot tea while watching snow fall, she'd feel different, but she had never had that luxury. From the time she and Bonnie had first moved to a part of the country that actually had four distinct seasons, she had been more concerned with the inconveniences and possible dangers of bad weather than its beauties.

It wasn't her job to get Gladstone prepared for a storm; there were other authorities to take care of that. But she had to get her people and the Sheriff's Department ready, and that took time. It was after seven-thirty when she went into the conference room to check on any progress in the investigation.

She knew before she opened the door that Bishop wasn't in the room — or in the building, for that matter — but asked as casually as she could when she found only Tony Harte there.

"He's at the hospital with Sharon," Tony replied. "Said he wanted to sit in on the autopsy. Didn't say why. I don't know, maybe he's got a hunch. Or maybe he's just looking for something to spark one."

Miranda sat on the table, unconsciously taking Bishop's accustomed place, as Tony worked on his laptop. "And you're trying to get something from the tire track?"

"Trying being the operative word. The good news is that we got a terrific clear cast of the treads."

"And the bad news?"

"It's one of the best-selling tires in the country. I've got someone back at Quantico trying to narrow down the possibles, but half the dealers aren't on computer yet. It's going to take days just to get a reliable list of retailers within a hundred miles who sold the damn things — never mind finding out from those dealers who their customers were and getting a list of them."

"Did we get anything else from the scene at the millhouse? Anything at all?"

"Not much. The bastard might not have been ready for us to find his victim, but he runs a pretty clean murder. We have the rope around Penman's ankles, which is your basic garden-variety hardware-store rope, and there was nothing fancy about the knot. We have a few — a very few — forensic odds and ends that might eventually help us build a case in court, but nothing helpful at this point. A few carpet fibers that could be from his car or his house; a couple of strands of hair we found caught in the door frame that may or may not match the victim's; a sliver of a footprint — without a distinctive tread." He shrugged. "What we can't interpret here we've sent back to Quantico for analysis. For what it's worth."

Miranda was silent for several minutes,

staring at the bulletin board already displaying the grisly crime-scene photographs from that afternoon. "Two things bother me," she said.

"Only two?" Tony's voice was wry.

"Well, two at the moment." She turned back to the agent. "What the hell is he doing with the blood — and what happens if we've really pissed him off by finding Steve Penman before he wanted us to?"

"For the first, I haven't a clue. I'd think the second was potentially more dangerous. Like I said out at the scene, I really don't want to see this guy pissed off."

"I don't either. But I'm afraid we will."

Tony pursed his lips. "Think he might find out how you got the tip?"

"If he listens to gossip, he'll certainly have a possibility."

"But is it something he'll believe?"

Slowly, Miranda said, "If Bishop's profile is accurate, it might be the only possibility the killer *can* believe. He thinks he's all-powerful and in control, that he seldom if ever makes a mistake. The fact that we found his latest victim before he was ready for us to will shake him. He might eagerly accept the idea that we had to use some . . . paranormal means to do it."

"It tracks," Tony admitted. "But if he believes Bonnie sent us out there . . ."

"Then she's a danger to him." Miranda's voice was grim. "Which is why she won't be alone at any time until this is over and done with."

"I know you're accustomed to taking precautions, but this has to be worrying you."

"You could say that." Miranda wondered almost idly what it would feel like *not* to be worried. After so many years, it was familiar, a normal state of mind.

"We'll get him, Miranda."

"Yes, I know we will." But would it be in time?

"You're doing everything you can," Tony reminded her.

"Am I?"

"The police work's all on target. Step by step and by the numbers. As for other things . . . we're using all the tools we've got. And so are you, right? Any insights?"

"Insights?"

"Vibes, let's say."

"I don't pick up vibes, remember?" she reminded him.

"Yeah, but you're precognitive. And even if you have burned out on that ability, chances are good there're still some residual flashes there."

Miranda hesitated, then shrugged. "None to speak of."

Tony was watching her steadily. "Because you're shut off?"

"Maybe."

"If so, this might be the time to turn it back on," he suggested lightly. "We can use any help we can get."

"I'll keep that in mind," she said, equally light.

Obviously realizing that pursuing that subject would gain him nothing, Tony tried another tack. "It's probably none of my business," he began.

Miranda half laughed. "Whenever somebody says that, you just *know* it isn't."

He grinned. "Touché. But I'm incurably nosy, so I've gotta ask."

"About?"

"Bishop."

Miranda told herself it was poetic justice for her to discuss him with his subordinates since they had obviously discussed her, but she was honest enough to admit to herself that wasn't why she readily answered. "What about him?"

"Well, he's becoming something of a legend — quietly — within the Bureau because of his success record, especially in the last few years. And he's far and away the most powerful and accurate telepath in the unit. So what most of us can't understand is how he could have . . . screwed up so badly eight years ago."

Miranda got off the conference table and went to pour herself a cup of coffee.

"I said it was probably none of my business," Tony murmured.

She was surprised to hear herself say, "So that's the general assumption, that he screwed up?"

"We all know the operation went south in a very bad way. That people — that most of your family died. And some of us know that Bishop blames himself for that. To be honest, it really doesn't sound like him to screw up that way. I mean, sure, he makes mistakes — but not like that. He's fanatical about making sure that anybody at risk is fully protected."

Miranda went back to the table and sat down again. "Mistakes are easier to make when you believe you have all the answers. When you've seen a vision of the future you absolutely believe will come true."

Tony thought about that. "He saw a positive outcome, and that's why he took the chances he did? But how? He's a touch telepath, not precognitive —"

"He was then," she said. "Just for a while . . . he was."

"He was temporarily precognitive?"

"Yes."

Tony blinked. "I don't understand. He's been tested, he isn't precognitive, not in the slightest degree. Abilities like that are born in us, not created. I mean, a head injury might trigger a latent ability — A head injury. That scar of his?"

Miranda shook her head. "No, the scar came later."

"Then there was no head injury? No unusual trauma to trigger a new ability temporarily?"

"Trauma." Miranda laughed under her breath. "I guess you could say that was it. An unusual trauma."

"What?"

"Me." Miranda lifted her cup in a mocking little salute. "I triggered it."

"How?" Tony asked.

Miranda wavered briefly, but finally laughed again, and took her coffee with her when she headed for the door. "I'm afraid that really is none of your business," she said. "Sorry, Tony."

"That," Tony said indignantly, "is really cruel."

"Life is unfair," she agreed. "Are you planning to be here awhile?"

He sighed. "Yeah, at least until the snow

gets good and started. Nothing to do at the Lodge but watch TV, so I'd just as soon work while I might be able to get something done. Both our rentals are SUVs and we know how to drive in bad weather, so we should be able to get around okay unless it turns into a real blizzard."

"Then I'll probably see you later."

She went to her office, absently leaving her door open, and sat down behind the big desk.

What on earth had possessed her? To talk about it at all, even to *think* about it, wasn't something she had allowed herself for so long. It was stupid, just plain stupid, to let herself get dragged back into the past.

Miranda sat there staring at the coffee cup on the center of her blotter, remembering so much more than she wanted to. She remembered his face transformed, hunger and tenderness naked in his eyes, in the bittersweet curve of his lips. She remembered how he had touched her hair, how he had held her against him all night, even in sleep.

Most of all, she remembered the unexpected force of his passion, the intense need that had half-frightened her. It had never been casual for him, not even in the beginning.

She hadn't even imagined what would

happen. Half-consciously pressing her cool palms to her burning cheeks, Miranda closed her eyes. Even Bishop, she thought, hadn't realized what passion would ignite between them.

Please, God, he hadn't known or even suspected, hadn't been *that* cold-blooded. . . .

"Randy?"

She jerked in surprise, hands falling, eyes opening to see Alex standing in the doorway.

"Sorry," he said. "But the door was open. I can come back later."

Miranda got hold of herself. Or tried to. The hand she used to pick up her cup was, she saw, shaking. "No, now is fine," she said, lying grimly. "What's up?"

Alex came in, closed the door, and sat in a visitor's chair. "Couple of things. The snow still hasn't started, but we're ready for it. The off-duty deputies went home to get a few hours' sleep in case they're needed later, but all are on call from here on out. We've set up a few cots in that empty office, and we have supplies enough to get us through a couple of days, just in case."

"Good."

"Tomorrow being Sunday, there won't be the usual traffic to worry about, especially since the churches will all cancel services if the weather's bad. We've raised the age for curfew to twenty-one, and asked that none of the kids go anywhere alone even before dusk. Safety in numbers, or at least we can hope there is."

Miranda nodded. "Then we've done all we can for the time being."

"Yeah."

She waited.

"I don't quite know how to put this, Randy, so I'll just say it straight out. The rumors are getting pretty wild, but I saw your face when I told you what Amy Fowler was claiming. I know you didn't get a phone call before you and Bishop went out to the old millhouse, and I know the only visitors you had were Bonnie and Seth Daniels." He paused. "I can guess the so-called anonymous tip came from them, and I have to assume there was at least some truth in what Amy claimed — as wild as it sounds. But I need to understand. About . . . uncanny hunches. About FBI agents who seem to know things they shouldn't. I need to know what's going on, Randy. And I'm asking you to tell me the truth about it."

"It won't make your life any easier," she warned bluntly.

"So what else is new?" He smiled faintly.

"Okay, then." Miranda drew a deep

breath and told him the truth.

Almost all of it.

Liz had decided to keep the store open past regular hours — until eleven or until it began to snow, whichever came first. Business was fairly brisk, both in books and in coffee, not to mention gossip, and she was hardly eager to go home and spend too many hours petting her cat and wishing for things she just couldn't have.

But she was also unwilling to provide a forum where some of the more hotheaded people in town could plan to do something stupid. So when Justin Marsh came in — ostensibly for a cup of coffee, but really to sound out his fellow citizens on the depth of their fear and fury — she did her best to head him off, before he could do any serious damage.

"Where's Selena, Justin?"

"Home," he replied.

"Here, have some coffee."

"Thank you, Elizabeth, but —"

"I hear it's getting really cold out there, so I'm sure you could stand something warm inside, right?" From the corner of her eye, she was amused to see a couple of her regular customers sidle out the door, clearly intent on avoiding one of Justin's tirades.

Justin caught her wrist even though she had made no move to walk away. "Listen to me, Elizabeth. Something must be done — there's an evil in our midst!"

"I don't think you'd get an argument about that, Justin. But it's not really our job to hunt down that evil, not with the sheriff and these FBI agents working so hard at it."

His fingers tightened around her wrist, and his pale eyes took on a more-than-usually fanatical gleam. "They are lost souls wandering aimlessly," he said, lowering his voice as though to bestow a confidence. "They can't recognize the evil they seek. But I can. I know the face of the evil."

Liz was tempted to ask him to draw the face for her, but overcame the impulse. "We all have our theories, I'm sure. But accusing anybody without cause is just going to get trouble started, you know that. Listen, we all know there's a storm on the way, and right now everybody is pretty worried about that. So why don't you drink your coffee and then go home to Selena, okay, Justin?"

He released her but shook his head, scowling. "Like lambs to the slaughter. They don't know. They don't know. . . ."

Liz went back to the counter, hoping he was in one of his brooding periods and no longer inclined to share his ideas and his wisdom with those around him — for the moment, at least.

John MacBride pushed his cup across the counter for a refill, murmuring, "Do you think if I sit very still, he might not see me?"

She smiled ruefully at the mayor. "It's worth a shot."

He sighed. "I should go, though. We're all set for the storm, but the voters don't seem to like to see their mayor just sitting around drinking coffee in the middle of a crisis."

"Half the town council is in here too," she pointed out. "Some looking for books, but a few just drinking coffee like you. And deputies have been in and out the last couple of hours."

"Have you seen the sheriff?"

"Not today. Between the storm and finding another body, I imagine she's pretty busy."

MacBride frowned down at his cup. "Yeah. I've gone by there a few times these last days, but she's always busy. And those FBI agents always seem to be around."

Liz knew the mayor had wholeheartedly welcomed the arrival of the FBI, and she knew why. But it didn't take The Sight to tell her he was a bit disgruntled by the continued presence of at least one of those agents, and by Randy's preoccupation with the investigation.

She felt a certain amount of sympathy, having herself waited with what patience she could muster for the man she loved to realize he hadn't been buried along with his dead wife. But all she said was, "I guess the harder they work now, the more likely they are to catch this killer quickly. We all want that."

"Of course we all want that." He must have realized how petulant he sounded, because he flushed and added quickly and with more positive emphasis, "Of course we do. It's Randy's job to make the streets safe for our citizens, and she's very good at her job. Devoted to her job. Of course."

"Mayor MacBride, I'd like to speak to you," Justin said forcefully from just behind his left shoulder.

MacBride's comical grimace of dismay almost upset Liz's composure, but she stopped herself from laughing. She left him to cope with Justin, which, to his credit, he usually did very well, and went on serving her customers.

At nine o'clock, the first flakes of snow began to drift lazily downward.

Bishop eyed Miranda's closed office door

as he passed, but the murmur of voices inside told him she wasn't alone, so he continued on to the conference room. He found Tony there sitting at one of the desks scowling at the screen of his laptop.

"There are," Tony said by way of greeting, "a hell of a lot of places selling tires in these parts."

"Any leads?"

"Not so you'd notice. Still trying to narrow the list to something remotely manageable. Anything new from the autopsy?"

"Sharon was right about the boy being injected with an anticoagulant — unfortunately, a fairly common one. It requires a doctor's prescription, of course, but we both know how easy it is to fake that sort of thing."

"Way too easy. There are places that never double-check the letterhead on a faxed request and never follow up on phone calls, so any prescription that looked legit was probably filled without a second thought." Tony shrugged. "I already checked with the Internet Crimes unit back at the office, and according to them it'll be virtually impossible to track the sale if he went that route. Backtrack if and when we find out who he is, possibly, but we won't find him working the other end. We can check local doctors and pharmacies, of course. Maybe we'll get lucky. Anything else?"

"Pictures on the way," Bishop said. "Everything in vivid color."

Tony grimaced, sensing the emotion rather than hearing anything in Bishop's calm voice. "Not a lot of fun, huh? I hate autopsies. Did you expect to learn anything by being at this one?"

"You mean spot something Sharon missed? Not hardly." Bishop poured a cup of coffee. "I don't know what I hoped to gain. If anything."

"Maybe you wanted to look at pure science for a while and avoid anything less . . . tangible."

"If I did, it didn't get me anywhere."

"Nothing at all unexpected about the body?"

"Nothing we didn't already know."

Tony fell silent for a moment. "I'm curious about something. Being a touch telepath, what happens when you touch a dead body?"

"Usually, nothing." Bishop sat down at his own laptop. "A couple of times, I've gotten a flash of images."

"A bright light?" Tony asked hopefully. "Anything that might possibly resemble the face of God?"

"That would be too easy, wouldn't it? The ultimate answer." Bishop smiled faintly. "Sorry, Tony."

"Yeah, well, it was a chance. Just something I wondered about now and then. You'd think with these so-called paranormal abilities of ours, we'd get a leg up on the rest of humankind once in a while. But no. We stumble around in the dark just like everybody else."

"No kidding."

Tony sat back in his chair and rubbed his face briefly with both hands. "Is Sharon done with the autopsy?"

"Except for a few lab tests."

"She's still at the hospital?"

"I left her there with Dr. Shepherd. She said she'd head back to the Lodge before the snow started, but I think he was leading up to a late dinner invitation, so maybe not."

"They're hitting it off, huh?"

"Looks like."

Tony grinned. "I guess she doesn't come across too many guys who could work up much of an appetite across an autopsy table."

"How many do you know?" Bishop challenged.

"None, to be honest. It's always struck me as gruesome work."

"And tracking down serial murderers and rapists isn't?"

"Well, I seldom have to touch them," Tony answered.

Bishop smiled, but said, "I'm not all that anxious to touch this one, but we definitely have to find him. And since we don't know what kinds of delays the weather might cause, I say we work while we can. Are you game?"

"Always," Tony said.

THIRTEEN

"So, can you *read* me?" Alex asked.

Miranda shook her head. "No. I can read less than half the people I meet, generally speaking. Think of it like radio waves from the brain, information transmitted by electromagnetic energy. I have a receiver, but I can only pick up the AM stations, not the FM."

"No way to switch, huh?"

"If there is, I haven't found it." Miranda shrugged. "For me, it's a normal thing, Alex. One theory is that people with psychic abilities are throwbacks to a more primitive age when the senses needed to be extremely sharp for survival."

"Liz said something like that."

"And it may be true. On the other hand, there's also a theory that humans are evolving toward psychic ability, and that those of us who already have it are just . . .

281

anticipating the rest of you. There are lots of theories. A normally dormant gene activated for some reason. An accident or illness in childhood that causes the electromagnetic field of the brain to be altered in some way. I've even heard it said that if we were all tested genetically, we'd find we share a common ancestor. Who really knows?"

"And who cares?"

"Well, I don't, to be honest. I was never interested in verifying it scientifically. I mean, what's the point? Present science knows pathetically little about the brain even when it functions according to accepted norms. Step outside those norms, and scientific understanding begins to break down in a hurry."

Alex looked at her curiously. "I gather growing up psychic wasn't much fun."

"Not much, no." Miranda resisted an urge to rub her temples. Confession might be good for the soul, but it hadn't helped her aching head. "Think about it. By the time you're seven years old, you've pretty much figured out that grownups get really nervous when you tell them about the pictures in your head. Especially when you've told them about something that hasn't happened yet — but does happen. So you stop telling them. Most of them anyway. My parents were understanding, otherwise it would have been unbearable."

"Your parents weren't . . ."

"Psychic? No, but both were highly intuitive, and both came from families filled with tales of paranormal things. They didn't automatically believe something wasn't real just because they didn't understand how it worked."

Alex had a sudden realization. "Bonnie — and that Ouija board. Jesus, you mean she really did get the information from a spirit?"

"When Bonnie was four," Miranda said, "she had an imaginary friend — or so we thought. A little girl named Sarah. She used to tell us all about Sarah, entertain us at the dinner table with stories about Sarah and her parents and her older brother and her dog. Then one day Bonnie casually told us that Sarah had been killed when her house fell on her. We were all startled, and Dad was curious. So he did a bit of research."

"And found Sarah?"

"Turns out our house had been built on a site where a previous house had been destroyed by an earthquake. And in that house lived a couple with a son — and a daughter named Sarah. She was the only one in the house to die in that quake."

"So how long did she hang around?"

"Bonnie never mentioned her again. Knowing what I know now about sudden deaths, I believe little Sarah just wanted to come to terms with what had happened to her. And Bonnie was the only one listening. Once the story was told, Sarah could pass on to wherever she was meant to go."

Alex shied away from questioning her on that last point, but did say, "What do you know about sudden deaths?"

"Most people who die suddenly aren't prepared to leave — especially if the death was violent. Some of them are mad as hell to find their lives cut short, and all of them want more time. Somehow, they're often able to get more time, at least in a sense."

"By haunting the living?"

"Only those who know how to look and listen."

"People like Bonnie."

Miranda nodded.

Alex thought about that. "Were there other ghosts?"

"Oh, sure, for several years. Then Kara and I were able to teach her how to shield her mind a bit, so that she only saw them when she was looking for them."

"And that was better?" Alex asked wryly.

"It's always better to be in control of this if

you can. Especially for Bonnie and others like her. Like I said, Alex — people who die suddenly can be angry. And negative emotions can be very destructive."

Hardly believing he was saying it, Alex said, "I guess that's why we won't be asking Bonnie to try and contact any of these dead teenagers."

Matter-of-fact, Miranda said, "With teenage victims of violent death, you not only get the anger of a life cut short but the caldron of emotions we all have at that age. When Bonnie's older, she may be able to handle it, but right now, with her own emotions so chaotic and her empathy so strong, she'd be in very real danger."

"What kind of danger? A ghost can't hurt you. Can it?"

Miranda hesitated, unsure how much he could accept. "They want to *live*, Alex. They want the life they were cheated out of. So if they see an open door . . . or an open mind . . . some of them come in never intending to leave."

Tony was pinning Steve Penman's autopsy photographs to the bulletin board, half-listening as Bishop talked on his cell phone to the agent leading a second team from the special unit, a team currently working on an investigation in Texas.

"You know you can't hypnotize her, Quentin," Bishop was saying. "You'll have to get at her memories another way. There's a form of conscious regression you can try, if you can find someone qualified to do it. It isn't always successful, but it might work in this case. Have Kendra check the data files. Yeah. No, we're not close to a resolution here as far as I can see." He frowned slightly. "Yes, the local authorities are being cooperative. Why?"

Tony glanced back over his shoulder, met Bishop's gaze, and was afraid he looked guilty.

Still speaking into the cell phone, Bishop said, "I'd appreciate it if you kept me advised on your progress, Quentin. Right. We'll be here. Talk to you in a day or two." He ended the connection and absently returned the phone to the pocket of his jacket. "Tony?"

"Yeah, boss?"

"Is there something you want to tell me?"

"Not really, no." Tony let the silence lengthen, then glanced over his shoulder again to find Bishop waiting with a patience he recognized only too well. "It's like you said, boss. Sometimes it's the pits working with people who can read your mind. Everybody was in the office when the request came in from Miranda."

"I wasn't even sure it was her," Bishop objected.

"Oh yes you were. I don't know how, since she'd changed her name, but you knew. How did you know, by the way?"

"I was . . . warned a couple of months ago. That I'd come back to Tennessee, and — Christ, Tony, everybody knows?"

"Well, you weren't being real subtle, if you want the truth." Tony went to the conference table and sat down. "I think you even asked how fast they could warm up the jet."

Bishop winced. "I don't remember that."

"I'm not surprised. Anyway, I wasn't sure what was going on since all I was picking up were emotions." He doodled on a legal pad and studiously avoided eye contact with Bishop. "But some of the others apparently got it loud and clear. And it's not like the story is a secret, you know, at least at the Bureau. So it's a sure bet the others are wild with curiosity by now. Wondering how you and Miranda are getting along. I guess Quentin couldn't resist asking — as casually as he could."

There was a long silence, and then Bishop said very carefully, "So I have . . . no secrets at all from the team, that's what you're telling me?"

"Really a bitch working with psychics," Tony murmured. "I told you before, boss. Being such a strong receiver apparently makes you an equally strong transmitter. If you and Miranda ever come to an understanding, you ought to ask her to teach you how to develop one of those shields. Hers works just dandy."

"I need a drink," Bishop said.

Tony tried hard not to smile. "If it makes you feel any better, we're all pretty exposed to each other. I mean, jeez, one of us gets a hangnail, somebody else is bound to know about it."

"It doesn't make me feel better. And if you tell me you knew that, I swear to God, Tony, I'll shoot you."

"It never crossed my mind. Or my radar, as the case may be."

"Just shut up," Bishop said.

Alex stared at Miranda. "Wait a minute. Are you telling me that a ghost can — can possess a living person?"

"If its spirit is stronger than the living person's, its will to live greater, it can overwhelm, control. I guess you could say possess."

"Is this just an assumption, or —"

"Oh, it's happened. The problem is that

medical science can't recognize it for what it is. So if a medium cracks up, well . . . they were crazy to begin with, weren't they? Psychotic maybe or schizophrenic. Or just plain nuts."

"But how can you be so sure that isn't the truth?"

"Because I'm a touch telepath." She drew a breath. "When I was about twenty-one, I was dating a psych student. He knew I was psychic and considered it just another sense, a tool I could use. And *he* could use. He was working in a psychiatric hospital, and he'd become fascinated by three of the patients there. Two of them were long-term, one was recent, but all had been diagnosed as dangerously schizophrenic — so dangerously that medication couldn't touch it. And all had a history of reporting clairvoyant and mediumistic experiences. It was the only other thing they had in common. He had a theory that the experiences were tied in with the schizophrenia, even dreamed that he might have discovered the cause of the condition."

"So what happened?" Alex asked.

"Well, there was no scientifically valid way to test his theory, but he really wanted to know if he was right. And I admit, I was curious myself. So he got me in there one night, secretly. I was just supposed to touch the patients — who were under restraints — and tell him what I got from them."

"What did you get?"

Miranda rubbed the nape of her neck. "I don't ever want to go through that again. It was one of the most terrifying experiences of my life. I touched these poor people — two women and a man — and I actually felt the other beings inside them."

"Maybe it was split personalities or —"

"No. I can't explain it in any way you'd really understand, but I knew, I know now, without a shadow of a doubt, that each of those people carried within them a distinct and separate other soul." She shook her head. "The sheer energy of two spirits fighting to occupy the same body was . . . incredible. No wonder their poor brains were literally misfiring."

Alex was wide-eyed. "You realize how farfetched all this sounds, don't you?"

"Of course I do. It's one of the reasons I've been keeping it to myself all these years."

"But since I asked?"

She smiled. "Yeah. Since you asked."

He brooded for a moment, trying to decide how much of this he really believed. "What about the agents? If all of you are psychic, can you read each other?"

She chose the simplest answer. "I don't know. I've sort of had my shields up since they got here."

"Because of Bishop?"

"More or less."

"Now that I know what happened eight years ago, I can't say that I blame you," Alex said.

Miranda hesitated, then heard herself say, "I don't want you to have the wrong impression about that, Alex. However . . . personally betrayed I might have felt, the truth is that Bishop was doing everything in his power to stop one of the most vicious killers in recent history."

"And that included sacrificing your family?"

"He thought he could protect them. He was wrong. No one could have protected them."

"Are you saying you forgive him?"

Again, Miranda chose her words with care, not quite sure if it was for Bishop's sake — or her own. "I'm saying that I can understand a little better now what he was up against, and why he made the choices he made. I don't agree with those choices, obviously. But hindsight, as they say, is twenty-twenty. If I had been in his position back then . . . maybe I would have made the same choices."

"And betrayed a lover?" Alex shook his head. "I don't think so."

Miranda didn't know what to say to that, so it was fortunate that her phone buzzed just then. She answered it, listened for a minute, then said thank you and hung up.

"Snow's started?" Alex guessed.

"Yeah. Listen, before it gets much worse I'm going to go home for a little while. I want to make sure Mrs. Task got out okay, then maybe take a shower and change before I come back."

"You don't have to come back tonight; your Jeep can make it easily even if the roads are lousy tomorrow."

"I know, but I'd rather be here. Besides, Bonnie is staying at the clinic with Seth and his parents, so there's no good reason for me to stay home."

"A little rest?" Alex suggested.

"I'm fine. Don't fuss, Alex."

He didn't push it. He walked with her as far as the bullpen, then went to his desk while she gave the deputy on duty at the reception desk a few instructions.

Alex had plenty to do. He'd had the librarian make copies of dozens of pages of classified ads, per his conversation with

Tony Harte; now he needed to read every ad in search of those a teenage runaway might have responded to.

"Hold down the fort, Alex," Miranda called as she headed out.

"I will. And you be careful."

"Yeah, yeah." She sent him a casual salute and left the building.

It was normally a ten-minute drive home, but that night it took Miranda almost twenty, more because she was observing her surroundings than because of the scant dusting of snow on the roads. She was glad to see that very few people were out; Liz's coffeeshop was still serving, from the looks of it, but there were only three cars parked out front and Miranda doubted anyone would linger much longer.

Other downtown merchants had closed shop, with the exception of the video store and a twenty-four-hour service station, both fairly busy as customers stocked up on gas and tapes.

Four Sheriff's Department cruisers were out patrolling, and she listened to her deputies' radio chatter without interrupting. Judging from their tones as much as the words, they were keyed-up but not dangerously so.

It reminded her of just how long and

eventful the day had been, and as she pulled into her driveway, she felt a wave of sheer exhaustion sweep over her. She was running on reserves and didn't know how long those reserves would last.

Long enough. It had to be long enough.

She didn't think it would be much longer. There had to be one more victim, she knew that. Five in all killed on her watch, and the last one unexpected in some way.

That death would mark the beginning of the end.

She unlocked the front door and went into the house. A cheerful message on the answering machine in the front hall told Miranda that Mrs. Task had made it home safely and that there was a big bowl of pasta salad and chicken in the fridge, and freshly baked bread in the bin.

It sounded great, Miranda decided as she walked into the living room and shrugged out of her jacket. As far as she remembered, lunch had been her last meal today. She removed her shoulder harness and hung it over the back of a chair. There were a couple of lamps burning, but it wasn't until she turned on another one that she saw the Ouija board on the coffee table.

Hadn't Bonnie said that they had been up in her room when they had used the damned thing? She was almost sure that was right, and could only suppose that Mrs. Task had brought it down here for some reason. It didn't sound like the housekeeper, who probably wouldn't have a clue how one was supposed to play such a "game," but Miranda couldn't think of another reason for the board to be down here.

Actually, she admitted silently, she was having trouble thinking at all. She bent down to absently move the planchette off the NO and to the center of the board, then went upstairs to see if a shower would clear her head.

Behind her, the planchette moved slowly back across the board and centered itself over the NO once again.

"Boss?"

"Yeah?"

"Do you realize you're pacing?"

Bishop stopped in mid-pace and frowned at his subordinate. "In case I haven't told you, you're a very irritating companion, Tony."

"Hey, I'm not the one wearing a path in the floor," Tony objected. He watched Bishop sit down decisively at his laptop, and added, "Something bothering you?"

"I hate storms."

"It isn't storming yet. I checked when I went to refill the coffeepot, and it's just snowing gently out there. Ground isn't even covered yet. Hell, the phones aren't even ringing with the sounds of worried citizens pestering their constabulary. Just nice and quiet, with deputies working industriously at their desks or playing poker in the lounge."

Bishop waited, but when it became obvious Tony was finished, he gave in and asked, "Where's Miranda?"

"Alex said she went home about half an hour ago. Supposed to be coming back, though. I gather she intends to spend the night here."

Forgetting that he wasn't going to pace anymore, Bishop got up and moved to the window. It looked out onto the lighted parking lot, which showed him a couple of cruisers and numerous other cars all dusted with snow. The snowflakes were getting larger and no longer falling straight down as the wind began to kick up.

"The storm is definitely coming," he said.

"And that's bothering you?"

"I told you. I hate storms." He was silent for a moment. "I don't know why the hell she doesn't just stay home."

"Feels her place is here, I guess."

"You said yourself nothing was happening."

"Yet."

"Even so."

Another silence fell, this one not interrupted until Bishop returned to the desk and picked up the phone.

"I guess you know her number," Tony said.

"Yes, Tony, I know her number."

Undeterred by the sharp tone, Tony watched him with interest. What he sensed in his boss wasn't dislike of the coming storm or mere restlessness but something a whole lot stronger and much less easy to define. And apparently contagious, Tony noted as he stopped his own fingers from drumming on the table.

Jeez, talk about tension.

Bishop hung up the phone. "The machine picked up."

"Maybe she's in the shower."

"Maybe." Bishop returned to the window.

"But you don't think so," Tony ventured.

For a minute it seemed he wouldn't answer, but finally Bishop said, "Something *feels* wrong."

"Feels wrong how?"

"I don't know."

"Feels wrong with Miranda?"

Bishop hesitated again, then nodded. "I used to — There was a time when I could feel what was going on with her. If she was happy or upset, I knew it."

"That's what you're feeling now?"

"No, this is different. It's like I saw or heard something I wasn't consciously aware of, something that's nagging at me now. Something I know that's just out of my reach."

"Something about Miranda?"

Bishop looked at the phone, his restlessness as clear as his reluctance to make a fool of himself. "I'll wait ten minutes and call again. In case she's in the shower."

Tony caught himself drumming his fingers again, and stopped. "Yeah," he said. "That sounds like a good idea."

The hot water made Miranda feel better, and by the time she'd dried her hair and dressed in jeans and a bulky sweater, even her appetite had returned. She looped an elastic band around her wrist to use later in tying back her hair.

In the living room she turned the television on for background noise and weather reports. It was only then that she noticed the Ouija board lying on the floor.

She grabbed her gun instantly, wondering why the game was the only thing disturbed in the room. An intruder would have taken her gun, surely; it had been clearly visible. Why knock a game board to the floor?

With her shields up and defenses cut off, Miranda could sense nothing unusual in the house. Which meant she would have to move carefully, room by room, turning on the lights, checking windows and all the outer doors, looking into closets and corners.

There was a quicker and easier way, she told herself. It wouldn't matter if she dropped her shields for just a moment or two. Just long enough to get a sense of the house, to make sure she was alone.

Miranda didn't fully realize the great strain of keeping those shields up constantly for so long until she allowed them to fall. For just an instant, the ache in her head intensified — and then vanished like a soap bubble. Her ears actually popped as though she were coming down from a high altitude, and her vision blurred before becoming so sharp that she blinked in surprise.

The moment of well-being was wonderful.

What came next was agony.

She dropped the gun, both hands going to her head, the red-hot jolt of pain making her sway. Even stunned, she instinctively recognized an attack, knew that something, some

299

energy, was trying to force its way into her mind. Just as instinctively she defended herself.

Her shields slammed back up, reinforced by sheer desperation, and in the same instant she made a violent mental effort to deflect that probing blade of energy. She almost saw it, white and shimmering and so rapacious it would cut its way into her. She almost saw it.

And then everything went black as pitch and as silent as the grave.

She never heard the phone begin to ring.

The last of Liz's customers left around nine-thirty, which gave her plenty of time to finish cleaning up before the snow got too bad. She left the front door unlocked, in case anybody needed to come in to use the phone, and kept the television above the counter tuned to local weather reports.

They weren't very encouraging, unless you liked a lot of snow.

Liz wasn't thinking about anything in particular, just letting her mind drift, when she suddenly understood what the white shirt meant.

Of course. Of course, it made *perfect* sense.

Her first impulse was to call Alex, but a

moment's thought made her decide on a trip to the Sheriff's Department. So she worked hurriedly, locked the front door and turned out the lights, then let herself out the rear door and locked it.

She always parked in back, in an alley just a few steps from the door, even though Alex had told her to park in front whenever she worked nights. Liz never worried about it. Just a few steps, after all, and she'd never been afraid no matter how late it was.

It was cold, much colder than it had been just a few hours ago. And the snow was beginning to thicken and blow about as the wind whined restlessly.

Liz started her car, then got out to brush the snow off the windshield while it warmed up. Her wipers weren't the best, and the defroster wasn't very enthusiastic, so she thought a little manual help was in order.

"You're going home late."

She turned with a gasp, then managed a shaky laugh. "And I have to go by the Sheriff's Department first. But what're you doing out —" Then she saw the gleaming knife.

"I'm sorry, Liz. I'm so sorry."

She barely had time to realize that she'd been wrong about the shirt after all when she felt the cold steel of the knife slip into her body with horrifying ease.

FOURTEEN

At first, Miranda ignored the voice. It was distant and hardly discernible, and besides, she was too tired to care what it was trying to tell her. She didn't know where she was, but it was quiet and peaceful. She had no reason to worry anymore and just wanted to be left alone there.

Miranda.

At the extreme edge of her awareness, she understood that something was touching her. She didn't feel it yet somehow knew the touch existed. And without thinking about it, she realized that without the contact she wouldn't be able to hear . . . him . . . at all. Not that she was hearing him, not really. She understood what he was saying, but not because her ears told her.

That was strange. She considered it idly, still not caring but mildly interested in the puzzle of the thing. All her senses, she realized eventually, had shut down. Shut down completely, turned themselves off. And because of that, her body was turning itself off as well. She had the vague impression of a heartbeat slowing down, of lungs no longer drawing in air, and other organs ceasing to function.

Miranda, listen to me. Hear me.

She didn't want to listen to him. He would hurt her again. She knew he would. He would hurt her and she never wanted to be hurt like that again.

You have to let me in, Miranda.

Oh, no. She couldn't let him in. It was dangerous to let him in. Because he'd hurt her again and because . . . because it wasn't time. Why wasn't it time? Because . . . something else had to happen first. That was it. Somebody else had to die. There had to be five, that was it, that was why she had to wait.

There had to be five.

Please, Miranda. Please let me in. Something's wrong, you have to let me in.

No. She couldn't. She turned away from him and drifted back toward the peaceful darkness. But there was a tugging deep inside her that she hadn't expected, and it was painful. She wanted so badly to let him in, to feel what she had never felt with anyone but him. But that frightened her too, her own need, the hunger that shattered control.

She shied away from it, tried to escape the demands of emotions she didn't want to feel. Tried to break the gossamer thread that seemed to connect her to something . . . outside . . . something . . . someone . . .

Miranda . . . you're dying. Can't you feel it?

She didn't want to listen to that, because of course she wasn't dying. She couldn't die, not yet. There was something she had to do, something . . . important.

Except nothing seemed to matter very much to her. Not now. The darkness was warm and peaceful, and she knew that outside held only anguish and worry and grief. And him. Him, making her life painful and prickly with complications she didn't need. Him making demands. She was so tired.

Let me in . . . God damn you, let me in . . .

She almost got away, got free, that faint connection so wispy and frayed it couldn't possibly hold her any longer. But then defenses she was barely aware of gave way, and something grabbed her, captured her. Other gossamer threads swirled around her, and where each one touched her she felt a jolt that was pain and pleasure and certainty that seemed to her inevitable. Struggle though she did, she was drawn slowly but inexorably out of the peaceful darkness.

She felt the cold first, a cold that was bone deep, and she knew it had been the beginning of death. Then the slow, heavy beat of her heart, uneven at first, gradually steadying, becoming stronger. Her lungs drew in air in a sudden gasp.

And she was back.

Miranda thought her head was going to explode, and every nerve in her body throbbed. She was cold and she ached, but she could hear again, hear the wind outside whining around the eaves and sleet rattling against the windowpanes. A familiar softness beneath her told her she was in her bed, though she had no memory of being brought upstairs. She knew if she opened her eyes she would see her bedroom around her. And see him.

"Damn you," she heard herself murmur.

"Damn me all you want, as long as you let me in."

She felt his hands framing her face, felt his mouth moving on hers, and no matter how much she wanted to resist she knew she was responding to him. Her body was warming, the cold ache seeping away, and she could feel herself opening up to him, accepting him now willingly where before she had simply given way to his urgent insistence.

There was a hunger in her greater than

her will to defy it. A hunger for him. His hands soothed her aching head and his mouth took hers in long, deep, drugging kisses more addictive than any narcotic.

"This isn't fair," she whispered when she could.

"Christ, do you think I care?" Bishop's voice was hoarse.

Miranda forced her eyes to open. She thought she had seen him in every mood, thought she would have recognized any expression his face could wear, but this was a man she had never seen before.

"I didn't let you in." She had to say it.

"I know."

"You promised you wouldn't —"

He kissed her again and said roughly, "Do you really think there's anything I wouldn't do to keep you alive? Even if it gives you another reason to hate me."

Miranda knew he'd find out soon enough that she didn't hate him, but she wanted to argue about this dying business because it didn't make sense to her. But his mouth was moving on hers and his hands were slipping beneath the covers to touch her, and all her consciousness focused on the need he was only feeding. Nothing else mattered.

Their eight years apart seemed to melt away, the clock turning back to a summer during which two new lovers discovered the most extraordinary intimacy either had ever known.

Their bodies remembered first, driven by an urgent hunger that had to be satisfied. Covers were pushed aside, clothing discarded, and they couldn't stop touching and tasting, couldn't get close enough to each other. It was familiar and yet new, their bodies altered by time and experience, more mature now, more aware of their mortality and less careless of life and the pleasures and pains it offered.

They explored the familiar and the different with the utter deliberation of two people who knew too well that each moment was a gift and that they might never get this chance again. They took what life and fate offered them.

Outside, the storm was building, wailing now, and inside there was warmth and intensity, another kind of force that raged silently.

It happened now as it had that summer so long ago, and Miranda was surprised and shaken all over again by the enormity of it. With the passionate physical joining came a mental union so deep and absolute it was as if their two souls merged and became a single entity.

In a flashing instant, Miranda saw his life in the years they had been apart, saw the pleasures and hurts of it, the triumphs and tragedies, the cases that had ended well and those that hadn't. She saw the faces of his friends and co-workers and enemies, saw the places he'd been and the things he'd done, and felt what he had felt. She knew that at the same time he was also reliving her life, her experiences.

It was a wildly exhilarating roller coaster of emotions, and coupled with the potent physical sensations of lovemaking, it pushed them toward an incredible peak so far beyond the reach of most humans that there were no words with which to describe the journey.

Except sheer joy.

Deputy Greg Wilkie was concentrating almost entirely on the tricky job of keeping his cruiser on the road, and probably wouldn't even have glanced into the alley if he hadn't been trying to keep a wary eye out for flying debris. He'd already nearly lost a side mirror to a flying branch. His only thought, when he saw someone moving around the car, was that Liz was leaving a bit late and that it was a good thing she had a front-wheel-drive vehicle.

He didn't worry much, but he was a serious young man and a dedicated, industrious cop, and on his next pass through town he was careful to check the alley again. He even altered his route so he could pass by Liz's house a few minutes later. Her car was parked in the driveway, and lights were on in the house.

Satisfied, he drove on.

One of the local pizza parlors had generously sent the last of the day's hot pies to the Sheriff's Department before the storm closed them down. And since the deputies expected to be awake most if not all night, none of them hesitated to scarf down pepperoni and onions even at ten-thirty.

"Sometimes I love my job," Tony confided. Sitting back with his feet on the conference table, he shared a pizza with Alex and watched a small TV the deputy had brought in and plugged into the building's satellite system. "Who knew cheerleading competitions could be so . . . enthusiastic?"

"I think that's the point," Alex observed.

"Ah. I've gotta get out more often."

A faint stab of guilt made Alex say, "We should probably be watching the Weather Channel instead of this stuff."

"Why? We know it's storming. We know

that sooner or later the storm will pass. The patrols outside are reporting in regularly to alert us in case of real trouble. And — Wow. Will you look at how high they can throw each other?"

Alex checked his watch. "How long's Bishop been gone?"

"An hour, give or take. He said he'd call if there was a problem."

"Maybe the storm —"

"These cell phones of ours work in anything short of atomic destruction." He looked over to find Alex staring at him, and added, "Joke. But they're pretty dependable. It wasn't a government contract."

"You have a strange sense of humor for a government agent," Alex observed, momentarily distracted.

"I think of myself as a cop, not a government agent."

"A psychic cop?"

Tony grinned. "I wondered when you were going to bring it up. Miranda told you, huh?"

"When I finally got around to asking, yes. But she didn't go into specifics about you guys. I mean, other than Bishop."

"Ah. So you want to know if I'm sitting here reading your mind?"

"Something like that."

"Nope. Not my thing. I just . . . pick up emotions from the immediate area."

"Which explains your *hunch* about our conflicted killer?"

"More or less. I'm also very good at interpreting data in the usual way."

Alex grunted and for several minutes stared at the TV. Then suddenly he said, "Randy told me she couldn't read me, but . . ."

"You feel exposed?"

"Yeah."

Tony shrugged. "You shouldn't. If she says she can't read you, then she can't. I might be able to guess what you're feeling at any given moment, but most people give that away with facial expressions anyway. Sharon might know the keys she found on the floor belonged to you, but that's about it."

"And Bishop?"

"I thought Miranda told you about him."

"I don't have to be psychic to know she wasn't telling me everything."

"Interesting." Tony nodded. "Okay. Bishop's a touch telepath, and a strong one. Stronger than Miranda. But he came to it later in life than she did. Some adepts don't really get a grip on their abilities until their twenties or so, whether because of denial or

311

lack of practice, whatever. So even though he's stronger, she has more control. She was able to block all of us, even Bishop. A very rare ability, believe me." Tony paused, then smiled. "And if you're worried about it, Bishop can't read you either."

"Randy said she could read less than half the people she met, usually. I always thought this sort of stuff sounded like magic. But it has its limitations just like everything else, doesn't it?"

"Oh, yeah. Just another sense. For instance, you can't see things that are out of sight in the distance or hidden behind other things, and if your vision happens to be genetically bad, what you do see is out of focus. You can't hear sounds except those within a certain really limited range, and even then what you hear can be distorted. Your sense of touch is affected by temperature, whether you're male or female, and a dozen other things; and your sense of smell is not only severely limited compared to most other animal species, but is so subjective that your own brain can trick you into believing you do or don't smell something. Every single psychic ability has limitations in the same way."

"Not magic at all."

"Nope."

After brooding about that for some time, Alex checked his watch again. "I'm going to give it another half hour, then I'll call Randy's house."

"Suit yourself." Tony was silent for ten of those minutes, then said musingly, "You know, there's been a lot of research done on psychic abilities in recent years. In putting our unit together, all sorts of tests and measurements were developed. We have files full of graphs and charts. Pages and pages of reports from doctors and psychologists and scientists. And case after case where psychic ability made the difference between success and failure. But for every fact there's a myth or a legend or just something we flat-out don't understand. Like telepaths, for instance. I've heard it whispered for years that when two telepaths make love, it's something pretty amazing. That it's like the difference between walking and flying — you get where you want to go either way, but once you've flown nothing else can ever compare."

Alex stared at him. "Is there a reason why you suddenly brought that up?"

Tony reached for the last slice of pizza and tested it with a finger to see if it needed to be nuked in the microwave. "Oh, no. No reason at all."

★ ★ ★

Miranda wasn't really asleep when the phone rang, just drifting pleasantly in a cocoon of warmth and contentment as she listened to the storm. Since she was on her side facing the nightstand she was able to reach for the receiver without even opening her eyes.

"Hello?"

"Randy, it's Alex. Are you — Is everything okay? When Bishop didn't check in, we got a little worried."

She opened her eyes and looked at the clock on the nightstand, only mildly surprised to find it was nearly midnight. "Everything's fine, Alex." She felt Bishop's arm tighten around her, and had to smile to herself at words that didn't begin to describe truth. "We'll wait out the worst of the storm here, though, and not try to get back until sometime tomorrow morning."

"From the weather reports we're getting, this thing may go on the biggest part of tomorrow," Alex warned. "But, so far, no major power outages and no other problems to speak of."

"Let me know if anything changes."

"Yeah, I will."

"And if Bonnie calls tomorrow before I get in, tell her I'm at home, will you, please?"

"You bet."

Miranda hung up, and for a moment or two just lay there enjoying the peaceful interlude. The warmth of Bishop behind her, his hard body pressed against hers, was a potent reminder of what they had shared and the undeniable truth that they were stronger together than apart.

She wondered if, even now, she was able to accept that.

She was aware of the easy connection with Bishop, of the complex weave of gossamer threads that linked their two minds, but she also knew that what had happened when they had first become lovers more than eight years before had happened again. Their minds touched just as their bodies did, but there was no active mental communication now, no exchange of thoughts or emotions. A kind of psychic overload had temporarily numbed every one of their "extra" senses.

The first time had been the strongest, leaving them unable to use their psychic abilities for days afterward — and leaving them understandably apprehensive about the cost of being lovers. Not that it had stopped them. And they had eventually discovered that the effects were short-lived, always fading within hours.

It was, Bishop had said, their own unique afterglow.

Miranda wondered how long the effects would last this time. Would it be days or hours before they could use their abilities again? And when they could, would they discover, as they had before, that their joining had created something remarkable?

Bishop moved behind her, and she turned onto her back to look up at him as he raised himself on an elbow.

"Wow," he said.

"I think you said that the first time," she observed.

"I wouldn't be a bit surprised." He touched her face gently. "I guess I'd expected all the years we were apart to change everything."

"Some things," Miranda said, not without ironic humor, "seem to be immutable."

Bishop smiled. "In this particular case, I hope you don't expect me to be upset about that."

Honestly curious and a little surprised, she said, "Then it doesn't bother you to be so . . . exposed?"

"To you? No," he answered without hesitation.

"It did once."

"I was an idiot then. I think I've mentioned it."

"I think you have."

He hesitated, then said, "I don't know how much came through just now, how much you've had a chance to think about, but you have to realize I never meant to go behind your back, Miranda."

"I know that." She had felt his regrets, so intense even after all these years that it had been painful. "I know that Kara agreed to help you only after you promised you wouldn't tell me." She paused. "But you did go to her without telling me, and you did that because you knew I would have said no."

Bishop didn't deny it. "I told myself she was old enough to decide what she wanted to do, that you were just being the protective older sister, worrying too much, and that once she helped us catch the bastard you'd agree it had been for the best. But I knew it was wrong. Going to her without telling you first was a . . . betrayal of you, a betrayal of everything we were trying to build between us. But —"

"But," she finished dryly, "you thought you could justify it."

"Yeah, I did." He didn't try to do that now, didn't argue as he had then that to catch a vicious killer virtually any means could be justified. He simply said, "I was wrong. Nothing could have excused hurting you like that, destroying your trust in me. Even if . . . even if it had turned out differently, it would have been over between us. It took me a long time to realize that. And understand why."

She was silent, watching him.

"And it was a professional mistake too. I closed my mind to all the facts I should have considered. You knew Kara far better than I did, understood her abilities in a way I never could have. You realized how vulnerable she was to a stronger mind, especially a psychic one."

"You had no way of knowing Harrison was psychic," Miranda reminded him. "None of us had."

He nodded, but said, "The difference is that it was a possibility you would have considered — if I'd given you the chance."

"Maybe."

He frowned slightly as he gazed down at her. "Miranda, you haven't spent all these years thinking any part of it was your fault, have you?"

"If we hadn't been arguing about it that last day, if I had just let you get back to doing your job, then maybe —"

"Miranda." His hand lay warmly against her face, his thumb moving in a gentle, soothing motion across her cheekbone. "It wouldn't have made a difference, you know that. You have to know it. There were two teams of agents and half a dozen plain-clothes officers stationed all around the house. I would have been outside with them. Even if I'd been there, I wouldn't have known what was happening inside until too late."

"Your spider-sense might have —"

"You're forgetting." His mouth twisted in self-loathing. "I wanted to confess, but I had some idiotic idea that you'd be more likely to forgive me if I confessed after we made love that morning."

She had forgotten that, which might have been surprising except for the utter chaos of the emotions that had followed during that endless day and all the days afterward.

"Very much a man thing, that sort of notion," she murmured, unable to resist.

"Apparently. And a stupid thing." He grimaced. "You know, I think it's one of the things I'm most ashamed of, that I had the colossal conceit to believe — honestly believe — that you wouldn't be able to stay mad at me when you were . . ."

"Weak with satisfaction?"

He closed his eyes briefly. "I don't believe I've ever been *so* wrong about anything in my life."

In retrospect, Miranda couldn't help but see the humor in it, but all she said was, "Let's call it a lesson learned and move on."

"Thank you," he said sincerely. "Moving on — since we had made love that morning, the spider-sense was temporarily out of order. Psychically, I was blind as a bat. So I wouldn't have had a clue that something bad was happening inside the house. Hell, I couldn't even sense a direct danger to myself." He briefly touched his left cheek. "Which is why I got this."

"I wondered. I knew you got it that day when Harrison — when he got past all the cops, but I never thought about how he was able to get that close to you."

"That's how. I never saw him coming. In any sense." Bishop paused. "He also got my gun. Killed four more people with it."

Miranda hadn't known about that. "I'm sorry."

He nodded. "Anyway, the point I was trying to make is that you weren't to blame in any way for what happened. It was my fault. Start to finish, it was my fault."

"Ultimately, it was Harrison's fault. He killed my family, Bishop, not you."

"Yes, but I made them a target. If I had gone to you first, it would have all been so different. I don't know if I'd have been able to convince you, but I do know that if you'd been involved, you would have been able to protect Kara, maybe even prevent Harrison from following that psychic connection back to her."

"I think you overestimate my abilities," she said, deliberately light.

"Do I?" He kissed her, taking his time about it, then said, "You knew this would happen. Us."

She didn't try to deny it, ruefully aware that he had mined that little nugget from her own brain during the wild kaleidoscope of mental communication. "I knew. And I wasn't happy about it, not then."

"What about now? Regrets?"

"No." She reached up to briefly touch his cheek, absently tracing the scar. "I don't know how I feel, except that I'm glad you're here. I'm not thinking past that."

"I'll settle for that. For now." He kissed her again, his brows drawing together as he sorted through the images and emotions stored in his brain. The exchange between them had been rather like viewing a video-tape in extreme fast-forward mode, and it was only now that they could begin to sift through and understand all the information.

"You knew we'd be lovers again," he said

slowly. "But there was something else, wasn't there? Something else you saw even before any of this started."

Miranda hesitated even now, not because she didn't want to confide in him but because she was uneasily aware that she might already have changed the future she had seen. Everything else had happened in the expected order, except for this. Five. Five victims, and *then* they became lovers again — that's what she had seen.

Had she changed the future? In building up her shields so strongly to close Bishop out and try to avoid any closeness between them, had she inadvertently caused the ideal situation that would make it possible for him to revive their relationship — and their bond?

And if she had . . . what would be the repercussions?

"Miranda?"

She smiled. "I don't know about you, but I'm starving."

"Miranda —"

"I'm not stalling. Well, not much." Whether or not she had changed the future, sooner or later she'd have to tell him what she had originally seen. Or he'd find the information stored in his own mind. And since she was reasonably sure of what would happen when he discovered it, any delay seemed wise. "I just think that since neither of us is sleepy and the storm may knock out the power at any time, we should take advantage of all the modern conveniences while we can."

He stared at her. "You aren't going to tell me."

"I really am starving, Bishop."

"Have I told you what a stubborn woman you are?"

"Once or twice." She threw back the covers on her side and sat up. "We'll argue about it later. For now, I'm hungry and I'd like to check the Weather Channel just to see what we're in for. And if you want a shower while the water's hot, I'd suggest now, just in case we do lose power."

He watched her gather their scattered clothing and leave it on the foot of the bed, then put on a thick terrycloth robe from the closet.

"I'd forgotten how beautiful you are," he said. "I thought I hadn't, but . . . Jesus. It's like a kick in the stomach."

Amused, she said, "You sweet talker, you." She found a pair of fuzzy cat slippers Bonnie had given her for Christmas and slid her feet into them. They looked absurd but were both comfortable and warm.

He grinned at her. "You still don't give a damn, do you? You're no more impressed by your looks than by your psychic abilities."

"Because I'm not responsible for either one. A genetic roll of the dice is. Ask me about my black belt or sharpshooter medals, or about my ability to finish a crossword puzzle in record time, and I'll brag a little bit."

"I wonder if you would," he mused.

"See you downstairs, Bishop." Halfway there, Miranda realized she was smiling. She had told him the truth: she really wasn't looking beyond the fact that she was glad he was with her right now. She didn't want to think about anything else.

She went into the living room to turn on the TV and got a weird sense of déjà vu. For a moment, she paused there, looking around with a frown. There was her shoulder harness hanging over the chair, the gun in it. Several lamps burning. The Ouija board on the coffee table.

She moved close to it, then bent and moved the planchette to the center of the board. She had the nagging sense that something was wrong with this picture, but couldn't figure out what it was. She also couldn't clearly remember last being in this room.

All she recalled was . . . coming home. And then being in bed with Bishop.

"I hope he can fill in a few of the blanks," she murmured to herself, and continued on to the kitchen.

Behind her, the planchette moved slowly back until it was centered over the word NO.

FIFTEEN

"If you had any sense," Alex told Tony, "you'd go on back to the Lodge and get some sleep."

"I'm a glutton for punishment," Tony agreed. "Besides, it hardly seems worth the bother at this point. The roads are so bad it'd take an hour to get there, and it's nearly two in the morning now. And storms are even less fun when you're all alone, that much I'm sure of."

"Um. Where did you say Dr. Edwards was calling from?"

"From your Dr. Shepherd's house. Not that I bought that old 'we only got this far before the storm stopped us' story. If you ask me, those two would have ended up at his house, storm or no storm."

Alex grunted. "You psychics seem to move awfully fast."

Tony grinned at him. "Think so? Sorry, pal, but it's not such an easy answer. In my experience, psychics actually tend to move more slowly than the average in romantic matters. Being more sensitive than most, wary of being hurt."

Alex decided he didn't want to pursue that subject. "Now that the pizza's all gone and we've run out of cheerleading competitions to watch," he said, "and since you don't want to call it a night, what do you say we try to get some work done?"

Tony sighed and propped his feet on the conference table once again, this time directing his attention to the bulletin board rather than the muted television showing weather reports. "It's all right with me. Assuming we can get anything done, which is doubtful. It'll be Monday at the earliest before Quantico can get us a workable list of tire dealerships in the area. And we've got three deputies out there reading through those copies of classified ads looking for a few our missing teens might possibly have replied to. I don't know about you, but I *don't* want to go down into the basement and hunt through more missing-persons reports, not tonight."

"No, me either. It's not the most cheerful place in the world even without a blizzard."

"So, we're left with brain work. Trying one more time to put the puzzle together."

Tony frowned at the bulletin board. "I wonder what it was the killer wanted from Adam Ramsay."

"You think Bishop's right about that?"

"I think he's a damned good profiler even without the psychic edge, and I've learned not to bet against him."

Alex gazed at the bulletin board. "With no more than the boy's bones as evidence, how're we supposed to figure out what might have had value to the killer?"

Tony twisted around to hunt through the stack of files on the table, finally producing a folder containing various interviews and the autopsy report on Adam Ramsay.

"How many times have you looked at that?" Alex asked.

"God knows. But maybe this time I'll see what I've missed every time before."

Alex shrugged and pulled another folder across the table so he could go through it. Before he opened it, however, he said slowly, "What does it say about a town that it might have hidden a monster for years? What does it say about us?"

Tony looked at him soberly. "It says this particular monster isn't wearing horns and a tail to make him easy to spot. They mostly don't, you know. They hide in plain sight, looking pretty much like the rest of us, daring us to see them, to recognize them for what they are. Problem is, even those of us with extra senses have trouble spotting the monsters, so don't beat yourself up about it. But I can tell you this much. When we do find him, his final victim will be this town, because none of you will ever be the same again."

"How did you find me when you got here?" Miranda asked as they sat at the kitchen table with coffee after their meal and listened to the storm wailing.

"Out cold," Bishop replied succinctly. "And I do mean cold. Your body temperature was dropping like a stone." He watched her, aware that she was edgy about something and that these first tentative hours together as lovers might well decide their future. It was the major reason he hadn't pressed her to discover what vision she had seen in the beginning. "Don't you remember?"

She frowned. "I remember coming home, letting myself in. I remember checking the machine out in the hall. And then . . . your voice in my head telling me I was dying."

Wary that she might believe he'd latched on to any excuse to invade her mind, Bishop said, "I found you in the living room, on the floor, as if you'd just fallen. No outward sign of injury. I'm no doctor, but I've seen plenty of dead and dying, Miranda. You were dying. It wasn't just the dropping temperature; your pulse was fading away, respiration slowing. It was like your body was just . . . stopping. Your mind had let go or been cut off somehow, was drifting away, and without it, all your systems were shutting down."

She accepted that only because she didn't have an alternate explanation. "But what caused it to happen? That's what I don't understand."

Bishop hadn't wasted much time in working it all out then, not with Miranda so still and seemingly lifeless. He hadn't thought about anything but getting her back, and had acted instantly and instinctively to do that.

But now he realized that her abrupt collapse was more than a little odd. "I assumed it was because of your shield. That all the energy you had trapped inside all this time had finally burst free. I knew as soon as I touched you that the shield was completely gone; that's how I was able to get through to you."

She got up to refill her coffee cup, still frowning. Instead of returning to the table, she leaned back against the counter near the sink and looked at him steadily. "No, that isn't what happened. I know it's what you were worried about, but I was able to control that energy without letting it damage me. Years of practice. There were side effects, sure — the headaches, for one. But nothing that could have caused that sort of ultimate collapse, and certainly not without warning."

"Then what did cause it?"

Miranda set her cup on the counter. "I was in the living room?"

"Yeah."

"Then whatever caused it must have been in there." She went into the living room and Bishop followed. They studied the room, which looked entirely peaceful and unthreatening.

Miranda sat on the couch, gazing at the Ouija board on the coffee table. "Why is this here? I could swear Bonnie told me they were up in her room when they used it."

"They wouldn't have carried it down here for any reason?"

"I can't think why they would have. Or why my housekeeper would have."

Bishop sat beside her. He reached out and idly moved the planchette to the center of the board. "If this is what they used to con-

331

tact . . . whoever it was they contacted . . . then it's a literal doorway."

She looked at him. "And maybe Bonnie forgot to close the door."

"Or closed it too late," he suggested. "I don't know too much about this sort of thing; like I told you, we've had trouble coming up with any viable tests or measurements, and the research on the subject is shaky at best. But I seem to remember you telling me once that there was no way for a medium to control what came through an open door."

"As far as I know, that's true. Sometimes a medium can partially block a doorway to narrow the opening, but that's it. And the danger is that it's usually the angriest, most negative spirit that rushes through the first open door it sees."

"The most recently and violently killed."

Miranda nodded. "Usually."

"Which in this case is likely to be Steve Penman, or maybe Lynet Grainger. Both were killed more quickly than the other two, with less time to even try to accept what was going to happen to them."

"True." Miranda thought about it for a minute. "Bonnie confessed that she and Amy had tried once before to contact someone who could help us locate Steve. It was a brief attempt, stopped pretty abruptly — but the name spelled out as their contact was Lynet's."

"She didn't strike me as the angry sort," Bishop said.

"No, she was a . . . very quiet, sweet-tempered girl." Miranda drew a breath. "But she died an adolescent, and the sheer emotional energy of that could easily be destructive. She could be desperate enough to live that she didn't stop to count the cost to anyone else."

Bishop tapped the board with a finger. "If this is the doorway Bonnie used, the place where she focused her energies, then her own mind was somewhat protected. Right?"

"Yes, especially if she raised her own shields immediately after they made contact. Kara and I taught her when she was very small how to protect herself as much as possible, and by now it's an automatic defense."

"Then what would happen if the doorway was open just long enough for a spirit to come through — but not long enough for it to find Bonnie's mind accessible?"

"Then the spirit would be . . . here." Miranda looked around. "In the house."

"Confined here?"

"Probably, at least for a while. Some are able to migrate to other places through connections with people they knew in life, but if this is where it came in, then it's stuck here until it gets its bearings and is able to gain and focus strength."

Slightly distracted by possibilities, Bishop said, "In that case, I hope the kid isn't a voyeur."

Miranda smiled. "According to Bonnie and other mediums I've talked to, spirits trapped in our world aren't completely *here*. They're only able to see the living people who are able to see them; the rest of us exist to them only as . . . the flicker of shadows caught out of the corner of their eyes."

Bishop grimaced. "The way most of us see them."

"Exactly. They don't drift around watching the living because they can't really see us. We just happen to inhabit the same space, I suppose on different dimensional planes."

Bishop thought about that. "Okay, that relieves my mind, at least on that point. Now — Bonnie and her friends make contact and then promptly leave the house. The only person left here is your housekeeper, who is probably not psychic."

"Definitely not psychic."

"Then she leaves. And the next person to come in — is you."

"Yes, but my shields were —" Miranda broke off, the wheels of memory almost visibly turning. "Wait a minute. I remember now. I came in here after taking a shower, and something made me think there might be an intruder in the house."

"What?"

"The board. The Ouija board was on the floor. When I first got home it was here on the coffee table. I knew I should search the house, but I . . . I decided to drop my shields instead. Just for a moment, so I could check the house faster and more thoroughly."

"And you opened a door," Bishop said.

With the clinic all but empty, they'd had their choice of rooms, but Seth's father had casually asked his son and Bonnie to sleep in the four-bed ward with the youngest patients, two little girls, and "keep them company."

Whether it was for the sake of propriety or in case the girls needed them, neither Seth nor Bonnie objected. In any case, Seth didn't intend to close his eyes, not tonight. Long after the girls and Bonnie had settled into sleep, he sat in the lounge near the door and listened to the storm raging outside the dim, quiet room.

As the hours passed, he fought off drowsiness several times, jerking awake to peer around the room uneasily, to listen the way someone snatched from sleep by a nightmare would listen for the stealthy footsteps of an intruder.

If asked, he couldn't have explained just what he was feeling. Anxiety over Bonnie, of course, because he thought this spirit business upset her more than she was saying. Lingering shock over the tragedy that had all but destroyed her family, and lingering astonishment that Steve's body had been found just where that damned Ouija board had claimed it would be.

A Ouija board, for Christ's sake.

He didn't believe in any of that shit. Well . . . he hadn't. But something about Bonnie's attitude had told him loud and clear that he'd better readjust his thinking if his future included her — which it most certainly did. And the damned thing had been *right,* there was no getting away from that.

Brooding, Seth shifted restlessly in his chair at least twice before it occurred to him that something was wrong. He didn't know what it was at first, but when the storm stilled for several minutes, he heard it. The sound was so low he'd noticed it only subconsciously, but now the hair on the nape of his neck was stirring, and he felt a chill of unease so strong it brought him up out of his chair.

He checked out the ward, moving slowly, pausing often to listen and silently cursing the storm as it picked up again. It was difficult to hear anything else, but as he circled the room and ended up at Bonnie's bedside, he heard it.

A faint rustling sound, almost like . . . whispering. It was low and quiet, but rose and fell, teasing his senses as he tried to grasp it and understand what it was. An insect? A mouse in the wall? A voice?

Seth bent over Bonnie and listened, but the hushed, rustling sounds weren't coming from her. She was sleeping, apparently peacefully, and he had to fight the urge to wake her just to make certain she was all right.

He forced himself to leave her in order to circle the room once again, and again ended up standing beside her bed looking down at her. That whispering . . . It wasn't an insect, and it wasn't a mouse, he was sure of that.

He was also sure of something else. Whatever it was, the sound was here. All around Bonnie. It wasn't coming from her, and yet . . . it was here. As if the very air above her relaxed, sleeping body contained something. . . .

A deeper chill swept through him, and he reached out to wake Bonnie, suddenly convinced beyond all reason that she was in desperate, deadly danger.

Before he could touch her, the storm quieted in another lull, and the silence of the room closed about him. He heard Bonnie breathing softly. Heard one of the little girls shift in her bed and murmur something unintelligible. Nothing else.

Seth drew back his hand and listened intently for several minutes, but there was only peaceful quiet inside and the storm outside.

Half under his breath, he said, "Daniels, you're losing it."

But he moved his uncomfortable chair closer to Bonnie's bed. And he didn't feel drowsy again, not for a long, long time.

"I'm not a medium," Miranda protested.

"No, which is why the spirit couldn't inhabit your mind," Bishop said. "But it tried. Tried to force its way, to cut your mind and spirit free of your body so it could have a vessel of its own again. And when your defenses slammed up, their normal strength magnified by all the force you'd been building inside . . ."

"It was too much," she finished slowly.

"My system couldn't handle it, physically or mentally. My spirit very nearly was cut loose, drifting away. And without that, my body was —"

"Dying. It makes sense. As much as any of this makes sense, that is."

Miranda smiled slightly. "So you did save my life. Thank you."

Bishop had a vague memory of growling something at her about doing whatever it took to keep her alive, and half hoped she'd forgotten that. He was fully aware that the ruthless aspect of his nature made her wary, and he wasn't sure if, given his actions in the past, she had any confidence in his ability to use that ruthlessness wisely.

"You're welcome," he said.

Miranda laughed under her breath, then went grave again as she looked down at the Ouija board. "So whatever spirit they contacted is probably still here, in the house." She kept her voice matter-of-fact, even though her skin crawled at the idea of a spirit so angry or desperate to escape, it had ruthlessly attacked her.

"Are you sure of that?"

"No. But I think we'd better assume it for now."

"And both of us are psychically blind as a couple of bats. Even if we were mediumistic, neither of us could open a door for it — to come into us or to leave here. So we're safe from it, at least for now. But when we regain our abilities we'll have to be careful; if it attacked you only because your shields were down, then anyone with any kind of psychic ability could be at risk."

"Bonnie can't come back here," Miranda said.

"At least not until we regain our abilities and figure out what to do about it," he agreed. "Young as she is, we can't take the chance she might not be able to protect herself — especially if, say, it's the spirit of Steve Penman, who by most accounts did have a lot of anger in his nature."

Recalling the force of the attack against her, Miranda felt a chill. Bonnie had good shields, strong shields, but they could be weakened by physical weariness or slip because of carelessness or inattention. Just a slight opening, a weak point in the defenses, and an angry spirit could force its way in — especially into the mind of a mediumistic psychic designed by nature to be receptive to the contact.

"She'll be all right, Miranda."

He was, she decided, getting entirely too good at reading her, especially without benefit of his extra senses. "I know."

"You said it would take time for the spirit to gain enough energy, enough strength, to leave here. Right?"

"Right." *As far as I know. But do I know enough to be sure?*

"Then we have a little breathing room. And there is a more immediate threat we have to consider."

He was right. Pushing aside the unknown, Miranda said, "Gossip is spreading fast about how we were able to find Steve's body. Sooner or later, the killer is going to find out Bonnie poses a danger to him."

"Yes — assuming he even believes in what she can do."

"You said it yourself, Bishop — this killer wants to think he's in control and all-powerful; it will only reinforce his ego if he thinks the only way we can interfere with his plans is by using paranormal means. That's right, isn't it? He'll be eager to accept the idea that the ghost of one of his victims sent us to find Steve Penman."

"He'll also be eager to make sure we can't use that tool again. Especially if it unsettles him to believe his victims can speak through Bonnie, can accuse him of his crimes. So I'd say we have far more to fear from the living than the dead, for the present anyway."

Miranda got up and moved across the

room to the big front window. The streetlights were barely visible through the swirling, blowing snow, and the moaning of the wind was constant.

"I hate this," she muttered. "We're isolated, cut off from everything, helpless to do anything but wait. While that maniac is out there somewhere, probably pissed and thinking about his next victim. I just hope to God he's trapped inside like the rest of us."

Bishop came up behind her and slid his arms around her. "You know, for an atheist you have an interesting relationship with God."

She was stiff for just an instant, then relaxed against him. "Oh, you noticed that?"

"I did, yes."

She chuckled, grateful for the momentary distraction from her worries. "Just habit, I suppose, to use the word. The name. No disrespect intended or offense meant. And no belief in a deity. Malign fate, maybe, but no benevolent intelligence watching over us."

"Yet you know something of us survives death."

"To me, that's not a religious thing — not a question of faith or belief, or any notion that surviving death is some kind of reward for a life well lived. It's a certainty. It's like knowing a tree sheds its leaves year after year, cultivating a new set each spring of its life cycle. The tree grows and sinks its roots deeper and deeper, and wears a new set of leaves each spring until it finally grows as large as it can, reaches the end of its life, and dies."

"Our bodies are the . . . leaves of our soul?"

"Why not?" She shrugged. "We tend to think what's real and lasting is only what we can see, but that doesn't mean we're right. Maybe our skin and bones and the faces we see in the mirror are really the most transitory things about us. Maybe we just wear our bodies the way that tree wears its leaves, our physical selves being born and maturing and dying over and over while inside our spirits grow and learn."

"It has its attractions, that theory," Bishop said. "And maybe it explains . . ."

"Explains what?"

He hesitated, and when he replied he made sure his tone was light. "Explains what I felt the first time I set eyes on you. Do you suppose one soul can recognize another even wearing a different set of leaves?"

After a moment, she said in an equally casual tone, "I guess that would depend on the soul. An old soul would probably have more practice at it, especially if you believe the karmic theory that says we travel through our existence surrounded by many of the same souls in life after life. Maybe we're psychic because we're old souls, and these abilities of ours are simply the result of a . . . spiritual evolution."

Bishop wondered if neither of them wanted to probe too deeply and question their own feelings because they were afraid of the answers they might find. But he accepted the tacit avoidance, and his own relief told him he was not yet ready to risk pushing Miranda in that direction.

"Another theory that has its own attractions," he said judiciously. "Nice to think of oneself as a highly evolved soul. Do you suppose an earlier set of my leaves might have been Charlemagne?"

Miranda turned to smile up at him. "More likely Rasputin," she said. "Although I suppose you could have been both, given the dates."

"The Mad Monk? Thanks a lot."

She slid her arms up around his neck. "There's just something about those eyes. Absolutely hypnotic."

"If you'll forgive a bad pun — look who's talking." He kissed her, then said, "We won't let anyone harm Bonnie, Miranda. Not in this life or from the next."

"Promise?" Immediately, she shook her head. "No, that's not fair. And not realistic."

Bishop lifted a hand to smooth a strand of her silky black hair from her face. He knew she was right, knew that to make such a promise right now, with everything that was going on around them, was unreasonable and even irrational. But he wasn't very surprised to hear himself say steadily, "I promise, Miranda."

Sunday, January 16

Deputy Sandy Lynch refilled her coffee cup and returned to her desk after a brief look out the window. The wind had finally died down, at least for the moment, and the snow had slowed to gently drifting flakes; if she'd been a fan of winter wonderlands, she would have loved it. But with a foot or so of snow on the ground and power outages being reported now that people were up and about, it promised to be a difficult, busy day for the Sheriff's Department.

Especially if, as the Weather Service was predicting, the back side of the storm blew through later today.

Sandy sipped her coffee and then rubbed her eyes wearily. Spending most of the night reading old classified ads hadn't been a lot of fun, but at least it had kept her occupied. Not that she really knew what she was looking for. As instructed, she was making a list of similar ads that had run around the time of each of more than a dozen reported disappearances of teens passing through the area. But in doing so, she had noticed that several businesses appeared to run ads all or most of the time — like the paper mill, for instance, which always seemed to need to hire more employees.

The car dealerships and garages also appeared to have a high turnover, the school system always seemed to be looking for bus drivers and janitors, and even the town of Gladstone itself offered a fairly constant stream of opportunities for transient labor such as street cleaning and litter control, grounds maintenance, and various kinds of painting and repairs.

Some time in the wee hours of the night, Sandy had compared some of the old classifieds with those in last week's paper, but nothing of particular interest had jumped out at her. Ads from years ago and those more recent appeared boringly similar.

"Dead bodies one day and paper cuts the next," she muttered sardonically to herself. "Talk about extremes. I just love my job."

The front door opened to admit a gust of

really cold air and one FBI agent, and since Sandy's desk was the nearest one occupied beyond the reception area, she got to chase blowing papers around.

"Sorry about that, Deputy," Bishop apologized.

Sandy got off her knees and back into her chair, wishing he didn't make her feel so flustered. "It's okay, Agent Bishop. Agent Harte is back in the conference room."

"Thank you." Bishop nodded courteously with a smile and went on past her desk.

Deputy Brady Shaw waited until the agent disappeared down the hallway before marveling, "Was that an honest-to-God smile? And me without my cameras."

"He's always polite," Sandy objected, ruefully aware of defending a man who could undoubtedly defend himself.

"Yeah, but he doesn't waste smiles — even on you, Sandy. At least he didn't yesterday." Brady nodded judiciously. "The test will be when Sheriff Knight comes in."

"What test?"

"To see if she's smiling too," Brady replied with a grin.

Sandy rolled her eyes and heaved a sigh. "Honestly, you men. Just because he's in a good mood you figure he got lucky last night."

"Give me another reason why he'd be in a good mood," Brady challenged. "We've got a killer running around out there and bodies piling up like cordwood, we're in the middle of a blizzard, the power is failing all over town — and the Bluebird Lodge sucks as a place to stay."

"I'm going back to work now," Sandy announced.

"I'll bet twenty bucks that Sheriff Knight is also in a good mood when she gets here."

"I'm ignoring you."

Brady chuckled. "Just wait and see if I'm not right."

Bishop walked into the conference room to find Tony leaning back with his feet propped on the conference table, and said, "Have you even moved since I left last night?"

"Of course I have." Tony looked at him with bright, speculative eyes.

"Don't even start," Bishop warned.

"I was just going to observe how much benefit there obviously is in a good night's sleep," Tony said innocently. "Last night you were pacing holes in the floor, and this morning you're . . . not nearly as tense."

Dryly, Bishop said, "Tony, you're about as subtle as neon."

Tony laughed. "Okay, okay. Where's Miranda?"

"She went by Dr. Daniels's clinic to talk to Bonnie and take her a few things."

"So the kid's stuck there for the duration?"

"She's safer there." Bishop briefly explained what he and Miranda believed had happened when Bonnie had used the Ouija board the day before.

Sobered, Tony said, "Poor kid. I always thought being mediumistic would be the least fun ability to have, even if it did confirm some kind of existence beyond death."

"It's one of the two abilities with the highest potential danger to the psychic, I know that much."

"What's the other ability? Being able to tap in to the mind of a killer?"

Bishop nodded. "I've known only two psychics with that ability. It killed one of them and damned near killed the other."

"Miranda's sister," Tony realized. "And the other — was that the psychic you told us about last year, the one in North Carolina?"

"Cassie Neill. When that case was over and done with, she had almost totally burned out psychically. It'll be years, if ever, before she regains any of her former abilities."

"You told us it was a good thing, for her."

"Yeah. She'd devoted her entire adult life to using her abilities to help the police, and she was about as close to a total breakdown as anyone I've ever seen. At least now she can have a shot at a normal life."

"Odd how some of us have few problems and others seem to be . . . almost punished . . . by psychic abilities," Tony mused.

"Why do you think it was so difficult to pull together an effective team of psychics that it took years to do it?" Bishop said. "Finding genuine psychics wasn't the problem; finding genuine psychics who could handle the work consistently was."

"Um. Which means we could really use someone like Miranda on the team."

Bishop picked up a sheaf of messages from the table. "She has a term of office as sheriff to finish out."

"And then?"

"We haven't talked about it."

Deciding not to push, Tony said, "Probably best to take things a day at a time for now." He saw Bishop frown down at the messages, and added, "You asked last night that the deputies taking phone calls note down any comments or questions about how we were able to find Steve Penman's body. There weren't many calls last night, but lots this morning."

"Have you looked at these?" Bishop asked.

"No, one of the deputies just brought them in a little while ago. Why?"

Grim, Bishop said, "Because the prevailing theory seems to be that we were able to find Penman's body because Liz Hallowell saw it in the tea leaves."

"Oh," Tony said. And then, slowly, "Oh, shit."

SIXTEEN

"No answer at her house or the store." Miranda cradled the receiver. "She's an early riser, she'd be up by now."

Bishop checked his watch. "Nearly ten. If the weather reports are on target, we'll get the back side of the storm by noon or a little after."

Miranda picked up a clipboard from the conference table and studied it with a frown. "Her house isn't in one of the sections reporting a power outage, but even if it were she'd still have the phone. Damn."

Tony said, "Unless he's stupidly out there now leaving tracks in the snow, or even more stupidly went out in the middle of the storm, he had to have acted fairly early last night, right? Just hours after we found Penman's body. Would he have felt threatened enough to move against her so quickly?"

"Believing it was possible she had a pipeline to his victims?" Bishop barely hesitated. "I'd say yes."

Miranda nodded. "Then we have to go out there, before the storm gets wound up again. Where's Alex?"

"The lounge," Tony answered. "When everything was so quiet a few hours ago, he decided to get a little sleep. Want me to wake him?"

"No. If we're very lucky, there won't be any reason to disturb his sleep now or later." She drew a breath. "In fact, I don't want to tell any of the deputies unless it's necessary. Liz is . . . very well liked. We'll keep it just between us, for now. Tony, if something has happened, first impressions could be very useful to us."

"Well, sure, but I'm not especially strong," he reminded her.

She gave Bishop a wry look, and he said, "At the moment, you have both of us beat."

Tony blinked. "Ah. I wondered why the transmitter was so silent that I was reduced to trying to read your stone face."

"Temporarily out of order."

"How temporarily?"

"A few hours, if we're lucky. A few days, if we're not."

"Receivers busted too?"

"Afraid so."

Tony looked from one to the other, having

little luck reading two very calm faces. "I see. I don't, actually, but since it's obvious I'm not going to get an explanation, never mind. The timing could be better, guys."

"No kidding." Miranda put down the clipboard. "There's some snow gear in one of the storage lockers. You'll both need boots, at least." She was already wearing hers.

"I'll get them," Tony said.

"Don't say anything to the others," Miranda told him.

"Gotcha."

When they were alone in the conference room, Bishop said, "Assuming we're right about this, none of us could have anticipated that he'd move so fast."

"I know, I know." But she was frowning.

And Bishop didn't like something he saw in her face, a tension or strain that hadn't been there just a few minutes ago. "Miranda, none of this is your fault."

She looked at him steadily. "But Tony's right about our rotten timing. We could hardly have picked a worse moment to have our abilities muted."

"We didn't pick the moment, it picked us." Bishop's voice was deliberate. "And I'm not sorry it did. The rate we were going, we were never going to get there without a nudge."

"It was more of a shove," she said.

It wasn't like her to be flippant at such a moment, and it told Bishop probably more than she would have liked about her state of mind. He crossed the space between them and lifted a hand to touch her face. "Are you all right?"

"There is," she said with a touch of grimness, "such a thing as being known too well."

"What's wrong, Miranda?"

"Me. I'm wrong."

"In what way?"

Miranda drew a breath and let it out slowly. "I thought I could change things. I thought I could . . . exert some kind of control over fate, even if only a little. And I thought I had. But if Liz is dead . . . if she died last night before you came to me . . . then it's all happening just the way I saw it happen, in spite of what I tried to do to change it. I can't change it. Apparently there's not a goddamned thing I can do to stop any of it."

Bishop felt a little chill that came from instinct rather than knowledge. "What is it? What did you see?"

Whether Miranda would have answered became moot when Tony returned to the conference room with the snow boots. She turned away from Bishop, becoming once again the brisk and efficient sheriff, and the moment for confidences passed.

Miranda made that even more clear when she decided they should take two vehicles — just in case one of them got stuck in the snow. It was a reasonable precaution, but it was also an obvious desire to be alone for a while since she rather pointedly suggested that Bishop and Tony take their rental SUV.

All the way out to Liz Hallowell's house, even as he concentrated on navigating in the deep snow, Bishop was trying to sort through the images crammed in his mind, all the emotions and events of Miranda's life during the past eight years. He felt frustrated, knowing that the answer was within his grasp if he could only identify it. But it was like searching for a single snapshot in a box filled with them when he wasn't sure what the picture was supposed to look like.

"Boss?"

Slowing cautiously to follow Miranda's Jeep around a corner, Bishop said, "Yeah?"

"If Liz Hallowell *is* dead . . . do we let the killer believe he succeeded in silencing our medium?"

"If it'll protect Bonnie, I say we damned well try. And you'll notice Miranda didn't send any of her deputies to the clinic; doing anything to draw attention to Bonnie before we know for sure what's happened could be a bad mistake."

"So could waiting," Tony offered soberly.

"I know. And so does Miranda."

Tony was silent for half a block; then, as he drew his weapon and checked it absently, he said, "Either the transmitter's beginning to recover, or you're worried as hell, because I can feel it."

Bishop tried experimentally to focus his spider-sense. "No, I'm still pretty much blind at the moment."

"And worried?"

"Let's just say I don't like the way things are shaping up."

"Can't say that I blame you about that."

Nothing more was said, and minutes later they reached Liz Hallowell's house. Bishop parked his vehicle behind Miranda's, and they joined her outside.

She was studying the smooth expanse of pristine snow covering the ground, Liz's parked car, and the small house. "Nobody's gone in or out of the house this way for hours at least," she said.

"I'll check the back." Tony headed off to make a wide circuit of the house. Minutes later, he returned. "Nope, no sign anyone's come or gone since the storm got serious last night."

"Feel anything?" Bishop asked.

"I don't feel anybody alive in there," Tony said reluctantly.

Miranda sighed, her breath misting the air. "Shit." The curse was too weary to hold any other emotion. "Anything else?"

Tony was silent for a minute, his attention and senses focused on the house, then frowned at the other two. "You know, for a murderous maniac, this guy has some peculiar emotions. What I feel most of all is intense regret. I mean, bordering on actual grief. He did not want to do . . . whatever it is he did."

Grim, Miranda said, "Let's go find out what he did."

They trusted Tony's sense of the place, but nevertheless drew their weapons automatically as they cautiously approached the house. They found the front door unlocked and went inside swiftly and silently, protecting one another and alert to possible danger.

Bishop didn't need his spider-sense to know there was no longer anything dangerous here, but he moved carefully, like the others, as he began searching the house. The big and open kitchen/dining/family-room area was easy to look over, and all that met their eyes was a placid cream-colored cat with chocolate points sitting on the back of the sofa; the cat didn't seem the slightest bit disturbed by strangers and was busily engaged in washing one brown forepaw.

They split up to check the other rooms. Bishop and Tony found nothing, and were just coming back up the hallway when Miranda emerged from the master bedroom. She leaned against the doorjamb, slowly returning her pistol to the hip holster she was wearing today.

Bishop felt an odd ripple in their connection, a flutter of emotions that marked the beginning of the return of his abilities. It told him much more clearly than her utterly remote expression that Miranda was badly shaken. It also told him why.

"Tony," she said, her voice carefully matter-of-fact, "could you do me a favor?" She wasn't looking at them but toward the living room.

"Sure," he responded instantly, his fixed attention showing that Bishop wasn't the only one whose extra senses were on the alert.

"There must be a carrier or crate for the cat around here somewhere. Could you look for it, please? And put the cat in it when you find it?"

Tony looked at the cat still busily cleaning its forepaw, then sent one quick glance toward the master bedroom. His face paled. "Yeah," he said a bit jerkily. "Yeah, I'll do that."

When he had gone, Bishop stepped to the doorway beside Miranda. He reached out and grasped her arm, needing to touch her.

"I'd read about it," she said. "Even saw a couple of pictures in a training manual. But this is the first time . . ."

"The survival instinct," Bishop said. "You can't blame the cat for that."

"Yeah. Except that somehow I do." Softly, without looking at him, she added, "Alex is not going to see that."

Bishop didn't argue. He squeezed her arm gently, then went past her into the bedroom. Wary of disturbing any evidence, he stepped inside just far enough to be able to study the scene.

Steeled by Miranda's warning, he wasn't shocked by what he saw, but he was somewhat surprised by a couple of things.

Liz Hallowell lay in the center of her double bed, for all the world as if she'd simply gone to sleep as usual. Had such care been taken for Liz's sake or because her murderer was trying to tell them something?

Guilt? Reluctance? Maybe this time,

whether consciously or unconsciously, he wanted them to know he regretted at least this murder, this death.

She looked so peaceful. The covers were drawn up to her chin, sheet and comforter folded neatly, the bed smooth and unblemished — except for the small circle of blood over her abdomen that marked the location of the wound that had killed her.

That must have been what first attracted the cat.

There were only a few flecks of blood on the pillow on one side of her head, the side where some of the skin had been peeled from her face. The cat had been neat.

And, apparently, not very hungry.

Bonnie came out of Amy's room and closed the door. Sedated again, her friend would sleep for a few more hours; it had so far proven unwise to allow her to be awake for long, since all she did was cry. Bonnie felt helpless, and it wasn't a feeling she enjoyed. She was also jumpy, and started when Seth put a hand on her shoulder.

"Hey — what's wrong?"

"You just startled me, that's all."

"I know the feeling," Seth said ruefully, taking her hand as they began walking down the quiet hall. "It must be the storm or something, but I've been jumping at shadows all morning."

"Shadows," Bonnie said.

"Yeah, you know what I mean. You get edgy and your mind starts playing tricks on you, starts telling you there's somebody behind you when there isn't. Like that." He didn't tell her about his imaginings of the night before.

Bonnie frowned briefly, but when she spoke, it was to say, "I promised your dad I'd read stories to Christy and Jordan, try to settle them down. They're jumpy too."

"The storm," Seth said. "According to the weather reports, this afternoon will be even worse than last night." He sent her a searching look. "You've been awfully quiet since Miranda came by here. Bonnie, if you'd rather be home —"

"No," she said, "I'd rather be here, with you."

"You're sure? Because I can take you to your house and stay there with you."

Bonnie hesitated, then said steadily, "Here is safer, Seth."

"Safer?"

"I know your dad thought Amy was just hysterical when she babbled all that stuff about me being a medium, but somebody must have taken her seriously; Randy says people are talking about how they were able to find Steve's body."

It took Seth only a moment to understand. He stopped walking and turned Bonnie to face him. "You mean the killer might think you're a threat to him?"

"It's possible. The storm is probably slowing the spread of gossip, but Randy wants me to stay here and not be alone just in case the killer hears something." She didn't add that Miranda had also warned her to keep her shields up in order to protect herself from another potential but more tenuous threat.

"Why isn't there a deputy here?" Fear for her made his voice angry.

"It would only draw attention to me, Seth. You know how garbled gossip gets; chances are, even if the killer hears something, he won't be sure what the truth is." She smiled at him. "If somebody knocks on the clinic door with a flimsy excuse, we probably shouldn't let him in — but other than that there really isn't much to worry about."

"Maybe for now," he said grimly.

Bonnie hesitated again, then said, "Randy thinks it's nearly over. If they can find out who the killer is before he has a chance to . . ."

"Come after you?"

"Before he has a chance to come after anybody else." She looked at him gravely. "We're all in danger, you know that. We have been all along. But Randy and Bishop will stop him."

"Will they?"

"Yes. I'm sure of that." But what Bonnie was less sure of was the cost. There was always a cost. Always.

"Okay, look," Seth said in a determined voice. "From now on, I stay within sight of you at all times. Promise me, Bonnie."

"I promise — as long as you allow me a little privacy in the bathroom."

He was young enough that some things still had the power to make him blush, but he said stolidly, "I'll wait outside the door."

She stood on tiptoe to kiss his chin. "Deal. Now, why don't we go see if we can calm down two sick little girls?"

Seth nodded and held her hand a bit tighter as they continued down the hall. As they passed a corner, he had another of those weird feelings, and almost told Bonnie that he could swear he'd caught a flicker of movement from the corner of his eye, as if a shadow had fleetingly reached out for them.

But he decided once again not to let his imagination get the better of his good sense.

Bishop stepped out onto the porch and zipped his jacket. The gray sky looked heavier and more threatening by the minute. It was just after noon; if the storm held off another hour they'd be lucky.

He was aware of the activity behind him, of Shepherd and Edwards, the muted sounds of voices and Brady Shaw's cameras, but he had gained all he expected to from the scene. Which wasn't all that much.

He looked down at the plastic evidence bag in his hands and studied the Bible through it. Old, dog-eared, and quite distinctive, he had recognized it the moment he'd seen it on Liz Hallowell's nightstand.

Under his breath, he muttered, "Just how stupid do you think I am?" Then he shook his head and tucked the bag inside his jacket.

The door behind him was shoved open wider and Sandy Lynch rushed past him. Bishop didn't have to catch a fleeting glimpse of her pallor or panicked expression to know she was about to lose her breakfast. She stumbled through the snow to just beyond the closest parked vehicle, which happened to be the hearse that would take away Liz's body, and disappeared behind it.

Poor kid. If she still wanted to be any kind of cop when this was over, it would be a miracle.

She came back to the porch a few minutes later and flushed a little under Bishop's sympathetic gaze. Jerkily, she said, "They turned her and I saw her face. I didn't think — but then the doctors were talking about it and — and — God!"

Both to inform and to give her time to compose herself, Bishop said, "You know, when kittens reach adulthood, their mother sees them as just other cats. She's done her job, her babies are grown — and they aren't her babies anymore. Maternal ties last only as long as necessary. That's a very practical idea in nature."

Sandy frowned. "But — but it *ate* some of her! I heard Dr. Shepherd say she'd had that cat for years, how could it do that? Was it so ravenous that —"

Bishop shook his head. "It had nothing to do with being ravenous and everything to do with being a cat. Experienced pathologists and cops will tell you it's more common than you might think. Die alone in your home with the family dog, and he'll wait until he's absolutely starving to death before he considers you a meal. Die alone with a pet cat, and he won't even wait until you're cold. Once dead, you stop being you and become just . . . flesh. It's his nature to be opportunistic; if there's food, he'll try it. Even if the food is the hand that fed him for years."

Sandy's face worked for a moment, and she finally muttered, "Oh, yuck. And I have a cat."

With a faint smile, Bishop said, "I like them myself. In spite of understanding them."

"I think," Sandy said, "I'll start closing my bedroom door at night. Misty can sleep on the couch."

Bishop didn't bother to remind her that given her age she was unlikely to die peacefully in her bed, at least during the probable lifetime of her cat. Instead, he merely nodded. "Probably not a bad idea, if only for your own peace of mind. For what it's worth, you don't have to worry that your cat is watching you and thinking of you as supper, Deputy Lynch. As long as you're a living being, she would never see you as a meal."

"Just don't stop breathing?"

"Something like that."

Sandy gazed past him at the doorway and drew a deep breath. "Right. And, for now, do my job. You don't have to say it."

"I think you're doing fine in a very difficult situation. Don't be so hard on yourself."

Obviously surprised, she flushed again and then ducked her head in acknowledgment as she went back into the house.

Tony passed her in the doorway and joined Bishop on the porch. "They just called to say the tow truck made it back to the Sheriff's Department with no trouble," he reported. "Her car'll be secured in the garage there, so we can take our time and go over it bumper to bumper."

Bishop nodded. "It took the direct route, right down Main Street?"

"As ordered. Brutal way for some of her friends to find out about Miss Hallowell. Calls are already coming in."

"Yeah. But I want this bastard to *know* we've found his latest kill."

Tony looked at him curiously. "And do you want him to think he's fooled us, at least for the moment?"

"If it'll buy us a little time, why not? If he thinks there's even half a chance somebody else could be convicted of his crimes, I'm willing to bet he'll sit tight and wait to see what happens."

"Pretty blatant, leaving that Bible," Tony mused.

"He hasn't shown much talent for subtlety, that's for sure. I don't know, maybe he's just trying to confuse things as much as possible. Killing someone who doesn't fit the previous victim profile and leaving evidence pointing to Marsh could be his way of slowing us down, distracting us."

"Is that what you think?"

Slowly, Bishop said, "I think he made his first serious mistake. I think he killed Liz because he was afraid of her, because he heard a garbled version of what happened yesterday, and acted on impulse to remove what he perceived as a threat. And it was only when he'd killed her that he realized he had to disguise his intent."

"Why?"

"So we wouldn't know he was afraid. He had to know that the only reason for *him* to kill Liz was an obvious one. Fear. When he saw that, he had to try to frame somebody else for the murder. Even if we believed Marsh committed only this crime, at least we wouldn't think the real killer was afraid."

"He didn't want us to think he was sexually interested in his victims, and he doesn't want us to think he's afraid of anything." Tony shook his head. "I guess homicidal maniacs are screwed up by definition, but this guy takes the prize."

"No kidding." Half consciously, Bishop turned to look toward the road.

"Miranda's coming?" Tony guessed.

"Yeah."

"I thought the transmitter was up and running again," Tony murmured. "So you two are sort of . . . linked?"

"You could say that." Bishop glanced at him, noted the professional as well as personal curiosity, and sighed. "It's like a corridor with a door at either end. With the doors open, we can communicate telepathically almost as easily as you and I are talking now."

"And with the doors closed?"

"There's just . . . an awareness. A sensitivity to mood, other emotions. Nearness."

"Ah." Tony nodded. "Mind me asking if the doors are open or closed right now?"

Bishop hesitated, then shrugged. "My side is open. Hers is closed."

"Could you open her door?" Tony asked.

"Probably. But it would be . . . a forceful act. An invasion of privacy. We all need our privacy sometimes."

"Jeez," Tony said seriously, "you just know communication between the sexes is a bitch when even telepaths with a direct line to each other have problems talking."

Bishop had to smile, even though he felt little amusement. "Like every other part of the human condition, Tony, it just makes things more complicated — not less."

"I guess so." Tony saw Miranda's Jeep turn into the driveway. "In any case, I certainly don't envy her the last hour or so, telling Alex about this."

"No. It wasn't pleasant."

As Miranda walked toward the porch, her face drawn and still, Tony murmured something about helping the doctors and retreated into the house.

"How's Alex?" Bishop asked her.

Miranda made no move to go inside. "Lousy," she said, not mincing words. "I left him at the office with Carl and a bottle of scotch. That song about not knowing what you've got till it's gone keeps running through my mind. Thinking he was still in love with his dead wife was such a habit, Alex never realized until today that he was falling in love with Liz." She sighed, then added immediately, "Do we have any preliminary reports?"

He told her what they had so far, along with his speculations on the killer's motives.

Thoughtful, Miranda said, "We've never publicly focused suspicion on anyone, so the killer might not have any idea that Justin Marsh has pretty solid alibis for the other murders. But I agree with you. I think he's less interested in offering us a suspect for all the murders and much more intent on making us believe he had nothing to do with this one."

"So we pick up Marsh. Pretend we've taken the bait."

Miranda rubbed the nape of her neck, frowning. "The only question is, either we do it now, before the storm hits, and suffer Justin's undoubtedly pissed-off company for God knows how many hours — or we take our time getting back to the office and let the storm logically and obviously delay things a bit."

"If you're calling for votes, I vote for the second option."

She smiled faintly. "Yeah, me too. Are they about done in there?"

"I think so. Sharon and Peter are going to take the body to the hospital and get started on the autopsy. We'll have her car to go over, and there are a few fibers and prints to sort through, but we can do that at the office. Tony took the cat to one of your local vets for now, by the way."

"Good."

"Miranda —"

The door behind them swung open, and Sharon Edwards joined them on the porch. "We're ready to move the body," she told them briskly. "Preliminary exam shows she died of blood loss due to a stab wound to the abdomen. From what I saw, most of the blood lost ended up in the backseat of her car, so we know how he transported the body here."

"He didn't take any of the blood with him?"

"I don't think so. If he did, it wasn't much. No signs of torture, no mutilation — other than that caused by the cat, of course."

"Of course," Miranda echoed flatly. "Did you pick up anything from the scene?"

"Nothing useful. The Bible must be one Justin Marsh has carried for years, because it practically screams his name. We didn't find the murder weapon, so there was no help there. And if the killer left anything else behind, it wasn't anything I could see or sense."

"Was the time of death last night?"

Bishop was conscious of an almost overwhelming urge to keep that question from being answered. But he couldn't, of course.

Sharon nodded. "I'd say sometime between nine and midnight."

"Between nine and midnight. I see."

. . . *if Liz is dead . . . if she died last night before you came to me . . . then it's all happening just the way I saw it happen, in spite of what I tried to do to change it.*

It was starting to snow again.

Miranda drew a breath. "It looks like we'd

better get moving. Sharon, we may end up snowed in for a couple of days, but you or Peter will call with the autopsy results?"

"As soon as we've finished."

"Thank you. Bishop, will you make sure the house is left locked, please?"

"Of course."

"I'll see you back at the office."

"Right." As he watched her return to her Jeep, all he thought of was Alex and those undiscovered, undeclared feelings; was it sheer, obstinate human nature to so often remain blind to the truth until it was too late?

Was it too late?

"Funny," Sharon said thoughtfully. "I mean, that she still calls you Bishop."

Gazing after the departing Jeep, he said slowly, "She's never called me anything else."

SEVENTEEN

The back side of the storm hit Gladstone just before two in the afternoon, and as promised it was proving to be even more vicious than what had gone before. The wind howled like something tortured, and snow mixed with sleet angrily pelted the windows, so much of it falling and blowing around that there was little to see outside except white. White everywhere.

Miranda stood at her office window, looking out at all the white and trying not to worry about all the things she couldn't control, when someone knocked on her door at a little after four o'clock. "Come in," she said, almost adding his name.

Bishop came in and closed the door. "Brought you some coffee," he said, moving around the desk to hand her a cup.

She accepted it. "Thanks. You know, I'd heard about white hurricanes but never saw one until now."

Instead of going back around to a visitor's chair, Bishop remained where he was, sitting on the edge of her desk. "The weather reports say it'll be another hour before the worst of it is past. That means the cleanup starts tomorrow."

"Most of the cleanup. As soon as the snow slacks off, I'll have patrols out, and there'll be power crews and snow plows starting on the mess. With most of the town without power, that'll be our priority."

"How long will the generators last?"

"We have enough fuel for several days, so there shouldn't be a problem here. Same goes for the hospital and the clinic. School's been canceled for tomorrow, like all shifts at the paper mill, and I doubt many of the other businesses will even make an attempt to open."

Bishop watched her profile, very aware of their connection and even more conscious of the closed door shutting him off from what she was thinking. Or feeling, for that matter; whether deliberately or not, Miranda's mind and spirit were both so still and quiet that they offered him no clue to her emotions. "I talked to Alex a few minutes ago. You know he never opened the bottle of scotch?"

"I know. He's not the sort to drown his

sorrows. He just keeps going blindly forward until he hits the wall."

"He's down in the basement digging through old files. Said he'd rather keep busy." Bishop paused. "But he's worse than walking wounded. I'd say that wall is close."

"Yes. I know. He was the same way when his wife died. Cancer. She was sick for months, but even with the time to prepare for the inevitable, he wasn't ready to let her go."

For just an instant, Bishop almost changed his mind, almost convinced himself that patience would be best. But remembering Alex's white face and numb expression drove him on. "I seem fated to always be advising other men to let go of the women they love."

"Is that what you told Alex? To let go?"

"No. But there've been other times. It was . . . easy advice to give. Rational, logical."

"But not welcome."

"No. Never welcome. Sometimes I think I said what I did to them only to remind myself. How impossible it is to let go. No matter how rational or logical it is. No matter how much time passes and how empty you feel, or how much you ache alone at night. No matter how many times you tell yourself what a fool you are."

"So we're going to talk about this," she said.

"I think we'd better, don't you?"

Miranda turned from the window at last and looked at him with a faint smile. "You have a captive audience this time."

"Yes."

"I can't grab my sister and run away. This time."

Bishop barely felt the edge of the desk biting into his hands. "No," he agreed. "Do you want to?"

"Run away?" She lifted her cup in a little salute. "It didn't help before, did it? Nothing was resolved, it all just . . . stopped."

"That isn't an answer."

"It's the only one I have."

"Miranda, you knew I loved you."

"Yes. And you knew that wasn't the problem."

"Trust."

She nodded. "You wanted what we had together, the euphoria of it, the incredible exhilaration, but afterward the closeness disturbed you. The intimacy. Being so . . . connected to another person. You didn't want to be known that well. You didn't want anyone to see or touch you that deeply. Not even me. So you closed the door."

"It wasn't always closed," he said roughly.

"Be honest, Bishop. It would have been closed even when we were in bed together if you could have figured out how to make that work. But you couldn't. Letting your guard down then was the price you paid for the thrill. And what do you think that was worth to me? How was I supposed to value a trust that was granted only reluctantly and when the barriers were torn down by passion? A trust you took back the instant you could."

He drew a deep breath and let it out slowly. "Don't damn me now for the man I was then, Miranda. I made mistakes and I made some lousy choices. But I'm not dumb enough to screw up a second chance. The door isn't closed now, not on my side."

"No," she said softly. "Now it's closed on mine. How does it feel, Bishop? To want in so badly and know you aren't welcome. To offer everything you are, and have it all thrown back in your face. How does it feel to be shut out as if you don't matter? How does it feel?"

Seth kept Bonnie in sight almost every moment as the day wore on, just as he'd promised. He helped her entertain the two young patients she had made her personal responsibility, and when they settled down for afternoon naps just before the storm intensified, went with her to one of the supply rooms to hunt for a few different games they could offer the girls later in the afternoon.

"It's going to be a long day," he warned.

"Yes. But at least we have things to do, keeping Christy and Jordan occupied." She sent him a quick smile. "If you can stand it, that is."

"I'm fine. I like girls."

"I know, and I should probably be worried about that."

"Not like them that way, Bonnie. Not the way I —" He saw her smile again, and added ruefully, "I walked right into that one, didn't I?"

"You're easy," she agreed.

He had to laugh, but sobered when he found a Ouija board on a high shelf. "Hey, here's another one of these things. I had no idea they were so popular."

Bonnie looked at the box, then at Seth. Her face was grave now. "It's just another game, at least to most people."

"But not to you."

"Not to me. We haven't really talked about that part of things." She looked at the checkers game in her hands with a faint frown.

"We have time," Seth reminded her. "I mean, just knowing that my girlfriend can communicate with dead people . . . well, that's a lot to — take in."

"You mean believe."

Seth hesitated, then shrugged. "I don't know, Bonnie. I guess I'd be quicker to believe you'd read the killer's mind to find out where Steve's body was. Maybe that is what I believe, since he was right where that damned board said he'd be. But the other options . . . Talking to the dead? Ghosts? I just don't know how I feel about that."

Bonnie summoned a smile. "Well, like you said, we have time."

Sensing that he'd upset her, Seth put the Ouija board back on its shelf and took her hand. "In case you're wondering about it, it'd take more than finding out you can read minds or talk to ghosts to get rid of me. I told you when we were kids that I was in this for life."

"Yes — but that's a promise I won't hold you to." Her voice was steady. "There are a lot more . . . complications . . . than you realize, Seth. It won't be easy, hitching your fate to mine."

"Who wants easy?" He lifted her hand and kissed it in a rare, graceful gesture. "I just want you. We'll be fine, Bonnie, I keep telling you. More than fine. We'll be great together."

Her smile this time was slow, and caught at his breath and his heart as always. "I know. I know we will."

"Good. Now — why don't we take these games back to the girls' room so they're handy when we need them?"

She nodded, and a minute later they were back out in the hall. But Seth had barely closed the door of the storage room behind them when they heard a muffled thud from inside.

Seth opened the door cautiously, peered inside, then relaxed with a laugh. "One of the games fell. I guess I didn't put it all the way back on the shelf or something. Or maybe the damned things are just haunted."

His tone had been light, but Bonnie frowned. "The Ouija board?"

"Yeah." He went back inside the room to replace the game on its shelf.

Bonnie was on the point of warning him that occurrences like this were rarely as innocent as they seemed, but in the end decided to say nothing. Seth had enough to consider.

But it bothered her. And she put a bit more effort into maintaining her shield, all the same.

Once, Bishop would have listened only to the words expressly designed to wound, and they would have cut him to the bone. He would have believed what she wanted him to believe, and responded in anger, retreating just as she had behind a closed door so that no communication at all could exist between them.

Once.

Her words still cut, but he could sense something else in her, pain or reluctance, even grief. Almost hidden from him in the stillness of her mind, but there and very real. Hardly the emotions of a woman wronged and hell-bent on revenge. And he was no longer that arrogant young man, careless of what he'd understood too late was precious to him. All of it — the hard lessons he had learned then and since then, the long, lonely years without her, his sheer determination, training and experience — combined now to focus his mind on solving a puzzle.

"Revenge, Miranda?" He spoke slowly, thoughtfully.

"Call it what you like."

"Vengefulness isn't part of your nature."

"Don't be too sure of that."

"But I am sure. I'm positive."

"Don't profile me, Bishop."

He smiled. "Why not? It's what I do. So

let me tell you what I think about someone who was born Miranda Elaine Daultry. I think that in most ways you're a very direct woman, Miranda. You say what you mean, and when there's a choice you'll always pick the most immediate and straightforward manner of handling a problem — whether or not it's the simplest. You don't postpone unpleasant chores as a rule, preferring to do what has to be done and put it behind you."

"What makes you think it's unpleasant?" she challenged. "They say revenge is sweet."

"Only to a vindictive nature. But there isn't a cruel or hurtful bone in your body. So if you *had* intended to get even, to strike back at me for how I treated you eight years ago, we'd be long past that by now. You would have gotten it over with in the first ten minutes."

"Maybe I wanted the punishment to fit the crime."

Slowly, still feeling his way through the intuitive process of understanding a unique personality, he said, "No, that's not you. You don't brood about things, don't let them prey on you. My guess would be that once you walked out of my life, everything you felt about me and what had happened was put aside while you got on with the necessary business of building a new life for you and Bonnie."

She was silent, but a flicker in her eyes told him he had scored a hit.

He said, "You tend to count pain as a lesson learned — and move on. Deliberately setting out to hurt someone else is completely alien to you. No, Miranda, you'll never convince me that getting even was ever part of the plan. Not then and not now."

"Never thought I'd have the opportunity," she said. "But once you showed up, well — how could I resist? I'm adaptable, Bishop. I revise my plans when necessary."

He shook his head. "No matter how much of an idiot I was, you valued what we had together. You knew how rare it was, how fragile. And to use your own definition — how intimate. No way would you have opened yourself up to that again just to punish me."

Miranda was silent.

"And there's one final thing," he said. "One thing I know absolutely about you. You don't stop loving someone because they hurt you or disappoint you, not you, Miranda. It's not in your nature. You're still in love with me."

Tony watched the fax begin to come

through, and said into the phone, "You guys were fast."

Dryly, Sharon Edwards said, "An autopsy isn't exactly something you want to linger over."

"Guess not. And I also guess you're stuck at the hospital until the storm's over."

"There are worse places to be snowbound."

"If you say so. Just for the record, the cots here are so uncomfortable, I'm actually missing my bed at the Bluebird Lodge. And you know how I feel about that bed."

"Things could be a lot worse."

"Oh, yeah? How?"

"The generator could go. And then you'd be cold and in the dark. It's all a matter of perspective, Tony."

"Yeah, I guess." He glanced at the small TV, which was currently showing a South American beauty pageant whenever the satellite signal could get through the whiteout, and grinned.

"I promised Miranda we'd report in as soon as we finished the post, so make sure she sees it ASAP," Sharon said.

"Anything we didn't already know?" Tony asked, making an effort to be professional while keeping one eye on the swimsuit competition.

"Not really."

"Then I won't disturb her just now."

"Why? Is something going on?"

"Well, let's put it this way. Bishop is in her office, the door is closed — and his transmitter is working at full strength."

"Tension?"

"Oh, boy. He prowled around in here for more than an hour, until it became obvious that Miranda was not coming out of her office. I don't know what's going on, what it was about Liz Hallowell's murder that made Miranda close herself off again, but he's flat-out determined to fix the problem."

"Some problems," Sharon noted, "can't be fixed."

"Don't try to tell Bishop that. I ventured a mild warning, and he nearly took my head off." Tony sighed, and began looking over the faxed autopsy report. "It's probably a good thing that we're all stuck inside until the storm passes. With nothing much else to do, at least they can get things sorted out between them."

"You mean they can try."

"Yeah. They can try."

"You son of a bitch." Miranda spoke quietly.

"Maybe. But I'm right, at least about this." There was no triumph in his voice, just certainty. "Christ, Miranda, you think I don't know you never would have let me get so close again if it wasn't true?"

She looked at the cup in her hand as if it were something alien to her understanding, then frowned and set it on the window ledge. "I always said you were a bright guy."

As badly as he wanted to, Bishop didn't move toward her. "You know something is going to happen, don't you? To one of us. It's what you saw in the beginning, the vision you've managed to hide from me. That's why you closed the link." He forced himself to let go of the edge of the desk, absently flexing his stiff fingers. "But which one of us are you trying to protect, Miranda? You? Or me?"

"A very bright guy," she murmured. Her face was still, those startling blue eyes fixed on him unwaveringly.

"What did you see? Tell me."

"You tell me something, Bishop. When you finally caught up with Lewis Harrison, was it the vision we both saw?"

He nodded. "A few minor details were different, but otherwise yes."

"Yeah, I thought so. No matter what we do or try to do, no matter how we try to change the outcome, it almost never works."

"What do you mean?"

"Our own actions create the future, even if we're given a glimpse ahead of time. You saw yourself catching up to Harrison, and you made it happen. I saw us become lovers again, and in trying to shut you out to stop it from happening, I created the very situation I was trying to avoid."

"You risked your life to try to shut me out." He had to say it.

"No. I told you I could handle the energy buildup."

"We both know it wasn't as simple as that. You could have destroyed yourself, Miranda. If that desperate spirit hadn't taken the decision out of your hands by attacking you, how long would you have let it go on? The pain, shutting off your extra senses, losing all your defenses. Sooner or later it could have killed you — or caused you to be killed."

Miranda shook her head slightly, more in resistance than disagreement, but she didn't protest aloud.

"Was it worth that to you?" It was something else he had to say, to ask. "Would you have rather died than let me get close again?"

"When it started . . . I thought so."

Bishop thought he probably deserved the jolt of pain he felt, but that didn't make it any easier to take. "I see."

Her smile was rueful. "I was angry, Bishop, even after all those years. Not because of what happened with my family. Bonnie was right, I never really blamed you for that. You were doing your job, doing everything in your power to stop a vicious killer. But I did blame you for . . . leaving me alone to cope with the aftermath."

"Miranda —"

"Oh, I know. I was the one who left in a physical sense. But I wouldn't have done that if you hadn't already drawn away."

"I felt guilty as hell, first about going behind your back to Kara and then about what happened to her and your parents."

"And you didn't want to feel my pain and guilt added to your own. I knew that. But it didn't help. You closed yourself off from me just when I needed you most."

Bishop wanted to tell her he was sorry. But what words were there to apologize for turning away from the woman he loved and allowing her to suffer alone and rebuild her life without his help or comfort? What possible words could he offer now?

Miranda didn't appear to expect any, and went on in a matter-of-fact tone. "So, yes, I would have done just about anything to shut you out when you came back into my life.

Even though I knew it was inevitable we'd be lovers again."

She drew a breath and let it out slowly. "I saw a series of events culminating in something else I wanted to avoid, but it's all happening. Every action I take, every choice and decision I make, just brings me closer to that future I saw. It's unavoidable."

"What future, Miranda? What did you see?"

"What's the use of knowing? You can't change it."

"Goddammit, tell me."

She left the window finally, crossing the space between them to stand almost between his knees. She lifted her hands and touched him, and with that contact the door that had shut him out quietly opened. "I die," Miranda said steadily. "I'm the killer's final victim."

As it turned out, the roaring storm made the little girls too jittery to be much interested in games, so Bonnie and Seth made a quick trip to the clinic's video library and returned with several tapes. It took only a few minutes to get the girls settled with snacks and the video they had chosen.

Under his breath, Seth murmured, "We don't have to sit and watch this, do we? I hate it when Bambi's mother —"

Bonnie made a hasty gesture to silence him, then drew him away from the two absorbed girls to the small seating area near the door. "I'd rather not leave them alone with the storm so wild," she said, "but we don't have to watch the movie."

"In that case, I'm glad we got the games. What do you feel like?" He bent down to sort through the boxes stacked on the coffee table. "Trivial Pursuit? Clue? I don't think we want Candyland, but what about Mah-Jongg? Or here's one with chess and checkers and — Hey. I must have grabbed this one by mistake when I went in to put it back on the shelf."

Bonnie stared at the Ouija board in his hand. "Did you?"

"I guess so."

"Seth . . . do you mind taking it back to the storage room?"

He looked at her gravely. "I wasn't going to suggest —"

"I know. I'd just feel more . . . comfortable if that board was somewhere else."

"But —"

"It's a doorway, Seth. I just don't want to be even unconsciously tempted to open it again, that's all."

"Would you be? Tempted, I mean."

"Yes. Because if that was Lynet we reached before, she might be able to tell us who her killer was. That answer would be worth opening the door — if I was sure I could control it afterward. But I'm not sure. I don't have enough experience to be sure."

"You opened it once before," Seth said, slowly enough to make his own doubts about the reality of that obvious.

"Yes. But Randy reminded me of just how dangerous it is to do that, and I promised her I wouldn't try again."

Seth opened his mouth, then closed it, hesitated, and shrugged. "Sure, I'll put it back."

"Thanks."

"Don't go anywhere while I'm gone."

Bonnie smiled. "No, I won't. I'll set up one of the other games so we can play."

"Good enough." Seth didn't exactly hurry as he left the room, but he didn't dawdle either. He strode down the hall to the storage room, and was careful to put the Ouija board on the highest shelf and shove it far back, so that no part of it hung out over the edge.

He came out and shut the door, absently jiggling the knob to be sure it was firmly closed. It was only when he took a step away that he heard it again.

The whispering.

Seth eased back to the door and pressed his ear against it, listening. He could hear it clearly, a muffled rustling sound that was like a voice or voices whispering rapidly, almost rhythmically.

It made the hair on the back of his neck stand up.

Seth hesitated, then reached for the knob and turned it slowly. The whispering continued. He jerked the door open.

Silence.

And a perfectly ordinary storage room, the Ouija board high on its shelf just as Seth had left it.

He waited a moment, heard nothing but the muted sounds of the storm, and closed the door. Still nothing. Whatever had made the whispering noise was silent now.

"Daniels, you're really losing it," he told himself out loud. But when he went back to Bonnie, he hurried.

EIGHTEEN

"No," Bishop said.

But he saw it now, the vision she had seen months ago, a rushing kaleidoscope of images and emotions and certainties. He saw the bodies discovered one by one, unable to see who they were but knowing what was missing from each: the blood, the organs. He knew as she had known that there would be five victims, the fifth one different from the others — and that after the fifth murder but not before, he and Miranda would become lovers and would restore the intense psychic connection they had once shared.

And after that, soon after that, the end would come with little warning. The images showed him what Miranda had seen from her perspective, a hazy background but Bonnie in clear danger, a hand pointing a gun at Miranda. And as she reached for her own gun, a shot echoing hollowly, the brutal shock of pain — and the utter certainty of death. Then, nothing.

Permeating all the rest, infusing every event throughout the vision, was another absolute certainty, a conviction so powerful there was simply no room for doubt. Bishop would save Bonnie. Without him, she would die as well. Miranda knew that, had known it all along. It was why she had contacted the FBI for help, knowing he would come.

"No," Bishop said again. He realized his eyes were closed, and opened them to find her watching him gravely. For the first time, he wished violently that their connection didn't allow him to see everything she had seen.

"You said once you'd take care of Bonnie if anything happened to me. I'm depending on you for that."

He didn't remember putting his arms around her, but now they held her tighter. "Nothing is going to happen to you. You are not going to die, Miranda. Not here, not now. Not for a long, long time."

As if she hadn't heard him, she said, "Bonnie's too young to go on by herself. She'll need someone. You'll be there for her, won't you, Bishop?"

He was unable to ignore that appeal. "You

don't have to worry about Bonnie. I swear to you, I'll take care of her. But this bastard is not going to kill you, Miranda."

She didn't reply to that but kissed him instead, and despite every other emotion crowded inside him, Bishop felt desire escalate so sharply that it threatened to push aside everything else. It had always been that way between them. The hunger was instant and total, and very little short of his fear for her could have kept him from responding wholeheartedly.

You're trying to distract me.

Would I do that?

He groaned and pulled back just far enough to make her look at him. "I'm not going to lose you again. Do you hear me? If I have to lock you in your own jail to keep you safe, then that's what I'll do."

Miranda smiled faintly. "No, you won't. Because you believe what I believe. The best way to deal with a vision is to make the logical decisions and choices as they come up, to stay where you are and go on with your life, and keep an eye out for warning signs. Do something drastic to change fate, and you always end up with a worse outcome than the one you originally saw."

"Worse than you being dead? I'll take that chance."

"But I won't." She stroked his cheek with a surprisingly gentle touch.

"Listen to me, and stop being such a god-damned fatalist. You told me years ago that your visions didn't always come true, didn't always happen the way you saw them."

"Yes. But so far this one has. There's no reason to expect the end to be different."

"There's a very good reason. Me. Where the hell was I in that scene? Because if you think I'll let you out of my sight until this is over, think again."

With a little chuckle, she said, "I wouldn't expect anything else. But you do realize, I hope, that we can't sleep together again in the meantime?"

Belatedly, he did realize that. "We can't take the chance of being without our abilities just when they're needed."

"It probably wouldn't be wise. We had an excuse last night, but not now. It may well be that the only edge we have is the psychic one."

Bishop eyed the white hurricane still going strong outside the window and wasn't all that surprised that he'd been completely unconscious of it for the last little while. "Nothing's likely to happen while it's storming," he pointed out, not really arguing.

"Not likely. Not impossible." She linked

her fingers together behind his neck. "Better to be safe than sorry, especially with a killer on the loose."

As badly as he wanted her, Bishop wasn't about to do anything that might put Miranda at greater risk; whether or not she had seen the actual future in that chilling scene, it was a foregone conclusion that both she and Bonnie were at risk, and he wanted all his senses at full strength. No matter what it cost him.

He kissed her, forcing himself to keep it brief. "This is going to be something we'll have to deal with in the future, you know. Maybe we'd better talk about it now and decide how we want to handle it. I mean, I have no intention of putting our love life on hold indefinitely just because we're both likely to be chasing after killers and other criminals most of the time. There is such a thing as sacrificing a little too much for king and country, so to speak."

Her smile wavered for just an instant, but her voice was calm when she said, "Why don't we talk about that later?"

"There will *be* a later, Miranda."

She nodded. "I'll try to stop being such a fatalist and think positively, okay?"

"That's all I ask. Well — that and one more thing. Stop calling me Bishop."

399

"I've always called you Bishop."

"I know."

"When we first met, you told me that everybody did. Except for your best friend from college, not a soul alive called you Noah. At least, not more than once."

He grimaced. "That was real subtle of me, wasn't it?"

"Let's just say I got the point. Would you like me to profile you now? Explain how being known only by your surname was one of the ways you used to keep people at a distance? Even lovers?"

"All right, all right. But the point is, I'm very different now and I don't want you at a distance. In any way, but especially emotionally and telepathically."

"You do recall there's a price to pay for that sort of closeness? If I should have another vision —"

"I'll have it too. Yeah, I know. They hurt, as I recall."

"That's still the same, I'm afraid, like a blinding migraine, though thankfully lasting only a minute or so."

"Now that you're no longer working so hard to shut me out, is another vision likely? You told Tony right after we arrived that you'd more or less burned out on the precognition."

"I lied."

Bishop winced. "And even years ago, once we were linked, you said the visions were more . . . intense."

"Uh-huh. And you're much stronger now than you were then as a telepath. So with your energy added to mine, we'll probably blow the top off that scale you guys developed at Quantico to measure these things."

He knew that was quite likely true. There had been so much going on the summer they had first become lovers, both around them and between them, that exploring the limits of what was psychically possible with their connection had not been uppermost in their minds. But what they had discovered in due course was that they shared each other's abilities even when apart, and that when they were in physical contact, the energy of each enhanced the energy and abilities of the other.

They had found out quite by accident that if they were holding hands or otherwise in physical contact and either of them touched someone whom neither had been able to read alone, they were sometimes able to read that person. Not always — but often enough to, as Miranda had put it, shift their combined range well over into the FM scale.

It made them, quite simply, more than twice as powerful together than either was alone.

Following his thoughts easily, Miranda said, "We're an odd pair, there's no question about that."

"I choose to think of us as unique, not odd." He drew her a bit closer, smiling. "And you never said you'd stop calling me Bishop."

"I didn't, did I?"

"Miranda."

She chuckled. "Well, it'll take some getting used to. You've always been Bishop." *Even in my mind.* Her mouth brushed his, then lingered. "But I'll work on it . . . Noah."

For a while, Bishop forgot everything except the aching pleasure of being physically close to her. Holding her and touching her, their mouths hungry, bodies straining to be closer despite the clothing and the necessity keeping them apart.

"Wow," Miranda murmured at last, her eyes darkened, heavy lidded, and sensual.

Bishop's arms tightened for just a moment, then he eased her away from him. In a hoarse voice he said, "Much more of this and I won't have any wits left to focus on trying to catch our killer. Jesus, Miranda."

"They say self-denial is good for the soul."

"Yeah, and I'll bet the ones saying it didn't have anything they hated giving up."

Miranda smiled, but said, "Maybe we'd better concentrate on work for a while. Storm or no storm."

"Maybe we'd better," he agreed. "We can try one more time to put the pieces of the puzzle together."

Monday, January 17

Amy Fowler opened her eyes and gazed blearily at the ceiling. Same ceiling. Same stupid, dull ceiling, industrial gray squares pockmarked with tiny black specks. She was really, really tired of looking at that ceiling.

At least the wind had stopped howling like something trapped alive, and sleet no longer pelted the windowpanes in that unceasing, unsettling rattle. The storm was finally over.

The sedatives had blurred time somewhat for Amy, but she thought it was probably Monday morning; the light coming from the single window in the room was very bright, sunshine reflecting off lots and lots of snow.

Two days. They'd found Steve's body just two days ago.

Under the covers, her hands crept down to cover her lower abdomen, and tears welled up in her eyes. Steve was gone. Steve was gone, and a baby was coming, and Amy was so scared. She wanted to just go back to sleep, not to think about it anymore, but Dr. Daniels had told her gravely last night that there wouldn't be any more drugs, that she had to face things.

Face things. Face her mom and dad. Face the pity of her friends at school, while her belly got big and she went every Sunday to put flowers on Steve's grave.

Oh, God.

"Amy?" Bonnie came into the room, her expression wavering between worry and hope. "Dr. Daniels says you should eat something. One of the nurses is going to bring you a tray in a few minutes."

"I don't care," Amy murmured, honestly indifferent. She found the bed's controls and pressed the button to raise the head several inches.

Bonnie sat in the chair beside the bed. "A snowplow went past a little while ago, so the roads are being cleared. I think . . . your mom wants to come take you home now that the storm is over."

"I guess there's no school," Amy said.

"No. Probably not tomorrow either."

Amy pleated the sheet between her fingers. "But sooner or later. And everybody'll know."

Reasonably but not without sympathy,

Bonnie said, "It isn't something you can hide for long. But you have choices, options. And you aren't alone, don't forget that."

"My dad's going to kill me."

"You know he won't."

Amy looked at her best friend and felt a little resentful. "I don't know that. All I know is that Steve is dead and he left me with a baby."

Bonnie didn't argue or point out that Amy had also helped create that baby. She merely said, "I'm sure if he'd been given a choice, he'd be here with you now."

"So I should be happy he would have chosen fatherhood over death? Great, that's just great."

"Amy, that isn't what I meant. I'm just saying that you can't blame Steve for not being here."

"You want to bet?" Amy laughed, vaguely aware that there was a shrill edge to the sound. "He couldn't leave well enough alone, that's what the problem was. That's what got him killed. He was always pushing, always going just that inch farther than he should have."

"What are you talking about?" Bonnie was frowning.

"I'm talking about Steve and his stupid,

stupid plots and plans. You think he wanted to work in the paper mill all his life? Oh, no, not Steve Penman. He wanted something bigger, something better. The problem was, he didn't want to earn it or work for it — he just wanted it. And he always had some kind of plan, some scheme for taking the best shortcut to get just what he wanted."

"Amy, are you talking about something specific? Do you have some idea who might have killed Steve?"

"I know *he* had some idea who it was that killed Adam Ramsay — and why."

"What? How long have you known that?"

Amy shrugged. "Just after they found Adam's bones, I guess. Steve hinted that he knew why somebody would have killed Adam. He wasn't going to tell me anything more at first. It makes . . . made him feel more important to know things other people didn't know. Me, anyway."

"What did he tell you?"

"He said Adam had a real talent for finding out things he shouldn't have, that he was always sticking his nose into the wrong places. He said he'd bet that's what happened, that Adam got too close to something dangerous. And he said he thought he knew how he could find out what it was that Adam had stumbled onto."

Slowly, Bonnie said, "Amy, why didn't you tell us any of this before?"

Amy went back to pleating the sheet between her fingers. "I don't know. I was so upset when he disappeared . . . and I don't really *know* anything else. I warned Steve not to go looking for whatever had gotten Adam killed, but he just laughed at me. He said he'd be careful." Her eyes filled with tears suddenly. "He said he'd be . . . but I guess he wasn't, was he? He wasn't careful enough."

"No," Bonnie said. "He wasn't careful enough."

"When are the deputies due back with Marsh?" Tony asked.

Bishop checked his watch. "Maybe half an hour or so, depending on the roads." Sitting on the conference table as usual, he returned to brooding over the bulletin board.

"Something bothering you?"

"Just trying to figure the bastard out. I keep coming back to the way he killed Lynet."

"Because he drugged her?"

"Because he drugged her and then beat her that way. If you look at what he did to the others — say, Kerry Ingram, for instance — what he did was deliberately torture someone who was acutely aware of what he was doing. It wasn't just physical torture but emotional and psychological as well."

Miranda came into the room in time to hear, and said, "But with Lynet, the torture was physical — and she was entirely *un*aware of it."

Bishop nodded. "So why did he bother? I mean, kill her, sure — once he grabbed her, even if it was a mistake, he had to follow through. But why beat her to death?"

"Because he's a perverted son of a bitch?" Tony offered.

"Because he was angry," Bishop said. "Not angry at her, or he would have made sure she felt it."

"At himself?" Miranda guessed.

"Maybe. Or his situation. Maybe he realized that Lynet was the beginning of the end, literally. Maybe she was the one who proved to him that he wouldn't be able to go on much longer if he had to kill kids he knew."

Tony shook his head with a snort. "So he's pissed at his poor victim because she's somebody he knows, and because he's pissed he beats her to death — but he drugs her first because he doesn't want her to know he's hurting her? Jesus."

"You're missing the point, Tony."

"What point?"

Bishop looked at him. "That uncontrolled rage. It's a change in him, in his behavior. If you look at the Ramsay boy and Kerry Ingram, what he was doing to his victims could almost be termed . . . clinical. Emotionless. He strangled Kerry again and again to the point of unconsciousness, then waited for her to revive and did it again. As if he was . . . studying her responses somehow. And even though we only have the Ramsay boy's bones, it's obvious from them that his killer came up with more than one creative method of torture. If it was torture."

Tony said, "What are you driving at?"

Bishop returned his gaze to the bulletin board. "Maybe I've been looking at this the wrong way. Maybe his goal isn't to torture as much as it is . . . to learn."

With a grimace, Tony said, "The way the doctors at Auschwitz wanted to learn?"

"Could be. It might explain how he's choosing his victims. How he rationalizes it, I mean. He may view teenagers as disposable somehow, as less valuable than adults. That could be how he justifies this to himself. Teenagers are . . . emotional, combative, driven by their hormones. They flout authority, assert their independence, cause

409

trouble for their parents and society at large."

"So he's using them as lab rats?" Tony shook his head. "But to what end? If he's convinced himself he's doing something noble and worthwhile for mankind, then what's the ultimate goal? Or am I being too logical?"

"No, he'd have a goal," Bishop said. "An ultimate aim or at least an avenue of pursuit."

"Just tell me he's not building a creature," Tony begged.

"No," Bishop said slowly. "No, I don't think he's doing that."

When he saw the Ouija box atop the stack of games on the coffee table, Seth thought that Bonnie must have changed her mind about using it. But then he remembered her voice and the expression on her face when she'd talked about how dangerous it was to be even unconsciously tempted to use it, and about promising Miranda she wouldn't try it again. And he knew it wasn't Bonnie who had brought the game back into the ward.

He stood there just inside the room, holding the juice he'd fetched for the two young patients. Across the room, Bonnie was reading them a story. No one had yet noticed his return. He'd been gone barely ten minutes.

What bothered Seth was a very simple question. If Bonnie hadn't brought the game, if he hadn't, and if neither of the little girls — confined to their beds — had done so . . . then who had? Who would have?

He looked at the stack of games again, and this time a feathery chill brushed up his spine.

The Ouija board was now out of its box, the planchette centered on the board and ready.

Christ, it even tempted him. To put his fingers on the planchette and see if it moved, see if the dead really could speak by spelling things out on a board . . .

With an effort, Seth snapped himself out of it.

He wanted to tell himself again that this was just a dream, a figment of his strained and anxious imagination. But he was standing there, wide awake, and a game that hadn't even been in the room ten minutes before had in the space of a few seconds arranged itself so as to be ready to be . . . played.

And if he listened intently, concentrated really hard and closed out the sound of Bonnie's musical voice reading the story, he was almost positive he could hear that unearthly whispering.

"Seth?"

He jumped slightly and looked toward the girls to find Bonnie gazing at him questioningly. "I didn't want to interrupt," he said, surprised his voice sounded so calm. He carried the juice to the girls.

"It's a good story," Jordan confided.

"Bonnie reads it real good," Christy said.

"We're about halfway through," Bonnie told him.

He nodded, glanced at his watch, and summoned a smile. "Dad's just down the hall. I'll go check with him, see how things are going."

"Okay," Bonnie said. "We'll be here."

As he turned toward the door, Seth realized that from where she was sitting Bonnie couldn't see the coffee table. He made a slight detour and replaced the board and planchette in the box, not surprised that his hands shook a bit.

He half expected the damned thing to bite him or something.

But the game appeared perfectly innocent now, and didn't do anything supernatural like jump out of his hands as he carried it back to the storage room and placed it on the high shelf.

"I'm not going to scare Bonnie," he muttered, stacking three other games and a bucket of wooden blocks on top of the Ouija board. "She has enough to worry about without some damned stupid game haunting her."

It was enough that it was haunting him.

He gave the box a final shove and left the storage room, closing the door very firmly. And pretended to himself he didn't hear a thing as he walked away.

Sandy Lynch poured a cup of coffee and used it to warm her cold hands. "How come I get all the crappy duties?" she demanded of the room at large.

Carl Tierney, lounging at his desk as he waited for the sheriff to buzz him, said lazily, "Because you're the baby deputy."

"That sucks," she said roundly.

"We've all been there, kid." He smiled at her. "Besides, it wasn't such a crappy duty. I was there too."

"You got to drive. I got to sit in the back and listen to Justin Marsh go on and on and on."

At his desk nearby, Alex said absently, "He does tend to do that."

Sandy, not quite certain how to treat the recently bereaved and cautious about trying, adopted what she hoped was a perfectly brisk and professional tone. "No kidding he tends to do that. And the man has radar when it comes to gossip, I'll swear he does. I heard things about people I really didn't want to know."

"For instance?" Carl probed curiously.

"Shame on you."

"Hey, it's better than being bored. Give."

"No." But Sandy couldn't resist adding, "Just tell me how he heard, from way out where he lives, that it was the sheriff's sister told us where we could find Steve Penman's body. I mean, gossip's probably spreading like wildfire by now, but way out there? And of all the screwed-up stories he might have heard, that's the one he believed?"

"That story's as good as any other," Carl said with a shrug. "I heard it from a guy who's married to one of the nurses at the clinic, so why not?"

"Why not? I'll tell you why not. Just how would that sweet girl know anything about a murder?"

"Tarot cards, I heard. Or maybe it was a Ouija board."

Alex looked up from the files spread out on his desk, frowning slightly. There was something he needed to remember, something he needed to say. But whatever it was drifted away before he could quite grasp it.

He was so tired he could barely think, his eyes were scratchy from staring at spiky handwriting, and his throat had nearly closed up from the dust.

Of course from the dust.

He'd barely slept in the last forty-eight hours, had downed enough coffee to put an entire platoon on a caffeine jag, and judging by the way his stomach was gnawing at itself and grumbling loudly he probably should have eaten something along the way.

Liz would have said he was just asking for trouble, letting himself get run-down like this —

No. He wasn't going to think about Liz. He wasn't ready to think about Liz. Close that door, just close it.

He forced himself to tune back in to the conversation between the veteran and the baby deputy.

"And what's the point of learning how to shoot if I'm never going to draw my gun?" Sandy was saying aggrievedly. "I push papers, I answer phones, I hold lights for FBI doctors, I listen to religious fanatics gossip about their neighbors, I even make the damned coffee. What kind of cop am I?"

"One just learning about things," Carl replied soothingly but with amusement.

"Give it time. Even the sheriff had to do the same sort of stuff when she first signed on."

"She did?"

"Sure, she did. All of us did. Of course, I don't recall her puking her guts out the first time she saw a body."

"Bones," Sandy reminded him coldly. "Horrible bones with bits of — of skin and hair still sticking to them. That's what I saw, Carl Tierney. Not a body. Bones. And you're one to talk; everybody knows you got sick too."

"That's slander."

"Not if it's true."

"It isn't. Vile gossip."

Alex tuned out the conversation again, wondering vaguely what had interested him the first time. He turned his attention back to the old file before him, trying to make sense of what he was looking at. He was dimly aware of people talking, moving through the room, phones ringing, but none of it touched him.

Could he survive this?

Would he?

"This is disgraceful!" Justin Marsh announced.

"It's just an interview, Justin," Miranda told him mildly. "A routine interview."

"Routine? Just an interview? You sent a

patrol car to get me, Sheriff! You had armed ruffians drag me from my own home before my stricken family!"

Miranda thought that both Sandy Lynch and Carl Tierney would have been appalled by that description of themselves, and that Selena probably had been more bewildered than stricken, but all she said was, "They didn't drag you, Justin. They asked you politely to come back here with them so we could discuss a few things. That's all. Just discuss."

"I'll have something to say about this to my attorney!"

"Go ahead and call him," Miranda invited, knowing very well that Bill Dennison would tell Justin to stop being such a fool and answer the questions.

Justin knew it too, judging by the glare he fixed on Miranda. "I'll sue you *and* the Sheriff's Department," he said, sounding more sulky than anything else. "Questioning me like a common criminal! And with an FBI agent standing over me in a threatening manner!"

Since Bishop was across the room leaning rather negligently against the filing cabinet, that was such an obvious exaggeration that Miranda could only admire it for a moment in silence. She propped an elbow on her desk and rubbed the back of her neck wearily.

Maybe if I drew my gun and pointed it at him? Bishop suggested telepathically.

Don't tempt me, she returned without looking at him. "Justin, the past couple of weeks have been a real bear, and this week isn't shaping up to be a whole lot better. I've got at least four teenagers dead, along with a lady I happened to like an awful lot, and I intend to get to the bottom of things."

"There's evil here, I've warned you —"

"So what I'd like you to explain to me is how your Bible ended up on Liz Hallowell's nightstand."

Justin paled, then flushed a vivid red. "Beside her bed? Sheriff, are you implying that my relationship with Elizabeth was in some way illicit?"

Miranda resisted an impulse to sigh. "I just want to know how she ended up with your Bible, Justin."

"I have no idea," he said stiffly.

"Well, when did you miss it?"

"I didn't."

Miranda lifted an eyebrow at him.

Flushing again, Justin said, "I've been preoccupied with the storm, Sheriff, like everyone else. We lost power in the first few hours, and I was kept busy tending to the fire, bringing in firewood and such. I didn't think about the Bible until you showed it to me."

"When do you last remember having it?"

He frowned at her, still indignant but reluctantly interested. "I suppose . . . it was at Elizabeth's coffeeshop. Just before the storm began. I must have left it there."

"Saturday night?"

"Yes."

"How long were you there?"

"Not long. Half an hour, maybe a little longer. It must have been about quarter after nine or so when I left."

"And after that?"

"I went home, of course. The snow had started."

"What time was it when you got home?"

"Nine-thirty, or a little after. I didn't dawdle. I knew Selena would be anxious."

It went without saying that Selena would back up what Justin said, and it was about what they had expected to hear. Miranda pushed a legal pad and a pencil across her desk to him. "If you wouldn't mind, Justin, try to remember everyone you saw or spoke to at the coffeeshop that night."

He picked up the pencil, but the frown remained. "You don't suspect me of killing Elizabeth?"

"Did you?" Miranda asked politely.

"Of course not!"

"Then why would we suspect you?"

"You brought me here to —"

"I brought you here to ask you about the Bible, Justin, that's all. We have to check out all the details, you know. Like the Bible. That was an anomaly, something out of place, and we have to try to explain how it ended up where it did. A list of everyone who had access to it and might have picked it up will undoubtedly be helpful to the investigation." Gravely, she added, "Thank you."

He stared at her for a moment, then muttered, "Of course, of course. Glad to help." He bent over the legal pad.

You ought to go into politics.

I'm in politics. She shot Bishop a rueful glance.

Oh, yeah — you are, aren't you? He stirred and said aloud, "Mind if I ask you something, Mr. Marsh?"

"I don't see how I can stop you," Justin said, far from graciously.

Miranda thought he probably remembered how easily Bishop had bested him in the contest of Biblical quotations, and his wounded vanity amused her.

If Bishop was also amused, he didn't let it

show; he was expressionless and kept his voice matter-of-fact. "You've been warning us about the evil in Gladstone for some time now. Is this just a general feeling of yours, or can you point to something specific?"

"How specific do I have to be?" Justin snapped. "People are dying."

"We know that, Justin." Miranda was patient. "And unless you have something useful to add as to who might be killing these people or why, reminding us continually that it's evil isn't entirely helpful. We know it's evil. We'd like to stop it. If you have any suggestions as to how we can do that, we'd appreciate hearing them."

His eyes on the pad as he quickly and neatly printed a list of names, Justin said calmly, "Then you might want to find out who ended up with Adam Ramsay's car."

NINETEEN

To get an answer from Justin unaccompanied by any religious or bombastic trimmings was so unexpected it took Miranda several seconds to respond. "There was no car registered to Adam Ramsay."

"That doesn't mean he didn't have one." Justin sent her a wry look. "Seventeen-year-old boys might not be able to legally own cars, but surely you don't expect that to stop them. I imagine his father probably registered the car in his name."

"Adam's mother specifically said he didn't have a car. That's why we never looked for one."

"Julie Ramsay doesn't have the sense to raise a pup, much less a boy. There was a lot she didn't know about him."

"How do you know about the car?"

"Cars were my business, remember? I notice them. I remember them. His was a green '89 Mustang."

Miranda looked at Bishop, who said, "Why do you believe the car is important?"

"Because it's never turned up, I suppose. And because whenever I saw the boy around that car, I always thought there was something sly about him, something sneaky. I raised two of my own, and I can tell you that boy was up to something."

"Anything else? Anything definitive, I mean?"

Justin pushed the pad across the desk to Miranda. "If there was anything definitive, I expect you would have spotted it by now."

Miranda honestly didn't know if that was a dig at her, the investigation, Bishop, the FBI — or merely Justin's way of slamming all of them.

Justin got to his feet. "I assume I can go now?"

Miranda pressed the buzzer on her intercom and stood up. "There are a few things we need to check out. I'm going to ask you to wait in one of our interview rooms, Justin."

He scowled. "You mean a cell."

"No, I mean one of our interview rooms." She nodded to Carl, who'd opened her office door and stood waiting. "Carl will get you some coffee and whatever else you need to make yourself comfortable, and I'll talk to you again later."

Justin protested bitterly but had little choice except to accompany the burly deputy.

When they were gone, Bishop said, "What surprises me most is that he raised two sons."

"Neither of whom chose to stay and make a home in Gladstone," Miranda commented dryly.

"Now, that doesn't surprise me." Bishop smiled faintly. "You may have to move him to a cell eventually."

"And I can only hold him for twenty-four hours without charging him. After that, he's out of here. And our killer will know for certain we haven't taken the bait."

"Before that happens, we'll make sure Bonnie is protected. This is hardly the most interesting place for a teenage girl, but —"

"But," Miranda finished, "she's better safe and bored. I won't take the chance of leaving her out in the open much longer. Gossip's probably even more garbled, and Liz's murder will make her involvement look more likely than not, but . . ."

She'll be all right.

Yes. Yes, of course she will.

But on some level far deeper than

thought, Miranda was afraid for Bonnie. Because of this flesh-and-blood killer walking among them and because of a spirit so desperate to live that it had nearly destroyed the first vulnerable psychic to cross its path.

Their killer was, as Bishop had said, the more immediate and direct threat, and Miranda was second-guessing herself every moment for not immediately having thrown a cordon of protection around her sister even if it *did* draw too much attention. She knew she wouldn't breathe easier until Bonnie was here under her eye, as safe as she could make her.

Except . . . Had Bishop realized, Miranda wondered, how it was tearing at her not to reach out with her shields and wrap Bonnie in psychic protection? It wouldn't protect her from a living killer, but it would protect her from a determined spirit intent on finding itself a living vessel in which to exist again.

It was a choice Miranda had made alone without talking to Bishop, but she knew he would have agreed, however reluctantly. She could not shore up her shields and extend them to protect Bonnie without psychically blinding herself — and now Bishop. And that was a possible edge they simply could not abandon if they were to prevent more murders.

Bonnie's own shields would have to be good enough to protect her, at least for the time being.

As they walked together to the conference room, Bishop said thoughtfully, "Interesting about the car, if it's true. It shouldn't take long to find out if Adam Ramsay's father did register one for him."

"I would say it's odd that nobody else mentioned a car, but we certainly didn't bring it up. Half the town could have noticed it at one time or another, and nobody said anything simply because we didn't ask the right question." Miranda shook her head. "His mother said there was no car, there wasn't one registered to him — so we never gave it another thought. Never asked anyone if they'd seen him driving or even knew that he owned a car."

"No reason you should have."

"Maybe, but —" Miranda broke off as the mayor appeared suddenly from the hallway leading to the front of the building. "John, what are you doing here?"

MacBride sighed heavily. "What do you think? Justin called me the minute your people showed up at his house."

Miranda looked at Bishop. "No wonder

he wasn't eager to call his lawyer. He'd already brought in the big guns."

"You have to admire his consistency," Bishop said.

"Has he been arrested?" MacBride demanded. "Justin?"

"He's being held here while we check out a few things, that's all," Miranda replied calmly. "Certain evidence at the most recent murder scene points to him."

"Evidence? What evidence?"

"John, you know I can't discuss that with you. Look, if you want to talk to Justin, go ahead."

"Of course I don't want to talk to him," MacBride said hastily. "I wouldn't even have come if I hadn't needed to go to the office anyway. But . . . Liz gone . . . Jesus, I couldn't believe it. Surely you don't think Justin could have —"

"I think I have to investigate every possibility, John. That's what they pay me for." Her tone was perfectly polite, but she had made no effort to invite him to her office or to join them in the conference room. "And I'm glad you're here, it'll save me a phone call." She looked at the legal pad containing Justin's list. "You were at Liz's coffeeshop Saturday night, weren't you?"

"For a few minutes, yeah."

"Did you happen to see Justin's Bible?"

Startled, MacBride said, "His Bible? Well, since it's always with him, I imagine I did. But if you're asking me if I remember actually seeing it . . . then I can't say that I do."

Bishop sighed. "Why do I get the feeling that'll be everybody's response?"

"Because nothing's been easy so far," Miranda told him.

"I wouldn't mind a little easy about now."

"Neither would I, but we aren't likely to get it."

"No, I suppose not."

MacBride glanced from one of them to the other, his mouth twisting, but his voice was easy when he said, "Can we talk for a minute, Randy? In private, if Agent Bishop doesn't mind."

"I'll be in the conference room," Bishop said agreeably. He took the legal pad out of Miranda's hands and went on without waiting for a response.

"What is it, John?"

"I just wanted to know how you were," he said with a touch of awkwardness. "We've barely talked in the last week, and —"

"I'm fine. Tired, but otherwise okay, all things considered." She smiled faintly. "Thanks for asking."

"You know I care about you, Randy."

Miranda was aware that Bishop was unabashedly eavesdropping, but it didn't disturb her because her response would have been the same even if the conversation had been a complete mystery to him. Quietly, she said, "I've always appreciated your friendship, John."

"Friendship."

"There was never anything more, you know that."

"There might have been, if not for —"

She shook her head. "It has nothing to do with anyone else, not really. We've known each other for years, John. Don't you think something would have happened long ago if it had been meant to?"

Unhappily, he said, "You're very sure, aren't you, Randy?"

"Very sure. I'm sorry."

"Yeah. Yeah, so am I." He settled his shoulders and tried a laugh that didn't quite come off. "I'd better get on to the office and let you get back to work."

"See you later, John."

Miranda stood there for a moment after he'd gone, then went into the conference room. Tony was on the phone, Bishop at his accustomed place on one end of the table as he studied the bulletin board.

It could have been an entirely silent conversation, but instead Miranda went to Bishop and murmured, "That was not exactly fair to John."

"Fair, hell." He smiled. "I told you I wouldn't let you out of my sight, and I meant it."

She eyed him. "Oh, that was why you eavesdropped?"

"Certainly."

"You'd better try it again in a more convincing tone."

Bishop chuckled. "Okay, so I had other reasons."

"Jealousy. I never would have expected it of you."

"Oh, I don't imagine it'll be a problem," he said calmly. "Once you fully commit yourself to me, that is, and tell me I don't have to worry about it anymore."

Miranda was trying to decide how to reply when Tony hung up the phone and said briskly, "Found it. There's a green '89 Mustang registered to Sam Ramsay — Adam Ramsay's uncle. Lives here in the state but not close by, and probably means to come in for the funeral when there is one."

"And pick up his car then," Bishop said.

"Yeah, or arrange to sell it, something like that."

"The question is," Miranda said, "where the hell is that car now?"

It took an hour to track down Sam Ramsay, who was indeed Adam's uncle and had indeed agreed about six months before to register a car in his name that was intended for his nephew's use.

"His dad paid the insurance," he told Tony somewhat truculently over the phone. "And made sure the car was inspected and everything. I am — was — holding the pink slip until Adam got old enough to put the car in his own name." He paused, cleared his throat, and added, "I'd planned to see about the car when I came to Gladstone for the funeral. Knew Julie wouldn't want it, and it's too much trouble to drive or ship down to Florida even if his dad was interested."

"Adam apparently didn't keep the car at his home," Tony said.

"No, Julie pitched a bitch at just the idea of him having his own car, really raised hell about it. Said he was too young. So Adam fixed it with a friend to park the car at his house."

"Do you know the friend's name?"

"Lemme think. Steve somebody. Can't remember the last name."

"Penman?" Tony suggested.

"Yeah, that sounds right — Steve Penman."

"Adam kept the car at Steve's house?"

"That's what he told me. I think they lived close by, so it wasn't any trouble for Adam to walk over and get his car when he wanted it."

"I see. Thanks, Mr. Ramsay, thanks very much. If we have any more questions —"

"I'll be here."

Tony cradled the receiver and reported the conversation to Bishop. "So that's the first real connection we have between the two male victims," he noted.

"Call the Penman boy's father," Bishop suggested. "See if he knows anything about that car."

"Right."

While Tony was doing that, Miranda returned to the conference room; she had been handling reports of a couple of fender-benders and checking on the progress of the power crews.

Bishop reported the latest findings aloud. The mental link between him and Miranda remained, but in order for them to concentrate on separate things without distracting each other, they had consciously eased their "doors" almost closed. Emotions and sometimes the flicker of a thought got through, but except for their questioning Justin, and Miranda's conversation with the mayor, they had settled on communicating verbally.

It was also less confusing for Tony that way.

He watched them as he waited for Steve Penman's father to come to the phone, fascinated as always by their relationship. Bishop had been characteristically brief in explaining why his transmitter had been rather abruptly muted, saying only that he was able to "borrow" Miranda's ability to shield selectively. Tony promised himself that when there was time and leisure to explore the matter, he'd ask a few nosy questions, but what he was really interested in was the apparently effortless telepathic link between Bishop and Miranda.

Now, that was really something.

They had emerged from Miranda's office late yesterday having obviously put at least one major hurdle behind them; she was oddly serene, no longer shut off or withdrawn, and Bishop no longer paced the floor — though something in his eyes when he looked at Miranda told Tony that not everything had been settled and that worries remained. In any case, they seemed entirely comfortable with each other, the only visible tension between them being of the electric, sensual variety.

Not, Tony reflected, that they were acting like a couple of horny teenagers, all secret glances and sweaty hands grabbing at each other. No, it was something a lot more subtle than that. Tony had the feeling that if he could see psychic auras, he'd see theirs merging, melding together whenever they were near each other — and eagerly reconnecting after they had been apart for a few minutes. Because that was the sense he got, that they were touching even when they weren't.

It was really fascinating.

The telepathic communication had become obvious rather quickly, and after the second or third time one or the other of them turned to him with a comment that had clearly been the end of a conversation rather than the beginning, Tony had strongly objected.

"Will you guys quit that? It's getting spooky. Not to mention confusing."

"He's probably right," Bishop had said, clearly amused. "Or he's just jealous that he can't do it."

Tony had made a rude response to that, even though all three of them knew it was at least half true.

"Hello?"

Recalled to duty, Tony said, "Mr. Penman? This is Agent Harte. I'm really sorry to bother you again, but . . ."

"So," Miranda said to Bishop, thoughtfully, "Adam did have a car. Since when?"

"Last July, according to his uncle," Bishop replied.

"A couple of months before he disappeared." She leaned her hands on the table and gazed absently toward the bulletin board. "Has anybody checked traffic violations?"

"Tony did. None on record. The kid was either a safe driver or lucky. Either way, there was certainly nothing to make any of your deputies notice that car and mention it later when he disappeared. I'm sure his friends knew about it but, like you said before, none of us asked the right question."

She nodded, then frowned at a stack of files threatening to topple over. "Is that —"

"More missing teenagers, yeah. Alex brought the files in a little while ago. We've gone back to '87 so far, and the count is up to twenty-nine."

Miranda sank down in a chair, visibly shaken. "Twenty-nine missing kids? In thirteen years?"

"Twenty-nine reported disappearances of

teens last seen within a fifty-mile radius of Gladstone," Bishop confirmed, more than a little grim himself. "We don't know for certain they even vanished, Miranda, much less vanished here. They could have resurfaced somewhere else under assumed names, or died of drugs or just life on the streets. We don't know."

"No, we don't know," Miranda murmured. "But there's at least an even chance that none of those kids got out of this town alive. My God . . . how could so many disappear without notice?"

"If you mean without official notice, consider that the disappearances averaged two or three a year over more than a dozen years. How many administrations in that time? How many strangers passing through Gladstone on their way to Nashville? And consider too that the old files weren't put on computer, where the pattern might have been seen before now."

"Still. We should have noticed. We should have seen *something.*"

There was nothing particularly reassuring Bishop could say, so instead he said, "One thing these files make more likely is that our killer has had a lot of practice. The steady stream of young people through this town for so many years, kids who wouldn't be missed or at least whose disappearance wouldn't be noticed by or tied to anyone locally, gave him plenty of time and opportunity to get very good at killing."

"And to get very good at disposing of the bodies." Miranda frowned. "That's another thing I don't get. If he's been successfully killing all these years, why suddenly begin leaving the bodies where they'd be found relatively quickly and easily? Both Kerry Ingram and Lynet were left in such a way that it was clear they'd be found sooner rather than later. Why?"

Bishop turned his gaze to the bulletin board and, slowly, mused, "The only thing we can be pretty certain about is that the new highway forced him to kill local kids, even kids he knew. As long as they were strangers, he could enjoy himself. But once he knew them, once he could call them by name and see their eyes or their smiles afterward in the faces of their relatives . . . maybe that was too much. Even if only subconsciously, maybe he's hoping we'll stop him."

Musing herself, Miranda said, "Adam was the first local kid to be killed. But he buried Adam just as — presumably — he buried or disposed of earlier victims, in such a way that his body wasn't likely to be found. So . . . did he bury him that way just out of habit? Because he hadn't yet even subconsciously realized he wanted to be caught? Or was there a different reason?"

Bishop thought about it, then said, "I still believe something about Adam or his murder will point directly to the killer. That's why he was buried how and where he was — because the killer knew we could discover something about him by studying that victim or that murder. And whatever it is . . . he doesn't want us to know it."

"We still aren't sure how he picks his victims," Miranda offered. "Maybe it has something to do with that? Maybe he grabbed Adam for all the wrong reasons, and knew or feared we'd discover that eventually?"

Nodding, Bishop said, "That's more than possible. It looks like he kept Adam alive the longest of the local victims, tortured him in the worst, most painful ways — like the chemicals to age his bones. Even if it was done for some other reason, that could also have been punishment, pure and simple, something inflicted to cause the most suffering. Didn't Sharon say that, that he probably did it just to see what would happen — for kicks?"

"Yeah, she did. And *you* said you thought the killer got Adam because he needed something from him."

"I still think that. Suppose . . . Adam knew something damaging or potentially damaging to the killer, and he either told the killer outright for some reason or else let his knowledge slip at just the wrong moment. And became a victim. He was punished for what he knew, and maybe tortured partly so he'd reveal everything to the killer."

"But did he reveal everything?"

"No. Although I can't at the moment tell you why I'm so sure of that."

"Instinct, maybe," she said.

"Maybe. Or sheer practice at understanding the methods and minds of monsters."

"Whichever it is, I think you're right. And it all sounds even more plausible when we add in what Bonnie called to tell us earlier — that Amy is sure Steve knew why Adam was killed, and that he went looking for answers himself. It can't be coincidence that Steve ended up a victim. That argues the possibility that there *is* — or at least *was* — some evidence or information for him to find. Maybe he found it. And maybe he died for it."

At that timely moment, Tony hung up the phone and turned to face them, saying briskly, "Mr. Penman is willing to swear on the Bible that Adam Ramsay never even parked his car at their house, much less kept it there."

Bishop eyed him. "I feel a 'but' coming on."

"You're so right. With a little prodding and skillful questioning from yours truly, he did allow as how the family owns quite a bit of property thereabouts — including an old barn a mile or so from their house. An old, supposedly unused barn not too far off the road that would provide fair shelter for a car."

"If it was there," Miranda said, "Steve must have known about it. Why say nothing all this time?"

Bishop said, "Maybe when Adam disappeared, Steve checked, saw the car was still there, and decided to bide his time and see if Adam turned up. When he turned up dead, Steve wondered about the car — and decided to check it out for himself."

"The arrogant stupidity of youth," Tony muttered.

"Maybe," Miranda said. "Or maybe Steve just made one mistake too many, like Adam." She got to her feet. "I say we go find out if that car is there."

Bonnie came out of Amy's room and closed the door.

Seth, who had been waiting nearby, asked, "Is she asleep?"

"Finally. I think she's dreading her mom's visit this afternoon. Your dad was right, though — with nothing much to do but think about things, she prefers sleep, sedatives or no sedatives."

"You must be pretty bored by now yourself."

Bonnie smiled at him. "No, I'm fine. Tired of being cooped up, I guess, but not really bored."

"Well, at least you can get some fresh air. Miranda just called. I don't know if anything new's happened — I mean, since Miss Hallowell was killed — but she wants you at the Sheriff's Department. She's sending a cruiser with two deputies, and we're not to open the door until we're positive it's them. I told her I was coming with you, and she said it was fine."

"Seth, you really don't have to —"

"Yes," he said, taking her hand, "I really have to. Don't argue, Bonnie."

She smiled at him again, and didn't argue.

The car was there.

Miranda, Bishop, and Tony found no marks in the deep snow surrounding the barn to indicate that anyone had been near since before the storm, but they were none-theless careful in clearing snow away from the wood-barred but not padlocked door far enough to pull it open.

A dusty green 1989 Mustang met their eyes.

They studied the car from the doorway for a few minutes, every sense each could claim probing and alert.

"There is," Miranda said, "something off about this place or that car."

"I don't get anything," Tony said.

"It isn't an emotion," she told him. "Something else."

Bishop added, "Something almost . . . primal."

Tony looked from one to the other. "Primal? You mean instinct?"

"No. I mean . . . basic. It's almost . . . I can almost smell blood, but not quite."

"This is a barn," Tony pointed out. "Probably been blood in here over the years, from animals being born or being slaughtered. Maybe that's it?"

"Maybe."

"Let's check it out," Miranda said.

Again, they were careful in approaching the car, each carrying a flashlight and wearing latex gloves so as not to disturb any prints they might have the luck to find.

Opening the driver's door, Miranda said abruptly, "If Steve *did* find something here in the car, what are the chances it's still here?"

"Fair to good, I'd say," Bishop responded as he opened the passenger's door. "Safer to leave it here until he decided what to do with it. Remember, the killer probably didn't have the chance to question the boy about what he might have known or found. It was undoubtedly a mistake when he hit his victim too hard initially, trying to subdue him."

"That," Tony said thoughtfully, "could explain the unfocused rage I felt out at the old millhouse. If he knew Steve had something on him and he had missed his chance to get his hands on whatever it is, I'd guess he'd be furious."

"Probably." Bishop took a seat as he began looking through the glove compartment. "One way or another, I figure he's been angry since he killed Lynet."

Miranda was checking behind the visor and under the mat, and to Tony said, "No keys. You'll have to pop the trunk the hard way."

Slightly offended, Tony said, "What makes you think I know how to do that?"

"Because you work for him."

Tony eyed Bishop, then sighed and dug into the pocket of his jacket for a small leather tool case. "He told us the skill might come in handy."

Miranda said, "He was right, then, wasn't he?"

Sighing again, Tony went around to work on the locked trunk. He didn't consider himself very adept at picking locks, but got the trunk unlocked quickly.

"Bingo," he said. "I think."

The other two quickly joined him, and all three gazed into the trunk at various items, including a tire iron, a half-empty plastic jug of what looked like water, possibly for a temperamental radiator, a spare tire so worn there was hardly any tread at all — and two burlap sacks that were quite obviously not empty.

"Not hacked-off limbs, please," Tony said, taking a step back.

"No," Miranda and Bishop said in one breath, then she added, "But there's something. . . ."

With two of the three flashlights directed into the trunk, Bishop leaned over and very carefully untied the twine holding the nearest sack closed. When he got it open, they could all see what looked like the top of a canning jar of the sort people had been using for generations to preserve food, except that this jar looked to be at least two quarts — unusually large for such a purpose. A piece of masking tape was attached to the lid, and across it in faded ink was written the date June 16, 1985.

Carefully, Bishop pushed down the burlap and tilted the jar back so they could see what it held. It seemed to be filled with what might have been preserves or jelly, so dark it was almost black. But as the jar moved, the contents also moved, sluggishly, and half a dozen small, round objects bumped up against the glass, their pallor in stark contrast to the dark, viscous stuff surrounding them.

Then Bishop tilted the jar back a bit farther, and three of the round objects turned slowly to reveal their other sides. Two were blue. One was brown.

"Oh, Christ," Miranda said. "They're eyes. Human eyes."

Tony cleared his throat, but his voice was still a little hoarse when he said, "On the whole, I think I would have preferred to find hacked-off limbs. An arm, a leg. Jesus."

"Be careful what you wish for," Bishop warned as he set the jar upright and reached for the second sack.

They were all braced for further horrors,

but what emerged from the second sack appeared quite ordinary, relatively speaking. There was an old cigar box with perhaps two or three ounces of some kind of ash inside, a slightly rusted pair of handcuffs, and a folded pocketknife.

Tony said, "We are sure, aren't we, that this isn't just some weird collection belonging to Adam Ramsay."

Miranda tapped on the lid of the canning jar. "In 1985," she reminded him, "Adam was three years old."

"Well, yeah — but the rest of this stuff?"

Bishop picked up the knife and studied it carefully. "Sharon might get something from touching this," he said, "but even if she doesn't, this is a collectible knife. They're often sold by hardware stores or pharmacies, especially in small towns."

Miranda didn't ask how he knew that; she merely said, "Steve Penman was near the drugstore when he vanished."

"Yes," Bishop said. "He was, wasn't he?"

TWENTY

The lounge of the Sheriff's Department didn't have a great deal to recommend it as far as Bonnie was concerned. One side of the long, narrow room held a kitchenette, while on the other were a couple of leather couches, two tables with chairs, and a bank of lockers. There was a dartboard on the wall, and several open shelves held a few board games as well as a caddy for poker chips and playing cards.

None of it appealed to Bonnie, even if there had been anyone around to join her in a game. Seth had crashed on one of the couches and was sleeping deeply; he'd gotten little sleep the last few nights, she knew, and she didn't begrudge him the rest. The deputies in the building were all working at their desks, busily coping with the aftermath of the storm and whatever duties might help identify the killer.

Randy would be returning to the office anytime now. And Bishop. Bonnie felt a bit wary of meeting Bishop again, talking to him — more so now than before. He and Randy were involved again, and even though Bonnie hadn't exactly discouraged the idea, she was anxious about it.

If it ended badly this time, Bonnie didn't know if Randy would be able to get past it.

Restless, Bonnie wandered out of the lounge. She looked into the big, open area at the front of the building they all called the bullpen, a small sea of desks turned this way and that, and the low dividing wall separating the office space from the reception area. There was a TV on a filing cabinet tuned to the Weather Channel, phones ringing at regular intervals, and the low hum of conversation.

The room smelled like coffee and pizza.

Everybody was busy, so Bonnie continued on. The conference-room door was locked, which didn't surprise her. Randy's office was open and empty. In another office just down the hall, a deputy sat with his back to the door, talking on the phone; judging by the cajoling tone, he was trying to mend fences with a sweetheart.

Bonnie smiled to herself and went on. One office was empty of office furniture but held half a dozen cots, though there was only one deputy, stripped to undershirt and pants, snoring softly. Another room was piled high with the boxes and other stuff that Bonnie remembered Randy had ordered removed from the conference room when the FBI had arrived.

Down some steps and along another hallway were several other rooms; since they were small and boasted small windows in the doors — and none in the rooms themselves — she gathered they were where suspects requiring privacy or more security were questioned.

She peeked into one and saw Justin Marsh sitting at the small table reading the newspaper, his frown and impatiently tapping foot mute evidence of frustration or irritation. Bonnie moved on hastily, not eager to attract his notice.

She looked into a couple more of the rooms, but all were empty. At the end of the hallway were three doors; two led to the cells, she knew, and the other led to the garage where impounded vehicles were kept.

Not interested in any of those areas, she turned and began to retrace her steps. She was just passing the little secondary hallway that led to an outer door to the side parking lot when she felt a rush of cold air.

Bonnie half turned her head but caught only a glimpse, a blur of movement. And then something struck her head, pain exploded, and everything went dark.

"I just don't believe it," Alex said hoarsely, shaking his head. "Right here? He took her from the fucking Sheriff's Department?"

"I should have stayed awake," Seth said, his younger voice thin with fear and worry and guilt.

"You? Jesus, kid, there were a dozen cops in this place — including me."

Tony said, "Never mind who's to blame. The important thing is to find him before — before —"

"Before he kills her," Miranda said. Her voice was very steady, but her eyes were blind.

Tony didn't know what to say to her; he thought it was quite possibly the first and last time he'd ever see Miranda Knight literally paralyzed, unable to do anything except sit there at the conference table and stare at the wall. And he was very relieved when Bishop came back into the room; he had been absent only a few minutes, checking the building for any sign that might help them because he didn't trust anyone else to do it.

Going directly to Miranda, Bishop knelt before her, his hands lifting to rest gently on her knees.

She looked at him, saw him. "I promised to protect her." She was talking to him alone, oblivious to everyone else in the room. "I swore I'd always keep her safe."

"Bonnie is going to be all right, Miranda. We'll find her, and we'll do it before that bastard can hurt her."

"You can't promise," she said almost wistfully.

"Yes, I can," Bishop said. He leaned forward and kissed her, equally oblivious to the watching eyes, then got to his feet and faced the others, one hand remaining on her shoulder.

"We don't have much time, but I think we have a little," he told them. "I don't believe he'll kill her immediately — he made that mistake with the Penman boy and lost the opportunity to question him. And he made a similar mistake with Liz Hallowell."

"With Liz?" Alex frowned at him.

Bishop looked at him. "He thought she was the one who told us where to find Steve Penman, and he didn't take the time to be certain. That haunts him, I'm sure."

"Haunts him?" Alex exploded. "He's a cold-blooded killer without an ounce of conscience, and you claim he can be haunted by a mistake? A fucking *mistake?*"

Remaining calm, Bishop said, "What I claim is that this killer is an intelligent, complex psychopath with a very definite set of rituals and rules governing his life and behavior. Carelessness caused him to make one bad mistake, and panic caused him to make another; he won't be quick to make a third. He'll need to assure himself that Bonnie is the threat he believes her to be."

Miranda stirred. "How? How can he assure himself of that? You said it yourself — talking to the dead isn't an easy thing to prove."

"Which is why we have a little time," Bishop said, holding her gaze steadily. "But not much, Miranda."

For just a moment she seemed to waver, but then her shoulders squared, her mouth firmed, and she stood up. "We have to find out if Steve asked anybody about that pocketknife at the drugstore the day he disappeared. We have the list of tire dealerships in the area to contact. We have to figure out if there's something, some place or action, linking all the missing kids together." She drew a breath. "And we have to find out how he could have discovered that it was Bonnie who was the threat — and how he knew she was here."

Alex gave a disgusted snort. "Hell, half the deputies out in the bullpen were discussing all the gossip this morning, and the consensus was that Bonnie being the one was as likely as anything else."

"A deputy didn't take her," Bishop said. "You're all accounted for. And Marsh is still safely locked in the interview room."

Alex said, "Granted, but anybody passing through could have heard all the talk, and we've had several visitors here at one time or another today."

Miranda stiffened suddenly. "John was here," she said slowly, looking at Bishop. "Remember? He said Justin had called him. And when we saw him, he was just coming from the direction of the bullpen. He could have heard them."

"We need more than supposition," Bishop reminded her. "We can't waste time chasing down blind alleys. Tony, track down somebody from the drugstore and find out about that knife, will you?"

"You bet." Tony picked up the bagged knife from the conference table and retreated to his desk to use the phone.

Remembering something else, Miranda said, "He was at Liz's store Saturday night before the storm. The gossip was starting up even then, so he could have heard the garbled version about Liz telling us where to find Steve's body. He had the opportunity to take Justin's Bible, and more than enough time to — to kill her and take her to her house before the snow got too bad."

"What about the profile?" Bishop asked her. "Does he live alone, or have a secure, isolated place where he'd feel safe?"

"He lives alone and has for years. Before that his father lived with him and was in very poor health virtually from the time John was a boy." Miranda spoke rapidly, frowning as she dredged up the facts she could recall. "His family home is a big, old house miles outside town, very isolated. He's been building a new place closer in, but says he'll never be able to cut his ties to the farm."

"He's the right age," Bishop said. "Old enough to have been doing this for fifteen years or more. Personality type could fit. Unusual to have a killer such as this one in a political office, far less a relatively high one, but it is possible. And he comes and goes here so freely as to attract little if any notice."

"He knew Lynet," Miranda said. "Dated her mother at one time, and not too long ago."

Seth, who had stepped away without comment to use one of the phones, hung up and said to Miranda, "I called the clinic. Dad said the mayor showed up there about an hour ago saying he just wanted to make sure everybody had weathered the storm. He went all through the place, said hello to the patients and nurses, even the kitchen staff."

"Looking for Bonnie," Miranda said.

"He asked about her. Very casual, said he thought she was there. Dad — Dad told him we were here."

Alex frowned. "Now that I think about it, I remember one of the guys saying this morning that he'd heard the story about Bonnie from somebody married to one of the nurses at the clinic. If MacBride over- heard that, he would have known to look for her there."

Tony hung up his phone with a bang and turned to the others. "Got it. I haven't tracked down a clerk who waited on Steve Penman the day he disappeared, but the manager is in the store and was able to check his books. This knife is a collectible, and there were only three of them sold in Gladstone. The serial number on this one identifies it as the one sold last summer to Mayor MacBride."

With all the snow on the ground, there

was no way it could be dark at three in the afternoon even in January, but a heavily overcast sky made it at least not quite as bright as it could have been. Bishop said he supposed they should be grateful for small favors.

Miranda frowned at the landscape spread out before them and said "Shit."

"We can't approach any way at all except on foot and even hope to get close without being seen," Bishop said.

"Then we go on foot." Miranda got out of the Jeep, wishing the snow didn't crunch so loudly underfoot, her gaze still fixed on the house barely visible through the thick forest of mostly pines all around it.

Bishop joined her. "How soon before you figure Alex tumbles to us being gone?"

"I'm counting on Tony to distract him as long as possible. There's no way I want him anywhere near here. He's just too wild to get his hands on Liz's killer. Much better for him and Seth to be concentrating on trying to find some connection to John in those files of missing kids."

Mildly, Bishop said, "We could have brought along another deputy or two."

"I don't trust anybody else to handle this," she said flatly.

"That's the nicest thing you've ever said

to me." He drew his weapon just as she had and checked it, thumbing off the safety. "I suggest we circle the house once we get under those trees, see what we can see without getting too close."

"Right."

They moved toward the house cautiously, careful of their footing in the deep snow, keeping to the shelter of trees and over-grown bushes wherever possible, and when they were close enough, they split up to bracket the house.

It was darker here under the shelter of the big old pines, and the house loomed above them. No light shone from any of the win-dows, though clear tire marks leading to the detached garage indicated that MacBride had left and then returned at least once today.

Miranda reached the back of the house before Bishop, and waited there, watching a greenhouse she hadn't even known was be-hind the place. It was a large structure, and the glass was either frosted or dewed with condensation, because it was opaque, but there was definitely a light on in there.

Bishop joined her in uncanny silence, only their connection warning her before he appeared.

"Where's your jacket?" she demanded,

keeping her voice barely above a whisper.

With the hand not holding his gun he gestured toward the front of the house. "Left it back there."

"Why? You'll freeze."

"It was too dark and too noisy. I never realized how noisy leather is," he told her. "Remind me to oil that thing or something. Later. In the meantime, I won't freeze unless we crouch here much longer. The greenhouse?"

"He's practically shining a beacon," Miranda said uneasily.

"Then he's either expecting us — or has absolutely no idea that we could be on to him so soon. Either way, what choice do we have except to go on in?"

"None that I can think of."

"Then we go in."

"He's talking, I think," she said, tilting her head slightly to try to focus all their extra senses on the building.

"As long as he's talking, his attention is occupied. It's the best we can hope for. I see two doors, one at either end. And the light's somewhere in the middle. Let's go."

There was no time to discuss a plan, but neither of them worried about that. Their connection was wide open once again, which made communication instant and silent and provided all the edge they needed to coordinate their approach and movements.

Opening the doors and easing inside was no problem, but then they discovered themselves in a virtual jungle, an overgrown forest of plants and trees draped with vines and nearly strangled by thickets of weeds.

Oh, great.

No choice but to go on.

It was impossible to see more than a foot or two ahead, and the place smelled horribly of rotting vegetable matter and damp earth. Trailing vines dangled slimy tendrils across them and thorns hooked at their clothing as they crept through the profuse growth, trying to follow paths that long ago had narrowed to mere memory.

It was their extra senses that told them they were nearly at the middle of the greenhouse, but even with that help it was impossible for them to know for certain what lay ahead. They paused, both trying to reach through the wall of greenery. The droning of MacBride's voice continued, a low muttering that sounded to them wordless, so they literally jumped when he suddenly spoke in a perfectly calm and even casual voice that seemed to come from no more than a few feet away.

"If you two would care to walk a few more paces, I'm sure it would be easier for all of us."

Goddammit.

Still no choice.

They moved forward as ordered, and emerged within the promised few paces into what looked like a clearing in the center of the greenhouse.

It must once have been a work area; there was still a rickety table at one side of the space holding a few rusting tools and empty clay pots. Hanging crookedly high above the table was a long fluorescent light, and though it flickered from time to time, it threw an almost painfully bright light over the scene below.

Bishop and Miranda standing frozen.

Mayor John MacBride smiling at them as though greeting welcome guests, his expression pleasant, his stance relaxed.

Except for the gun he held, cocked and ready, at Bonnie's temple.

Bonnie was clearly frightened but amazingly calm, pale but not crying. She even attempted a smile at her sister, obviously wanting to reassure her that she was okay.

Miranda had a sudden, overwhelming sense that this was the place she had seen in her vision, and she had a helpless awareness of fate rushing, of events carrying her toward whatever destiny was intended for her. She didn't look toward Bishop, but she was very conscious of their connection, and of his absolute certainty that she would not die here.

Still, she knew that if what she had seen was right, the abrupt severing of their link could be as devastating for the living as the dead; gently and without warning, she closed the door on her side.

"You might want to drop the guns," MacBride suggested.

Neither of them hesitated. They dropped their guns. Not only because of the gun he was holding to Bonnie's temple but also because of what he held in his other hand. It was obviously an explosive device — some kind of small but undoubtedly deadly grenade, with the pin out.

A dead man's switch.

"Kick them toward me," he instructed.

They did so, and when MacBride gestured commandingly with the gun, Bishop moved closer to Miranda until he was hardly more than a couple of yards away from her. MacBride could cover them both easily now. They were facing him across fifteen feet or so of rotting mulch and little else, with the tangled jungle all around them

461

seeming to hover, to press inward. That and the sour smell of rotting vegetation made the place feel so claustrophobic it was difficult to breathe.

Or maybe, Miranda thought, that was just her terror. It clogged her throat, cold and sour. And her heart thudded against her ribs with heavy urgency.

She had promised to protect her sister. She had *sworn*.

Bonnie's hands were tied behind her back, her ankles tied together. She was completely helpless. And she looked very small to her sister, very fragile. She still wasn't crying, but there was something resigned about her calm, something fatalistic.

Miranda hadn't told her all that she'd seen, but she had always suspected Bonnie had guessed the rest.

Conversationally, MacBride said to them, "I keep asking her if she can really talk to the dead. But she won't tell me. I thought it was Liz, you know, when I heard the story that night at her coffeeshop. I thought she had helped you, had told you where to find Steve's body. But it wasn't Liz. Poor Liz."

"You made a mistake." Miranda was surprised her voice sounded so calm. "Don't make another one, John."

"I didn't want to hurt Liz. I liked her. You

know I liked her, Randy. But what choice did I have? I was careful with her. And I didn't take anything." His tone was reasonable but held a hint almost of pleading, as though for her approval.

Miranda tried not to gag. "You mean no body parts or blood? That was big of you, John."

"You don't understand," he said, shaking his head.

"Then make me. Make me understand." She had no idea if it was even wise to keep him talking, but a glance had shown her that Bishop's expression was unreadable, so she was following her instincts.

"You're a cop, you know all about the need to deal with threats," MacBride said. "Liz was a threat."

"No, you only thought she was. And you were wrong." She saw a faint quiver disturb his complacency, and concentrated on that chink in his armor. "You were *wrong*, John."

He smiled suddenly. "I know what you're trying to do, Randy. But it won't work. I'm sorry about Liz, but that's past now. Done. This" — he gave Bonnie a little pat, almost friendly — "is hardly a mistake. I can learn so much from Bonnie."

"No. You —"

"Because if she can talk to the dead, that

opens up a whole new avenue to explore. I've been thinking about it for some time, you know, about what to do next. I'd already realized I couldn't go on finding my subjects around here."

Your subjects? But Miranda couldn't say it, couldn't force a word out. Her fear was choking her again.

Bishop either knew or guessed, because he spoke up then, his voice steady. "Because you knew them. Knew their names, their faces. Their mothers and fathers."

MacBride responded to that easily, almost eagerly. "That proved to be . . . surprisingly difficult. Adam wasn't so bad, the sneaky little bastard, but Kerry . . . she kept crying and asking me why. And then there was Lynet, little Lynet. . . . I liked her."

"But you killed her anyway," Bishop said.

"I had to. Once I'd taken her, well . . . she had seen me. I couldn't let her go. But I made sure she didn't suffer."

Miranda swallowed hard and said, "That might earn you a cooler corner of hell, but I doubt it."

"You still don't understand. It was research, Randy, that's all. Study."

"To figure out what makes bodies tick? Sorry, John, but medical science has pretty much got that pegged."

"Do you think so? I don't agree. There's still so much to learn. I wanted to learn." His expression darkened for the first time. "I wanted to be a doctor. But they said my grades weren't good enough in college. My *grades*. Idiots. I've learned more on my own than any school could have taught me. All it took was a certain amount of . . . detachment."

Bishop said, "We've been wondering about something. Why take the blood?"

Not at all reluctant to supply the information, MacBride said, "I was working on various ways to naturally preserve organs and flesh. I thought blood might do it. But I haven't found quite the right combination of blood and chemicals just yet."

Bishop nodded gravely. "So I guess you were experimenting with the chemicals when you discovered how to age bones?"

MacBride shrugged dismissively. "I used the chemicals to clean the bones, but I noticed how it aged them. I wondered how the formula would affect a living subject, so I tried it on Adam. I'm afraid it was very painful — but he deserved it, the little sneak."

"He found out about you."

"Little sneak. Poking his nose into places he had no business being. If he'd just done the yard work I hired him for, everything would have been fine. But, no, he had to snoop. He took my knife. One of my jars. Other things, probably." MacBride laughed suddenly. "The little bastard wanted to blackmail me, can you believe that? Wanted me to pay him to keep his mouth shut."

"So you killed him," Bishop said. "But he didn't talk, did he, MacBride? He didn't tell you where he'd hidden the things he took from you."

"No. He seemed to have it in his head that as long as he had that stuff hidden he'd be all right in the end. Idiot." MacBride shifted slightly and, perhaps tired of remaining in the position, stepped back away from Bonnie. He didn't push her to the ground so much as guide her down with his gun hand until she was sitting. He kept his gaze steadily on the two people in front of him.

Miranda wanted to go to her sister so badly that she could feel her muscles tensing, and forced herself to relax as much as she was able. It wasn't time to act. Not yet.

MacBride no longer held the pistol to Bonnie's head, but he still had the grenade.

He straightened, the gun held negligently but not so carelessly as to offer Miranda any hope. "Of course, I didn't like not knowing where the stuff was, but that kid was so sly and sneaky, I doubted he'd told anyone about it."

"A chance you were prepared to take," Bishop said. "Until Steve told you he had it."

"He didn't mean to tell me," MacBride said with a shrug. "It was an accident, really — a very fortunate accident. I ran into him in front of the drugstore, and he asked me about the knife. He knew I collected them, so he thought I could tell him who else in town did. I said I had a collectibles catalog in my car, and he went with me to see it. After that, it was easy."

"Too easy," Bishop said. "You hit him too hard."

"Well, I figured the kid would have a thick skull, as big as he was. I was wrong, worse luck." He frowned suddenly and glanced down at Bonnie, his thoughts obviously having come full circle. "I was surprised when you found him so soon, before I wanted you to. But if she did it . . . that does open up new possibilities. Maybe I don't need lots of other subjects. Maybe just one will do."

Miranda felt a chill so icy that she went cold to her bones. Bonnie in the hands of this madman, the subject of his insane "research" for God only knew how long?

No.

"She can't help you," Miranda said.

"She can if she can really talk to the dead," MacBride said in a reasonable tone. He seemed undisturbed as he put the pin back in the grenade and dropped it negligently into the mulch. "That's an aspect of the human experience I haven't explored yet. I understand the death of the flesh, but not what happens to the mind and spirit." He glanced down at Bonnie. "Is there a heaven? A hell? A God?"

Very quietly, Bonnie answered, "All three."

That reply startled Miranda, but MacBride was, for the first time, visibly shaken.

"You're lying," he accused, his eyes now shifting back and forth between his captive and the pair facing him.

"No." Bonnie's voice was still quiet. She even smiled. "It's the truth. Didn't you know? Didn't you realize there'd be judgment and punishment?"

Miranda had to bite her lip to keep from saying, *Be careful! Don't push him too far! Don't frighten him!*

Obviously trying to recapture his earlier

clinical tone and only partially succeeding, MacBride said, "Your brain must be different if you can talk to the dead. That would be interesting to study, your brain."

As if she hadn't heard him, Bonnie said, "Your victims would love to judge and punish you. They're just looking for a door so they can come back."

"Door?" MacBride was frowning, plainly uneasy.

"Between our world and theirs. Victims of murder are unhappy souls, and angry. They stay in limbo for a long time, unable to move on."

"Dead is dead." He didn't sound nearly as sure as he obviously wanted to. "I know. I've watched death again and again. It's just like flipping a switch. Alive — then dead. There's nothing after. Nothing."

Bonnie turned her head and looked up at him with an oddly serene smile. "Nothing? Then how did we know where to find Steve? You thought it was Liz, reading tea leaves. But it wasn't. It was me. And Steve. Poor dead Steve."

MacBride's throat moved convulsively.

"Shall I open the door again, Mayor? Shall I let poor dead Steve and all your other victims back in?"

Don't frighten him, Miranda thought

again. MacBride was like a cornered animal when he was frightened. . . .

"Ghosts can't hurt me," MacBride scoffed, only a faint quiver betraying his apprehension.

"Are you sure about that, John?" Miranda asked, trying to draw his attention away from Bonnie. "Are you really sure?"

"Sure enough." But a white line of tension showed around his lips, and his eyes were still moving restlessly as though searching the profuse vegetation all around them for something threatening.

"They want back in," Bonnie said softly. "They want to . . . talk to you, Mayor."

"There's nothing after death." The gun in his hand moved until it was pointed at Bonnie. "Nothing. No heaven. No hell. No ghosts." His voice was suddenly toneless, and dawning in his face was the look of a man confronting a nightmare he hadn't dared to imagine.

Miranda could almost hear the screams of his victims, and knew that John MacBride heard them. She saw his finger tightening on the trigger, and understood in a moment of utter clarity that he would kill Bonnie because he dared not leave her alive.

Bonnie could talk to the dead. And John MacBride couldn't bear to hear what the dead would say to him.

Miranda knew she had to act, and now. But she also knew that the extra pistol she had stuck into the waistband of her jeans at the small of her back was too many long seconds away from her hand because of her heavy jacket.

She also knew there was no choice.

She went for her gun.

Seeing or sensing a threat more immediate than Bonnie, MacBride moved with lightning speed, his gun jerking around to point at Miranda. He fired, and in the same instant Bishop was there in front of her, throwing his body between her and that lethal bullet. As her fingers closed over her own gun, she heard the shot, heard the sickening wet thud as the bullet struck Bishop. Everything in her cried out in desperate, violent protest, but it was too late. With dreadful suddenness, their connection was severed, his hot agony washing over her and through her, and Miranda could barely see as she drew her gun and leveled it at MacBride.

And it was her vision. Bishop lay on the ground, momentarily out of her sight. Bonnie tied up and helpless, the gun aimed at Miranda, a shot echoing — and the agony of death.

But not hers.

She fired three times, hitting MacBride

dead center in his chest, and even as he fell she was dropping her own gun and kneeling at Bishop's side.

Terrified by the deathly pallor of his face, she stared at his once white T-shirt, horribly marked by a spreading scarlet stain. She fumbled with the shirt, pulling it up so that she could see how bad it was. The wound was a small, round hole in Bishop's chest, neat, hardly bleeding now.

It looked so innocent. So minor. But Miranda knew all too well the irreparable damage a bullet did to the human body. The ripped muscle and shattered bone, the internal organs torn beyond repair . . .

She pressed both hands over the wound, bearing down, trying with all her might and will to hold life in his body. He couldn't leave her. He couldn't.

"Randy, you have to untie me," Bonnie said.

"I have to stop the bleeding," Miranda said, vaguely surprised that she sounded so calm.

"That won't help him now." Bonnie's voice was very thin and very steady. "Look at where the wound is, Randy. His heart's already stopped."

"No."

"Randy —"

"No!"

"Listen to me. You have to untie me. Now, before it's too late."

Miranda was trying to listen for another voice. "Noah?" She touched his cheek with bloody fingers. "Noah, please . . ." She looked at her sister with blind eyes. "I can't *feel* him anymore, Bonnie."

"I can."

Miranda blinked, saw her sister clearly. "You can feel him? Then —"

"It's not too late. You have to come untie me, Randy. Hurry."

"I don't want to leave him," Miranda whispered. But even as she said it she was crawling across the damp, sour mulch to Bonnie, finally understanding her sister's urgency. She worked on the ropes, the task made more difficult by the bits of dirt and bark sticking to the blood that coated her fingers.

"Hurry, Randy. There isn't much time left."

"You can't," Miranda protested.

"Yes, I can."

Fiercely, Miranda said, "Do you think I could bear it if I lost both of you?"

"You won't lose either of us," Bonnie promised, her voice holding steady.

The knots finally gave way, and Miranda was still protesting as they hurried back to

473

Bishop's sprawled, motionless body.

"You'll have to go too deep, give too much of yourself —"

"You can pull me free before it's too late." Kneeling on one side of Bishop, Bonnie looked across at her with absolute trust. "But not until he's back. Promise me."

"Bonnie —"

"Promise me, Randy. You know what could happen if you pull me free too soon."

Miranda closed her eyes briefly, desperately aware of critical seconds ticking away. "All right. Just do it, Bonnie."

Bonnie leaned forward over Bishop's body and placed both hands over the wound in his chest. She drew a deep breath and closed her eyes, and Miranda saw her shudder, saw the color seep from her face as she poured everything, all her strength and will and her vital life force, into the effort to heal a mortal injury.

Miranda put her hand against Bishop's cold cheek and prayed silently to a God she had never believed in.

TWENTY-ONE

When Alex and Tony burst into the green-house, the brilliant fluorescent light over the onetime work area provided more than enough illumination to see clearly. The body of John MacBride lay sprawled on a mound of rotting mulch, his bloodied shirt and open, staring eyes mute testament to the sudden violence of his death.

A few feet away, Miranda sat with Bonnie's head in her lap, gently stroking her sister's hair with one hand. Behind her, his arms wrapped around her and his scarred cheek pressed to her temple, was Bishop. He was almost rocking her in an oddly intimate, comforting embrace.

Tony felt a bit embarrassed looking at them, which surprised him somewhat. He felt like an intruder.

Miranda looked up at them calmly. "What took you so long?"

"We were miles away." Tony hunkered down to check MacBride's carotid pulse just to make sure. "But that's a hell of a transmitter you've got there, lady. Even at that distance, it jerked me up out of my chair when you called."

"Did I call?" she asked vaguely.

Tony tapped his temple with two fingers as he straightened.

She grimaced. "Sorry. I wasn't even aware of doing it."

"Yeah, that's what makes it remarkable," Tony said dryly.

Alex said, "Hell, even *I* heard it. Jesus, Randy."

Miranda wondered if she was, even now, broadcasting like a beacon, but didn't worry too much about it. She was so tired she doubted she had enough psychic energy left to disturb anybody, at least for the moment.

"Is she all right?" Tony asked, staring down at Bonnie's relaxed face.

"She will be. But we should get her off the cold ground, I think."

Tony gazed at her steadily. "So it's over?"

"Just about," Miranda said.

Bishop stirred for the first time, easing away from Miranda and climbing to his feet, and it was only then that the two other men saw his bloody shirt.

Tony eyed him for a few seconds, then said, "Cut yourself shaving?"

Alex was open-mouthed with astonishment. "For Christ's sake. Liz got it right. I *swear* I forgot all about it, but even the white shirt —" He grunted suddenly and looked oddly amused. "It wasn't symbolic at all. It was literal."

Politely, Miranda said, "Alex, are you telling me that you knew this would happen?"

He grimaced. "I'd forgotten all about it, but Liz — had a vision. She said even before he got here that Bishop would give his life for somebody here in Gladstone. Not that he looks all that dead to me."

"Next time," Miranda said to her deputy, "you might want to share information like that."

"I didn't really believe it at first," he said apologetically. "And then, when I did . . . things were happening and I sort of forgot about it." He looked at Bishop again with a slight frown. "That's definitely a bullet hole. And a lot of blood. So, if you'll forgive me for asking — why aren't you dead?"

"Let's just say I had a guardian angel," Bishop replied.

Tony knelt down and studied Bonnie for a moment. He lifted one of her hands, saw the bloodstains, then looked at Miranda intently. "Wow. Her other ability."

"Yes," Miranda said, meeting his gaze just as seriously. "But that stays between us. She hasn't the strength to heal the world, so she just helps some of those who cross her path. Which is as it should be."

After a moment, he nodded. "Definitely as it should be." With surprising strength, he gathered Bonnie in his arms and rose to his feet. "We have a cruiser coming right behind us. I say we leave the deputies to stand guard over this place for the moment while you three have a chance to get cleaned up and maybe rest an hour or so. I'd say you've earned it."

Bishop helped Miranda to her feet. "I don't think you'll get an argument," he said. He didn't let go of Miranda's hand.

A little less than two hours later, with Bonnie still sleeping under the care of Dr. Daniels at his clinic — and a stubborn Seth standing guard over her — all three FBI agents and most of the Cox County Sheriff's Department were in Mayor John MacBride's secluded house.

The place was lit top to bottom. The first quick search had shown them that most of what they were interested in was in the basement. Part of the large room was perfectly ordinary and held the usual clutter of unused and broken furniture, shelves weighted down with old tools and other items that could mostly be classified as junk.

But a padlocked wooden door gave them access to an equally large and far less cluttered space with neat cabinets along one wall, open shelves along the other, two actual cells complete with iron bars, and numerous pieces of gleaming stainless-steel equipment that Sharon Edwards confirmed were usually found in hospitals, morgues, and funeral homes.

"Talk about a lab experiment," Alex muttered.

The scope of the "experiment" became clearer as they studied what was stored on the open shelves. Bottles of chemicals, neatly labeled. Tools and instruments. Supplies. And records.

Nearly twenty years of records.

Miranda pulled one file off the shelf at random and looked inside. The neat handwriting didn't surprise her, given what she knew of John MacBride, but little of what she read made sense to her.

"Sharon, this looks more like your bailiwick than mine."

The doctor looked at the file and frowned. "We'll have to go over all these, of course, but here it looks like he was experimenting with various kinds of preservatives."

"Yeah, he mentioned that."

Alex opened one of the cabinets and took a step back. "Oh, shit. Look what the crazy bastard was preserving."

They all saw clearly, because when the cabinet was opened an interior light came on to reveal what was stored there.

More canning jars. Lots more. Some contained clear and semiclear liquids, others more viscous fluids, but all had grisly contents made up of various human body parts.

Miranda didn't waste much time. Turning to the others, she said, "This is too much for a small-town sheriff's department, and I'm guessing you guys didn't come prepared for anything like it."

"You can say that again," Tony said.

Bishop said, "Calling in Quantico would probably be the best option. They're the only ones well-enough equipped to send a team down here capable of dealing with this."

"That suits me fine," Miranda told him. "I'll have a big enough headache dealing with the town when the news breaks tomorrow. This part of the mess can be somebody else's nightmare."

Bishop nodded. "Then we lock up, post a couple of guards, and clear out. The less we touch, the better."

Nobody argued.

The deputies chosen to stand guard weren't happy about it, but given both the grimness of the chore and the threatening weather, Miranda promised a four-hour duty rotation, and they accepted that.

The rest departed, and as they drove back to town with Alex and Tony, Miranda said, "Why is it that I don't feel much of a sense of closure? It's over. The monster's dead."

"That won't sink in for a while yet," Bishop told her from experience. "As brutal as it'll be, finding out a bit more about how his mind worked will help. It's human nature to always try to understand the monsters, to neatly label them before we lock them away in a drawer. Luckily for us, this monster left a record of his horrors."

"It won't be pleasant reading," Alex said.

"No, but the answers we need are there. And none of us will be able to put this behind us until we have those answers."

"But for tonight," Miranda said, "it's time to stop thinking about it, if only for a few hours."

They returned to the Sheriff's Department for nearly two of those hours, out of necessity. Bishop had to call Quantico, and given the magnitude of John MacBride's crimes that call was a lengthy one. Miranda had to talk to her deputies about the situation and set up the temporary duty rotation, then she had to get in touch with members of the town council.

It wasn't a responsibility she enjoyed. No one had suspected MacBride, no one had felt even a tinge of doubt, and the shock and grief of the councilmen as they were informed was deep and honest. It wasn't just a political matter or even a betrayal of trust; John MacBride had destroyed the faith of those who had believed in him — and in the basic goodness of their fellow citizens.

Finally, the necessary calls had been made and duties finished, at least for the moment. Exhaustion had caught up with Alex at last, and he was sleeping deeply on one of the lounge couches, but Carl Tierney assured Miranda he could keep an eye on things until Alex awakened or she returned. And Tony volunteered to remain there overnight as well, saying wryly that the cots weren't too bad.

"Go home, Sheriff," he said. "And take my boss with you. After all, he's been dead. That's very tiring."

So it was after eight o'clock that night when Bishop parked Miranda's Jeep in the driveway of her house and they climbed wearily out.

"Sometime soon," she said, "I want to take a week or so and just sleep."

"I couldn't agree more." He took her hand as they went up the walk together, adding, "It looks like your housekeeper was here as promised."

"I told her to leave the lights on for us. And, knowing Mrs. Task, there'll be a full meal in the oven or fridge."

"Good. My appetite may just be coming back."

They went into the house, and Miranda was a little amused to realize that both of them reached immediately to unfasten their weapon holsters as soon as they stepped into the living room. She was going to comment but was distracted by an unexpected sight on the coffee table.

"Look. Mrs. Task left the Ouija board out," she said. "I should have remembered to ask her to take it —"

The planchette began to circle the board wildly.

Miranda looked at Bishop as he came to stand beside her and frown at the board. "I'm not doing that," she said.

"Neither am I. That spirit, maybe? The one trapped here?"

"But communicating without a medium? That would take so much focus and determination —" She shook her head and looked back at the board. "No use arguing with reality. Who are you?"

L . . . Y . . . N . . . E . . . T.

"Is it her?" Bishop wondered.

"I don't know. But whoever it is, we'd better pay attention," Miranda said. "What is it you want, Lynet?"

Bishop picked up a pad and pencil from a nearby table and jotted down the letters as Miranda spelled the response aloud.

WARN YOU.

"Warn us about what?"

BONNIE.

Miranda felt a chill. "What about Bonnie?"

IN DANGER.

Miranda looked at Bishop, then returned her attention to the board. Holding her voice steady, she said, "You mean Bonnie's still in danger, Lynet?"

YES. FROM THE OTHER.

"What other?"

ANOTHER CAME IN WHEN THEY OPENED DOOR FOR ME.

"Lynet —"

BAD MAN. VERY BAD MAN. WANTS BONNIE.

Miranda had a sudden, frantic realization that in the relief of all of them surviving the confrontation with MacBride, she had forgotten something vitally important. The danger to Bonnie that wasn't flesh and blood. The danger of a spirit so desperate to live again it had nearly killed her. She looked at Bishop. "I thought Bonnie was only at risk here in this house, at least for a while, but —"

"Look," he said.

The planchette circled madly, stopping several times on NO, and then began spelling slowly.

DANGER NOW. HE'S BEEN WITH HER ALL ALONG. WATCHING HER. WAITING. HE KNOWS SHE'S TIRED NOW, WEAKENED. HE MEANS TO GET HER TONIGHT.

"Jesus," Miranda whispered. "But . . . how? Who would have a connection to her strong enough that he could find her so quickly?"

"Who is it, Lynet?" Bishop demanded. "Who is this bad man?"

The planchette was motionless for several seconds, then spelled slowly: LEWIS HARRISON.

Miranda and Bishop didn't waste another moment asking questions, they just ran for the door.

Halfway to the clinic, Miranda broke the tense silence to say, "Six and a half *years?*

Dead all that time and he's still a threat to us?"

"Bonnie was the one who got away, literally," Bishop said. "The only one of his victims to actually survive. He was psychic — he must have known or realized at some point that she was a medium. Maybe he even touched her mind there at the last moment, established a connection she wasn't even aware of. So all these years he's bided his time, waited for her to open a door for him. If you hadn't protected her in every sense of the word, he would have gotten to her years ago."

"And when she opened the door to let in poor little Lynet, he came in too. Bonnie told me she had a bad feeling about it. That's one of the reasons she got Seth and Amy out of the house so quickly. But he got to her anyway. The house couldn't hold him."

"We'll stop him, Miranda."

"Stop him how?" Her voice was shaky. "Noah, I've been in contact with people trying to fight off an invading spirit, remember? I know what hell they're trapped in. What I *don't* know is how to free them from that torment."

"We'll find a way. You saw this, Miranda, remember?"

"I didn't see this," she protested.

"Of course you did. It wasn't a visual image but an absolute certainty. You've known for weeks that I'd save Bonnie's life."

"You've already saved her."

He reached over and took her hand. "Think about it. You're the one who saved Bonnie, Miranda. You took down MacBride before he could hurt Bonnie. I saved *your* life. His gun was pointed at you."

Miranda wasn't sure he was right, but she stopped arguing. Of course they would save Bonnie, somehow. Anything else was just unthinkable.

Abstractedly, she said, "Have I thanked you for that, by the way?"

"You will," he said cryptically.

There was no time to question him now, since they had reached the clinic. They hurried straight to Bonnie's room and found a distraught Seth watching his father examine Bonnie. She was lying in the bed, still and silent — but her eyes were wide open.

"I was about to call you," Seth told Miranda, his voice cracking. "She was okay, she was sleeping, you'd told us she'd probably sleep all night without waking. But all of a sudden she made this little sound, like something hurt her or scared her — and her eyes opened. She's been like that ever since."

Colin Daniels straightened and frowned as he gazed down at Bonnie. "I don't understand this. Her pulse and blood pressure are normal, pupils normal, reflexes." He looked straight at Miranda. "I know what she's capable of, what she did today, and I know how much it drains her, but this is something different."

"Something very different. Her body is fine, Colin," Miranda said, stepping to the side of the bed. She started to reach for her sister's hand, but Bishop spoke before she could.

"Let me."

Miranda knew he was the stronger telepath, and since their connection had been severed so brutally hours before, she couldn't borrow that strength, so she merely nodded.

Bishop took Bonnie's hand, and almost immediately his face tightened. Half under his breath, he muttered, "Goddammit, it is him. I touched his mind once before. Cold and slimy, so black with evil it's like a bottomless pit." He concentrated, then said, "He hasn't won yet. Bonnie's protecting herself, at least partially. But she's weakening."

Bewildered, Seth said, "He? You mean someone's — *inside* Bonnie's mind?"

"An old enemy," Miranda said. "We think

he's been waiting, watching her. Now that she's vulnerable . . ."

Seth caught his breath and let out an anguished groan. "I *knew* there was something here, something not right. I could hear it sometimes, almost see it. And the way that damned Ouija board kept turning up like it had a mind of its own and wanted Bonnie to use it —"

"Don't blame yourself," Miranda said. "There was nothing you could have done to prevent this, Seth."

"I could have warned her," he said miserably. "She didn't seem to feel anything, any threat, not like I did."

"No, she wouldn't have. Her mental shields were up in order to protect her. That . . . makes us sort of blind to a threat like this one."

"Dammit," Seth muttered. "Dad, can't you —"

Colin Daniels shook his head. "Some things are beyond today's medical science, son. This is one of them. I can't help her. It's up to them."

Seth gave his father a faintly surprised look, though whether that was due to the admission of the limitations of science or to the clear acceptance of the paranormal, he didn't say. He just returned his anxious attention to the bed where Bonnie lay and muttered another helpless curse under his breath.

Miranda waited until Bishop gently released Bonnie's hand, then said as steadily as she could, "I still don't know how to save her."

"I do." He put his hands on her shoulders and turned her to face him. "I've fought him before, Miranda. I crawled inside his head until I could predict what he'd do before he thought of it himself. Tracked him, hunted him. And killed him. I killed him once, I can do it again."

"After what happened today, you can't possibly have the strength to —"

"With your help. Your strength and abilities added to mine will be enough to fight him and win. He can't withstand both of us."

"The connection was destroyed," she reminded him. "It can only be rebuilt in a physical joining."

"No, there's another way. Something else can forge a bond, and even stronger than the one we had before. If we let it."

She stared up at him for a long moment, and even in her desperate need to save her sister, vital seconds ticking away, the last lingering tinge of fear made her hesitate.

Bishop looked at her steadily, and waited.

In the end, Miranda realized her hesitation was only a reflex, an instinctive urge to protect herself. But that wasn't necessary anymore. She had known the truth long before now. She held out her hand, and when his fingers closed over hers, she smiled at him. "Let's get the bastard."

He smiled in return. "Reach for me, Miranda. Reach out with your mind."

Miranda obeyed, closing her eyes to concentrate better, opening her mind to him.

It was astonishingly simple. Her mind and spirit knew his so well that reaching out to him was virtually involuntary, and when he met her halfway, his mind wide open and welcoming, she had a curiously fateful sense of having come home. She could feel the gossamer threads of energy and awareness forming between them, touching and twining, stronger and more solidly anchored than ever before so that their connection was deep and sure.

Ready, love?

Ready, she affirmed.

Let me fight him. Lend me your strength and will, but don't take an active part in that; force him to concentrate on me while you help Bonnie.

Miranda wasn't at all surprised to realize

that she knew, now, how to help Bonnie. And her trust and confidence in Bishop were absolute. *I know what to do. Get him.*

Eyes still closed, they reached out their free hands and touched Bonnie.

"What —" Seth began, but his father grasped his arm and sent him a warning glance.

"Wait," he murmured. "Just wait."

Miranda wasn't even conscious of them. She was entirely caught up in what she and Bishop were trying to do. The only direct mind-to-mind connection she had ever known was the one with Bishop, so she was surprised at the very different sensations when she slipped with him into Bonnie's mind.

It was dark, but that dimness was shot through with flashes and pulses of energy like red lightning. They didn't brighten the darkness so much as slice through it. Angry. Hungry. And it wasn't silent. Almost below the level of awareness was a rustling sound, a kind of rhythmic whispering that rose and fell, sometimes intense and sometimes fading.

It's him, Miranda realized. *He's everywhere.*

No, it only seems that way. His energy is scattered, diffused. He thought she'd be an easy target, but he was wrong. Here — look. There's Bonnie.

Miranda looked where he indicated, and saw in a far corner of the darkness what appeared to be a small, crystal cocoon. It was opaque, hiding what lay within, but it gleamed, the red tendrils of Harrison's frustrated anger glancing off it harmlessly.

Like a diamond, Bishop observed. *She imagined the hardest substance she knew and hid herself within it. You taught her well, love.*

Miranda wasn't at all sure this was anything of her teaching, but there wasn't time to think about it.

Go to her, Bishop said. *Be ready. When I have Harrison contained, help her free herself. It will take all three of us to throw him out — and all the way to hell.*

Thought was deed here; Miranda found herself kneeling by the crystal cocoon. She put one hand on the cool, polished hardness of one of the facets, and turned her head to watch as Bishop stalked the killer.

She thought later how odd it was that so much of what happened was visible to her, but decided in the end that it was only the human mind's way of understanding, interpreting the pure electrical impulses of the brain as images.

It was fascinating. And terrifying.

Bishop, the one she knew best, was wholly visible to her, lithe and powerful as he moved through the darkness, his spirit luminous with energy and purpose. Harrison, his energy diffused as Bishop had said, was at first only the red lightning flashing through the darkness, scarlet tongues of flame that began licking at Bishop as his threat was sensed and understood. Then the flames became brighter and hotter as Harrison concentrated his attack on Bishop, circling him, seeking a weakness in his defenses.

Without even being consciously aware of it, Miranda sent more of her energy through to Bishop, knowing without having to think about it that the attack was a deadly danger not because Harrison was stronger but because Bishop was intent on fighting — not on defending himself.

Again and again the flames circled and probed, darting in to reach for Bishop. He seemed to sense every attempt a bare second before it was made, eluding the threads of energy with an almost mocking ease. Miranda could hear the angry hiss of energy as Harrison was thwarted, and just as she realized that Bishop was deliberately baiting his adversary, Harrison abruptly took on a ghostly human shape and launched himself at Bishop with a roar of insane rage.

Miranda waited only long enough to see

the two spirits literally locked together in a struggle so fierce and powerful that threads of white hot and angry red energy arced from them continuously. She quickly turned back to the crystal cocoon and sent an urgent summons.

Bonnie? It's all right, sweetie, we're here. Come out.

Heartbeats passed, seconds during which Miranda had the fearful awareness that Bishop's struggle was taking a toll on him even with her energy bolstering his; Harrison wanted to live again, and that was a drive so primal it made him almost too strong to fight.

Almost.

Abruptly, the crystal cocoon vanished and Bonnie was there, pale and frightened, but calm, just as she had been when another killer had held her hostage.

Tell me what to do, Randy.

Miranda took her hand, connecting them as they had never before been connected in their lives. *Concentrate. We need all your will, all your determination to be rid of this bastard.*

I hate him. Bonnie's spirit was surprisingly strong. *He killed Mama and Daddy and Kara. I want to destroy him, Randy. I . . . want . . . him . . . gone!*

Miranda felt those emotions, that utter

determination, flow through her, the energy sharp and powerful as it coursed in a dynamic surge through the link to Bishop.

Miranda saw Harrison's spirit weaken, saw his frustrated rage, heard his howl of wild protest as Bishop's hands closed around his throat with new power.

This time, Bishop told him with relentless certainty, *I'll send you straight to hell.*

To Seth and his father, silently watching, the struggle was no less dramatic for being utterly silent. Bishop and Miranda held hands, their free hands touching Bonnie, their eyes closed. And slowly, as the minutes ticked past, things started to happen. Their faces drained of color. Their bodies seemed to sway.

Seth shifted uneasily and whispered, "Do you feel that?"

His father nodded and held up his arm. The fine brown hairs stood straight out from the skin. "And there's a hum," he murmured. "I can feel it more than hear it. Like —"

"Current," Seth said. "Electrical current."

They watched intently for another full minute. And then, abruptly, Miranda and Bishop caught their breath and opened their eyes.

Colin and Seth both jumped, and at the same moment the room's door slammed shut with a bang.

"He's gone," Miranda murmured. "This time for good."

"Jesus," Colin said.

"Did it work?" Seth demanded.

He was answered when Bonnie blinked and murmured shakily, "Has anybody got an aspirin?"

Seth more or less launched himself at her, his relief overwhelming, but his father's attention was on the two standing on the other side of the bed.

They held on to each other, barely able to keep on their feet and clearly on the point of exhaustion, their faces drawn and weary but also quietly triumphant. They looked like two people who had literally fought a war and emerged in some way stronger and more complete.

But there was something else, one more thing that drew Colin's gaze and held it in a fascination that was only partly clinical. "I guess," he said, "there's always a cost, isn't there? A scar earned in battle."

Miranda blinked at him, then looked up at Bishop. She was only a little startled by what she saw, and reached to touch his left temple, where a vivid streak of white hair had appeared.

"Family trait," he said.

EPILOGUE

Monday, January 24

"Well," Tony said, "in case we needed it, we have verification that MacBride's car has the right set of tires, that he ran ads looking for 'willing hands for light work' up until he got involved with the town government ten years ago and then apparently found some of his victims among those answering town and county ads, that both the knife and handcuffs we found in Ramsay's car can be traced to him, along with the ash in that cigar box — which came out of his own personal crematorium — and that the hairs we found out at the old mill-house belonged to him."

"Nice to know," Alex responded gravely, "that good old-fashioned police work can accomplish so much." He was grateful to Tony; the very talkative and humorous agent had kept his mind engaged during the past days — and off a loss he still wasn't ready to face.

"Isn't it?" Tony buffed his fingernails on his shirt.

Accepting his role as straight man, Alex continued. "Of course, given that we also have more than thirty jars holding various body parts, seventeen years' worth of meticulous files detailing every atrocity, and MacBride's journal in which he waxed grotesquely poetic, I'd say everything else is pretty much superfluous."

"You just wanted to use that word," Tony accused.

Alex was saved from having to defend himself when Miranda walked into the conference room. She handed Tony a sheaf of papers, saying, "Add this to the file on MacBride. They're still reading and analyzing his journal, but it appears that what he told us about Adam Ramsay being hired to do yard work and getting a little too curious was the truth. Adam was hired to trim back the bushes around the basement. Apparently, he did a little exploring. And it seems he was very good with padlocks." In a wondering tone, she added, "I'll never understand how anyone could look at the horrors in that room and not run screaming."

"Instead of collecting select items for blackmail purposes?" Alex shook his head, equally baffled. "I guess it takes all kinds.

499

The same town that produced Adam Ramsay also produced our very own Frankenstein. Except that MacBride wanted to tear bodies apart rather than stitch them together." He refused to allow himself to think about Liz.

Not yet. Not yet.

Not until he could stand the pain.

Miranda sighed. "I'm just glad most of the press is camped out around his house instead of here. I'm tired of having microphones stuck in my face and questions shouted in my ears, and I hate seeing myself on the evening news."

Coming into the room just then, Bishop said, "No way are they going to stop aiming cameras at you, love. They've found their hook. Beautiful sheriff hunts down vicious serial killer and makes her town safe again."

Miranda lifted an eyebrow at him. "You forgot the 'aided by handsome, enigmatic FBI agent.' That was today's addition."

To Alex, Tony said, "Don't you feel invisible?"

"And unloved," Alex said sadly.

Looking at Bishop, Miranda said, "We've got to separate these two. They're getting worse every day."

"I thought we were getting better," Tony

said, injured. "A little comedy to leaven the tragedy hereabouts."

Deadpan, Miranda said, "A very little comedy."

Alex sighed. "Misunderstood again. It's very disheartening."

Bishop shook his head at Miranda. "I told you to just say the word and I'd take you away from all this. Well, from part of this — Tony's on the team, I'm afraid."

Tony brightened visibly and grinned at Miranda. "Oh, are you coming to play with us?"

"I have a term as sheriff to finish," she said.

As if she hadn't spoken, Bishop went on, "After all, we've solved our little telepathic problem, so we'll be able to work together without ever having to worry about . . ."

"Self-denial?" Tony finished limpidly.

Miranda eyed him. "You weren't supposed to figure that out."

"I'm very bright," he apologized.

Not quite under his breath, Alex muttered, "Hell, even I figured it out."

In a determined voice, Bishop said, "After helping Bonnie, we ended up with a much tougher and more durable link, that's all I meant. Nothing mutes out abilities these days, and there's no denying we're stronger together than either of us is alone. So there's nothing to stop us working together."

"Except my job. And Bonnie. I'd hate to take her out of school, and I doubt I could take her away from Seth."

"Seth is going to college in the fall," Bishop reminded her. "Lots of great universities in Virginia. And I have a hunch Bonnie wouldn't mind the move too much."

Miranda, who knew, said, "Yes, but there's still my term as sheriff, and —"

"I bet Alex would love to be sheriff," Bishop said. "No slight intended — especially after recent events — but chasing down bad guys on a national scale is a much better use of your considerable talents. And I need you."

Miranda drew a breath, but whatever she intended to say was cut off when both she and Bishop suddenly paled, winced, and closed their eyes.

"What?" Alex demanded, alarmed.

"I think," Tony said, watching them with interest, "they're having a vision."

"Nobody told me they hurt," Alex said, looking from one to the other warily.

"Ouch," Bishop said distinctly after several moments.

"I guess they hurt," Tony said.

Miranda opened her eyes and lifted her

hands to rub her temples. "I warned you," she said to Bishop. "They come out of nowhere."

Bishop smiled at her. "I don't think this one came out of nowhere, do you? I think fate just answered the question for you, love."

Unwilling to admit defeat, Miranda said, "Not necessarily. My visions aren't always accurate."

"This one will be."

She stared at him.

He crossed the space between them and kissed her, then repeated, "This one will be. You can't escape destiny, Miranda. Not this destiny. I won't let you." Without giving her a chance to answer — at least out loud — he turned and left the room.

"What destiny?" Tony demanded.

Miranda sat down at the table. "Never mind."

He grinned at her. "I can guess."

"Hell," Alex said, "even I can."

"You're both full of it," she told them.

Tony started laughing. "Miranda, I hate to tell you this, but back at the office we started taking bets ages ago concerning the questions of one, would Bishop ever find you, and two, when he found you, would he ultimately persuade you to join our team professionally — and him personally."

She almost smiled. Almost. "And?"

"And the odds always favored Bishop. By a wide margin." He grinned and shrugged. "What can I say? The man knows how to win."

Slowly, Miranda smiled. It was the first time Tony had ever gotten a true look at the warmth and vitality she normally kept hidden beneath professionalism, and for a moment or two he tried to remember what they were talking about.

All of a sudden, he totally understood why Bishop had asked how fast the jet could be warmed up the moment he learned of her whereabouts.

"Oh, hell," Miranda said, and there was sheer delight this time in giving in to destiny's plan for her. "Alex — you want to be sheriff?"